The
Consequences
of
Choice

LOST AND FOUND

By
Sheryll Gent

Southern Scribe
Press

Contents

As a teenager navigating some tough obstacles, my best friend introduced me to his mother, Sheryll Gent, assuring that she could offer guidance. Over coffee and pastries, I found not only a mentor and role model but also an incredible, lifelong friend. Sheryll's unwavering faith, compassion, and strength have continued to inspire me through the years. When she first decided to write a novel, I was thrilled to support her, and now as we celebrate the re-release of her novel I am overwhelmed with the honor of being her publisher.

The story you are about to read explores the profound *Consequences of Choice*, a theme woven into every facet of our lives. It reminds us that the decisions we make—whether good or bad—shape our journey and often reveal unexpected blessings. It follows the Parker family as they navigate personal loss, economic struggles, and societal challenges, all while steadfastly living for God's glory. The heroine, Sandy Parker, embodies the author's heart and faith, reminding readers of the power of resilience and the importance of a Christ-centered life.

Even more remarkable is how this author continues to mirror her beloved character, thirteen years later. Just as Sandy faces trials and heartbreak, Sheryll has encountered profound challenges and personal loss throughout the years, much like the nation she loves so deeply. Yet, she continues to rise above it all, never losing sight of her goals and maintaining her unshakable faith. Her perseverance and hope shine through in her writing, inspiring readers to reflect on their own lives and choices.

Though the world has changed drastically over the past decade, the values and struggles presented in this novel are more relevant than ever. In a time of uncertainty and division, this book calls us to reflect on our faith, embrace community, and work together to rebuild what we've lost. It's a timeless reminder that, as believers, we are part of an unbreakable body, capable of bringing hope and transformation to the world.

"I predict future happiness for Americans if they can prevent the government from wasting the labors of the people under the pretense of taking care of them."
- Thomas Jefferson

CHAPTER 1

WAVES OF HEAT SHIMMERED above the dusty road, promising yet another sweltering day in the Sandbox, a name commonly used by deployed soldiers to describe the Middle East. On this Sunday morning, the fighting had abated, and Staff Sergeant Joe Parker paused for a moment to consider the stillness. Could it be that even the enemy would hold this day sacred? He shook his head at the ridiculous notion. This enemy held no day sacred. Every day was a day to kill the infidels.

A small band of soldiers trailed stealthily behind him, their weapons held in check, tight against their chests. The stifling heat that radiated off their heavy Kevlar helmets made them feel as if their heads were strapped into a pizza oven. With each step, the powdery desert dust rose and fell in soft clouds, coating them from their sweat-drenched faces to their worn and beaten boots. If the heat and dust were irritants to them, they did not show it; their attention focused solely on the man leading them as each cautious step brought them closer to the darkened doorways and windows ahead.

The Marines had come through several days earlier and cleared the small, militant village that now lay barren and silent before them. Yet, as effective as the Marines were, experience had shown these soldiers that the enemy was quick to return to the fight. Staff Sergeant Parker stepped aside and motioned to the soldier directly behind him, "Nelly! Take point!" His command was nothing more than a whisper. Once his rank position was filled, Parker fell back to bring up the rear. His eyes constantly scanning across the openings in the buildings - dark, menacing black eyes bordering both sides of the street, peering out at the soldiers, taunting them.

Tom Connelly, or 'Nelly' to his friends, nodded and stepped forward to the front of the line. From here on, there would be no voice communication, only hand signals. The men moved cautiously through the village, checking each building before they passed. As the last structure came into view more than one prayer of thanksgiving was whispered. Staff Sergeant Parker quickly glanced around as they approached the darkened entryway of the building at the end of the street. He couldn't help but feel they were walking into a trap. Could his trained instincts be telling him something that the others were not aware of? He trusted his men and their abilities but could not shake the feeling that something was about to go terribly wrong. Quickly pushing the soldier in front of him against the mud-covered building, he moved to the front. As they arrived at the last entryway, he motioned to Connelly to fall back and have the men circle the building.

By all appearances, it was just like every other structure they had passed, or so they thought. As they drew closer, Parker heard a scuffle from within. Could he have imagined it? After all, his instincts and adrenaline were peaking. Any sound, no matter how minute, would be magnified ten-fold in this desolate place. The sound became louder as it drew closer to the doorway. Fine dust particles floated out from the shadowed door that yawned before him. Parker pressed his back hard against the building, gripping his weapon.

The scorching heat continued its assault as sweat poured from his brow, stinging his eyes. He dared not move. His muscles strained and his trigger finger fell into position, ready to react. He held his breath, pointed his weapon into the building, and peered into the shadows from the door frame. Even with his polarized sunglasses, the darkness within made it difficult to determine who or what was in there. Each second seemed an eternity before his eyes adjusted to the drastic change in lighting. He knew he couldn't just fire blindly. What if a family or child was hiding inside? No. He must wait. Once again, his fate and that of his men were in the hands of his Creator.

A movement from the corner of the room suddenly caught his eye. A mongrel puppy, no more than three months old with hopeful eyes and a wagging tail, peered out of the darkness at the Staff Sergeant. The pup was the same muddy color as every other building on the street. Staff Sergeant Parker smiled softly and let out a shaky sigh. "Just another victim of the War on Terror." He bent down slowly, scooped up their new charge, and passed him back to Connelly. "Don't ever say I didn't give you anything, Nelly." Tom Connelly smiled back at Parker and kissed the puppy on the top of his head. He readjusted his weapon for battle before tucking the dusty mutt securely in the crook of his left arm. With nerves still tense, the men regrouped to continue their sweep. Suddenly a shot pierced the silence, sending the soldiers scrambling for cover into the building previously occupied by the homeless pup.

"Sound off!" Parker yelled. The men called out their names. "Johnson! Where's Johnson?"

"He was right behind me," Whitaker whispered hoarsely. His throat tightened as he recalled Johnson crying out just before he ducked into the shelter. He turned to the soldier that was behind Johnson, "Did you see Johnson go down?"

The soldier shook his head, "No man! I was running for cover like everyone else!"

In the meantime, Staff Sergeant Parker positioned himself at the doorway. "I see him! He's still breathing. Davis! Get on the radio! We need air support and Medivac! Whitaker, cover me! I'm going out! Where's my sharpshooter?"

"Right here, Staff Sergeant!" Tom Connelly passed the pup to Jenkins.

Parker motioned to Connelly, "Check the northeast window! See if you can get a bead on that son of a gun!"

Whitaker and Connelly locked their sights in the direction where they suspected the sniper was holed up. Meanwhile, Staff Sergeant Parker edged toward Johnson's stock-still body, keeping his head low and crawling tight against the wall to avoid the sniper's crosshairs. Every breath filled his lungs with the fine dust that had been a constant nuisance to the soldiers since their arrival. He was continuing his snail's approach toward Private First-Class Kyle Johnson when another shot rang out, flashing up dust near his face and blinding him momentarily. The sniper's shot was just enough to give away his position to Whitaker and Connelly. They began a rapid-fire assault as Parker advanced on the wounded soldier. After what felt like an eternity, Parker finally reached his teammate, "How you doin', Johnson?"

"I think I'm okay, Staff Sergeant, but I can't feel my legs."

"It's probably just temporary, son. C'mon, let's get out of here." Parker jumped to his feet, grabbed the young man from beneath his arms, and dragged him quickly toward the doorway of their shelter while Whittaker and Connelly continued their attack.

"I'm out," Connelly hissed and paused in his firing to reload. The brief pause of one rifle offered just enough opportunity for another report from the sniper. Parker's movement was just enough to offer an opening in the body armor. The sniper's shot found its mark deep in Staff Sergeant Parker's chest. He collapsed hard against the door jamb, still holding onto Johnson and moaned, "Take him."

Whitaker tossed his M16 to a teammate and ran to catch Johnson before he fell from Staff Sergeant Parker's grip. "Martin! Gomez! Bring in Staff Sergeant!" he barked.

During all the commotion, Connelly locked in on the sniper and fired. "Got him." Within three minutes of their call, the low rumble of Apache helicopters roared in with their M230 chain guns blasting, reducing the buildings along the once silent, dusty street to nothing more than smoldering rubble.

Whitaker removed Kyle's helmet and loosened his flak jacket. "Hey buddy, how are you doing?"

"Where's Staff Sergeant? Where is he?" Kyle tried to wrestle himself from Whitaker's hold, but in his weakened state, only fell hard against him.

"He's here, Johnson. The medics will be here any minute; you just lay quiet."

Three medics rushed into the weathered shack. Two attended furiously to Johnson removing his flak jacket and running his vitals. After a quick, but thorough examination, the medic slapped Johnson on the shoulder and said, "You'll live, soldier," and gave the all-clear to transport him to the waiting chopper.

The senior medic went straight to Parker and began pulling off the body armor that should have protected him from any fatal wounds. The armor did not come off quickly and he thought fiercely of the precious time being wasted while he struggled with the heavy covering. "These things can be a curse or a blessing!" He swore under his breath. When the armor was finally removed, the medic saw what he had feared. A brilliant patch of crimson spread quickly across the wounded soldier's camo blouse. He looked grimly at Connelly.

Tom Connelly came to relieve the soldiers who had caught Parker before he hit the ground. "Hey Staff Sergeant, I'm here. I'm gonna take off your Kevlar, okay, man?" He stooped down behind Parker, propped him up against his chest and removed the helmet carefully, and laughed nervously, "Looks like they missed your hard head."

Parker chuckled hoarsely and focused his eyes on his friend. Connelly spoke softly, "We got him, sir, and the medics say Johnson will be all right. Connelly glanced nervously at the man working on Parker, but he just shook his head. A sob welled up from deep within Connelly's soul, but he choked it back and tightened his grip on his friend. Tears began to stream down his dust-covered face, but he quickly wiped them away. "You stay with me, sir." Connelly's voice rose in desperation but softened again as he whispered to his brother-in-arms, "Sandy will have my head on a platter if --" Nelly could not finish his statement. He could not say out loud what he feared the most, certain that too soon it would become a reality.

"You tell my girl that I love her, Tom," Parker whispered. His breathing labored in short gasps as he fought to stay alive just a little longer. He wanted to make sure his best friend would take his message to his wife.

"You tell her yourself, Joe. We'll be home before you know it. You told me so yourself. Then Sandy can make one of those awesome pies you always talk about." Connelly whispered as he tightened his hold on his friend.

"You do what I asked okay, Tom? Tell her I've gone on ahead and I'll be waiting on her." Staff Sergeant Parker's body shook violently as he struggled for one more breath. One never came and he died quietly in Connelly's arms. Connelly pressed his cheek against Parker's damp head. Overcome with grief, he held his friend in a tight bear hug and let the tears fall.

Suddenly, a firm hand gripped his shoulder, pulling him back from his anguish. "You're next in command, sir." The medic said sadly.

Connelly looked up and let out a ragged breath, "Right." He loosened his hold on Parker and stood to face his men. He was not the only soldier who mourned the loss of Staff Sergeant Parker. "MOVE OUT!"

John 15:13 "Greater love has no one than this that he lay down his life for his friends."

CHAPTER 2

Dear Joe,

I pray this letter finds you safe. The boys and I are doing just fine. They start spring break next week and both are fit to be tied. Not to worry though, darling. They may be looking forward to not having school, but there are plenty of chores for them. I've been making a list, so we can surprise you when you come home. We're counting the days until then, honey. It's been quiet here and the weather has been good to us. We had a pretty good rain the other day and the garden is sprouting already. One of the mares will be ready to foal in a few weeks.

Mr. Olsen asked about you at church today and Miss Laney sends a prayer and a hug your way. We are all praying for you and your unit, darling, and praying that you are all safe and strong.

Mr. Beechum finally broke down and bought that John Deere tractor he'd been wanting for months. Mrs. Beechum, of course, would rather have gone to Dollywood and she didn't mind telling all the ladies about it after church. Mr. Beechum must have put his foot down.

Sandy smiled to herself as she wrote the last line, recalling Mrs. Beechum's not-so-subtle remarks about her husband taking a stand for what he wanted. She continued her letter to her husband of fifteen years, reporting the news of their small town in Western Maryland, and the latest antics of their two sons.

Well, my love, that's about it. Have I told you how much I love you? Let me tell you now. Sandy penned another full page to her husband and closed her letter the same way she had since their early years when Joe was in boot camp; with a soft mist of perfume that he had bought her for her birthday and a gentle kiss at the bottom to seal it.

The half-mile stroll to the mailbox helped to clear her head as she enjoyed the quiet stillness of the woods. She absently brushed away a lone tear that slipped from her emerald, green eyes. As with many of the others, she didn't notice this one. It was just a part of how her life was these days; all the days since Joe started deploying. There were good days, and bad days; sometimes tears all day, and sometimes they just slipped out unannounced and unnoticed. She let out a deep sigh. Dusk was quickly approaching, and it was time to go find her sons. They were out on the property somewhere, and she had a pretty good idea where. When they ran off like this, it was usually down to the pond with their fishing poles and Shadow, their German shepherd.

For some reason, Sandy could not take her mind off her husband tonight. Normally the day-to-day chores crowded out the lonely times, but evening was falling, and it was then that she missed him most. "Joe, I think this is the most difficult part when you are so close to coming home."

Sandy stopped at the front porch and filled her lungs with the cool evening air. Spring was certainly on the way, but there was still a chill in the air. She stepped back into the house and lifted Joe's old worn denim jacket from the hook by the front door. It was too large for her petite frame, but she felt Joe's closeness in every thread, every fiber of the garment. She shrugged into the jacket and wrapped it tight around her. Closing her eyes, she imagined his arms, strong and safe, enveloping her. The combined scents of horse and wood smoke crowded her nostrils and mind with memories of the days when she and Joe ran the ranch together. A lump filled her throat and threatened to come up, but she swallowed hard and squared her shoulders like a good Army wife. "Hang in there, kiddo, just another few weeks and he'll be home."

Sandy stepped down the wood plank stairs of the wrap-around porch and surveyed the property, thinking again of the repairs that would need to be done before Joe came home. The fence back in the woods by the road needed mending, the porch needed painting, and the barn doors needed repair. She gazed out over the fifteen acres of partially wooded rolling hills and ten acres of fenced lush pasture. Dotting the landscape were three milk cows, a two-year-old stallion, two geldings, and two brood mares, one of which was about to foal in a matter of weeks, grazing lazily in the cool afternoon air.

Joe and Sandy had purchased the ranch a year after they were married after he had returned from his first tour of duty in Iraq. She remembered their conversation vividly. Anticipating the birth of their first child, they were lying together on the couch like spoons in a drawer; her back pressed tightly against his front. Joe picked up a lock of her chestnut brown hair and twirled it around his calloused fingers and kissed it softly before he spoke. "Sandy, you know how much we love horses and the wide-open spaces?"

"Mm-hmm," She murmured, and clumsily rolled over to face him.

"Well, what do you say we buy a ranch?" He said, searching her eyes for a hint of excitement, or agreement. She dropped her gaze from his and bit her bottom lip. Joe smiled. He recognized the look. She did it whenever she was uncertain or troubled. He made note of it, and gently pressed on. "Honey, I want a home for our kids, not some rental house in the 'burbs.' I want to teach them to fish and ride and do all those things that we did growing up." The look in his eyes as he spoke was hopeful, excited, and determined.

"I'd say that's a wonderful idea, Joe," Sandy said, nudging closer. "But can we afford to buy a ranch? I mean the rent on this house, and I use the term loosely, is tough enough to make, and with the baby coming . . ." Sandy's voice trailed off.

Joe chided her, "Oh ye of little faith. Come on, Sandy. I'll be getting a raise soon and we've got the GI Bill to buy our first house. Besides, I've been praying on it, and I believe this is what God wants us to do."

Sandy looked intently into his deep brown eyes and was reminded, "Trust in the Lord with all your heart and lean not on your own understanding." She smiled and kissed him. "Well then, if you think that is what God wants, then who am I to say no?" She wrapped her arms tight around her husband's muscular chest. "When do you want to start looking?" It was Joe's turn to fall silent. She jerked her head up and peered suspiciously at him, "Joe?"

"Now Sandy, you know I would never make a huge purchase like that until I spoke with you," Joe said, "but I did find a ranch I want you to look at. The mortgage payments would be only about one hundred dollars more than what we're paying for rent, and with the extra money I'll be making, we can do that easy," Joe's voice softened to a whisper. "Just don't say 'no' until we see it together, okay, darlin'?" He brushed her cheek softly, anticipating her answer.

Sandy stroked his whiskered face and whispered. "When do you want to go see it?"

"How about right now?"

Sandy smiled, thinking back on the drive out to the ranch and the first time she laid eyes on their new home. Joe turned their old truck down the dirt road that wound its way through the tall maples and oaks that would soon be their property. She took his free hand that rested on the gearshift and brought it to her lips, then turned her gaze to her husband, her eyes moist with emotion. She knew at that moment that this was what God wanted for them. They were home.

Joe helped her out of the truck and wrapped his arms around her from behind, "You see darlin,' it's not too big. It's just big enough for us and all the babies we're going to have." Joe smiled broadly at his bride and kissed her on the top of her head. "I already checked with the realtor, and he said the structure, foundation, and roof are solid."

"The porch needs some help," Sandy smiled ruefully and nodded toward the sagging wrap-around porch.

"Yes, it does, and the interior needs paint, too," Joe said matter-of-factly. "We've got a barn, a stable for ten horses, and a nice big shed for me. They are all in fair shape, they just need a fresh coat of paint, and a few window replacements on the storage shed, and stable. All together what do you think?"

"I love it." She smiled up at her husband and laughed out loud when he let out a holler and swept her up in his arms, swinging her around. "That's my girl," he shouted.

Sandy giggled wildly as he swung her. When he finally stopped and placed her back on her feet, she was still laughing and trying to catch her breath, "Now you do know that all this work has to be done before your next deployment."

"Oh, you bet. We've got ten months."

They slaved, sweated, and sacrificed for nine tough, grueling months until finally, they were able to step back and see what they had accomplished. Of course, there would always be work that had to be done, but the house was now a home. The old hardwood floors throughout the house were scrubbed and polished and new vinyl floors were laid in the kitchen, mudroom, and two bathrooms. During the frigid winter months, they would enjoy the coziness of the fireplaces in the living room, and master bedroom, and the wood stove in the kitchen.

The kitchen was open with a dining area large enough to accommodate a polished oak dining table that seated twelve. French doors opened onto the wrap-around porch and paned windows stretched from the floor to the ceiling on either side of the French doors bringing the outdoors in. Another door, just to the right of the kitchen stove connected the kitchen to the mudroom with ample room for a washer, dryer, and folding table. Between bartering, trading, and purchasing, Sandy and Joe were able to acquire half a dozen chickens, a rooster, a cow and a couple of horses to get started. It wasn't long after they finished the farm that he was called back to duty.

A cool gust of wind put an end to Sandy's reminiscing. She checked the shed to confirm what she had already suspected, the fishing poles, and tackle box were missing.

Gray, rain clouds gathered on the horizon as Sandy made her way toward the bass pond, quickening her pace beneath the ever-darkening sky.

1 Peter 5:6 "Humble yourselves, therefore, under God's mighty hand, that He may lift you up in due time."

CHAPTER 3

"HERE, LET ME HELP you." Fifteen-year-old Joe Jr. reached toward the fishhook and nightcrawler in Ben's hands.

"No Joe, I can do this," Ben pushed his brother's hands away.

"All right, but don't be all day about it. The rain will be here before you get that worm on the hook."

Ben's concentration locked on the worm and his tongue wriggled and writhed right along with the wriggling and writhing bait he was attempting to wrap around the hook. Finally, with the worm securely gaffed, the eleven-year-old boy turned happily to his big brother, "Watch this cast," Ben said. With his tongue still working furiously, he dropped the hook with the impaled nightcrawler, reeled the line up slightly, drew the fishing pole back carefully, then with one sweeping motion, sent the bait, sinker, and bobber sailing away flawlessly across the pond, slapping the water with a soft plop.

"Nice cast little bro'," Joe exclaimed.

Ben smiled with pride at his big brother and they both settled on the sloping bank. They sat silent for a moment or two, and then Ben spoke, "Joe, do you miss daddy?"

"Sure, I do. Why?"

"I don't know. I just miss him. It doesn't seem like he'll ever come home." Huge teardrops threatened to spill over. "I feel like crying sometimes but I don't want to cry around Mom."

"That's okay, Ben, I feel like crying too, sometimes. He'll be home soon. Remember what mom told us the other day?"

"Yeah, it just feels like a long time," Ben said.

Joe, Jr. laid his arm across his little brother's shoulders. "It'll be all right, Ben. Just you wait."

Sandy stayed back and observed the interaction between her two sons. Joe Jr. was born shortly before his father left for his second deployment. She and Joe were convinced that the work they did on the ranch brought on the delivery a week ahead of schedule, and although Joe was ordered to leave sooner, the Army was gracious enough to allow him to be with his wife for the birth of their first son. But as happy as Joe was to be with his wife and newborn son, he was anxious to return to Iraq and finish the mission with his men.

Joe Jr. had matured quickly from taking over a lot of his dad's responsibilities on the ranch. His shock of raven hair drew out his green eyes. He was tall for his age and took pleasure in the fact that he was taller than his mom. He hoped one day to reach his dad's six-foot, three-inch height.

"Just think, Ben, by the time summer is here dad will be home. You just keep thinking about that. Okay?"

"All right Joe, I guess you're right. I just get these awful feelings in my gut sometimes." Ben looked up at his brother and gave him a weak smile. "I believe you, Joe. I'll just think about summer."

"Good," Joe said with a nod of his head. A chill wind reminded them that the storm was approaching. "Come on, Ben. We've got to get going." Joe watched the bobber jerk and skirt its way across the pond, leaving a tiny wake as his brother reeled in his hook.

Ben absently brushed a wisp of light brown hair from his eyes and looked at his big brother. As much as he tried to be independent, he had a strong dependence on him for emotional and moral support. Along with all the normal qualities of the average eleven-year-old, Ben also possessed a gift of knowing things. He didn't always tell his mom, but he confided in his brother often. Joe didn't understand Ben's gift, but he believed him and felt a strong responsibility toward him. He remembered the things that frightened him when he was Ben's age during his dad's deployments. The sense of loss when their father deployed grew less and less for Joe, but Ben felt a strong loss every day. Sandy noticed that Joe didn't cry anymore when his dad left, and she knew it bothered him. She had tried to talk to him from time to time, but he kept his fears and feelings tucked safely inside. She chalked it up to his age and took comfort in the fact that he did confide in Steve, their minister.

Sandy glanced up at the approaching storm and trotted toward Ben and Joe Jr. When old Shadow, spotted his mistress, he struggled to get up. A pang of sadness came over Sandy as Shadow lumbered toward her. The hip dysplasia was taking its toll, and she couldn't bear to see him in so much pain. Soon, she would have to make the difficult decision to put their loyal companion down. When he finally reached her, she grabbed his large head and rubbed him gently under his gray chin. Shadow succumbed to Sandy's affections and lay down slowly in the soft spring grass, offering up his belly for her to rub. "Oh, you big baby," Sandy laughed. "Let's get the boys before this storm explodes. I'll rub your belly later." She stooped next to Shadow and gave him a quick rub anyway. Thunder rumbled over the mountains. Quickly she got to her feet and trotted toward the pond, with Shadow following.

"Let's go, boys. The last place we want to be is in this open field," Sandy said.

"Mom, you should have seen Ben's cast. It was perfect!" Joe Jr. exclaimed as he reeled in his line. A quick inspection of his hook revealed that he did nothing more than feed the bass in their pond.

"You guys catch anything," Sandy asked.

"Nope," Ben answered, obviously annoyed with the non-compliant bass in the pond.

"Well at least you provided supper for a few fish," Sandy joked. "Now let's go see about ours." Sandy tousled Ben's hair, and the four of them turned toward the house. By the time they reached the house, the first big drops of rain had begun to fall. "Just leave the poles and tackle box in the mudroom, boys," Sandy shouted over the rain, "we can put them away tomorrow." She held the screen door open while her brood tumbled up the wood plank steps. Suddenly, a sharp clap of thunder sent Shadow bolting between the boys, slamming Joe into the screen door and sending Ben sliding across the mudroom floor where he stopped just short of the washer.

"Shadow, will you watch where you're going, please?" Ben shouted and picked himself up off the floor. Shaking his head he muttered, "You crazy dog."

Sandy laughed, "Okay, okay cut old Shadow some slack, Ben. You know how storms scare him."

"Oh, all right. Sorry, Shadow." Ben got on his hands and knees and crawled under the kitchen table where Shadow had retreated and cuddled with his dog. He kissed the old shepherd on his gray nose and wrapped his arms around his thick neck. "I love ya, boy." The boy and his dog curled up under the table and drifted off to sleep until the smell of their supper awakened them. Hamburgers, fried potatoes, and sliced tomatoes.

Sandy set the table for three, *"Won't be long, there will be four place settings. Oh Lord, please bring him home safe."*

"Okay fellas, go wash up," Sandy called over her shoulder as she prepared the plates.

"Mom," Ben said as he crawled from under the table, "do you think daddy will be home before my birthday?"

"Well, Ben, since your birthday is three months away, I would say yes, but you know we've talked about this, haven't we?" Sandy stroked his cheek and looked tenderly at her youngest son. She knew his fear all too well.

"Yes Ma'am," Ben lowered his head and pretended to examine the hole in the toe of his sock.

Sandy quickly put the plates on the kitchen table and knelt in front of him. He had his mother's mouth and her smile, but tonight the corners of his mouth were turned down into a frown and his bottom lip trembled. Looking into his deep brown eyes, she felt as though she were looking into her husband's eyes.

Large tears welled up and spilled over. "I miss daddy." The boy stepped forward, threw his arms around his mother's neck, and began to sob. "I don't know what it is mom; I've just got a bad feeling tonight. I'm sorry!"

Sandy held him close to her and bit her bottom lip until she tasted blood. *"A little help here, Lord."* "Honey, listen. Do you remember what daddy told all of us before he left?"

"Yes," Ben took a deep breath and wiped his eyes on his sleeve, "he told us to be brave for him, and to take care of each other because if he knows we're okay, he can do his job better."

"That's right," Sandy said. "And what is the Scripture verse he asked you to memorize?"

"Psalm 56, verse 3," Ben said, "When I am afraid, I put my trust in You."

"Right again. We must have faith that God will bring daddy home. Even when it feels like he'll never come home. Okay, sweetie?" Sandy gave Ben a reassuring hug and held his face in her petite, calloused hands. "Go and wash up now before your supper gets cold."

Ben left his mother's arms and brushed past his brother without looking up. Joe could see that Ben had been crying and looked to his mother for an explanation. Sandy stood up, keeping her back to Joe and wiped her tears on her apron. She pretended not to notice Joe's inquiring gaze. "Where've you been, Joe?" she asked.

"Prepping the fireplaces in your room and the living room," Joe said. "Is Ben all right?"

"Yeah, he just misses daddy real bad tonight." Sandy poured milk into three glasses.

Joe Jr. reached into the refrigerator and took out the ketchup, mayonnaise, pickles, and mustard. He placed them on the table and then busied himself with the wood stove. Without looking up he spoke, "We talked down by the pond. You know how he gets, Mom? Sometimes he gets feelings about things."

"I know, Joe, he mentioned it, but we don't want to go there tonight. Okay?" Sandy knew the feelings that Joe was talking about. She had had them several times that day but brushed them off as just a passing annoyance. Now she wondered whether something had happened.

Psalm 56:3 "When I am afraid, I put my trust in You."

CHAPTER 4

THE BLACK SEDAN ROLLED silently through the small town of Willow Creek, its windshield wipers slapping furiously against the onslaught of rain.

"I wonder if they roll up the streets every night, or just during thunderstorms," Private Dreyfuss queried, more to himself than to his passenger. The passenger did not respond. Words of condolences and sorrow filled his head. As many times as he had performed this heart-breaking duty, it never got easier. A woman and her children would learn within the hour that her husband and their father would not be coming home this time. Because it was Dreyfuss's first assignment of this kind, Captain Graham could not blame him for the remark.

"Okay, I think this is the turn, the mailbox says 'Parker'." Dreyfuss moved his face closer to the windshield as if being closer would coax more light from the headlamps. "Man, it's dark out here," he said as he maneuvered the sedan carefully into the drive, only to be stopped by the cattle gate. He put the car in park and looked to the captain, "Be right back." Dreyfuss sprinted to the gate, unwound the chain from the post, and pushed the gate wide. The sedan continued down the dirt road that led to the Parker Ranch. The captain remained silent.

"Captain Graham?" Dreyfuss said quietly. The captain turned his head to look at his driver.

"Captain, I've never done this before. Is it customary for me to go to the door with you or should I wait in the car?" Dreyfuss hoped that the captain would tell him to wait in the car.

"You will need to come to the door, Private. Just pull around the driveway there and turn off the car. We don't know how long we will be."

"But I'm soaking wet, Captain."

"I doubt she'll notice, son."

Before the car made it to the front door, Shadow announced their arrival with loud bellows and scrambled from beneath the kitchen table. Ben and Joe Jr.

stopped clearing the table and looked quickly up at their mother. Sandy stood at the sink drawing water to wash the dishes. She looked back at them, frozen in fear.

"Mom! Maybe it's Dad," Ben shouted and raced to the door behind Shadow before Sandy could stop him.

"Ben! Wait!" Sandy yelled.

Seeing the anguish on his mom's face, Joe turned and ran down the hall to catch his brother. Ben swung open the front door, mindless of the storm still thrashing outside. The captain and private stood stone-faced at the door. Suddenly the world around Sandy fell away and she stared down the hallway, seeing nothing but the men standing at the end of it. She floated toward the door, toward the men, unaware of her movements as her feet carried her from the kitchen to the soldiers; her eyes glued to the captain. "Boys, run upstairs please," she said without realizing it.

"But, Mom," Ben cried "Why? Where's Daddy?"

Joe Jr. knew why the soldiers were there and looked up at his mother; tears already forming in her eyes.

"Joe, please take Ben upstairs." Sandy tried to swallow the lump that had settled in her throat. She lifted her chin and focused on the two men. Her mind was a jumble, going in a thousand different directions, unable to focus on a single thought. She suddenly found it strange that the private was soaking wet, and the captain was not. She realized that the gate must have been closed, and then wondered, "Why am I thinking such things?"

Captain Graham waited until the boys were up the stairs. He could still hear them crying softly and knew they were waiting just around the corner at the top of the stairs. He stood before Sandy with his cover in his hands, and the drenching rain falling in sheets behind him. His voice was sorrowful when he spoke, "Mrs. Parker?"

In her sorrow, it didn't occur to Sandy to invite the soldiers in, "Yes?"

"May we come in?"

Sandy stepped aside, still numb, her head swimming. The men entered, grateful for the warmth. "Mrs. Parker," Captain Graham began, "it is with my deepest regret to inform you that your husband was killed in a firefight today. He was shot saving the life of another soldier in his unit."

Sandy's knees buckled and Captain Graham moved quickly to catch her before she fell to the floor. He slipped an arm around her slender waist and walked her to the kitchen table. The dishes were still waiting to be washed, and the table was still waiting to be cleared. The smell of fried potatoes and hamburgers still hung thick in the air. Private Dreyfuss hurried to the cupboard and brought Sandy a glass of cool water from the kitchen faucet. She took it gratefully with trembling hands.

"Mrs. Parker, is there anyone we can call?"

Her voice was thick, "I have a sister in town, and my minister, Steve Barnes."

Still disoriented from what was happening, Sandy could not remember her sister, Tanya's, phone number and went to the rolltop desk to find her address book. She tried Tanya's number twice, but her hands shook so badly, and her vision was so distorted that she misdialed twice. She finally surrendered the phone to the captain. He patted her hands gently, took the phone, dialed the number, and then passed the phone back to Sandy.

"Tanya," Sandy said weakly.

"Hey Sandy, how are you making out with this storm?"

"Tanya, I need you to come over," she pleaded.

Tanya did not hear the pain in her sister's voice, "Come out in this weather? You're crazy!" Tanya exclaimed.

Sandy finally broke into heaving sobs, crying uncontrollably.

Captain Graham took the phone, "Ma'am, this is Captain Graham, United States Army. Mrs. Parker's husband was killed in action today."

"Dear God. No," Tanya whispered.

"Your sister needs you here. Can you contact her minister?"

"Yes, of course. Thank you, Captain. Will you stay with her until we get there?"

"We'll be here."

Tanya's mind raced as she grabbed her purse and keys and bolted to her car. The storm was beginning to subside, but Tanya didn't notice. All she knew was that she needed to get to her sister. Once she was in the car, she dialed Steve Barnes's number.

"Hello, Steve?" Tanya's voice began to break.

"Tanya? What is it?" Steve said, hearing the despair in her voice.

"Steve, Joe's been killed. There is a Captain Graham at Sandy's house now. He just called me, and she needs us both there. Can I pick you up?"

"Yes, yes. I'll be waiting outside."

Steve ran out the front door and into the pouring rain just as Tanya pulled up. He quickly slid into the passenger seat and looked at the woman next to him. "Do you know anything more than what you told me, Tanya?" He asked, placing his Bible on the seat between them.

"No, I'm afraid not," Tanya said, pulling away from the curb. "Sandy called me and said she needed me to come over. Then she just started crying. That's when Captain Graham got on the phone and told me that she needed us there right away."

"Wasn't this his last deployment?" Steve said.

"Yes," Tanya said. They drove in silence until they finally arrived at the ranch. Tanya quickly wiped the tears from her face as she turned into Sandy's driveway.

Steve laid a hand on her shoulder and squeezed. "You'll need to be strong for her, Tanya. Can you do this?"

"Yeah, I'll be all right." Tanya gave him a faint smile and put her attention back on the dark road in front of her.

All the lights were on in the farmhouse and the smell of wood smoke hung in the cool air when Steve and Tanya arrived. Sandy looked up when she saw her sister and Steve come through the door and the tears began to fall again. Tanya ran to her and sat gently next to her, wrapping her arms around her. Ben and Joe had come downstairs and were seated on the couch next to Sandy. When Ben saw his Aunt Tanya and Steve come in, he slid over to make room for them next to his mother.

Captain Graham rose from where he sat in the wingback chair by the fireplace and introduced himself. "Good evening, ma'am, sir, I'm Captain Graham. This is Private First Class Dreyfuss."

"Thank you for being here, Captain." Steve shook the officer's hand and turned to shake hands with Dreyfuss. "I'm Steve Barnes, Sandy's and the boys' minister. This is Tanya, Sandy's sister."

The soldiers remained standing after the introductions, "Mrs. Parker, on behalf of the United States Army, and Staff Sergeant Parker's unit we thank you for his service and offer our heartfelt condolences for your loss. May God be with you."

Steve sat next to Ben and put an arm around him and then turned his attention to Joe. The young man sat at the far end of the couch, his expression was blank and unemotional. Steve could see he was withdrawing. Fighting to hold back the emotion that was about to overwhelm him.

Sandy turned her red, tear-stained face to the officer and took his hand, "Captain, the soldier whose life Joe saved, is he all right?"

"Yes, ma'am he is."

"May I ask his name?"

"His name is Johnson, ma'am. Private First-Class Kyle Johnson."

"Thank you."

Once outside, Private Dreyfuss took a moment to wipe the tears from his face. The captain didn't miss it, "That's all right, Private, it happens to all of us."

As the black sedan pulled away from the farmhouse, Sandy Parker's life, as she knew it, would never be the same.

Revelation 21:4 "He will wipe every tear from their eyes. There will be no more death or mourning or crying or pain, for the old order of things has been passed away."

CHAPTER 5

The aroma of freshly brewed coffee pulled Sandy from a deep, but fitful sleep. The reality of the previous night swept over her like a smothering blanket, casting her into a dark world where the morning could not reach her. She rolled over to Joe's side of their sleigh bed and wept softly into his pillow. Dread filled her and she was afraid, afraid of facing life without her soul mate.

Down the hall, Joe Jr. stared out his window at the same hopeless morning. Tears rolled down his already moist cheeks and into his soaking wet pillow. "Dad, why did you have to go back? What's going to happen now? It was all right when I knew you'd be coming home, but now . . ." He stifled a sob, "God, why did you take him from us!" In his anger, Joe slammed his fist into his pillow and rolled over, turning his back to the window, to the beautiful spring day and God.

Ben sat staring into his bowl of Cheerios. "Aunt Tanya?"

"Yes, Ben," Tanya said as she poured herself a cup of coffee.

"I saw Daddy last night. I had a dream about him."

Tanya sat at the table next to her nephew and stared at him. "No kidding?" Her voice was still tired from the long night, "What was the dream about, Ben?"

"Well, I dreamed that he was sitting next to me on the bed, and he was smiling. He looked so happy. He told me not to be sad and that we were going to be all right." Ben wiped the tears on his cheek before they dropped into his bowl of cereal. "I wish I could see him for real."

Tanya took the child's hand, "Ben, look at me." He turned his face to her. "Ben, you understand that your dad didn't die in vain, don't you?"

Ben sniffed, "Uh huh."

"And you know that if he could come home to you, your brother, and your mom that he would?"

"Yeah, I know."

"I think your dad came to see you last night to let you know that he still loves you all and he wants you to know that he is happy where he is." Tanya reached out and took him in her arms. "You are a very special boy, Ben. How blessed you are that he came to see you."

Ben wiped his tears on his arm, and sat back down at the table, putting his attention back to his Cheerios; playing with the little 'O's' floating in the sweetened milk, pushing them under, and watching them bob back up.

Tanya looked up from her coffee when she heard the shuffle of bedroom slippers across the hardwood floor in the hallway. She went to Ben, "I think your mom is awake," she said as she pulled his chair away from the heavy oak table. "Why don't you go see if Joe is up?" Sandy scuffled into the kitchen, her thick terry bathrobe wrapped tightly around her, and the collar pulled close around her neck.

Without a word, Sandy sat down heavily at the kitchen table and stared with red, tired eyes at the steaming mug of coffee that Tanya had just placed in front of her. The sorrow that had settled into them would remain with her for a lifetime.

Ben looked sadly at his unresponsive mom, then at Tanya who offered him an encouraging smile. He nodded but didn't speak and left the room in search of comfort from his big brother.

The eleven-year-old padded upstairs and down the hallway to Joe's room. He took his time to consider the pictures that lined the hallway on both sides; photographs of him, and his brother together or with their mother and father. He stopped in front of his favorite picture and got lost in it, as he always did. In the picture, he, his brother, and their dad are standing together on the bank of the pond with their fishing poles in hand, happy smiles across their faces. His mom had taken it one autumn day, just before his dad left for his last deployment. It had been a wonderful day. They had ridden the horses through the trails in the woods surrounding their property and then stopped at the bass pond for a picnic. Ben reluctantly pulled himself away from the picture and went to Joe's room. Quietly he put his ear to the door and turned the knob slowly.

"Who is it," Joe muttered.

"It's me, Joe. C-can I come in?" Ben stammered.

"No."

Discouraged and yearning for comfort from his big brother, Ben retreated from the door and skulked toward his room.

"Ben?" Joe called out.

"Yeah," Ben said, hopeful.

"You can come in," Joe said.

Relieved, Ben swung open the door into the sun-drenched room and saw his brother curled up with his back to the window. Since Joe made no effort to move, Ben sat cross-legged on the floor in front of him. "Are you okay?"

"I don't know, Ben. I don't know how I feel."

"Yeah, me neither. Aunt Tanya made me Cheerios, but I wasn't even hungry for them."

Joe grinned slightly, knowing his little brother's love of Cheerios. "Wow. That is bad. Is Mom up?"

"Yeah, she just came down, and then Aunt Tanya sent me to get you."

"How is she?"

"She seems to be fine. Like I said, she made me Cheerios."

"No, you goof, Mom!"

Ben looked down at his stocking feet, "She looks tired, and she didn't say anything. She just kinda stared at her coffee."

"Where's Steve?" Joe asked.

"He's tending to the horses," Ben said. "Do you think we should go help him?"

Joe thought for a moment, "How long has he been out there?"

"Well, he was already out there when I got up," Ben said.

"Don't bother then." Joe said, "He's probably done already."

Tanya sat at the table with Sandy and waited for her sister to speak. When she didn't, Tanya spoke. "Steve's turning out the horses and milking Emily, Daisy, and Josie. He should be in shortly."

Sandy gazed absently into her steaming cup of coffee but couldn't form any words. She looked up at Tanya and opened her mouth to speak, but all that came were the deep, relentless sobs that had haunted her throughout the night.

Tanya rose quickly and went to her, pulling her close, "There, there, Sandy. You go ahead and cry it out." Tanya wept softly, trying not to let her sister hear her; after all, she was the big sister. She was supposed to be the strong one. She felt Sandy pulling away from her and loosened her hold on her.

Sandy took in a deep breath, "I'm okay, Tanya. I'll be all right." She rubbed her face with her hands, and then laid her head on the table, her chestnut hair spilling across her face and onto the table. "This can't be happening. I was certain that he'd be coming home, that we'd spend the rest of our lives together and grow old on this ranch."

Steve came in from outside and saw Tanya kneeling next to Sandy. He rushed over and helped Tanya up and then pulled a chair over and sat facing Sandy. He didn't speak but bowed his head and prayed.

When he was through, Sandy looked up at him and erupted into fresh tears, "Oh, Steve, why can't I stop crying?"

"You'll stop when it's your time to stop, Sandy. It will take some time," Steve said, still holding her hands. "Are the boys up yet?" Sandy looked at Tanya for the answer.

"Ben is up. I sent him to check on Joe," Tanya offered.

Steve and Sandy climbed the stairs and stopped in front of Joe's door. Steve knocked softly, "You guys up?"

"We're up." Joe sat up in his bed.

Sandy and Steve came in and sat on the bed next to Joe while Ben got up and sat next to Steve. Sandy put an arm around her oldest son and pulled him close to her allowing him to snuggle next to her. A sob began to bubble up from deep down but try as he could, Joe couldn't stop it. She held him while he cried and saw that Ben, his little shoulders heaving with each sob, had his head buried in Steve's shoulder. She ignored the fierce, building heat of the sun beating through the window warming her back beneath her robe, but spoke softly to her sons, keeping her voice low and controlled. "Joe, Ben, we talked about this, didn't we? We talked about how this might happen, and we needed to be strong."

Joe interrupted her, "Mom, you said if we prayed, God would bring dad home."

Steve reached for Joe's shoulder and spoke gently, "Joe, God didn't want to take your dad from you. That's not what He does, and I believe you know that. God's tears were the first to hit the floor when your dad was killed and even though He didn't want to take him away from us, He is welcoming him now in Heaven. That is where he will be when we go to meet him. God will never abandon us, Joe -- not you, Ben, your mom, none of us. He will always be here with us. We can't turn our backs on Him now. Do you understand that?"

Joe nodded to Steve and his face softened into sadness rather than anger.

"Mom?"

"Yes, Ben."

"Are we going to have to move from the ranch?"

Sandy had asked herself that same question, just minutes before.

There were so many decisions to make, and so much to do. "For now, no, Ben, we're not going anywhere. There's going to be a lot to do, but we have Aunt Tanya and Steve. We just need to take this one day at a time, but the first thing we need to do is pray."

Psalm 6:9 "The Lord has heard my cry for mercy; the Lord accepts my prayer."

CHAPTER 6

A soft summer breeze glided down from the mountains that surrounded the green pastures of the Parker ranch. It passed gently across the family burial plot where Joe Parker was laid to rest just seven weeks ago. It continued its journey through the barn, gathering up the sweet smell of hay and carrying it through to the corral where Joe Jr. and Ben groomed the horses.

"Ben, just pick the hooves and comb their tails. Leave the rest to me. You're too short to do the rest."

"Well, I won't be short for long," Ben bragged. "Mom says I'll be tall as daddy someday. After all, I'll be twelve next month."

"That's fine, but for now you're still too short," Joe replied curtly.

"Joe, what's the matter? It seems like you're always mad." Ben moved around to the gelding's rear legs and leaned into him with his shoulder. Familiar with the routine, the horse offered his hoof freely to the boy.

"I'm not mad, Ben. I just miss daddy. I wanted our summer vacation to be like it used to be when we went fishing, or to the pony auctions on the Eastern Shore." Joe ducked under the horse's head and started to work on the mane, combing out the knots. "I feel like Mom expects me to do everything he did, plus my chores, and I'm just tired is all. I guess I'm just ticked off about everything, but I'm not mad at you, little bro'." Joe tousled his brother's hair.

"I can help you with more of the chores," Ben offered.

"You already are. Don't worry about me, Ben." Joe smiled at his brother and went back to grooming Pilgrim, a tall bay gelding.

Sandy hung up the phone and turned to Tanya and Steve sitting at the kitchen table with the breakfast dishes still in front of them. "That was Miss Laney from church. She said she just came from Willowdale and all the grocery stores, including the members' only one, have shortened their hours. They're going to start closing at five o'clock and limit the days they will be open. What do you suppose is happening?"

Tanya turned a questioning look to Steve. "Have you heard anyone talking about it?"

Steve thought for a moment. "I would imagine because of the fuel and food shortages caused by the floods, fires, and storms across the country, not to mention the failing economy, stores are hurting." His attention was divided between the women sitting at the table with him and the cows grazing lazily in the pasture.

"I'm glad we planted a bigger garden," Sandy replied, as she cleared the table. "Now, we just have to pray for a good crop. Steve, you want to put in a good word, please?"

"I'll see what I can do." Steve smiled, drained his coffee cup and went to put it in the porcelain sink.

Sandy watched the way her sister followed Steve's every movement with an interest she had not noticed before. He was, after all, a very handsome man and not what one would think the town minister should look like. His dark, brown hair lay thick and wavy, and fell softly over his forehead and ears. A closely trimmed mustache and beard defined his strong facial features. Standing at a full six feet two inches, his tanned, muscular frame towered over Sandy and Tanya. "Well, ladies, it's time I got some work done. Sandy, you take care, and I'll pray for rain." He planted a small kiss on her cheek and gave her a firm hug. "I'll be in touch." He turned to Tanya and smiled. "I'll talk to you later."

"Wait, Steve. I'll walk you out. Sandy, be right back!" Tanya called over her shoulder and followed Steve out the door.

Sandy watched them as they walked toward the barn and was suddenly taken aback when Steve took Tanya by the hand. A sudden rush of . . . what? Jealousy? Envy? "Oh, forgive me, Father. I should be happy that my sister found such a good man." Sandy turned and went to the mudroom. There was laundry that needed to be done and things that needed her attention. "I must stay busy." She filled a wicker basket with wet towels from the washer and loaded the washer again with the sheets she had pulled from the beds earlier. She slammed the lid shut on the washer, hoisted the basket up on her hip, kicked open the mudroom door. Not realizing the force she had used, the door slammed hard against the outside wall. Sandy paused for a moment shocked at her behavior. "I'm so sorry Father, please forgive me for whatever I'm feeling. Lord, I don't even know!"

Tanya joined her sister at the clothesline. "Hey, need some help?"

"Sure." Sandy moved the laundry basket between them with her foot and grabbed a towel from the basket. "Well?" she said, raising an eyebrow and giving her sister a sideways glance.

"Well, what?" Tanya asked, trying to hide the smile that crept across her lips. Her hazel eyes danced with joy at the thought of Steve Barnes, and she knew very well what her little sister was talking about.

"I saw you two holding hands and he made the first move. Plus, you couldn't take your eyes off him all morning." Sandy said quietly.

Tanya caved. "Truth to tell, Sandy, we've been interested in each other for quite some time now. We were going to tell you, but then Joe died and, well, we just didn't think it was the right time. Please don't be angry."

Sandy bent to pick up another towel and then looked at her sister. Her words were soft, but Tanya could see the hurt that still lingered in her eyes. "I'm not angry. I'm just upset that you felt you had to hide it from me."

"I'm so sorry, Sandy," Tanya said.

Sandy felt the pain come back again and buried her face in the wet towel. The heaviness of the towel muffled the sobs that escaped from deep down inside her. After nearly two months the ache had slowly subsided, but the grief still overcame her when she least expected it.

Tanya quickly stepped over the laundry basket and wrapped her arms around her little sister. "Oh, Sandy, please forgive us. We didn't mean to make you sad."

Sandy shook her head, causing Tanya to step back. "No, you and Steve didn't do anything wrong and there is nothing to forgive. It's just that," she paused to swallow hard, "it still hurts sometimes that's all. I'm afraid I'll be doing this for a long time."

"You take all the time you need, Sandy." Tanya took her sister back in her arms and held her while she cried. A moment passed and she felt the sobs subsiding and Sandy relaxing in her grip. She stepped back once again and took her by the shoulders, "You hang in there, kiddo. We'll get through this together."

"Thanks, Sis." Sandy patted the tears from her face with the towel she was still holding, and then hung it on the clothesline. She suddenly felt the need to see her sons, "Let's go find the boys."

When they had finished hanging the towels on the line, they strolled toward the barn. The warm summer breeze caressed their faces and Sandy smiled and closed her eyes, as God wiped her tears. "Thank you for looking after us, Father." She gave Tanya a nudge. "So, are you going to see Steve tonight?"

"Yes, he's cooking supper for me," Tanya said.

"Mmm, I hear he is a terrific cook."

"He is," Tanya smiled. "Mrs. Olsen is bringing by her famous chicken casserole tonight, isn't she?"

"Yes. I'm grateful for the help from everyone but I need to get back into taking care of things myself around here." Sandy said, "I can't keep depending on the congregation to keep the place running."

"Well, for now, take the help while you have it. I saw Mr. Beechum at the general store yesterday and he said not to put the livestock in the lower field tomorrow. He'll be by in the morning to mow." Tanya said. "No doubt Mrs. Beechum will come too." Tanya laughed. "Half the time she pretends to be angry with the poor man, but you know she dotes on him like I've never seen."

Sandy smiled softly at the memory of her last letter to her husband, telling him about Mr. Beechum's tractor. They emerged from the barn into the corral, "Hey, fellas."

"Hi, Mom," Joe greeted her with a smile. It pained her to see that his smiles weren't as bright as they used to be and that an expression of sadness had settled over him. He nodded to Tanya, "Hey, Aunt Tanya," and turned his attention back to grooming Buck, a stout, buckskin gelding.

At times Sandy felt he was withdrawing from her, and her first instinct was always to go to him as she had done before, but Tanya took her arm as she stepped toward him. "Sandy, wait. Let Steve talk to him. He's dealt with this before, and I think sometimes the boys need someone besides their mom. "No offense," Tanya said apologetically.

"None taken, Tanya. You're right."

"Steve will be here tomorrow," Tanya reassured her.

2 Corinthian 1:3-4 "Praise be to the God and Father of our Lord Jesus Christ, the Father of compassion and the God of all comfort, who comforts us in all our troubles, so that we can comfort those in any trouble with the comfort we ourselves have received from God."

CHAPTER 7

My dear Sandy,

I pray all is well with you, Joe Jr., and Ben. Are the boys minding you? If not, tell them daddy will be home soon to whoop 'em. Just kidding, honey. If there's one thing, I'm sure of, it's you keeping them on the straight and narrow. It's been quiet these past few days. We have a sweep scheduled for tomorrow, Sunday. We don't expect a lot of action but know that's something we can never count on. My men are all doing well, and they loved the snacks and cookies you sent. They send their love and thanks to you and the boys. They always ask to see the pictures of you, the kids, and the ranch. To some of them, those are the closest thing to home they have, and they always say what a lucky man I am, but I already know that. Well darlin', it's almost time to relieve Johnson. I told you about him in my last letter. This is his first tour in country, and a good man. He's only twenty-two so the seasoned soldiers have taken him under their wings.

Tom Connelly says hello and is looking forward to one of your apple pies I've told him about.

Stay strong, Sandy, and know that I love you no matter what.

Tell all the folks at church I said hello and thank them for their prayers and support.

Love, Joe

P.S. Pay close attention to the things that are happening in Washington. I have a feeling things are going to start happening soon now that the new guy is in office.

Sandy sighed and sat back in her chair at the kitchen table. "Joe must have written this the day before he was killed," she said looking up at her sister. "What do you suppose he meant by 'pay close attention'?"

Tanya rose quickly from the table and poured herself another cup of coffee.

"Tanya, what is it?" Sandy asked, puzzled by Tanya's unexpected silence.

Tanya stared down into her coffee cup and shook her head, then looked at her sister with a look of disbelief, "Sandy, you are amazing to me; the way you are handling all of this," she began. "I mean, for pity's sake you lost your husband of fifteen years and here you are three months later reading his last letter to you and you're keeping it all together. I know your faith is strong, but just knowing how much you loved him . . .," Tanya shook her head. "I don't know how you do it." She sat back down at the table and wiped the tears from her face.

"Love him," Sandy corrected her sister.

"What?" Tanya looked up at her.

"Love him." Sandy said, "I still love Joe, Tanya. I'll always love him. And you don't see me all the time. I've cried until there were no more tears left in me, and I've gotten downright angry with God. We both know it wasn't His fault, though." Sandy patted Tanya's outstretched hand. "Today is a good day. Steve said the grieving process would take some time. All we can do is take it one day at a time." Sandy stared hard into Tanya's eyes. Her older sister wore her sadness on her face in the tiny lines around her eyes and mouth. She appeared tired and worn down and it was obvious that her worry for her little sister was beginning to take its toll. "Tanya, listen to me," Sandy continued. "I didn't get to this place by myself. I have you, Steve, Joe Jr., and Ben, and I have God. If we didn't have Him, and all of you," Sandy's gaze fell away from Tanya and remained distant for a moment then she focused back on her sister, "Well, I don't know what we would have done. We're in this together, right?"

Tanya patted Sandy's hand, "You're right. How did you get to be so wise?"

Sandy just smiled, "I learned from my big sister," she said and turned her eyes upward. "I expect mom and dad were there when Joe arrived in Heaven." Suddenly the smile left her face when she noticed Joe's letter on the table, bringing her back to what had troubled her. She picked it up and handed it to her sister, "I'm still concerned about the last words in his letter though. What do you make of it?"

Tanya took the letter and smiled to herself; the soft, powdery sand that covered everything in Iraq had found its way to the United States by way of Joe's letter; making Tanya feel that much closer to her brother-in-law. She rubbed the sand between her fingertips thoughtfully and then re-read the last line of his letter. "I suppose he means just that, Sandy. Something's happening; and I know you can feel it, too. The stores are changing their hours, food and gasoline prices are through the roof, and even unavailable at times. To be perfectly honest, the excuses the media offers don't seem to hold water with me. Times are changing; and I think Joe was right. It will be happening soon.

Days turned to weeks, weeks rolled into months, and the small town of Willow Creek buzzed with speculation and worry. The new Commander in Chief had been in office for seven months and the promises he made during his campaign were coming to fruition, but not in the way the people had expected. The changes were subtle at first, but in the stifling heat of mid-summer, things began to change dramatically. The taxes imposed on the small businesses were too much for many of them and they were forced to close their doors. Seeing the opportunity to provide for the people where the small businessman could not, the bureaucrats in the Supreme City, as it was now called, quickly took advantage of the losses, and funneled the surplus of goods to their government-run stores. The more the media reported that what was happening was for the good of the people, the more the people believed them. It wasn't long before much of the country was following the Supreme Leader like sheep to the slaughter.

Things were no different in Willow Creek. The few banks that remained in business were merged into the ones owned and operated by the regime. Bill's service station, which had been in town for twenty years also closed, leaving the other mom and pop station to fend for itself with little gas and high taxes. Everyone in town knew it would be only a matter of time before that station closed, too.

The morning sun was just cresting over the horizon, burning off the humidity of the evening, when Joe and Ben ran out the back door to do their chores.

Once the horses were groomed and turned out, and the cows milked and turned out as well, the boys returned to the house with buckets of milk in each hand, their stomachs growling at the aroma of frying bacon.

"Breakfast sure smells good, Mom," Joe said, stopping in the mudroom to pour the milk into a larger container. "I'll put this on the truck; do you want the vegetables and eggs to go, too?"

"Yes, please. Thanks, Joe." Sandy said.

"Mom, are we breaking the law?" Ben asked as he poured salsa over his eggs. "I thought the President said that he would be responsible for taking care of the needy people."

Sandy was alarmed by the question, "We're not breaking the law, Ben. Why would the government want to keep us from providing food for hungry families in our community?" With Ben's question, Sandy was beginning to question herself. She certainly didn't want the federal government telling her who she could and could not help in their town. "Look," she said, frustrated, "finish your breakfast. We need to get going."

"Mom, can I drive?" Joe asked as they walked out the door.

"On the way home. Okay?" Sandy said as she climbed into the truck. Ben climbed over the tailgate and took a seat between the milk cans and baskets of vegetables while Joe sat in the cab with his mom. He looked at her thoughtfully. "Mom?"

"Yes, Joe?"

"You look worried," Joe said.

Sandy looked at Joe and smiled, "You're just like your father. Do you know that? He could always read me like a book."

Joe grinned. He liked it when his mom compared him to his father. Then his expression turned somber, "I think Ben was right. We should be more careful," he said.

"What do you mean?" Sandy said.

"I mean, we are breaking the law by doing this. I've heard talk about it at school," Joe said.

Sandy shook her head in disgust, "Well you know what? I am doing what the Lord has asked us to do, so the government can just live with it." When they arrived at the church, Sandy pulled the truck in front.

Joe looked over at his mom, "It'll be all right, Mom. Don't worry." He leaned over and kissed her cheek then got out of the truck and went to the back to help Ben. Between them, they carried a large basket of corn and ran up the stairs through the big oak double doors. They nearly ran into Steve.

"Hey guys, where are you going in such a hurry?" Steve gave them each a strong hug.

"We brought the food and milk for the community warehouse, Uncle Steve," Joe said. "Where do you want us to put it?" He was now as tall as Steve, from a growth spurt that struck in late spring.

"Bring it inside, guys. I've got some folks coming for it soon." Steve strolled down the stone steps of the church and leaned into the truck on the passenger side. "Hey Sandy, the boys look good. Happy." He smiled.

"Yes, the summer months have been good to them," Sandy said, "and Joe's love of God has returned, thanks to your gentle counseling." She looked gratefully at Steve, but he could tell something was weighing heavy on her mind.

"What is it, Sandy?"

"Steve, Ben asked me this morning if we were breaking the law by providing food for the needy, and then Joe just told me that there was talk at school about it."

Steve looked at her curiously.

"Why are you looking at me like that?" She asked.

"I'm sorry, I didn't mean to." He looked around then back to Sandy.

"It's just that --" he paused.

"Steve, what is it?" Sandy said.

Steve leaned closer into the truck and lowered his voice, "Sandy, government officials are monitoring what people are purchasing at the grocery store. They are not saying why right now, but I have a hunch we're going to find out soon." He glanced at a man walking by, nodded 'hello,' and then continued, "I'm thinking this ought to be our last load for the season, okay?" Steve watched the boys carrying the baskets of vegetables into the church, then smiled at Sandy. "But on the bright side, it looks like you've got a pretty good one. Are you sure you're leaving enough for yourselves?"

"Absolutely," Sandy said, "God has blessed the ranch this season. Annie gave birth to a healthy filly, and we've got about a dozen chicks and the garden thrived."

Ben climbed into the bed of the truck while Joe stood at the driver-side door. He smiled sweetly and held out his hand. "You said I could drive."

"So, I did." Sandy dropped the keys in his open hand, "Here you go, but remember you have your little brother in the back and your mother right next to you."

"Sandy, can I make a suggestion?" Steve said.

"Of course, Steve, what is it?" Sandy said as she slid across to the passenger side.

"I've heard some talk about the bank. I'm not at liberty to say who told me or go into any details but do this for me. Go to the bank and take out as much as you can without closing the account."

"Okay, but what about the future deposits from Joe's Social Security?"

"The news said this morning that Social Security, including survivor benefits for our military, will be put to a stop soon. I'm looking into something safer to put our money into, but for now, I think it would be safer with you. As soon as I research some more, I'll let you know." He leaned in and kissed her lightly on the cheek. "Tanya and I will stop by tonight if that's all right."

"That will be great, Steve. How are you two newlyweds doing?" Sandy asked.

Steve's face lit up, "Wonderful. Thanks for asking. I never thought I'd be this happy. Your sister is a blessing and so are the rest of you," Steve said ruffling Ben's hair when the boy poked his head through the rear window and into the cab.

"I'm glad," Sandy said, "You two are a perfect match."

"That's true. We both had to wait, but God's timing is always perfect," Steve said.

Sandy smiled, "Yes, it is. Thanks for the information, I'll see you tonight."

Steve nodded to Ben to sit down in the back of the truck then slapped the passenger door of the truck. "See you all later."

Sandy turned to Joe, "Ready?"

Joe nodded, put the truck in gear, and slowly pulled away from the curb.

"Do me a favor, Joe, swing by the bank before we head home," Sandy said, as she dug through her purse looking for her wallet.

Joe watched her carefully; her face was drawn with worry, "Sure mom. What was Uncle Steve saying about the grocery store?"

She looked squarely at her son, "You and Ben were right. He said there were government officials at the store, checking what people were buying. He wasn't sure why, but I expect we'll all know soon enough. I'm sure it has everything to do with what we were just talking about. He also said that our money wouldn't be safe in the bank much longer. That's why I'm going to take our money out." Sandy laughed nervously, "Of course, there isn't much in there, to begin with, but it'll be safer at our house than at a government-run bank."

Joe stopped the truck in front of the bank and Ben poked his head through the sliding rear window of the cab again, "Mom, we're almost out of Cheerios. Can we get some more?"

Suddenly panic filled her; a few minutes ago that question would not have bothered her, but after what Steve just told her, she didn't want to let her sons out of her sight. "Okay, but you boys come right back here do you understand? I'll be right across the alley at the bank.

Mind Joe, and don't talk to anyone." Sandy said.

"All right, Mom. Don't have a cow." Ben said, exasperated.

"Here, take this." Sandy handed him a ten-dollar bill. "You might as well get a couple of boxes, the way you eat."

"Thanks, Mom," Ben kissed her cheek, jumped out of the truck, and ran after his brother, toward the grocery store. When they walked through the automatic, sliding glass doors, Joe was surprised to see that there were only two cash registers open. Ignoring the men in black suits that were standing at each aisle and each register, Ben went straight to the cereal aisle. Joe could sense that the men were dangerous and quickly caught up with his brother, grabbed him by the shoulder, and escorted him to one of the registers. He recognized the woman at the register and smiled cautiously. She had been working there for years, but her usual cheerful face was shrouded in a veil of fear. A faint smile barely formed on her lips, but her eyes did not reflect it.

The man standing behind her watched them carefully. "Did you find everything you needed?" he asked Ben.

"Yes, sir," Joe answered.

"Is that all you're getting?" The man grinned. His eyes were dark, and they danced when he spoke, but there was an evil gleam about them that Joe didn't like.

The question was again directed at Ben, but again Joe spoke for him, "This is all we need for now, thanks."

"Very well. Have a nice day, boys." The man nodded.

The cashier handed the change back to Joe and nodded. "Thanks for coming in," she said softly.

Joe nodded back, gave the man a hard look and took his brother by the shoulder again, and led him out.

"Good morning, Mrs. Parker."

"Good morning, Stephanie, how are you?" Sandy said as she walked to the teller's window.

"I'm just fine thanks; and yourself?" Stephanie Miller answered.

"I'm doing well, thank you." Sandy pulled her wallet from her purse and began writing out a check for all but fifty dollars in her account, signed the back of the check, and slid it beneath the bulletproof glass toward the woman.

The teller examined the check carefully and then looked back up at Sandy. "You want to take this much out, Mrs. Parker?"

"Yes," Sandy said. "Is there a problem?"

"No. No problem at all." Stephanie turned to her drawer and began counting out the cash. She looked up from time to time as though she were looking for someone.

Sandy knew the security cameras were on her and tried her best not to look suspicious, but the teller's behavior was making her nervous. Barry Manilow sang softly to 'Mandy' through the overhead speakers while the teller continued to count. Needing something to do with her hands while she waited, Sandy took an envelope from the stack on the counter and prepared to receive the money. Then deciding the single envelope wouldn't hold all the bills, she picked up two more. She continued to watch Stephanie count as Barry sang, "Oh Mandy, you came, and you gave without taking . . ."

"Here you are, Mrs. Parker." Stephanie counted out the money again in front of her, "One hundred, two hundred, three hundred . . . Is there anything else I can do for you?"

"No, Stephanie, this will be all."

Stephanie continued to smile, but Sandy could tell there was something very wrong. "Goodbye, Mrs. Parker. Have a nice day."

"So long, Stephanie." Sandy looked a second longer at Stephanie then turned toward the exit. She had to use every bit of self-control not to turn around again.

The teller watched Sandy leave out the front door and then picked up the phone. She held her hand closed over the mouthpiece when she spoke. "Yes sir, five thousand dollars. Thank you, sir."

Sandy crossed the alley and went to wait by the truck for the boys. She could see them through the big plate glass windows of the grocery store as they finalized their transaction with the cashier. On their way out they were joined by Mr. Beechum. He approached her in the truck, "Mornin,' Sandy. How you folks doin' today?"

"Not bad today, Mr. Beechum," Sandy said. "How about you and Mrs. Beechum, is everything all right with you two?"

"We're doin' the best we can. She's worryin' more and more these days, you know. Says she wishes Jesus would just come and bring us all home." Mr. Beechum shook his head in dismay. "I have to say, for once I agree with her. Those Regulators in the market are gettin' downright irritating."

"So that's what they're called," Sandy thought.

Mr. Beechum pulled a tattered handkerchief from his back pocket and mopped his brow, already glistening with sweat in the early morning heat.

Sandy smiled softly at the old gentleman, "Well, you two hang in there. I'm sure things will straighten out soon enough." She felt as though she lied.

Mr. Beechum stared down at the dusty parking lot and scratched his balding, sun-freckled head. "I suppose so, Sandy." He turned his gray eyes up to the blue sky and squinted, and then looked back at Sandy, "I'd best be gettin' home."

"Let me give you a lift, Mr. Beechum. It's too hot for you to be walking."

"Thanks, Sandy, I'd appreciate that. Truth be told, I'm surprised you still have fuel in this old truck."

"Truth be told, Mr. Beechum," Sandy laughed, "this is probably our last trip to town in the old truck. I'll have to put her out to pasture with the horses." She looked at Joe and Ben. "Guys, can you think of anything else we need from the store while we're here?"

"Nope," Ben answered. Joe just shook his head, not in any hurry to go back into the store and helped Mr. Beechum climb into the cab of the pickup truck with his groceries.

"You know, Sandy," The old man said once he was settled, "the wife and I are movin,' and I'd sure like to know my tractor is being cared for. Would you be interested in it?"

Sandy's jaw dropped as Joe pulled the truck out onto the main road toward Mr. and Mrs. Beechum's farm. "Mr. Beechum, why would you want to get rid of your tractor? You love that tractor! And besides, where are you going?"

"Of course, I love the tractor. That's why I want to give it to you. You've got plenty of fields and that tractor knows them probably better than you do." He chuckled, and then looked at Joe, "Son, you wouldn't mind mowing the fields with a brand-spankin' new John Deere, would you?"

Joe smiled broadly, keeping his eyes glued to the road, "No sir!"

"Mr. Beechum, will you at least give it some thought?" Sandy pleaded.

"I have, Sandy and that is why I'm telling you. I want you to have it. As far as where we go, I reckon Willowdale, or The City as they call it now. There's talk that folks like us will have an easier time there in our later years. The farm has gotten to be too much for us, and our health isn't as good as it was." The old man paused, and Sandy wondered whether his Cancer had come back. He continued, "I just think it's the best thing for us at this stage in our life. I'll bring the tractor by in the morning."

"When are you leaving, Mr. Beechum?"

"We'll start packing up tomorrow and should be out by the end of the week." The old man sighed and stared out the window, fearful of the uncertainty so late in his life.

On the drive back home, Sandy contemplated their future. "Lord, we're coming into some uncertain and scary times. I trust in You and know You will take us through this, but I pray that it will not be too difficult for folks like the Beechums."

Proverbs 3.5 "Trust in the Lord with all your heart and lean not on your own understanding. In all your ways acknowledge him, and he will make your paths straight."

CHAPTER 8

Tom Connelly adjusted his rucksack before he stepped off the C17 transport plane. There were times when he felt like a pack mule, but it never bothered him. Everything he carried in the worn duffel and pack had been necessities over the past twelve years. With his pack situated, he hoisted the fifty-pound duffel over his shoulder and proceeded toward the arrival gate. His M-16 was slung over his other shoulder and Lucky followed him closely. Tom looked around the tarmac. There was no parade and no welcoming committee. No joyful families with signs or bands playing patriotic songs. There was just people going about their business, oblivious to the heroes in their midst.

He thought of the homecoming from his first deployment and of several after that. The people had been so happy to see them. There had been greeters, handshakes and many tears. Back then he believed they were working toward a goal, but now there was no love, no appreciation for the lives lost or those returning from the war. Coming home now wasn't a choice for him. He was ordered home by a government he didn't understand. With all the military removed from the Middle East and other areas around the world, Tom and many others would have to adjust. It would be difficult leaving the structured life of the military, but he knew he could adapt to whatever this changed world threw at him.

"Staff Sergeant Connelly!" Tom turned to see Kyle Johnson limping across the tarmac towards him, struggling with his duffel, pack, and rifle.

"Johnson, it's good to see you," he smiled.

"Good to see you too, sir. Hey there, Lucky." Johnson paused to catch his breath and scratched gently under the puppy's chin, "What do you think about all this nonsense, sir?" he said, still winded.

"Johnson, I'm not your superior anymore. You don't have to call me Sir or Staff Sergeant." Tom said. "As far as what's going on, I know a little bit, but now is not the time to talk about it. We need to get this government-issue gear turned in before they have us arrested."

After the men turned in their weapons and other equipment, they gathered the few items that were their own, including the duffel bag, compliments of the U.S. Army, and made their way to the base bank.

"Should we just clean out our accounts, Staff Sergeant?" Kyle asked, as they walked into the bank.

Tom Connelly shook his head and chuckled to himself. "I'd better get used to it. I don't think he'll change any time soon." He smiled at the younger soldier limping next to him, "That's what I'm thinking," Tom said. "From what I've heard already, I don't trust this new system."

"Good idea. I'll do the same," Kyle said.

The teller smiled at Tom when he approached her window, "Good afternoon. How may I help you?" she asked.

"I need to close my account, ma'am," Tom said, as he filled out a withdrawal slip. When the teller didn't respond, he looked up from what he was doing and grew puzzled at her expression. "Is there a problem?"

"No, sir, not exactly," she said. Her chubby face was expressionless, and he knew enough about body language to see that she didn't approve of him or his request. "I just need to see some ID, Mr. --," she paused, her eyebrows raised in mock curiosity.

"Connelly." Tom said, already growing irritated at being a civilian. He reached into his back pocket and withdrew his wallet, flipped it open and tossed his military ID onto the counter.

She picked it up and scrutinized it carefully. The picture on the ID didn't do him justice, she thought, as her eyes went from the plastic card to the man standing in front of her. His face was tanned from years spent in the desert. His green eyes had a gentleness about them, and his light brown hair, nearly shaved off in the picture, was now an inch or two longer, trimmed in the typical military fashion.

Tom watched her intently while she took her time examining him and his ID card. "Well?" he queried.

Finally, she returned his card and smiled, "Thank you, Mr. Connelly. I just need to make a call." Without waiting for a response from him, she quickly turned her back to him and picked up the phone. After several minutes of whispering and listening, she hung up and turned back to him. "Thank you for waiting, Mr. Connelly. I can close your account now."

"What? Did you have to get permission from someone?" Tom snapped.

"It is just a precaution, sir," she said handing him the stack of cash.

Tom took his money, thanked the girl, and stepped away from the counter.

Kyle had watched the interaction that took place and was ready for the same treatment. "You might as well call that person back Miss, because I'm closing my account, too."

The teller took Kyle's withdrawal slip and followed the same procedure. When she had counted out the bills, she handed them to Kyle with a smile. "Thank you for coming in, gentlemen."

Kyle watched Connelly pull a fifty-dollar bill from the thick wad of cash and then stuff the rest of his savings deep inside his duffel. Kyle did the same. When he was sure the money was well hidden, he grabbed his bag and hurried after Tom who had already left the building. "Now what are we going to do?" he asked when he had finally caught up to him.

"Now I go buy me some wheels." Connelly said shortly, "What's all this about 'we'?" He was still agitated with what had just happened in the bank.

Kyle bowed his head as they walked, and Tom softened. He couldn't help but think of how Johnson reminded him of Lucky with his sweet demeanor. He remembered the first day the kid showed up in Iraq. The young soldier always had a smile on his face and was still very green. It was, after all, his first deployment. All Tom knew about him was that he came from a small town in North Georgia and had joined the Army right out of high school. He never mentioned parents, and when mail call came around, Kyle always slipped away quietly, knowing there would be no mail for him.

Kyle's recovery from the gunshot wound had been slow, and when it was finally time for his release, he fought with his superiors to be sent back to his unit. Although they had only a few months left in country, his request was approved, and he was shipped back to Iraq where he fought fiercely with his brothers against the enemy.

"I've got nowhere to go, Staff Sergeant." Kyle said.

Tom jolted back to the present time; it happened often. He would think of his men or the days in Iraq and he would instantly be transported back there.

"I was kinda hoping I could tag along with you," Kyle continued. "You never know when you'll need back-up these days."

Tom watched him walking along-side him with his gimpy leg and hopeful eyes, and realized that, like Staff Sergeant Parker, he had grown fond of the young man and suddenly he felt the Spirit move in him. *"Look after him, Tom."* He grinned and said, "Oh, all right. I guess I could use you, but you have to do one thing."

"What's that, Staff Sergeant?" Kyle asked.

"Stop calling me Staff Sergeant. It's either Connelly, Tom, or Nelly. Got it?"

Johnson lifted his head, and the spring came back in his limp. "Got it, Nelly."

They purchased a twenty-year-old truck for a fraction of what it was worth. Tom wondered why the used car dealer gave them such a good deal. He assumed it was one of two things, either because they were paying cash or because the truck was such a gas-guzzler, the dealer wanted to unload it to the first person that asked about it. After an hour of paperwork, they made a quick stop at a grocery store for food, water, and dog food, and then packed it all in a box in the bed of the truck. Tom pulled a large tarp over the box, secured it with bungee cords and then climbed back into the cab. As he pulled away from the store he glanced over at Kyle, "We've got one more stop to make."

"Okay." Kyle studied Tom's face. It was always hard to tell what he was thinking about. He was a quiet man who never said much, but Kyle could always count on him to tell the truth in any situation. That was one of the things he admired about him. Another was a quiet strength that seemed to come naturally to him, and his men drew from it like a well while they were in Iraq.

Tom parked the truck behind the pawn shop and turned in his seat to face Kyle, "Listen, before we go in, there's something you should know."

Kyle cocked his head in question while he held Lucky, "What do you mean, Connelly? Does it have something to do with all this government trouble?"

"Yeah, I'll tell you more about it later, "Tom said, "but for now just don't talk too much. Okay?"

"Yeah, sure." Kyle nodded his head.

They entered the dark, musty pawn shop through the back door, and the smell of decay and age from the antiquated items surrounded them. Thirty-year-old televisions were lined up on metal shelves with an assortment of outdated VHS players, DVD players, and tape recorders. Eight track tape players sat on the shelves beneath them. On the far side of the room, a whole wall was dedicated to VHS movies of every variety. Behind the counter an old gentleman watched them curiously. He was a short, stout man. A small fan hanging just above him blew fair strands of white wispy hair wildly around his head. "You boys just get home?" he asked through false teeth.

"Yes sir," Johnson replied, remembering what Tom had just told him.

"Well, welcome home," the old man replied. "I'm sure you didn't get any of that when you set down."

"No, sir, we didn't, but thanks," Tom said.

What can I do for you today," the shopkeeper asked.

"We're looking for weapons," Tom said.

"Well, you've come to the right place," the old man said. He turned around and went about pulling handguns and rifles from behind his counter and laid them out on the counter. "Take your pick, boys. These should serve you well. We've got a Mossberg 500 12-gauge shotgun, a Winchester 30.06 rifle, a Glock nine-millimeter semi-automatic, and my personal favorite, a Smith & Wesson .357 Magnum Revolver." Tom picked up the Glock and checked the aim on it.

"Where you headed?" the shop owner asked Tom.

"No place in particular," Tom answered quietly, keeping his eyes fixed on the nine-millimeter.

"That's good," the grizzled old shopkeeper replied with a wink. "You just keep it that way. The less folks know about your doin's these days, the better off you are. Just take a little advice from an old soldier; stay off the main roads and travel under cover of dark as often as you can. Do you have any night vision goggles or comm's equipment?"

"No sir," Connelly replied, surprised at the advice and the question. "We turned all that in."

The shopkeeper held up a knurled arthritic finger. "Hold on for just a second." He shuffled into the back of the store.

Johnson shrugged his shoulders and gave a questioning look to Connelly who shook his head in return. Neither one spoke.

Moments later, the man, hunched over from years of standing at the same counter, emerged from the back of his shop with a case that looked nearly new, and a battered cardboard box. He placed the box on the floor, then lifted the case and placed it carefully on the glass counter. He opened it toward Tom and Kyle.

"Night vision goggles! Nice!" Johnson exclaimed.

"They're yours." The shopkeeper announced. "Some grunt turned 'em in over a year ago for some cash and never came back for 'em." He shook his head as he considered his words then continued, "I expect he was killed in action. It's hard to imagine anyone not coming back for these. Here take these, too." He bent over and lifted two hand-held radios from the box on the floor. "UHF PRC152's. I've had them in my shop for years. When all that computerized stuff took over no one wanted 'em." He let out a chuckle and continued, "Now that the government has taken control of all satellites, GPS, and the like, you can't use fancy radios anymore without being tracked. If you want to stay 'under the wire,' these radios should do the trick. They'll work with any other UHF or green gear if you can find them." The old man laid the radios on top of the NVG case and pushed them toward Tom. "Take 'em. I have no use for 'em. As a matter of fact, I'm going to make a gift out of all of this. Consider them gifts for coming home alive."

"But we've got to give you something," Connelly protested.

"You know what you can give me?" The old man said, "You can get a band of your brothers together and get our country back. The government has gone crooked, and I fear like I've never feared before, and I'm retired military, so you know we don't scare easily. You stay safe and strong and find others who are willing to fight for the country we used to have."

A chill raced up Johnson's spine and he wondered whether it was a ghost from his wound or something worse.

Connelly gathered up the radios along with the case, "Thank you for everything, sir." He shook the hand of the old man and could feel the fight still in it. Kyle collected the remaining weapons and ammunition and looked at Tom. His eyes spoke volumes.

Johnson nodded slightly. He understood everything. He grasped the shopkeeper's hand and shook it. "Thank you, sir."

"You're welcome, son. Be careful now."

The truck followed the black ribbon of highway that wound its way through the southern West Virginia Mountains. The high beams revealed dense forest on either side and Tom was certain that the shoulder fell off sharply to his right. Lucky was lying on the seat next to him with his head resting on Tom's thigh. From time to time, he would open his big dark eyes to check on his companion. Satisfied that all was well, Lucky returned to his nap. The only thing Tom could find on the radio was some ranting talk show about how the condition of the country had vastly improved. Frustrated with the lies that spewed from the host, he switched it off and glanced over at his companion.

Kyle snored softly from the passenger seat, his head bobbing softly against the jacket that cushioned it from the window. "Wake me up in a couple of hours," he had said, but Tom drove on. He knew sleep would evade him as it had for the last four months. He knew it would be a long time before he could experience that sweet, peaceful retreat from the reality of this world. He checked the gas gauge, a half a tank. He would have to top it off at the next station if they were open. No sooner did the thought cross his mind, than a town appeared in the moonlight in the valley below. He considered letting Kyle sleep but decided against it. Times were strange and he wasn't comfortable approaching an unknown situation without backup.

"Johnson," Tom shoved his shoulder. Lucky, startled by the sudden movement, rose sleepily sat up on the seat and looked out the front window. Tom shoved harder. "Johnson, wake up, man."

"I got him, Sarge! He's in my sights!" Kyle yelled.

"Johnson!"

Kyle sat bolt upright. His head swiveled sharply as he first looked out the passenger window, then out the windshield at the road and then rested on Tom. "What's up, Nelly?"

"We're getting low on gas," Tom said, glancing at his companion. "There's a town ahead, but I'd rather not go through blind. Keep a close watch, will ya? Where's your sidearm?"

"I got it right here." Johnson pulled the .357 Revolver from his right boot, "Do you think we'll run into any trouble?"

"I don't honestly know, but I don't want to take any chances either." Tom said. "We just need an open gas station." Connelly squinted trying to see clearer through the darkness.

They drove slowly down the hill into town. Connelly thought it looked morbidly like the abandoned streets in Fallujah, only the buildings weren't made of mud. The side streets veiled in shadows gave no indication that life existed there.

"So far it looks like the whole place is abandoned." Kyle shook his head with uncertainty.

"Abandoned or just shut down for the night?" Tom questioned.

"I'd have to say abandoned, Connelly. Look." Kyle pointed toward the northeast side of the road. "The windows are busted out of that store and over there, that car's just sitting in the middle of the road with the doors sitting wide open. This is creepier than anything I've seen in the Sandbox. We need to clear out of here right now. I'm getting a bad feeling about this place."

"We'll clear out now," Tom said, "but we're not going far. We need to find out what happened here." Tom said.

"Well, we sure ain't stayin' here are we?" Kyle asked. "I'm not in the mood to mix it up tonight with a bunch of non-friendlies."

"We'll pass through, then pull off the road and hide out in the woods 'til morning," Tom said as he maneuvered the truck off the road. He drove slowly down an old fire road that took them deep enough into the woods to keep them out of sight for the night. "No campfire tonight, Johnson."

"That's fine with me, Nelly. God only knows what's out there." Kyle laid on his back with his head on his rucksack and foul weather jacket between him and the damp forest floor. He gazed up at the blinking blue stars suspended in the velvet night sky. "Connelly, what's going on?"

Tom Connelly sat against a tree next to Johnson and poured some water from his canteen into a bowl for Lucky. "The government that's in place now doesn't believe this country should be as strong as it once was. They are under the delusion that the American people want to be taken care of, rather than work for what they have. And to make matters worse, there are folks around, a lot it seems, that would rather follow blindly behind a leader that claims he will take care of them. Honestly, I think folks have just gotten lazy and they are tired of fighting to do the right thing. What they don't realize is that if they let the government do whatever it wants, it will take total control, making it harder to regain that control."

Kyle nodded in agreement, "You're right, Connelly, it doesn't seem like we are as strong as we once were." He was still puzzled, "But why go around busting out windows and ruining people's livelihoods?"

"Think about it, Johnson." Tom explained, "Those folks who did those things, busted out the windows, they were most likely the same ones who believed that following this new leader would bring them peace and prosperity. Anyone who chose not to go along with them was their enemy. The folks on the receiving end, who got their windows broken, were the ones who didn't want to follow along. They were perfectly content with working their jobs, supporting their families, and living their lives. They weren't willing to blindly follow someone they didn't trust."

Tom shook his head in disgust, "The media isn't helping either. They're building the administration up to be something positive, for the good of the country."

Kyle rolled his head over to look at Tom, "How do you know all that?"

Tom hesitated, "Staff Sergeant Parker's wife wrote to me. She gave me a few details and I filled in the blanks."

Kyle sat up and gawked at Tom, "She wrote to you?"

Tom was perturbed at Johnson's obvious surprise. "Shut your mouth for crying out loud, Johnson! You're gonna catch a bug in it."

"Sorry, Nelly. I didn't mean to react like that." Kyle said, leaning back against the tree. "I didn't know you'd been in contact with her."

"I wasn't. She wrote to me. Apparently, Staff Sergeant Parker told her we were good friends."

"Brothers, you mean," Johnson corrected, knowing the relationship between the two men.

Connelly's attention strayed to his boots as he recalled his last day with his best friend.

"Did you ever write her back?" Kyle asked.

"No." Tom said quietly.

"Well, why not?" Kyle said, still trying to grasp the idea that Staff Sergeant's wife had written to Tom.

"She just wrote to thank me for looking after him, for being his friend," Tom said. "She warned me that things were going bad while we were away and that we should be prepared for when we came back. She's a good military wife. She understands how we can be removed from the reality of home when we're so far away."

"Is that where we're going now, Tom?" Tom nodded but didn't say anything right away. "Is she expecting us?" Kyle pressed gently.

"I doubt it, but I made a promise to Staff Sergeant Parker, and I aim to keep it."

Johnson felt his heart break for the hundredth time, not only for the loss of his brother in arms, the death he was still convinced he was responsible for, but for the loss that Joe Parker's wife must have suffered and most likely, was still suffering.

Tom knew Johnson still carried an enormous amount of guilt about that day. He watched the soldier withdraw into himself as he always did when thinking of Staff Sergeant. "Johnson, you know he would have risked his life for any of us. Besides, if I hadn't stopped firing to reload, that Sniper may not have gotten that shot off."

Kyle swiped a tear from his face. "You were just doing your job, Tom. It's not your fault you had to reload. If I had been quicker on my feet, I wouldn't have been shot and he would still be here." Kyle held his head in both hands as if to the memory away. "I just can't get it out of my head that I killed that wonderful man. I widowed his wife and orphaned his sons!"

Johnson, it was his time. You didn't do any of that." Tom said, knowing his words would offer no comfort.

"Well, it sure appears that way to me." Johnson tilted his head back against the tree trunk to keep the tears from spilling out from his dark blue eyes, but it didn't work. He didn't mind crying in front of Connelly. God knew they'd all cried together at one time or another, including the day they'd lost Staff Sergeant Parker.

"I don't know how to take that away from you, Johnson, but know that God is lookin' after his family." Tom said.

"I wish I could be as certain as you about such things. I wish I could get over this hurt." Kyle said without looking at Tom.

"Try to get some sleep, Johnson," Tom said quietly. "I'll take the first watch."

Johnson turned on his side with his back to Connelly and didn't say another word.

Tom prayed, "Lord, please give this man peace. I ask you Lord to give me the words and wisdom to share your forgiveness with him. If not me, Lord please put someone in his life that will help him." Tom sighed heavily and stared up into the sky. Heavy clouds had rolled in, covering up the stars and moon, promising rain. His heart was heavy thinking of how he would approach Sandy Parker and her sons. He knew the Lord would put him in the best position possible, but the anticipation of what was coming ate away at him.

His thoughts drifted back again to Iraq and Staff Sergeant Parker, the man who had shared his family with him when he had no one. At eight years old, Tom had lost both his parents in an automobile accident. With no other family, he had bounced from one foster home to another, dragging his few possessions in a garbage bag. He never again felt the closeness of family ties until he joined the Army and was assigned to Joe Parker's unit.

Staff Sergeant Parker was fond of all his men, but it was Tom that he would go to when he needed quiet conversation. He would talk in detail about his family and how much he missed them and always shared the care packages, pictures, and cards that his wife sent. Through those simple touchstones from home, and the stories that Joe shared, Tom felt as though he had another family outside the Army.

Hebrews 14:27 "Peace I leave with you; my peace I give you. I do not give to you as the world gives. Do not let your hearts be troubled and do not be afraid."

CHAPTER 9

SANDY PUT THE LAST jar of green beans she canned on the pantry shelf, removed her apron and hung it on the hook near the mudroom door. Joe and Ben had been in school for nearly six weeks now, so she was left to run the ranch on her own during the week. Over the summer months the boys had been a tremendous help, but as much as she needed their help, she didn't want to take time away from their schoolwork. Sandy grasped one of her large baskets she used for harvesting the vegetables and started for the back door. The squash and pumpkins were ready to be picked, but the boys would have to help her with the pumpkins. She set her booted foot across the threshold when the phone rang. She contemplated answering, but something told her to take the call. "Hello?"

"Hey, Sandy?"

Sandy could already hear the tension in her older sister's voice. "Hi, Tanya. What's up?

"Did you know Mrs. Olsen is moving?" Tanya said.

"No kidding? Why?"

"She says she's moving to Willowdale because all the food and fuel shortages are scaring her. She thinks she'll be better taken care of in the city where they've started a new program."

"What new program?" Sandy suddenly felt nauseous as she let the basket fall to the floor.

"She and her kids are signing up for this new program that's being tested in the larger cities first. It's called the Government Funded Life Care program."

Sandy pulled out a kitchen chair and sat down hard, "Tanya, do you remember what Joe wrote at the end of his last letter?"

"Yes," Tanya replied. "He said to keep your ears open. Is this what he was talking about? How could he know about this?"

"You know, I honestly don't know. I always chalked it up as one of his conspiracy theories, but he had that gift of knowing things. He began talking about it shortly after we bought the ranch. He said one day the government would try to take over everything and put it under the guise of helping people who can't or won't help themselves. The bottom line is, they gain control of the needy people first, their accounts, property, if they have any, and they say government contractors and financial advisors will manage it. Once they gain control of everything, they give people the minimum of what they need to scrape by, leaving those folks in a terrible situation. They are too poor to leave the program, so they're pretty much stuck."

Sandy suddenly gasped, "Oh my gosh! I just had a thought."

"What?" Tanya exclaimed.

"Do you remember when I told you Mr. and Mrs. Beechum were moving to Willowdale?" Sandy paused, giving Tanya a moment to think back on the conversation.

"Sandy! You don't suppose it was starting way back then, do you?"

"It's a possibility, Tanya. This had to have taken some planning. It began subtly at first, but now it seems as though they are gaining momentum. I mean, if you think about it, they already own the only bank in town and Bill and Ellie's gas station dried up two months ago.

"But what about this program," Tanya questioned. "Won't there be some folks who won't want to go along with it?"

"I would certainly hope so," Sandy said. "We need to be those people, Tanya. We can't fall prey to what they are trying to do. And we need to inform those who may not understand and believe it is a good idea."

"I need to talk to Steve about this." Tanya muttered almost to herself. "Maybe we can have a meeting after church. Can Steve and I come over tomorrow night? We need to discuss more about it."

"Sure, come for supper." Sandy said, already pre-occupied with plans for the following evening.

"Okay, great." Tanya said, "I'll do some research on this program and bring what I find."

"How can I help?" Sandy asked. The news had left her feeling frightened and threatened.

"You've got your hands full with the ranch," Tanya said. "Rest assured, Sandy, you do plenty. We'll talk more about it tomorrow night. Do the boys know anything about this new program?"

"No, I don't think so; at least they haven't mentioned it." Sandy said.

Tanya huffed in disgust, "Well, it wouldn't surprise me if they started bringing it up at school."

"If I hear anything I'll let you know," Sandy said. "Has anyone else left Willow Creek?"

"I don't know, but the attendance at church has dropped considerably."

"Yeah, I remember from last Sunday. Has Steve been around visiting to find out why?"

"That's where he is today. No one has called, but with the sudden drop in attendance, well, it's very suspicious."

Just then the front door swung wide as Ben and Joe burst into the house and ran into the kitchen still wearing their backpacks. Their faces were flushed and sweating from running down the half-mile lane toward home. Obviously, they had news to tell that couldn't wait. Ben was waving a piece of paper in his hand while Joe stood anxiously clutching the mail. His face was drawn with concern.

"Look, Tanya, the boys just got home from school. I'll call you later."

"Okay sis, kiss them for me."

Sandy smiled, "Will do."

Before she could even disconnect the call Joe began, "Mom, you won't believe what happened at school today!"

"Believe what? What's got you guys all fired up?" Sandy was still spooked about the conversation she had just finished with her sister. "Slow down you two. Joe, you go first."

Joe began cautiously. Laying the mail on the kitchen table he took a deep breath and looked directly at his mom. "Mom, some kids at school were talking today about how their folks are going to sell their houses to the government and move to the city, a lot of kids, Mom. If it were just a couple I wouldn't have noticed, but there are at least ten kids whose parents have signed up with the government for a new program designed to help families in need."

Ben spoke up, worried, "Mom, are we going to have to move to the city?"

"Absolutely not!" Sandy sprang from her chair and paced the linoleum floor to calm herself, "So many questions with no answers." She saw the uncertainty in her sons' faces. She had to remain steadfast, not only for her own sanity, but for them as well. She crossed the kitchen to the coffee pot and poured herself a cup, then loaded some homemade chocolate chip cookies on a plate and brought them, with two glasses of milk to the table. She sat across from Joe and Ben and looked at each of them carefully. "You need to tell me as much as you know." They both moved to speak up again, but she held up her hand, "One at a time. Ben, what is that in your hand?"

"There's a meeting at school."

"I can only guess what's on the agenda." Sandy took the wrinkled notice from Ben and read it carefully. As she read the notice, Joe Jr. watched her face as confusion melted into concern. She laid the letter on the table and rubbed her temples. "Joe, what else can you tell me?"

"I know some of the kids aren't too happy about moving, but most of them think it's a great idea. They say they won't have to worry about anything because the government will take care of them. It doesn't sound so good to me, mom. There's something else, too."

"What is it, Joe?"

He hesitated for a moment knowing she would hit the roof.

Sandy watched him and waited patiently for him to find the words.

"They are monitoring our meals at school now, even what we are bringing from home."

She felt the blood rush to her face, "Are you kidding me? When did they start doing that?"

"It's only been this week," Ben offered, "and they don't seem to mind what you've been putting in our lunches."

"That's not the point, Ben. They aren't taking any of your food away, are they?"

"No, they just monitor." Joe sat at the table next to Ben and drained his milk glass. "What are we going to do?"

"I don't know, Joe. Aunt Tanya and Uncle Steve are coming over tomorrow night. We'll have to talk about it then." Sandy picked up the announcement again, "When is this meeting?" she said more to herself, "Monday." She looked at her sons. "At least that will give us the weekend to investigate this. Okay guys, grab a basket. Joe, will you back the truck up to the garden please? We can take the pumpkins to town this afternoon for the church pumpkin patch and go to Lee's Market tomorrow morning."

As they walked out together, Sandy noticed the look of concern on Joe's face, and put her arm around him, honey, don't worry. We'll get through this."

Joe looked at his mom, and for the first time she saw the young man as he held the keys to the truck in his large, calloused hand. His hair had been growing out for the winter, and a shadow was beginning to form on his young face. Not only the shadow of approaching manhood, but a shadow of concern. Concern that no sixteen-year-old should know. "I know we haven't been much help on the ranch since school started, Mom, and I hate to see you doing so much. I just wonder if this government thing is something we should consider."

Sandy stopped abruptly and locked her gaze on Joe, "Is that something you want, Joe, or is it just because you think the ranch is too much?"

"I just think the ranch is a lot for you. I can always quit school and help you."

"You'll do no such thing, Joe." Sandy wrapped her arms around her oldest boy. "We'll be fine, Joe. Whatever is happening we will get through it with God's help? Am I right?"

Joe hugged her back, "Yes ma'am."

Sandy pulled the truck around to the loading dock behind the market where she sold and traded her vegetables, milk, and eggs. It had turned out to be a fairly lucrative business since the government stopped paying her husband's benefit checks. She checked her side view mirror and saw Lee, the owner of the store, coming out to meet her. His normally round and cheerful face was now drawn and worrisome.

"Mom, we've got a lot of stuff today, don't we?" Ben commented, bringing her back to the task at hand.

"We sure do. I'll need your help unloading it." She put the truck in park and turned to see Lee standing next to her window.

"You must leave, Sandy!" His voice was low and hoarse but there was urgency in his statement that frightened her. "No sale today. You go, now!"

Ben's face went white as he peered out the back window of the truck and saw a man in a dark suit approaching them. The man was smiling broadly, sporting a bright red carnation in his lapel. "Mom, go!"

Startled by Ben's sudden outburst, Sandy slammed the truck in gear and spun tires out of the parking lot, leaving the stench of burnt rubber and shredded tire in her wake. She checked the side view mirror as she sped off but could not make out the image of the man who approached them.

Lee jumped back to avoid the speeding truck and backed into the man that now stood behind him.

"Now, Lee, what was that all about?" The man's voice dripped with kindness, but Lee knew better. He bowed his head and waited for his punishment. The man grabbed Lee's slender wrist twisting his arm behind his back. He pushed Lee toward the back of the market with the muzzle of his gun jammed into Lee's back, not speaking until they were inside. "What did you tell her, Lee?"

"Mr. Garrison, I just told her new policy of dropping food and no pay for her. She get angry and she leave."

"I'd rather you waited until I could talk to Mrs. Parker myself, Lee. You know the drill, right?"

"Yes sir, I know drill. I sorry, Mr. Garrison, I will not do it again."

"I'm sure that you won't." Mr. Garrison left Lee in the back of the store trembling and praying that he would have a chance to talk to Sandy again.

Once they had rounded the corner and were out of sight of the market, Sandy stopped the truck and turned sharply to Ben "What on earth was that all about, Ben?"

"He was one of the men from school, Mom." Ben said, quickly looking out the back window to make sure the man hadn't come after them. "He's one of the guys who checks to see what we eat. He's not a nice man, Mom."

Still trembling, Sandy put the truck in gear and headed toward home. Her mind was a whirlwind of questions, but her main question was why Joe couldn't be there to help her through this. Of course, she already knew the answer to that. God was there to help her. Ben stared silently out the window not sure whether he should try to talk to his mother or just leave her to her thoughts. He wished his brother were there. The man in the black suit had made him nervous at school when he roamed around the lunch tables, but to see him outside of school in a place that Ben never expected, well, that was just too creepy for him.

1 Peter 4:12 "Dear friends, do not be surprised at the painful trial you are suffering, as though something strange were happening to you. But rejoice that you participate in the sufferings of Christ, so that you may be overjoyed when his glory is revealed."

CHAPTER 10

Clouds gathered and tumbled one over another as the early morning sun attempted to shine through the ever-darkening sky, however the rain-laden clouds won the battle, and the sun slipped reluctantly behind the rolling gray billows. The strong smell of rain pulled Kyle from his sleep. He quickly rolled up his sleeping bag and collected his things while Tom slept fitfully. Hearing the activity in camp, Lucky poked his head out from deep within Connelly's sleeping bag.

"Good morning, little buddy," Kyle whispered.

Lucky crawled out of the sleeping bag, stepping on Tom's face in the process, and then happily trotted into the woods. Tom awoke with a start until he realized where he was and then began clearing the site as well. Just as the first heavy raindrops began to fall, Kyle scooped up Lucky when he returned from the woods, and he and Tom sprinted toward the truck.

"That came up quick," Kyle said once they were safely in the cab of the truck. "Did you get any sleep, Tom?"

"The usual," Tom said. "What about you?"

Kyle knew the 'usual' amount of sleep for Connelly was only about three to four hours, if he were lucky. "Yeah, I slept all right. It'll be nice to actually sleep in a real bed at some point though, instead of on a cot or on the ground."

"I hear you," Tom agreed. "Of course, we don't know when or where, but hopefully soon." Tom looked out the window toward the sky, "We need to go into town and check it out."

"Let me run point," Kyle said.

"No problem," Tom said, "just remember, this is just like the Sandbox. We don't know who or where the enemy is."

"Understood," Kyle said.

The men donned their ponchos, checked their weapons, and ammo, then proceeded toward town using the cover of the woods, while Lucky remained in the truck with a chew toy and his breakfast. The rain continued to pour, creating streams of reddish-brown mud that flowed down the mountain slope into the street while a crow's incessant caw echoed through the still, silent morning. The men made their way through the thick brush with the stealth of the well-trained soldier. When they reached the edge of town, Tom peered out from behind a massive oak tree at the empty street. Checking his watch, he thought to himself, "It's oh-seven hundred on a Friday morning. There should be some kind of activity, people going to work or school something."

"I'm telling you, Tom, this just ain't right." Kyle whispered.

"Keep your eyes peeled. Once we investigate this and get some fuel, we're out of here." Tom said. The rain tapered off to a soft drizzle, but the temperature had dropped considerably, sending a chill breeze through the trees, but neither Tom nor Kyle noticed the sudden cold; adrenaline had taken over.

They crouched low and ran toward the cover of the first building. It sat on the corner of the street and was part of a row of shops whose windows were either broken completely or had sharp shards of glass hanging threateningly from their frames. A large wooden sign weathered by years of exposure to the elements hung askew on its chain just under the pink and white canvas awning. The sign read 'Betty's Dress Shop.' Kyle slowly poked his head around the corner, wishing he had the protection of his Kevlar. As his field of vision cleared the corner of the store, he found himself staring face to face into lifeless, black eyes. His heart skipped half a beat until he realized it was just a mannequin that had fallen over.

He continued his visual search of the dark store through the broken plate glass window. Once he was satisfied that it was clear, he motioned for Tom to follow him. They climbed through the gaping hole in the window, stepping over the large rock that was obviously used to break it. A thorough search of the store revealed nothing more than vandalism and a molested wall safe and cash register.

When they were convinced that the store was free of any threat, Kyle relaxed a little. "It's too bad about the store, but I'm glad we didn't find any dead bodies," he admitted as they moved cautiously toward the door.

"You and me both," Tom agreed. "Come on, I have a feeling we'll find more of the same."

"Let's just gather what we need and get the heck out of here." Kyle checked over his shoulder as they exited through the front door. By the time the soldiers reached the other side of town, they were certain that the people of this small town were forced out, the only questions gnawing at them were, by whom and why.

Still on their guard, they began the return trip back to the truck, making a quick detour through the food store, drug store, and hardware store. They were able to gather a decent cache of supplies that would at least get them through several weeks, if they rationed it. On the way out of the hardware store, Tom noticed a wide variety of vegetable and flower seeds on a rack by the door. A thought came to him, *"You will need these."* He didn't hesitate; grabbing two handfuls he stuffed them in a canvas bag he had picked up earlier.

The rain had subsided, and the sun was trying to break through, when they stepped out of the shadows of the store. Spying two gas pumps across the street, Tom headed toward them carrying two five-gallon gas cans he absconded from the hardware store, while Kyle kept watch up and down the street.

"There isn't any!"

The men froze at the sound of the female voice. Kyle turned slowly in the direction from where it came and saw a young woman barely out of her teens shakily holding a shotgun on him, eyeing him suspiciously from a second story window over the drug store. She had apparently been watching them for some time. "Turn around slowly and keep your hands where I can see them!" She called out to Tom. "And put down those gas cans! You won't be finding any more gas in these parts!"

Tom did as she ordered and turned slowly with his hands out and palms up. Kyle clutched the bags of groceries and first aid supplies in one hand and his firearm in the other. They watched the girl and the gun warily, Tom spoke carefully, "We don't mean you any harm, Miss. We're just passing through. Now, why don't you just come down from there?"

"I'll come down, but I'm not lettin' go of this shotgun. You move from where you're standing, and I'll shoot ya!"

"No problem, Miss. We'll wait right here for you."

Kyle put down his sacks but kept his pistol, not knowing what this young woman was all about. When she finally emerged from the drugstore, she still had the gun pointed at them.

"Now, Miss, if you lower that shotgun, I'll lower my pistol then we can just talk; okay?" Kyle said gently.

"I'd listen to him if I were you. He's a pretty good shot," Tom commented.

"Well, I'm a pretty darn good shot too -- at this range." She looked carefully into their eyes. When she did not sense any threat from them, she slowly lowered her shotgun, but in doing so Kyle saw her bottom lip begin to quiver. Her hold on the shotgun loosened and her knees began to buckle. Kyle quickly holstered his weapon and raced forward to release the shotgun from her trembling hands. Tom rushed over to receive the weapon from him so Kyle could catch the falling girl before she hit the pavement. His strong right arm slipped easily around her tiny waist as the girl melted into Kyle's arms and began to sob heavily. He held her while she cried.

Tom looked nervously up and down the street; time was getting short. His instincts were telling him they had to leave. "We need to get out of the open, Johnson. Come on. Let's get back to the truck. She'll be all right if she stays with us." Tom ducked inside the General Store to pick up another backpack for the girl and a few items he figured she might need and then gathered the rest of their bags.

Kyle pulled gently away from the girl and held her firmly by the shoulders until she could get her balance, "Listen, everything will be all right, but you need to come with us." He took the shotgun that Tom handed him and put his free arm around her to keep her steady. By then the rain had picked up again and when they arrived back at the truck, it had turned once again into a steady downpour. Kyle helped their new charge into the truck where Lucky greeted her happily with kisses and nuzzles. Once she was settled, Kyle went to help Tom quickly pack their supplies carefully in the bed of the truck underneath a heavy tarp.

When everything had been tied down sufficiently, Tom slid into the driver's seat and looked her over. He carefully noted the torn jeans, muddy tennis shoes, and filthy sweater ripped at the shoulder. Her face would have been pretty had it not been stained with tears and the same reddish-brown mud that poured down the mountain into the street. Her shoulder-length, dark hair was matted and oily.

She didn't speak but could feel his eyes on her -- scrutinizing her. She buried her face in the soft fur of Lucky's neck and began to weep.

"We need to find out what happened here, Miss." Tom began softly. "We realize you are upset, but you must talk to us."

She looked up at him and then at Kyle. Her eyes were dark; haunted. Fresh tears began to fill them. She shook her head sharply as though she were trying to cast out the horrific memories that lived there.

Kyle wanted to comfort her but dared not push too much. "Let's just drive for now. Maybe Sandy can tell us more," he suggested.

"Well, whatever it is, it's certainly worse that I thought." Tom pulled the truck off the fire road and onto the highway, hoping and praying that they could find some answers.

They drove silently with their new charge through the back roads, working their way toward the Parker Ranch in Willow Creek, Maryland.

"My uncle has a ranch about twenty miles north of here." The sudden break in silence made both soldiers jump. Tom had been watching the gas gauge for the last ten miles and she could tell he was getting concerned about where they would find fuel.

Tom turned to her, "Does he have fuel pumps?"

"No." Her eyes clouded over. "But he has horses or used to have horses." She lowered her head.

"When was the last time you spoke with him?" Kyle questioned.

"About three weeks ago. He called to tell me that no matter what, I needed to stay close to home and not trust any newcomers coming around. He talked to my dad, but I was never told what was really going on until "they" showed up." Her voice trailed off.

"We know this will be hard on you, but before we start blazing trails with you, we need to know everything that went on back there, and how you came to be the lone survivor. But first things first, what's your name?" Tom said.

"Fair enough," the girl stated. "My name is Morgan, Morgan Ellers."

"I'm Tom Connelly and that bald-headed guy next to you is Kyle Johnson."

"And who is this?" Morgan asked, holding Lucky up to her face to kiss his nose.

"That's Lucky," Tom answered, "he's a stray pup we picked up over in Iraq."

"Are you soldiers?" Morgan asked, still cuddling Lucky.

"Yep," Tom said.

"I guess that explains your bald head," she smiled at Kyle.

He rubbed the stiff fuzz on his head and returned the smile but didn't say anything; he was too busy taking in her pretty smile.

"We'll find a place to get off this road and you can tell us over breakfast what happened here."

Just the mention of the word triggered angry growling in Kyle's stomach. He hadn't realized how hungry he was.

They drove another five miles down the road until Tom found another fire road where he could pull off. From there he took the trail deep into the trees until he was certain they couldn't be seen from the road. "Kyle, you keep watch but stay out of sight of the road. Okay?"

"Don't worry about me, Connelly, just don't forget to call me for breakfast," Kyle smiled.

Tom laid the bacon in the large cast iron skillet while Morgan prepared the coffee. From time to time, he would glance at her as she worked. She didn't look any more than twenty at the most and hoped that she hadn't lost her family in whatever tragedy that took place in the little town where they found her.

"I want to thank you, Tom, for bringing me with you." Morgan said suddenly.

Tom kept his attention on the bacon, "It's not like we could have just left you. When Kyle gets back are you going to be okay to talk about it?"

Morgan nodded her head, the strands of her dirty hair brushing against her cheeks, "Yeah, I'll be all right. I need to tell someone, or I'll go crazy."

"Do you mind me asking how old you are?" Tom queried.

Morgan pressed the lid onto the coffee pot and placed it on the grate that Tom had laid over the fire. "Didn't anyone ever tell you it's impolite to ask a woman her age?"

Tom looked up from what he was doing, "I'm sorry, Morgan. I didn't mean any disrespect."

Morgan chuckled, "I'm just teasing, Tom. I'll be twenty next month." She cast her eyes down, and sadness swept over her. "It feels good to smile, but at the same time it doesn't feel right. Is that weird?"

Tom smiled gently, "We're livin' in weird times. I believe if something makes you smile, I say go ahead and smile. Heaven knows there hasn't been much of that in quite a while."

While Tom and Morgan were preparing breakfast, Kyle had walked out to the road and stood back in the trees, out of sight. He couldn't get over how desolate it was. The rain had finally stopped, and the sun was shining down, drying out the forest after the downpour. Kyle filled his lungs with the musky air, "Thank you, Father, for the beautiful day."

"Kyle?" He jumped at the sound of Morgan's voice behind him.

"I really gotta quit sneaking up on you guys," she giggled.

"No kidding," he smiled back at her. "Is breakfast ready?"

"Yes." She turned and walked with him back to the campsite feeling safer and more secure than she had in a very long time.

When they had finished breakfast, they relaxed around the campfire with their coffee. Tom spoke up first, "So tell us what happened back there, Morgan. Take your time and try to remember everything. It's important that we know all the details."

Morgan took a sip from her coffee before she began. "It started out very quietly at first. There was the usual town talk about the lack of gasoline, food, and banks being taken over. Everyone in town was worried, businesses started cutting hours or shutting down altogether, and then people started to leave saying they were going to the city. One day these men came to town; there were five of them. They looked suspicious, but they had a way of talking to the people that made them feel comfortable. Most of the town folk trusted these men, even my mom and dad." At this Morgan closed her eyes and shook her head. Tears began to stream down her cheeks, but she was determined to get her story out.

She took a deep breath and continued the account in her soft West Virginia drawl. "The people of the town, at least most of them, were convinced by these men that help would be provided for them if they left these 'backwoods' as they called them and came to the city where they would be properly taken care of. Most of the folks went with them, my folks included. They waited until I had gone to visit my Uncle Walt, the one I told you about."

Kyle interrupted her, "I don't understand why they would just up and leave their daughter behind, Morgan. Why would they do that?"

"Because they weren't sure themselves, I think. They knew I didn't approve of the men and their talk of leaving. That's when I started going to Uncle Walt's on the weekends. While I was away it seemed like everyone just up and left. When I came back home the town was nearly empty."

Tom spoke up, "It sounds like they were trying to protect you, Morgan."

Morgan just shrugged her slender shoulders and continued, "There were a few who stayed behind, but by that time the power to the town had been turned off and food and fuel deliveries had stopped. We were completely cut off. Then one night a big truck came through, you know, one of those military looking trucks."

"Maybe a seven ton," Kyle whispered.

Connelly nodded.

"So, this truck came through town with these men, and they were wearing some sort of uniform. They didn't look like soldiers, though. They couldn't have been. All the soldiers I've ever known were decent and cared about people." At this she smiled softly at the two men in front of her, then she continued, "These men were cruel. They vandalized the shops, throwing rocks or whatever they could find through the windows. They hollered through a bullhorn that the town needed to be evacuated, and everyone had to leave immediately. The residents were forced to go with them. They even went into people's homes and dragged them out and put them in the truck. Lots of folks just dropped everything and ran for the church. When the men saw where they had gone, they barred the doors of the church and they -- they set the church on fire."

Morgan began to weep, "I watched from the woods, but there was nothing I could do. I wanted to help them. They were screaming, but . . ." Morgan covered her face with her hands and wailed. "I just don't understand what is happening. What do they want from us?"

Kyle tossed the last of his coffee into the fire. He wanted to believe her, but his instincts told him to proceed with caution, "How did you come to be the only one left in town?"

"I ran to the woods with some of the others, but we were separated. When I was sure the men were gone, I came back to town."

"You look like you've been out in the woods for quite some time, Morgan," Tom said.

Morgan self-consciously ran her hand over her tangled, matted hair. "When they cut the water and the power . . ." Her voice trailed off, "I guess I could have gone to the creek to clean up, but I was afraid to leave the house during the day for fear I'd be seen. Then when night came, I didn't want to go into the woods alone. I felt like a prisoner, but there were no guards or bars on the windows. I was so afraid," she cried. Suddenly, Morgan lifted her head, took a deep breath and squared her shoulders, "But this morning, I woke up and told myself I wasn't going to be afraid anymore. I was going to get my dad's shotgun and do whatever it took to fight back." She shrugged, "Then I saw you guys."

"Tom, did Sandy mention anything about this?" Kyle sat hunched over with his elbows resting on his knobby knees.

Tom looked squarely at Kyle and Morgan, "This new government is hell-bent on gaining control of our Country and the people in it. We could be living under complete Marxist control before we know it. Just think of it. The people of the United States will be serving under their government instead of their government serving under them, and it will have power and money over them to get or do whatever they want."

Morgan drained her coffee cup and stood up. "All this talk is scaring me. Do you guys trust me now? Can we please go check on my Uncle Walt? We'd be smart to get his horses and pick him up, too, if he's still there."

"Okay, I guess we can trust you." Tom gave her a wink and they broke camp.

The drive to Uncle Walt's farm was another half hour. When they arrived, Morgan sat forward and studied the scene. "His truck is still in the driveway, but the front door is wide open. I don't like the looks of this," Morgan said warily. "Pull around to the back by the stables."

Kyle checked his weapon while Tom pulled around to the back of the house and turned off the truck, then faced Morgan, "You wait here."

"I don't think so!" she exclaimed. "What if someone comes?"

Tom chambered a round in his nine-millimeter, "Fine, but do as I tell you and nothing else, got it?"

"Got it." She picked up Lucky and carried him with her.

The trio exited the truck and moved as a group carefully, but quickly toward the house. Tom tapped Kyle on the shoulder and motioned for him to go around to the other side of the house, while he moved around to the front of the house. He peered through the open front door and what he saw made his heart sink. It looked as though Morgan's Uncle Walt was in the middle of preparing his breakfast, the smell of bacon still hung heavily in the air. He turned to Morgan, "Hunker down right here at the kitchen door and do not move," he whispered sternly. He surveyed the kitchen one more time and then stepped quietly across the kitchen floor toward the interior of the house. After a thorough inspection, he spied Kyle coming in the back door.

"Outside is clear, at least from what I can see from the porch," Kyle said, "but the woods are pretty thick. You really can't see anything in there without going in. Where's Morgan?"

The men rejoined Morgan where she was still seated on the floor by the door. "Well, that's it," she said taking Kyle's hand as he helped her up, "He's gone."

Kyle looked down at her. Her face was drawn with worry, "Morgan, any ideas?"

"None. Evidently, he left in the middle of breakfast, but his truck is here. Kyle did you see the horses?"

"No, but if they're still in the stable, I wouldn't have," Kyle said.

"If his truck is still here then he obviously left on foot, horseback or he was taken," Tom suggested.

Morgan gasped at the thought of her beloved Uncle Walt getting kidnapped. "We need to check the horses." She walked hurriedly toward the back door that led to the stables, but before she got to the door Kyle grabbed her arm.

"Wait! You can't just stroll around anymore, girl. Don't you know there are dangerous people out there?" Kyle poked his chest with his thumb, "I'll check the horses."

"You do that," Tom said grinning, "then report back here. Morgan, we might as well take advantage of what we've got. You can have the shower first if there's water. You've got fifteen minutes. Then it's my turn." He smiled when he looked back at her.

Morgan went down the hall to the bathroom, shed the dirty clothes she had been wearing and turned on the hot water as hot as she could stand it. She knew her fifteen minutes would expire long before she was ready to come out and it would take a lifetime for the memories of the last week to wash away. She jumped when someone banged on the door.

"Times up!" It was Tom.

"Okay, okay, I'm done." Morgan stepped out of the shower and wrapped a towel around her. When she opened the bathroom door Tom was waiting for her. "Towels are in the closet to the left."

"Is there any hot water left?" He raised an eyebrow.

"Don't know." She replied smartly. "You can wear some of Uncle Walt's clothes, but you'll probably need a belt to hold up your drawers," she chuckled.

Meanwhile, Kyle had come in the back door. "Tom!"

"Yeah! I'm in the shower!"

"There better be some hot water left!"

"Tell Morgan, she went first and probably took it all!" Tom hollered from the bathroom. "What's the situation with the horses?"

"There are four horses in the stable. They seem all right."

"Kyle!" Morgan called from the bedroom.

"What is it, Morgan?" Kyle walked down the hallway toward Morgan's voice. "You decent?"

"Yes, come in. I found something you and Tom should see."

Kyle stepped up to Morgan and took the piece of paper she was holding and watched her wipe fresh tears from her face. She was actually quite pretty with clear tanned skin and deep brown eyes. Her wet hair rested on her shoulders with soft bangs already dry that wisped across her forehead. He read the letter and laid it on her dresser. "He's a Marine? At least he is alive, Morgan. We can be grateful for that, and he says he'll see you again.

Morgan dropped her head and began to weep, "I should have stayed with him."

Come on, you gotta stay strong now, Morgan. These days aren't what they used to be." He rubbed her back.

"I know, Kyle. I'm just worried about him. He is retired Marine, so I know I don't have to worry about him, but I still do."

"Next!" Tom hollered as he came out of the bathroom. "Hustle up, Kyle. We need to get going."

"Tom, you need to come see this." Kyle said as he came out of Morgan's bedroom.

The two men passed each other in the hallway. "Whew, man you smell!" Tom laughed and gave Kyle a shove.

To Kyle, it somehow felt wrong to be laughing when the world around them was falling apart, but he appreciated what Tom was doing.

"So, what's up?" Tom said.

"Morgan found a note in her room," Kyle said just before he closed the bathroom door.

Tom entered Morgan's room with his towel still wrapped around his waist. When he saw her, she was bent over tying on her hiking boots. "Whatcha got, Morgan?"

She didn't say a word but nodded toward the dresser where the letter lay open just where Kyle had left it.

Tom picked it up and read it.

Dear Morgan,

By the time you get this letter, I will be gone but I will be safe. I got word that the Regulators were coming, so I had to leave quickly. I've taken two of the horses, you take the rest and whatever you can find that will be of use to you. Stay off the main roads. Check the root cellar and the basement. Be careful of who you meet, your best bet is Christian believers. They seem to be the only ones who haven't fallen under the spell of these monsters. Be strong, Morgan. I will be seeing you very soon. Semper Fi!

Love,

Uncle Walt

Tom handed the letter to Morgan, "You, okay?"

Morgan nodded, "I'm fine now that I know he's safe. Let's go check the root cellar and basement, I don't know what we can expect to find, but he may have something we can use."

"I'll get dressed and meet you down there," Tom said as he left the room.

Kyle had finished his shower and headed toward the kitchen where he found Morgan and Tom loading the saddlebags. "What'd you find?" he asked, buttoning up a borrowed shirt from Walt's closet.

"Radio, batteries, some dried beef, canned goods, and water. Time's wasting, we really need to get going," Tom said.

With the horses saddled and packed, Tom led the way with Lucky perched in front of him. Morgan rode in the middle and Kyle brought up the rear with the packhorse in tow. Each one hoped that more answers would be forthcoming when they arrived at their destination.

Psalm 62:8 "Trust in Him at all times, O people; pour out your hearts to Him, for God is our refuge."

CHAPTER 11

SANDY GAVE THE STEW a final stir and placed it on the back of the stove until Tanya and Steve arrived. The biscuits, warm out of the oven, were nestled in a towel in a basket and placed on the back of the stove next to the pot of stew. With the table set for five, Sandy made one last check to see if anything was missing. As she counted the place settings, she felt a pang of sadness when she counted five instead of six; a sixth setting for Joe, who should have been there. She quickly brushed the thought away and went to see about the dirty dishes in the sink, just as her sister and brother-in-law came through the front door.

"Hey, Sandy!" Tanya called out.

"I'm in the kitchen!" Sandy wiped her wet hands on her apron and went to greet them.

"Hi, sis? How are you doing?" Tanya gave her little sister a hug. "Oh, it feels good in here," she said, taking in the warmth of the woodstove and the tantalizing aroma of homemade biscuits and beef stew. "It's downright cold outside. I think it's going down to the thirties tonight."

"You're right; I remember the news saying there would be a cold front coming through." Steve wrapped his arms around Sandy and hugged her tightly. "How are you doing, kiddo?"

That was one of the many things she loved about Steve. He was a hugger and as strong as he was, his hugs were a great comfort and source of security. "Not bad. Staying busy today."

He could tell she had had a difficult day and smiled tenderly at her.

She smiled back and returned to the sink before he could see the tears welling up. "We still had a lot of squash in the garden, so I picked them this morning." Sandy took a deep breath as the loneliness passed. "What'd you guys find out?"

"Not so fast." Steve's eyes were hopeful. "What did you do with all that extra squash?"

Sandy chuckled, "Not to worry, Steve. I put them in a basket by the front door for you and Tanya, so you won't forget them when you leave. I'm surprised you didn't see them when you came in."

Tanya burst into laughter, "To be honest, Sandy, I saw them, but they were so pretty I thought they were just your autumn decorations!"

Sandy shook her head, "Tanya, you are a nut. Are you hungry?"

"Of course," Steve replied. "Where are the boys?"

"They're putting up the horses. They shouldn't be too much longer. Listen, there's something I need to tell you."

Steve pulled a chair out for ladies and then took one for himself. "What's up, Sandy?"

"Ben and I went to the market to drop off some produce today." Sandy retold the story of the man with the red carnation and Lee; the anxiety built up inside of her as she described the account of how frightened Lee was of the man.

"Did you recognize the man, Sandy?" Steve questioned.

"No, I didn't get a good look at him, but, like I said, Ben saw him, and he recognized him from school. Steve, do you think the boys will be all right at school?" Her voice trembled with emotion.

"To be honest with you, Sandy, I don't know. What I do know is that we need to trust God to protect us. For now, I'd say lay low, see what develops, and take in as much information as we can. I'm sure they will be fine. What about you?"

"Yeah, I'll be all right." She nodded her head and let out a heavy sigh. "So, tell me, what did you find out?"

"The talk around certain blog sites says that things will get much worse before they get better." Tanya looked at her husband, then back at her sister. "This thing that's going to happen, the moving of the people and taking control . . ."

"Has already begun," Steve finished her sentence.

Tanya nodded in agreement, "We were able to find out from these sites that this is not about helping the people in need, but it's about taking control of everything, just like Joe had said. They take in the folks who are struggling under the guise of helping them through their financial difficulties, and then slowly take control of their lives. The people are at the mercy of a new system designed to make them completely dependent on a government whose only goal is to take, take, and take. It will pay them just enough to get by, but not enough to get ahead. The people aren't going to know what is happening until it is too late."

"Kind of like the idea of the 'Company Store'," Steve offered.

"That is just what we talked about the other day, Tanya! Remember?" Sandy exclaimed.

"Right," Tanya agreed again. "And folks that have the money, who don't want or need the help of this program, are being run out of their homes. At first, they are told to leave quietly and become part of the 'greater good' as they say." At this, Tanya exaggerated quotation marks with her fingers and continued, "If folks don't leave, then they are forced out. I don't think it's gone violent, yet, but here's what's strange. They are calling the places where they move the people, 'The City.' Not like you would refer to just a 'city,' but the actual name of the place is The City. That's what all the sites are calling them. And they're scattered all over."

Sandy's head started to ache as she tried to process this frightening news. "Well, once they drive everyone out of their homes, then what? What do they do with the empty houses, the lives of those they drove out? And why are the news programs not saying anything about it?"

"No one knows for sure, Sandy." Steve's voice was low and calming. "Do you remember how they were when this guy was running? They were all over him. They built him up to be someone who could do wonderful things. Where vacant homes are concerned, we think their plan is to use them for housing. Of course, it's not like people will live independently. There will always be someone controlling them. Watching them."

Sandy's mind was all a jumble as her mind raced to ask the next question, "How can we stop them?"

"That's the problem." Steve continued, "No one is standing up against any of it. What few of us will be left," Steve paused, "well, it is frightening, but when I think of David and Goliath, then I have hope. There is always hope, Sandy, but it will be hard."

Steve had always been so sure, so confident, and full of faith, but tonight . . . Sandy saw uncertainty, "Do you know if anyone has been in contact with any of the people who went into The City?"

Tanya and Steve shared a glance, "I went there yesterday morning." Steve spoke softly, knowing her reaction.

"You did what?" Sandy kept her voice low because she heard the boys coming, but her eyes were screaming as she looked at the two of them. "What was it like? What did you see? Steve, wasn't that dangerous?" Then Sandy turned on Tanya, "How could you have allowed him to go?"

Tanya looked at her sadly, "Sandy, we both knew it would be dangerous, but these are dangerous times."

"Mom!"

All three adults jumped when the back door slammed and the boys stormed in. Sandy pointed a warning finger at Steve and Tanya, "Not a word," she whispered, as she stood up.

"Mom, we're hungry. Is supper ready?" Ben yelled as he ran up the stairs.

"Yes, go wash up fellas," Sandy yelled from the kitchen sink.

Sandy cleared the table of the dinner dishes while Tanya poured coffee for Steve, Sandy, and herself. After Joe brought in more wood from the back porch and stoked the wood stove in the kitchen, he sat down at the table next to his brother.

The conversation at supper had been light; focused mainly on crops and the upcoming holidays, but now that everyone had settled, Steve began the discussion. "Boys, has anyone at school spoken about this new program? Have any of your friends or teachers talked about it?"

Joe spoke first, "I told mom the other day that a lot of my friends have already left. Their parents moved their families to The City because the officials told them life would be easier there. They'd all have jobs with good pay, insurance, and a good education for their kids and nice homes to live in. And they're calling the place The City like it's the actual name. I don't understand."

Steve looked around the table, "That's exactly right, Joe. They are naming all of them like that."

"My teacher is telling everyone to come to the meeting, and that we will talk about it then," Ben interrupted. "She said there would be two guest speakers."

"Ben, did your teacher say anything more, like whether people should go?" Steve asked.

"Well, yeah, she wanted everyone to go to the meeting."

Sandy smiled, "No, honey. Uncle Steve meant to leave their homes and go to The City. Did she say anything about that?"

"No. Not really. She said she was going to go with her parents, though. She said they were older." The adults exchanged glances.

"Let me tell you what I saw when I went to The City," Steve said.

"Uncle Steve! You went?" Joe asked, surprised.

Steve nodded and continued, while Sandy got up to pour more coffee. "I went to see Mr. and Mrs. Beechum. I'm afraid Mr. Beechum's cancer has come back, and he is not doing very well. Mrs. Beechum is doing the best she can under the circumstances, but they haven't got much freedom, and they miss the church. They send their love to all of you."

A faint smile crossed Sandy's lips as she recalled the last conversation she had with Mr. Beechum about his tractor.

Steve continued, "Apparently there isn't any type of worship service offered so Mrs. Beechum reads to Mr. Beechum from her Bible every morning and evening. At least, that way, they can receive some kind of spiritual food. I suggested that she try to meet with others in their building, but she said there is a strict schedule in the building, and they are all confined to their rooms promptly at eight o'clock p.m. Oh and get this, there is a wall surrounding The City now. I have no idea how they got it up so quickly, but the wall stands about twenty feet high or more and there are armed guards at the entry way, but you don't really see them until you get inside."

"What are they armed with, Steve, could you tell?" Sandy asked.

"They were M-16's Sandy. The type of weapon our military uses, or I should say, formerly used. There must be a surplus now that they've brought all the soldiers back. Anyway, as I approached The City, I saw a gate. You know the kind they use at railroad crossings. I had to leave my truck parked outside the gate and walk in."

"Frankly, I'm surprised that they let you leave, Steve." Sandy replied.

Steve chuckled, "Frankly, I'm surprised they did, too." He took a sip of coffee and continued. "So anyway, I got there and the man at the gate asked me whom I was there to see. I told him, he made a call, let me in, and gave me a key card. He said it was the only way to get into any of the stores and buildings and that I had to return it when I left. Then some fellow in a golf cart picked me up at the front gate and brought me to a gray building about ten stories high. In front of all the residential buildings, including the Beechum's, were what I can only assume were 'doormen.' He was huge and wore a black suit and over coat. He asked for my key card, swiped it through a magnetic slot by the front door and let me go in." Steve took another sip of coffee and set it down to cool. As he looked around the table all eyes were glued on him. "Is this frightening you, guys?" He looked at Ben and Joe.

"Yeah, a little bit," Joe said. "But it's a good thing you went in. I mean, wouldn't it be best to know what they are up to over there?"

Steve nodded his head in agreement. He wanted to wrap up the story now that he saw the effect it was having on the kids. "I took a little walk when I left the Beechum's and found the grocery store, and Leon's gas station is still there, too. I even had to use the key card to go in there. I poked my head in the door to say 'hi' to Leon, but I didn't see any sign of him. There were just a couple of guys that I'd never seen before. Oh! And one more thing, I stopped by the bookstore to satisfy a curiosity I had, and lo and behold, guess what they had removed from the shelves."

"No, they didn't!" Sandy exclaimed, "The Bibles?"

"You guessed right, Sandy. Anything to do with Jesus, God or the Old or New Testament has been removed. Instead, there are books on the leader's philosophy of life and every other type of man-made religion or self-help book. This is all very disturbing." Steve shook his head, "We must go to their so-called 'informational' meeting tonight and listen for anything that will help us."

"Uncle Steve, what if they try to make us leave the farm?" Joe asked.

"We won't go. We'll have to stand firm against them," Steve said decidedly.

Tanya took Steve's hand into hers and exchanged looks with her family.

"Are you boys up to this?" Sandy asked, scrutinizing the expressions on her sons' faces.

"By God's Good Grace we'll do this," Joe said quietly.

Sandy looked at him lovingly, "You are your father's son."

1 Peter 5:6-7 "Humble yourselves, therefore, under God's mighty hand, that he may lift you up in due time. Cast all your anxiety on him because he cares for you."

CHAPTER 12

TOM PULLED A STAINED, worn envelope from his breast pocket and checked the return address and the handwritten map on the back with a quick scan of his flashlight. "We need to follow this two-lane to a dirt road on the right and that should lead us to the Parker Ranch driveway." The night riding had started out difficult, especially when they had to keep to the unfamiliar woods, but after three days on the road, they and their horses had grown accustomed to one another and to the noises that only came in the dark and uncertain terrain.

"Hey, Nelly," Kyle whispered.

Tom quickly put a finger to his lips and led his horse off the road into the woods. The others followed him deep into the thick brush until he stopped next to a huge, fallen maple tree and motioned toward the road they had just left. Kyle and Morgan turned in their saddles just in time to see a seven-ton rumble slowly up the deserted street. In a turret above the cab, a guard was standing, flashing a powerful spotlight into the empty buildings and shops that lined the main street. Morgan's horse blew and shook his head noisily, the halter and bridle rattling in the dead silence of the woods. The three riders froze. Morgan leaned forward in her saddle and rubbed her horse's ear trying to quiet him. The seven-ton continued its mission, the driver and guard seeming not to notice the riders.

Steve checked the fires in the fireplace and woodstove while the others were getting ready for the meeting at the Community Center.

"Are we good?" Tanya asked when she met him in the hallway.

"We're good. Are Sandy and the boys about ready?"

"Here we come," Sandy called as she, Joe, and Ben bounded down the stairs.

Tanya was happy to see that her little sister had regained some of her curves over the past couple of months. After Joe died, she had lost too much weight, and with all the work required on the ranch, it was no wonder. Sandy was always smaller than her sister and she remained that way, but at least she was at a healthier weight now. Her chestnut hair had grown longer too, the deep color offsetting the dark green in her eyes. Normally, she kept her hair pulled back in a tight ponytail, but tonight she let it fall in thick tresses down her back. "You look nice, Sandy."

"Why, thank you, sis. I've just got my old jeans on," Sandy smiled.

"Well, you still look nice." Tanya gave her sister's shoulder a squeeze before they stepped out the door.

"I'm locking the door, Mom!" Joe called out.

"Thanks, Joe."

They all piled into Steve's four-door dualie and headed toward the Community Center in town, each of them anxious about what was in store. The town was quiet as they drove slowly through the deserted streets. When they arrived, they were shocked when Steve pointed out the seven ton that was blocking the exit to the Community Center. They all knew that what lay ahead for them was not going to be good.

Together they walked into the auditorium. By the number of empty chairs, it was obvious that many of the townspeople had already left for The City. Steve guided Tanya and the others to the back row where there were five seats together. The metal folding chairs scraped the linoleum floor and people chattered about the upcoming meeting or whatever was happening in their lives at the time. Mostly though, the talk was about what would happen after tonight and the uncertainty of it all. After ten minutes passed, the school principal finally came to the podium.

"Good evening and thank you for coming," the woman began. "Some of you already know who I am, but for those who do not have children at the Willow Creek School, my name is Ms. Thompkins. We have been called here tonight to get answers to questions that I'm sure a lot of you have. To help with those questions, we have two gentlemen with us tonight, who were kind enough to brave the cold and come to Willow Creek to inform us of a wonderful new plan and to answer your questions. Please welcome Mr. Garrison and Mr. Smith."

Tanya and Steve exchanged amused glances at the mention of 'Mr. Smith.'

Three men emerged from the shadows of a side door. Two of the men stayed up front at the podium while a third found his way to the back of the room. Keeping her focus on the men up front, Tanya leaned over and whispered to Sandy, "I thought she said there were two men."

"Maybe the other guy is security," Sandy answered. She continued to stare at one of the men at the podium. There was something unsettling about him, as though she had seen him before. She tried to push back the fear that began to take hold of her; "I must stay focused." She pulled out the small notebook and pen she always carried in her leather bag and settled back to listen; the familiarity of the man still gnawed at her. Ben suddenly grabbed her hand. When she looked down at him, his face had gone white. "Ben, what is it?" She whispered.

"It's him, Mom. It's the guy from the market," Ben whispered.

Sandy looked up at the man and realized that the market was exactly where she had seen him. She leaned into Tanya, "Tanya, that's the guy from the market."

Tanya nodded her head in question, "Are you sure?"

"Positive," Sandy answered.

Tanya laid her head against Steve's shoulder and whispered to him what Sandy had just said about the man on the stage.

Steve nodded his head ever so slightly in reply but did not speak. He could feel the eyes of the man behind him watching them.

The man whom they would come to know as Mr. Garrison stepped up to the microphone, "Good evening, ladies, and gentlemen; thank you for coming tonight. We have news that we think will make you all very happy." Mr. Garrison waved his hands dramatically as he spoke, "We all see how our friends and neighbors have been suffering through some very difficult life situations; and our Leader in Washington has also witnessed your suffering and wants to give you relief from all your strife, pain, and uncertainty. With the help and support of our friends on Capitol Hill, he has come up with a plan where there will be food, fuel, and clothing; anything, and everything you and your families will ever need."

Garrison continued, "Jobs will be provided for you with the best of benefits, including dental." With his last remark he flashed a bright, sardonic smile. Sandy wondered whether she was the only one who saw it that way. Several people in the room chuckled at his attempt at humor, but the others continued to eye the men suspiciously.

He pressed on with his pitch. "Some of you may ask, 'How can this be? How can our President do this?' Well, this is the dawning of a brand-new day, my friends. Our president is no longer our president; he has chosen instead to be called our Supreme Leader. He wants to lead us into peace and prosperity for all mankind. Our old society has proved time and again that it cannot provide for all men.

Our Leader has arranged that every man, woman, and child, no matter the age or station in life, will be well taken care of for the rest of your days. All he needs from you is your dedication to his cause and your cooperation. You folks in Western Maryland will be joining with your neighbors in West Virginia. Our Cities will be set up from previously existing cities and they will be strategically developed to better serve their residents."

Someone raised a hand, but Mr. Garrison continued his speech. "We will take questions at the end of the meeting. Those of you living within the city limits of Willow Creek will be the first lucky folks to relocate to your new homes. Those of you living on the outskirts and surrounding areas will be notified by mail of your relocation schedule.

Judging by the empty seats, I think it is safe to assume that some of your neighbors have already taken advantage of our new system."

Sandy felt her stomach start to churn. "Don't throw up, oh my gosh don't throw up!" Ben sensed her discomfort and took her hand. He looked up at her and smiled, but his face was still pale. She gave his hand a squeeze and returned the smile. If her sons only knew how much strength she drew from them.

"Your housing will be provided for you," Garrison continued, "beautiful, spacious homes. You will want for nothing. Imagine getting up and going to work at a job you absolutely love and without a care in the world. You will be coming home to your family, without any worry of getting those bills paid or putting your child through college. You will be able to send your children to a university of their choosing. No longer will you have to decide on a college for its low tuition because it's all you can afford. Imagine the future you can provide for your family."

"He means, the future the government will provide," Steve said shortly. "He sounds like a used car salesman." Steve's comment sent Tanya into a fit of giggles that she couldn't control. She bit her lip in an effort to keep them away, but they continued to bubble up despite her efforts. The man with no name had wandered to the other side of the room, but when he noticed the commotion in the back row, he made his way down the aisle toward them. Steve squeezed his wife's hand to get her attention. When she spied the third man approaching, she quickly gathered her wits. For the rest of the meeting, he stood behind the back row, watching them.

Garrison went on, "Our leader has received the approval from the Congress and the Senate, and they are all in agreement that this plan is the best for our Country. We can take your questions now."

"What will become of our homes here, our belongings?" Someone called from across the room.

"You will take your belongings with you, of course!" Garrison answered. "The homes and the heavy mortgages that go with them will be dealt with by our administration. Some homes will be used for housing and the homes not used right away will be reserved for future purposes at the discretion of our leader and his advisors."

"What about our animals?" An elderly woman asked.

"They come with you. Smaller pets like cats, fish, and birds; you can keep with you in your new homes. Larger animals and large breed dogs will be kept at a public shelter. You can visit them anytime you like, and they will be well taken care of. After all, our leader is an animal lover himself. Too many of our beloved pets have been turned over to kill shelters because their owners couldn't afford to take care of them. That problem has been resolved."

"What about folks who don't want to leave; who want to stay in the homes they've grown up in?" Steve stood up when he addressed the man at the podium.

"Of course, you would want what is best for all the families of your community, Pastor Barnes. As much as you would like to meet the needs of your flock, I'm sure you will be the first to admit that you have fallen short."

Steve's face flushed with anger, "Have you not heard sir that the Lord will provide for all of our needs?"

"Yes, Pastor, I am well aware of that quote, but you must admit there are folks in your town that have already left because their needs could not be met by your almighty." Nick Garrison's reply dripped with sarcasm as it echoed through the hall.

Steve clenched his fists, but he held his tongue and sat down. The anger that this man had generated in him was like nothing Steve had ever experienced before. He closed his eyes and prayed silently for the strength they would surely need.

After witnessing the exchange, Ben leaned over to whisper to his mom but froze when he noticed that the man who stood behind them raised his hand to get the attention of the speaker at the podium. "Mr. Garrison, I believe this young man has a question for you."

Ben looked up at his mother and stammered, "Mom, I--

Sandy held her hand up to quiet him. "It's okay, honey." She stood up to address Garrison, "My son only had a question for me, his mother. I apologize for the interruption." Sandy sat back down. Her heart was pounding, and she could feel the man's glare boring into the back of her head. She looked at Ben and gave him a reassuring smile.

Several more questions were answered to the satisfaction of nearly everyone in the hall. As they began to file out at the close of the meeting, they talked excitedly amongst themselves. The atmosphere was electric.

Sandy and Ben walked together behind Steve and Tanya while Joe, Jr. brought up the rear. When they arrived at the exit, they saw that Mr. Garrison was standing by the door, chatting with the people as they left. They had no choice; they had to walk past him.

"Good evening, young man," Garrison extended his hand to shake Ben's.

The eleven-year-old kept his hands clenched tight by his side and gazed cautiously up at him. "Hullo."

"Did you enjoy the meeting tonight?" The man asked.

"Uh huh," Ben looked down at the floor and examined a scuff mark beneath his shoe.

"It was very informative," Sandy interrupted. "Thank you for your time. We really need to get these boys to bed, school tomorrow you know." Sandy attempted to move Ben along, but Garrison was persistent.

"How do you feel about home schooling, Mrs. Parker?"

Sandy's breath caught in her throat, "How did you know my name?"

"We make it our business to know everyone here in Willow Creek, Mrs. Parker, and in every other town we come to."

By this time Steve and Tanya had stopped and gone to stand next to Sandy and Ben. Joe, Jr. stepped in closer. "We like our school just fine. Thanks," he snapped. He did not like the way Mr. Garrison had spoken to his Uncle Steve, his mom, or his little brother. And he especially didn't like the way the man had mocked God. No, to Joe these men were very bad news, and he had already made up his mind that he would do whatever it took to stop them from destroying his town and his country.

"I was just going to say that with this wonderful new program, you don't have to go out on those freezing winter mornings. You can attend school in your PJs."

Joe Jr. rolled his eyes and took his mom by the arm. "Come on Mom, we need to go."

"Good night, Mrs. Parker, Joe, Ben." The man stepped aside and allowed them to leave. He watched them carefully through squinted black eyes as they exited the building.

Once they were outside, Steve hurried them to the truck. "In the truck and lock the doors," he whispered. Joe opened the back door to the truck and climbed in after his mom and Ben. As Steve pulled out of the parking lot, he checked his side view mirrors, certain that they would be followed. "Okay, what happened back there?" he asked nervously, looking back at Sandy.

"I don't know, Steve. Maybe they found out our names from the school records or by asking around town, maybe at Lee's Market. How would he know your name, though?" Sandy's voice shook with fear.

"Well, since I'm the Pastor of the only church in town, it couldn't have been very hard to figure me out."

Ben looked at his mom with pleading eyes, "I didn't mean to start any trouble."

"Honey, you didn't start any trouble. Those men are bullies, and they found someone they could pick on."

They rode in silence for the rest of the trip home, but the thoughts and fears that ran through their minds were all the same; the government had only one goal; to gain total control of the people and their possessions. Steve pulled the truck into the drive and drove slowly down the half-mile lane. As they neared the farmhouse, the headlights bounced across the yard. A lone figure quickly dipped behind the southwest corner of the house. "What was that? Did anyone else see it?"

"Now you're really scaring me, Steve. What are you talking about?" Tanya leaned forward in her seat and squinted into the darkness.

Steve stopped short in front of the house and slammed the truck in park. "Wait here!" He reached under the seat and pulled out his revolver, then slipped quietly from the truck. He peered hard into the darkness where he had spotted the shadow. Suddenly another movement caught his attention. "Freeze!"

A voice from the end of the house called out, "We don't mean any harm!"

"Who is 'we' and what do you want?" Steve called back.

"My name is Tom Connelly. We're looking for someone. I was told she would be here."

"Connelly?" Sandy cried and scrambled out of the truck behind Joe.

Romans 15:5-6 "May the God who gives endurance and encouragement give you a spirit of unity among yourselves as you follow Christ Jesus, so that with one heart and mouth you may glorify the God and Father of our Lord Jesus Christ."

CHAPTER 13

"Mrs. Parker? Yeah, it's me, Connelly! I've got a couple of friends with me."

"Steve, Tanya, it's okay. It's Tom Connelly, Joe's Army buddy from Iraq. Come on out, Tom!" Sandy sprinted up the porch steps to open the door and paused for a moment to watch the tired riders emerge from the edge of the porch. It was too dark to really see their faces, but once she opened the front door, a welcoming light and warmth spilled out across the porch.

The three travelers and their mascot cautiously moved out of the darkness into the light, relieved to have finally reached their destination.

Once everyone was in the house, Steve locked the door behind him and proceeded to stoke the fireplace and wood stove for the long night ahead.

Sandy began the introductions, "I'm so happy to finally meet you, Tom. I feel as though I know you already from Joe's letters."

Tom was exhausted and relieved to have finally arrived, but he wasn't prepared to meet Sandy and her family. He was taken aback and left speechless by her excitement and natural beauty. The pictures that she sent Joe hadn't come close to showing her true self.

Realizing his fatigue, Sandy took him by the hand, "Look, I'm babbling. Let me introduce you to everyone. These are our boys, Joe Jr. and Ben," Sandy beamed as she touched the shoulder of each son and continued. "My sister Tanya and her husband and our town minister, Steven Barnes."

Finally finding his voice, Tom reached out and shook hands with everyone, "Pleased to meet all of you," then he turned to his friends.

"This is Kyle Johnson. He served with Joe and me in the Sandbox, and this is Morgan Ellers. We sort of ran into her on our way here. Her uncle was kind enough to leave us his horses. We put 'em up in the empty stalls. We didn't think you'd mind."

"No problem at all," Sandy smiled with a wave of her hand. "And who is this little guy?" She knelt next to Morgan and stroked Lucky as he impatiently stood wagging his tail, waiting for someone to notice him.

"This is Lucky," Tom grinned softly at the pup. "He came back from Iraq with us." He considered how he came to have Lucky but thought that story should be saved for another time.

"You guys want some coffee?" Sandy asked her new guests.

"That's a great idea, I'll get it." Tanya exclaimed, then went to the kitchen and busied herself with the coffee and snack preparations.

"There's so much to discuss and so many questions I have for you, Tom. I really don't know where to begin." Sandy sat in the rocker next to the fireplace. "First I want to thank you for coming all the way out here, and I believe you are the man whom my Joe saved." Sandy gazed at Kyle who was sitting on the couch next to her chair. "I remember the night Captain Graham came to see me; I asked him the name of the man . . ." she stopped suddenly when she saw the pain etched in Kyle's young face. It spoke volumes, "You fool!" she thought, "Can't you see he's already so hurt by this?" "Oh Kyle, I'm so sorry. He loved his men very much, you know. He wrote to me about you." She smiled. "He said you were a good soldier."

Kyle felt the lump grow in his throat. "I can't tell you how terrible I feel about what happened, Mrs. Parker. I loved Staff Sergeant. We all did, and I'm honored to finally meet you. I just wish it were under happier circumstances."

Sandy laid a gentle hand on the soldier's arm, "Kyle, please don't blame yourself for Joe's death. What he did was out of love, and I believe you know that he would have done it for any one of his men."

"Mrs. Parker, I have a message that Staff Sergeant Parker wanted me to give you." Tom said. He had seated himself on the couch next to Kyle.

"Oh?" Sandy turned a tearful gaze to Tom.

"He wanted me to tell you that he loves you, and he's gone on home to wait for you." Tom lowered his gaze. He couldn't look into her eyes without the guilt eating him up.

Sandy fought desperately to smile through her tears. It was a bittersweet reunion for all of them. Tom noted how she bit her bottom lip and remembered Staff Sergeant Parker telling him how she did that when she was worried or troubled. Unable to speak for fear of breaking down, she looked back to Kyle and Tom and nodded her thanks. Morgan buried her face in the softness of Lucky's scruff to keep from crying.

"Well," Sandy wiped the tears from her eyes and looked at her boys. They too were recovering from the message from their father to their mother. She smiled gently, "Fellas, I think it's time for bed. You have school tomorrow."

"Mom, I don't want to go to school tomorrow. Those men, they didn't feel right tonight." Ben turned pleading eyes to his mom, then to his Uncle Steve.

Sandy turned her attention to Joe, Jr. who looked back at her, just barely shaking his head. Steve witnessed the silent exchange between mother and son and offered a word. "Sandy, I think we should listen to Ben. I don't like the thought of the boys going anywhere alone after tonight. I think they should stay home at least until we can figure something out."

As Morgan observed the interaction between the mother and her sons, she glanced over briefly at Tom and Kyle. Noting their concern also, she asked Steve, "Why don't the boys want to go to school? What happened tonight?"

Steve gave the chilling report of everything that transpired during and after the meeting. When he had finished, the room was hushed, with just the crackling of the fire filling the void. He continued, "That's why we were so skittish when we came home and found you here. We don't normally scare that easily, but under the circumstances -- "

"I can see why." Tom said.

Sandy got up from the rocking chair and corralled the boys toward the stairs, "Off to bed then, I'll let you cut school tomorrow, but it's still late and it's been a long, long day. I'll be up in a second."

Joe and Ben said goodnight to everyone, then headed for the stairs. When they reached the top, Joe turned back to his mom, "I'll share Ben's room tonight so someone can have mine."

"Thanks, Joe. Good night."

Tanya returned to the living room with a tray of fresh coffee, cups, and thick slices of warmed apple pie. "Here you go. You three must be starved." She smiled at her husband, "Steve?"

"Let's give thanks for our new friends and ask a blessing on the snack." They bowed their heads and clasped hands. "Almighty God, we thank you for the safe arrival of Morgan, Tom, Kyle, and Lucky. Thank you, Lord for guiding their steps and that no harm came to them on the road. Please, Father, watch over us and guide us in these troubled times. Help us to be a light in this dark and broken world. Bless this food to our bodies, Father, and bless those who prepared it. In Jesus' name we pray. Amen."

"Amen," the group responded together.

"I'm going to go tuck in the boys," Sandy said. "I'll be right back."

Tom watched her as she climbed the stairs and shook his head. "Steve, it's almost frightening how much Joe looks like his dad."

Kyle nodded, "You can say that again. The boy is the spittin' image of him."

Steve took Tanya's hand, "You guys are going to need a place to stay the night aren't you, Tom?"

Tom looked at Kyle and Morgan, then back at Steve, "We haven't given it much thought. We were just anxious to get here, but yeah, I suppose we will."

"Tanya and I live in town. We have a couple of spare rooms," Steve explained. "We'd love to have you, and Kyle come stay with us. You'll be quite comfortable, and Tanya makes some pretty good coffee."

Tom tasted his coffee and smiled, "She does at that. That'd be great, Steve. Thanks."

Sandy poked her head into Ben's room, "Hey guys, you still up?" She stepped gingerly over Joe who was already in his sleeping bag on the floor.

"Yup," Ben moved over in his bed to make room for her to sit next to him. "Mom, what do you think is going to happen? Are those men going to make us leave the ranch?"

"Of course not, Ben." Sandy exclaimed.

"Mom," Joe rolled on his back to look at her, "I've been thinking, and I've changed my mind. I don't think it's a good idea to stay home tomorrow."

"No, Joe." Ben interrupted.

"Why's that, Joe?" Sandy asked.

"If we start changing things now and stay home from school, especially after what happened tonight, it will just draw more attention to us."

Sandy considered his statement, "You're right, Joe. And right now, that's something we don't want to do." She leaned over and stroked his cheek. "How did you get to be so wise?"

"I have good teachers." He smiled back at her, but his eyes reflected sadness; he was still thinking about his dad and the message that Tom delivered.

Sandy's heart swelled with pride at Joe's remark and thanked God for blessing her with so much. She turned her attention to Ben, "We just need some time to figure out what we need to do next. For now, we'll just have to trust God, follow along and see where He takes us. Okay?"

"All right." Ben rolled over and turned his back to his mom and brother.

Sandy leaned over and kissed him goodnight and whispered softly, "It'll be all right Ben, I promise."

Ben rolled over, reached up and kissed Sandy on the cheek, "Okay, Mom."

"Did you guys say your prayers?"

They muttered together, "Yes, ma'am."

"Good. Joe, Ben, I love you both." She stroked their heads gently before she left.

"Night, Mom," Joe yawned.

Sandy pulled the door shut and turned to look at the family pictures on the wall. "Oh Joe, I sure wish you were here," she whispered. She turned and headed downstairs to where the others were talking softly.

"Did the boys get down all right?" Tanya asked Sandy as she entered the living room.

"Yeah, but Joe made a good point, and as much as I don't like the idea, he's right. He thinks they should go to school tomorrow. He doesn't think it's a good idea to draw attention to them now that those men have already noticed them."

"He's a very wise boy for his years," Tom's voice was low.

"Yes, he is." Sandy looked at Tom. "He's had to grow up so fast."

Steve saw the conversation going in a direction that would make the evening difficult for his sister-in-law. "Sandy, you know it's late. What do you say we let you turn in? Tom and Kyle are going to stay with us."

"All right, that sounds good," Sandy, said cheerfully.

Tanya stood up and stacked the dirty dishes on the tray. "Sandy, I'll knock these out and we'll be out of your hair."

"Nonsense, Tanya, let me do that." Morgan stood up and stretched. "I need to earn my keep." She smiled at Tanya as she took the tray from her.

"Thanks, Morgan," Tanya followed Morgan into the kitchen and picked up the kitchen towel while Morgan filled the sink with water. "You know, Morgan, I can't tell you how happy Steve and I are now that you are all here."

"Well, we're just glad we got here when we did. It's getting pretty bad out there, Tanya. When we came in tonight there was a seven-ton military truck patrolling the streets with a floodlight. I've seen what they can do. It will turn violent if people don't leave."

"Yeah, we saw the truck at the Community Center, and we all wondered what it was doing there. Do you think the boys will be all right at school tomorrow?"

"I think so," Morgan said. "Sandy is right. For now, you don't want to do anything that will draw attention to yourselves. We need to 'keep under the radar' as they say. As far as the trucks go, you'll be seeing many more of those."

With the dishes put up and the coffee pot prepped for the next morning, Morgan dried her hands on a kitchen towel. She looked all around the kitchen at the crown molding and French doors, "Sandy sure does have a beautiful home."

"Yes, she loves this ranch. I honestly can't see her ever living anywhere else. She and Joe bought it when she was pregnant with Joe Jr. She has a lot of wonderful memories here."

Morgan cocked her head and smiled softly at Tanya, "Well, hopefully when this is all over, she'll be able to make some more memories."

The others were already gathering in the hallway to leave when Tanya and Morgan joined them. "Okay, we're all done." Tanya turned and gave Morgan a firm hug, "Morgan, thanks for helping with the dishes. It is so nice to have met you and, like I said, we are very happy you are all here." She stepped away from Morgan and turned to Sandy, "You sleep tight tonight, and we'll see you first thing in the morning. What time do the boys leave for school?"

Sandy returned her sister's hug, "The bus picks them up at seven-thirty."

"We'll be here," Steve kissed Sandy softly on the cheek and gave her a hug. "Sleep well, Sandy."

"I will, thanks for everything tonight." Sandy looked up at Tom and Kyle, "I'm so glad to finally meet you both. Thanks again for coming so far. I really hope you plan on staying on for a while." Sandy extended her hand and shook hands with Kyle, then with Tom. The huge paw of Tom's hand swallowed up her smaller one. Judging by the calluses on her hands, the thought crossed his mind that she must run the ranch pretty much on her own. He didn't speak but nodded his thanks.

When at last everyone had left, Sandy walked Morgan upstairs. "Morgan, Joe keeps his room fairly clean, but if you give me a couple of minutes, I'll change out the sheets." Sandy whispered as they walked past Ben's room.

"Sandy, that's not necessary," Morgan assured her. "I've been sleeping on the ground with the horses for nearly a week. I can't tell you how much we all appreciate your hospitality."

"I'm just glad you and the guys made it through without any problems," Sandy said. She looked Morgan up and down; "here, come into my room for a minute." Sandy opened her dresser drawer and pulled out some flannel pajamas.

"I think you are just my size. I've got some other clothes we can go through in the morning."

"Thanks, Sandy. I really hadn't planned on going so far from home, but to be honest there was nothing left for me there. Then when Tom and Kyle showed up and they offered to take me with them, it felt like the best option, so I never looked back. I'll tell you what I'd love right now though is a hot shower."

"Oh, by all means! The bathroom is just across the hall and there are towels and washcloths in the closet behind the bathroom door. Take whatever you need. Whatever you can't find, just holler. Thankfully, the hot water heater runs off propane, so we still have hot water for a while." Sandy gave Morgan a hug, "Good night, Morgan."

Morgan hugged her back. How was she going to tell these gentle people about the horror that was coming?

Sandy turned out the lights, hit her knees, and thanked God for the blessings of new friends and their safe travel. "Lord, please watch over my boys tomorrow; please watch over all of us."

Morgan stepped from the shower and sighed, still fretting about what the future might hold. Despite the frightening world they were currently living in, it had been a very good day. Although she was grateful for her new friends, she worried for Ben and Joe. She was troubled by all of them because she knew what the Regulators were capable of doing. When should she tell Sandy and the others? Should she, Tom, and Kyle leave in the morning? There were so many questions that she just didn't have the answers to.

"Well, I can't think about this tonight. I need sleep." Morgan slipped into her donated flannel pajamas, delighted with their softness and warmth. When she slid into the crisp, scented sheets she smiled, Sandy had changed them after all.

Steve pulled the truck into the driveway and checked the dashboard clock before he turned off the truck; "Ten-thirty! It's late. You guys must be exhausted."

"Just a bit," Kyle yawned.

"You should be quite comfortable tonight," Steve said, "and hopefully it will be a nice change from what you're used to."

Kyle and Tom brought in their gear from the truck while Steve stoked the fire in the woodstove in the kitchen. When he finished, he found them standing awkwardly in the front foyer.

"You have a beautiful home here, Steve," Tom said.

"Thank you, Tom. Tanya and I love this house. I've had my eye on it for years, but you know with my meager minister's salary, it took me quite a while to save up for the down payment."

"It looks like it was well worth the wait." Tom replied.

"It most certainly was." Steve smiled at him and motioned for them to follow him, "This way, guys."

Kyle studied the family pictures that adorned the wall as he followed his host up the wide hardwood staircase. Next to a photograph of Steve and Tanya's wedding day was a picture of his Staff Sergeant in uniform with his beautiful bride on their wedding day. Kyle's gaze settled on them for a moment more before moving on to a photograph of Staff Sergeant, Sandy and the boys together by a large pond. The last item on the wall was a family picture of whom he could only assume was Sandy's and Tanya's parents.

"Here you go, Kyle." Steve opened the door to a small, but comfortable room. Four overstuffed down pillows on a double bed, covered with a thick homemade quilt presented a warm welcome.

"Thanks, Steve." Kyle entered the room and dropped his duffle and backpack on the floor. He sat on the bed. He didn't dare lie down just yet. He knew that if he did, he would pass out from exhaustion.

Steve opened the door to the room across the hall. "Tom, you can stay here. The bathroom is there at the end of the hall and the towels are in the closet just outside the bathroom. There's shampoo, soap, and whatever you need under the bathroom sink. If there's anything else you need, just let me know." Steve clapped Tom on the shoulder as he turned to leave.

"Thanks, Steve." Tom nodded and stepped into the room. Similar to Kyle's room, a colorful quilt and flannel sheets covered the bed. Tom couldn't wait to crawl in.

"Do you and Kyle have fresh clothes for tomorrow, Tom?" Tanya asked as she came down the hall.

"Not exactly, ma'am. Whatever we have in our packs, is what we've been wearing for the last week or so."

"Well, tell you what, you leave the clothes you want to wear tomorrow outside your bedroom door, and I'll toss them in the wash before we go to bed."

"You really don't need to go to that trouble, ma'am," Tom protested, embarrassed. "We can get it tomorrow."

"Nonsense, we're going straight back to Sandy's in the morning, so there won't be time." Tanya noticed the way he shyly focused on the hardwood floor without wanting to look at her. She laid a gentle hand on his arm and spoke softly, "Listen, Tom. I would say you have all had a very rough time these past few weeks. Not to mention all those months you and Kyle spent in Iraq, protecting us, and helping others in need. Please, let us take care of you now."

Tom raised head, met her eyes, and smiled. "Yes, ma'am. Thanks for all you've done for us already."

"It's our pleasure." She smiled as she and Steve left him at the bedroom door.

While Tom showered, Kyle went back downstairs to help Steve bring in some firewood and stack it against the brick wall next to the fireplace. "Steve, there's something you all need to know about the people who are moving everyone out."

"I think I've got a pretty good idea already," Steve said, "but I think we should wait until we are all together. Then you can each tell your story. How about tomorrow after the boys have left for school? Would that be a good time?"

"Yeah, that'll be fine." Kyle said.

Steve studied Kyle's face, "But what about you, Kyle? How are you doing?"

"I'm doing all right, I suppose," Kyle said, keeping his attention on the logs he was stacking.

"I see you walk with a limp," Steve said. "Is that a result of your injury?"

"Yes sir. There was a lot of damage done, but the doctors were able to fix me up pretty good. All that's left is a limp and some pain during the cold winter months." Kyle hesitated, and knelt down next to Steve, "There's something else I'd like to talk to you about, Steve."

Steve paused in his stacking and gave his full attention to the soldier next to him.

Kyle continued, "It was so hard to look at Sandy tonight. I'd like to, you know, talk about that sometime, if that's all right?" Kyle dropped his gaze and put his focus back on stacking the wood.

Steve's heart was saddened, and he laid a reassuring hand on Kyle's muscled shoulder. "Sure, Kyle, we'll find some time tomorrow."

Hebrews 10:22 "-- let us draw near to God with a sincere heart in full assurance of faith, having our hearts sprinkled to cleanse us from a guilty conscience and having our bodies washed with pure water."

CHAPTER 14

NICK GARRISON HESITATED BEFORE knocking on Commander Baroam's door. He had just arrived back in the Supreme City and received a message that the Commander wanted to see him. Although Garrison was a cruel man in his own right, something about the man who waited on the other side of the door took evil to a completely new level. Garrison was more than willing to carry out the orders he received from his boss, always believing his reward in the end would be control of his own 'City', but coming face to face with Baroam was the one thing he tried very hard to avoid. He took a deep breath and rapped sharply on the heavy walnut door.

"Enter!"

Nick opened the door, stepped inside, and closed the door behind him. "You called for me, Commander?"

"Ah yes, Mr. Garrison. Welcome back. I trust things are going well with the creation of our new Cities?"

"As well as can be expected, sir. We've run into a few snags with the high amount of security that's required, but I'm confident that we will resolve them quickly."

"Good, very good, Mr. Garrison," the Commander purred. Sitting in an over-stuffed leather chair, Baroam kept his back to Garrison. The heavy drapes and dark paneling in the room seemed to muffle their conversation and Garrison strained to hear the words that spilled from the Commander's lips. "I've decided to give you your own City, Mr. Garrison. How would you feel about that?"

Nick was visibly stunned. He opened his mouth to speak but couldn't find the words soon enough.

"What? No response? Are you not grateful for the gift I am giving you?" Baroam asked.

"Sir, no, I mean, yes," Garrison stammered. "I am grateful. I'm just surprised, sir."

"Are you questioning my judgment, Mr. Garrison?"

"Of course not, Commander," Garrison moved forward, expecting a withdrawal of the offer. As he did, the leather chair spun around suddenly and the Commander sprung to his feet forcing Garrison to step back to where he stood before, "I just had not expected it so soon."

Commander Baroam stood less than five foot six. His paunchy mid-section revealed his fondness for sweets . . . pastries especially, and his thin blonde hair in a comb over, did little to conceal his flushed, balding head. Looking at him, one would not feel threatened by his physical appearance or his slight lisp, but he had the one thing that no one else had. This inept-looking excuse of a man had the ear of the Supreme Leader. As a result, Baroam had an army of men at his disposal. Men who would eagerly follow their Commander's bidding including making anyone who disappointed him, or the Supreme Leader 'disappear.' Baroam locked his fingers behind his back and turned to the window overlooking the Supreme City. "Mr. Garrison, I received your reports on the various Cities going up and there is one, in particular, that I need you to run. It is not very big I am afraid, but the people will be the challenge."

Garrison couldn't believe what he was hearing. He stood rigid, waiting.

Baroam continued, "A lot of them are God-fearing, as they are fond of saying, and it has been difficult, to say the least, to convince them to convert to the beliefs of our Supreme Leader."

At the last remark, Garrison knew where the conversation was going and found it nearly impossible to contain his excitement.

Baroam turned to face him. His black eyes drilling hard into his subordinate, "I trust you will not disappoint me or the Supreme Leader?"

A shiver snaked up Garrison's spine. He ignored it and tried to keep his eyes locked on Baroam, "No sir. You can count on me." He extended his hand expecting Baroam to shake on the deal, but Baroam turned back toward the window.

"Do you not want to know where you will be going, Mr. Garrison?" Baroam's voice took on a higher tone.

"I'm sure anywhere you send me will be more than satisfactory, sir." Garrison said, anxious to hear the words.

"I believe you were just there." Baroam said.

A nefarious smile began to spread across Garrison's face, "Yes, Mr. Baroam?"

"Pack your bags, Mr. Garrison. Your friends from Willow Creek await you."

Nick Garrison couldn't be more pleased. He left the Commander's office delighted in the fact that the Supreme Leader trusted him enough to assign him his own City.

When the whole idea of the Government Funded Life Care Program began, he was convinced that it wouldn't work, but by pure dumb luck and a lot of help from the mainstream media, the majority of the people, even those who did not favor the idea at first, made the decision to go. They followed the Leader to the Cities that seemed to have miraculously sprung up overnight. For those who weren't so eager to give their lives over to the government, the Regulators were there to 'encourage' them.

In the beginning, when his followers elected the Supreme Leader to office, the Christians and believers were certain he had ulterior motives, and they were right. They began to challenge the leader, but the more they questioned, the louder the supporters became. His cronies in the Supreme City backed him up on every decision he made, making it virtually impossible to slow his momentum. The Supreme Leader had a deadline and time was growing short. By the end of his first year, he wanted the citizens of the United States assigned to their new Cities. The Regulators began to move faster and became more aggressive.

Garrison grinned to himself, thinking back on the last few months and the progress they had made. He exited the warmth of the building onto the frigid city sidewalk. The day was cold and gray. People hurried by, anxious for the warmth of their homes. Looking around, he noticed that there were many more Regulators than there were civilians. Baroam wasn't wasting any time getting his Cities in place. Garrison breathed in deep, relishing the crisp afternoon air. A sense of satisfaction filled him. Finally, there would be order. The government would be in complete control. No richer versus poorer or 'haves' and 'have-nots;' all the people would be on equal footing. Everyone in The Cities would be in the same class, with the proper food and energy budget for each family and the Supreme Leader would have control over all of it.

Garrison's thoughts turned to his City. Would the residents go quietly? Some were already in their units. Those were the anxious ones. How would it go for the rest of the residents? His thoughts began to race as he recalled the stories told by the other Regulators. One especially humored him. "They were just like cockroaches when the lights turn on," the spiteful man had said. "The people scattered when they heard the trucks coming." Garrison looked forward to a similar experience when he began the final process in Willow Creek. There was something about the people of that town that struck a nerve with him, and he was thrilled that he would be exercising his power over them. Yes, he was looking forward to going back to Willow Creek because there was a certain family that he desperately wanted to see again.

Job 36:20-21 "Do not long for the night to drag people away from their homes. Beware of turning to evil, which you seem to prefer to affliction."

CHAPTER 15

DAWN BEGAN COLD AND windy as John Smith waited outside the big double glass doors of the Hyatt Hotel. The smell of fresh paint and wet concrete told him that the construction of the new City that was once known as Willowdale was complete. The twenty-five-foot-high security wall that surrounded The City was finished. Now all that remained was to round up the residents still outside The City. He stamped his feet and wrapped his arms around himself against the cold and decided to wait inside the building. His new boss was late. John had never met him before but had heard of the man. John was not looking forward to the encounter. Just as he took hold of the cold bronze handle of the glass door, a sudden screeching of tires jerked his attention back to the street. A black Jaguar skidded to a stop in front of the building where John was standing. He stared at the driver who emerged from the luxury car and hoped that this was the man he was waiting for. He had a broad smile on his tanned, rugged face and appeared very happy; not half the monster he was expecting. He scrutinized him further and detected a glint of evil, which hid a more sinister edge behind his smiling eyes. "This is one man I definitely do not want to cross." Smith extended his hand as Garrison approached him.

"Good morning! You are my new assistant, I presume?" Garrison gripped Smith's hand in a bone-crushing handshake.

"Yes sir, my name is John Smith." Smith braced himself for the loud guffaw, which always seemed to follow whenever he introduced himself.

Garrison did not disappoint him. "John Smith! You have got to be kidding me! Tell me that is not your real name." Garrison doubled over, laughing, while Smith just rolled his eyes and waited. When Smith did not respond, Garrison looked up and apprised his assistant more seriously. "What? Did your parents have no imagination?"

"Actually, Mr. Garrison, it's a family name that dates back to the eighteenth century."

Garrison bowed low in mock humility. "A thousand pardons, Mr. Smith. Come on, let's get out of this cold."

The two men entered the deserted hotel, crossed the plush carpeting of the ornately furnished front lounge, and strode toward the elevators. As they rode up to the top floor the men made small talk. "When we're all through with the construction, there will be microphones and video cameras planted in every elevator.

John made a mental note to keep his hands in his pockets and his mouth shut anytime he rode the elevators.

Garrison stepped out of the elevator first and went directly to his office and living quarters. "Now, this is what I'm talking about," he shouted as he entered the suite, noticing the mahogany paneled walls immediately. "What do you think, Smith? Does this pass inspection?"

John Smith looked approvingly around the room at the cherry wood desk and credenza. Behind the desk was a wall, fully dedicated to monitors. He could only presume they would be connected to the thousands of security cameras installed around The City. "It is beautiful, sir."

"Yes, it is. Come on, let's take a walk and you can pick out your quarters. If you're going to be my right-hand man, I'll need you close by."

Garrison's boisterous personality was nothing like Smith's quiet, subdued persona, but Garrison had specifically requested Smith to be his personal assistant. Like himself, Smith had a reputation among the others of being quite a ruthless adversary and Garrison wanted him by his side where he could keep an eye on him. Besides, Smith shared the same animosity toward the people of Willow Creek that he held.

Smith opted for a room two doors down from Garrison's quarters. They took a tour of the rest of the hotel, including the fully stocked gourmet kitchen and the basement, which Garrison had converted into a jail. "Why keep the jail here, boss? There's plenty of room around the City."

Garrison turned from the cell he was examining. "Two reasons, Smith. First, I want to keep offenders close by. Do you see those cameras?" He pointed to the small cameras installed in the corner at both ends of the hall. "I will be able to see everything that goes on down here. Second, if, and I mean 'if', there is going to be any escape attempts from here, I want to be the first to know. But the way things have been going, I doubt seriously that any of these folks would have the wherewithal or the nerve to even consider an escape."

Smith nodded. Garrison was right of course. He'd seen some of the people brought into The City already and they were harmless. He was convinced, along with Garrison, that this would be one of the easiest Cities to control.

Psalm 7:14-15 "He who is pregnant with evil and conceives trouble gives birth to disillusionment. He who digs a hole and scoops it out falls into the pit he has made."

CHAPTER 16

THE SUN HAD NOT quite crested over the tree line when Steve started on his second cup of coffee. The woodstove was well stoked and roaring on this cold crisp morning, heating up the old Victorian home. During the winter months the house was difficult to keep warm, especially the upstairs so the master bedroom's stone fireplace roared throughout most of the winter. Steve always made a point to relight the fire in the morning before Tanya woke up and she never failed to thank him. He thought to himself how lucky he was. He smiled to himself, "Dear Lord, thank you for my beautiful bride and our beautiful home."

When he bought the house, he had no idea that he would be married to the love of his life within two years. The day he laid eyes on Tanya, he told himself that she was the girl for him and prayed that God felt the same way. Obviously, He did. Steve smiled over his coffee, thinking back on the day and the expression on her face when he had asked her out for the first time. He had been nervous to say the least, but it soon passed when he witnessed her reaction. At first, she had seemed apprehensive; he was, after all a preacher. However, her misgivings gave way to the truth that she was attracted to him in a way that she had never felt before, and she had accepted his invitation to dinner.

Steve pulled himself back to reality and unrolled the newspaper.

The headline read, "TOWN OF WILLOW CREEK TO MAKE THE BIG MOVE!' He nearly choked on his coffee and didn't hear Tanya pad into the kitchen. "Hi, honey, thanks for my fire." She kissed him on the top of his head as she walked by on her way to the coffeepot.

Steve jumped at her voice, but she didn't notice. "Well, they certainly didn't waste any time, did they?"

"Waste any time on what?" she asked, taking a seat across from him at the kitchen table.

He handed her the paper and watched her jaw drop as she read. "Steve, this is happening way too fast! Those guys said the town would have a week to prepare. This article says the town must be cleared out by Friday and its already Tuesday. I don't understand."

"They are trying to move everyone out faster so they can gain control faster, Tanya. People are rushed, they forget to do things, and the government will step in and say, 'Here, let us help'."

"Mornin,' folks." Tom strode into the kitchen wearing the clean clothes that Tanya left at his door. He went straight to the coffee pot and took one of the mugs that Tanya had set out the night before. After he poured himself a cup, he moved to the table and slid into a chair between Steve and Tanya.

"The paper says they're pushing to move the townspeople out by Friday," Steve said. "Take a look. It won't be long; they'll be knocking on our door."

Tom took the paper that Tanya offered him and read carefully. "I expect it will be a lot sooner than any of us want. You need to talk to Morgan. Her town was cleared out and it wasn't pretty." Tom took a sip of his coffee and smiled gratefully at Tanya. "Good coffee."

Tanya returned the smile. "Thanks, Tom."

"How'd you sleep last night, Tom?" Steve asked. "Were you warm enough?"

"Oh yeah, I was plenty warm and literally slept better than I had in years. Thanks. Those nights in Iraq got downright frigid. We were lucky when we got to sleep in a tent. Most times we curled up under a truck or in a bombed-out building."

Steve got up to retrieve the coffee pot to top off Tanya's cup and shook his head, "Well, Tom, for what it's worth, thank you for serving so others could live free."

"The living free part in our country may be debatable in the next few weeks, but thanks, I do appreciate it." Tom took a deep swallow of coffee so Steve could top off his cup. He nodded his thanks and then turned back to Tanya. What time do the boys leave for school?"

Tanya checked her watch. "Soon. If we want to see them off, we should leave shortly."

"I'll go check on Kyle." Steve rinsed his coffee cup and set it on the counter next to the coffee pot. Tom followed suit and went back to his room to pack.

While Tanya was finishing making the bed, she suddenly heard shouting coming from down the hall. She ran to Kyle's room where she found Steve pinning

Kyle down, trying to wake him. Kyle was drenched in a cold sweat and shouting, "Get him, Nelly! Shoot him! I can't see him!"

"Kyle, wake up! Wake up!" Steve shook the screaming soldier. Suddenly Kyle opened his eyes and the terror staring back at Steve was something he had never encountered in his years of ministering.

Tom rushed into the room. "Let me; we've been through this before." He sat calmly on the bed and grasped Kyle firmly by his shoulders. "Johnson!"

Steve quickly went to stand with his wife in the doorway. What they witnessed would stay with them for the rest of their lives.

Kyle was still lying on the pillow with his arms flailing out in front of him, ready to fight the enemy that lived in his head; horror filled his eyes. "Nelly! Did you get him, Nelly!?"

Tom grabbed Kyle's arms with both hands and brought his face down, filling Kyle's field of vision. He whispered in his ear, "Kyle, it's okay; we got him. We got him, Johnson." He continued the gentle speak until his friend finally settled and relaxed his arms.

"Is Staff Sergeant okay, Connelly? Is he going to be all right?" Kyle's eyes remained open, but they were shadowed, not seeing yet.

Tom's face remained just above Kyle's. "Johnson! Wake up, soldier!" he shouted. Steve and Tanya had jumped at the sudden outburst, but slowly Kyle began to come around. Tom breathed a sigh and turned to their hosts who stood frozen in the doorway. "He's all right. There are still some unsettled memories he needs to deal with."

Kyle stirred and the terrified shadow that had previously blanketed his eyes lifted. He looked up at Tom. "Thanks, Nelly. That was a bad one." His voice was still shaky. A movement at the corner of his eye startled him. He turned and saw Steve and Tanya standing in the doorway. The worry on their faces told him that they had witnessed his nightmare. "Oh God, I'm sorry. I'm so sorry." Kyle covered his face with his large, calloused hand to hide the shame.

Tom nodded his head, motioning the minister and his wife to leave. They turned silently and left the room. After they had gone, He turned back to Kyle and spoke softly, "Don't worry about it, man." He rubbed Johnson's blond hair. It had grown out and was nearly touching the tops of his ears. "You need a haircut, soldier."

"Do you think they'll ever stop?" Kyle asked.

"They'll stop. It'll just take time," Tom said. "Come on, we need to hustle up. Sandy's boys will be leaving for school soon. I'll get you some coffee. You can drink it on the way."

Steve drove the truck down the driveway and saw Sandy and the boys walking toward them. He stopped, allowed them to drop the tailgate and climb in, and then backed up until he reached the main road where the bus would pick up the boys.

"Hey guys, good morning." Sandy greeted everyone as they emerged from the truck. "I'm glad you made it. The boys were really looking forward to seeing you this morning."

"Sorry we're late," Kyle said. "I --"

"We slept in a little," Tom interrupted. "It sure felt good."

Steve walked up to Ben and Joe, "Listen up, boys, I probably don't have to tell you but be very careful today. If you see anything out of the ordinary, take note of it and let us know when you come home. Stick together when you can and watch your backs when you are separated. I'm not trying to scare you, but you need to be very aware." Steve looked over at Kyle and Tom. "Is there anything you guys want to add before they leave?"

Tom stepped forward and looked down the main road. "The bus is coming. You just look after one another when you can. Okay? Stay focused."

Ben looked worried. "What if they don't bring us home today, Mom?"

"Today they will bring you home," Steve reassured him.

The bus came to a stop in front of the driveway and the boys started across the road. Tom walked over and stood next to Sandy. "Is that the same bus driver they always have, Sandy?"

Sandy quickly diverted her gaze from her sons to the driver and was relieved. "Yeah, he's the regular." She gave him a wave and he tipped his ball cap back at her.

"Is that normal behavior? What about the expression on his face? Is he usually that grumpy looking?"

Sandy chuckled, "Yes, he's a little grumpy by the time he gets to our stop."

Tom smiled back at her, and then watched the boys as they made their way down the aisle on the bus. They seated themselves on the side of the bus facing their family and new friends. Ben sat next to the window and Joe sat next to him on the aisle. The boys peered out the dirty bus window and waved good-bye to the adults. Sandy couldn't shake the feeling that she had made the biggest mistake of her life. "Oh God, please watch over them today. Please give them comfort and strength to do what is needed."

Tom watched her expression. "God will protect them, Sandy. They'll be fine."

"Yes, you're right." She smiled and joined the others at the truck.

Tanya climbed into the truck and slid over next to Steve, allowing room for Sandy in the front seat. Tom and Kyle climbed into the back. Tom remembered the pictures that Staff Sergeant used to share with him in Iraq and could now see for himself the peaceful serenity of the ranch. As they approached the house, a curl of white smoke rose lazily from the chimneys. Last night, the darkness concealed the beautiful pastures. Now Tom could see the horses, covered with warming blankets, as they grazed contentedly in the lush pasture they shared with the cows.

"Did you guys have breakfast?" Sandy asked, interrupting Tom's thoughts.

"No, we were all running a little late this morning," Tanya answered. Did you see the paper yet?"

"No, not yet." Sandy replied. "I don't usually check it until after the boys have left."

2 Timothy 3:8-9 "Just as Jannes and Jambres opposed Moses, so also these men oppose the truth -- men of depraved minds, who, as far as the faith is concerned, are rejected. But they will not get very far because, as in the case of those men, their folly will be clear to everyone."

CHAPTER 17

JOE AND BEN TRIED their best not to look scared, but they suddenly realized that they were not the only ones. Charlotte, a blond-haired, blue-eyed girl in Joe's class came to sit across the aisle from them. Her voice quivered. "Hi, Joe. How are you?"

"All right, I guess." Joe answered, not in the mood to talk.

Charlotte didn't notice, "What do think is going to happen, Joe?" She asked, "Is your family going to get moved to the city tomorrow like the rest of us?"

Joe looked at her sharply, "What do you mean tomorrow? I thought it wasn't going to happen until next week."

"We did too, but mom and dad got a call real early this morning. They told them to be ready to go by tomorrow. I don't want to go, Joe. I'm scared."

"It'll be all right, Charlotte; try not to worry about it. Did they tell your folks anything else?"

Charlotte looked around cautiously and whispered to Joe, "Well, they said that they would send a truck by tomorrow morning and take us directly to the transfer station. I don't know what that means."

"I don't either," Joe said. "Are you going to school tomorrow, Charlotte? Did they say whether you would be taken to school?" Joe tried to control the urgency in his voice.

"No, but I don't think we'll be going. It sounds like the trucks will be at our house first thing in the morning. They're not going to let us bring Sasha, Joe." Hot tears stung Charlotte's eyes and spilled over her long lashes. Joe's heart broke for her. Sasha, Charlotte's beloved Akita-Husky mix, had been with Charlotte since Sasha was a puppy. Her parents had picked up the dog from the shelter and the two had been inseparable through the years. The girl wiped her eyes and continued, "The men said that she would be safe, and we could see her after we were settled into our new quarters."

"I'm sure you'll get to see Sasha again, Charlotte. Like I said, try not to worry about it." Joe put a reassuring hand on her arm.

"Will you try to find me when you get transferred, Joe? I'm going to miss you." Charlotte said shyly.

"I'll try, but I don't know where they'll put us." Joe said. Charlotte's tears made him uncomfortable. "I'll try. Okay, Charlotte? You just stay close to your family when you get to where you're going. Do you understand what I'm telling you, Charlotte? I think it will get dangerous. Don't do anything foolish. Okay? I'll find you; I promise."

The young girl smiled sweetly at him through her tears, smoothed her hair, and wiped her face before she turned to gather her books.

The bus pulled in front of the school and ground to a halt, the air brakes hissing sharply. While gathering his backpack, Ben noticed the men from the night before and nudged Joe with his elbow. "Joe, look. There they are. Do you think they're looking for us?"

"I doubt it, little bro. They're probably watching everyone. You watch your back today and I'll see you in the hall or after school, okay?" Joe gave his little brother a shove on his shoulder, his subtle way of showing affection.

"Okay, Joe. I'll see you around. See ya, Charlotte." Ben shouldered his backpack and followed them. Once they were off the bus, the kids went their separate ways, but Ben noticed that the man who spoke with them the night before was studying him carefully. "I'd better tell Mom about this."

Joe watched his brother go down the hall until the boy disappeared around a corner. Joe then hurried to his locker to pull the books he would need for his first three classes. He was still thinking about Charlotte when he slammed the locker shut and found he was standing face to face with Mr. Smith. Joe cursed him silently for scaring him. The man was dressed in a black suit, black pressed shirt, and black necktie. He didn't seem to notice that he had startled the boy and smiled maliciously at him. The carnation in his lapel stared stupidly down at Joe. "Good morning, Joe Parker, Jr."

"What do you want and how do you know my family?" Joe snapped at the man.

"You'll be surprised at what I know, Joe. Just a little heads up for you, son. Bring all your books; you'll be turning them in today."

"I'm not your son; now get out of my way!" Joe, anxious to get rid of the man, skirted around him and walked swiftly to his homeroom class. He thought his heart would pound right out of his chest, but he kept walking, not wanting to look back.

Smith grinned as he watched Joe hurry down the hall.

Sandy and Tanya prepared breakfast while Steve, Kyle, and Lucky walked out to see the horses. Tom had settled himself at the kitchen table and watched intermittently between the ladies cooking and the back pasture. He stretched his long legs out in front of him and leaned back in his chair. "Joe was a lucky, lucky man," he thought, and then turned his attention to Sandy. "What does this house run on, Sandy? Is it electric, gas, oil?"

"It's oil and gas mostly, but we use electricity for the lights. Why do you ask?"

"They turn off all the power." Morgan shuffled into the kitchen, still in her borrowed flannel pajamas. "They shut the town down completely. Is there any coffee?"

Startled by Morgan's comment, it took Tanya a moment before she remembered her manners. "Oh, sure. Here you go, Morgan." She poured a steaming cup and handed it to her. "Cream and sugar are on the table."

"Well, are they going to do it here, Morgan?" Sandy asked.

"Eventually," Tom said, not wanting to cause any alarm just yet. When Morgan's story was told he wanted everyone to be present.

"Thanks, Tanya." Morgan gratefully accepted the hot coffee. Taking a seat next to Tom at the kitchen table, she sleepily added cream and sugar to her coffee and stared out the window at nothing in particular. She felt Tom's eyes on her as she absently stirred her coffee. She rolled her eyes and turned to him, "What? Do I have bedhead or something? Why are you looking at me?"

Tom chuckled, remembering from the trail that Morgan was never in the best of moods when she woke up. "I was just going to say good morning, Morgan. Did you sleep all right?"

Morgan, with her hair all askew, flashed her eyes at Tom. "Yes, I slept great. Where's Kyle?"

"He's out with Steve and Lucky, looking at the horses." Tanya smiled at the interaction between Tom and Morgan. "They should be back shortly."

"I'm sorry I missed the boys. Did they get off all right?"

It was Sandy's turn to answer, "Yeah, they weren't real happy to go, but I'm sure for today they'll be all right."

Morgan continued her surveillance of the back pasture and then sipped her coffee carefully. After determining that it was still too hot, she blew softly into it.

She tasted it again and was satisfied. "Sandy, I don't think you should send them to school tomorrow. What time does the bus bring them home?"

Sandy turned to look at Morgan. "Three-thirty. Why? Morgan, is there something we should know? What happened in your town?"

Silence fell over the kitchen as Morgan looked at Tom, then Tanya, and finally rested her gaze on Sandy.

Steve and Kyle walked leisurely out to the pasture to watch the horses graze. The morning was clear and crisp, with a cold breeze coming down from the neighboring foothills. Neither man spoke as they walked along the fence line toward the pond. Kyle dug his hands deep into the pockets of his denim jacket as they walked. Even with the sheepskin collar turned up around his neck and ears the chill still found its way in through the small gaps left by the buttons that pulled against the fabric. "Staff Sergeant Parker used to show us pictures of this ranch, and of Sandy and the boys," Kyle began. "He was so proud of those boys, especially Joe Jr. He told us once that he didn't worry much about Sandy because he knew Joe would take care of her no matter what. 'Little Ben, he's got a gift,' Staff Sergeant would say. And this ranch . . ." Kyle paused for a moment to take in the quiet beauty of it. "He told how he brought Sandy out here to look at it and she just fell in love with it. He always said that if it weren't for her, he didn't know where he would be in this world. He said that this place was his heaven on earth and that it's what got him through the war."

Kyle lifted his head and looked hard at the minister standing next to him, "My God, Steve, he was so in love with her, and I got him killed!" Kyle bowed his head and leaned his back against the fence. He let the tears fall freely to the ground now, not caring whether Steve saw them or not. He kept his hands deep in his pockets and sniffed hard trying to get his emotions under control. When he was finally able to speak again, he opened up, "Steve, I've asked God to forgive me so many times. Tom has talked to me about it and said that God doesn't have to forgive me because I haven't done anything wrong, but why do I feel like this?"

"Kyle, it's no surprise you feel the way you do, but remember, you were shot. You were the responsibility of Staff Sergeant Parker, and he knew that. If he were standing here right now, he would tell you that he was just doing his job, and I think you know that; don't you?"

Kyle wiped his tear-stained face. "Yeah, I do know that, but why can't I forget it, Steve? The nightmares are going to drive me crazy."

Steve laid a gentle hand on Kyle's shoulder. "Kyle, it's not a matter of forgetting. That's something you'll never forget. I believe it is a matter of learning how to live with that memory. And above all, you're going to have to forgive yourself."

"I don't think I can do that." Kyle's eyes pleaded with the minister. He shook his head and turned away. They walked silently up the hill, the wind whipping sharply around them, while Lucky bounded across the pasture after a field mouse.

Steve continued his talk, "Kyle, would it help if you spoke with Sandy? Do you understand that she doesn't blame you and the boys don't blame you either? You know Joe was just as proud of his men as he was of his family. He told his family about all of you; he loved you. He wouldn't have died any other way, Kyle."

"Did you know that it was Staff Sergeant Parker who taught me about the Bible and how God sent his Son to save us? He even baptized me in Iraq. Did you know that?"

"No, Kyle. I didn't know that." Steve said quietly.

Kyle nodded, "Yeah, he sure did. We had one of those rare nights when it was quiet and Staff Sergeant and I stayed up late, talking and reading from the book of Acts. He explained to me about baptism, and I told him I wanted him to . . . well, you know we had to improvise, being in the middle of the desert and all, but I was baptized." Kyle's voice trailed off. When he looked around, he realized they were standing at the family cemetery. He turned to Steve, with despair in his eyes, "Is this where --?"

"It is." Steve said gently. "Sandy spent days up here after they brought Joe back. Then the days turned to hours, and she finally was able to go a day or two without coming up here."

"What about the boys? How did they take it?" Kyle asked, afraid to hear.

"I won't lie to you; it was very tough on them, especially young Joe. He was angry. He felt saddled with all the extra work on the ranch and then felt guilty for feeling that way. We spent a lot of time together after his dad died; he got through it. Ben has grown up a lot, too, these last few months and his dad was right. He does have a gift. The night they got the news of Joe's death, Ben said that his dad came to see him. He said Joe came to him, told him not to worry, that he was happy, and that everything would be all right.

I'm telling that to you now, Kyle. Staff Sergeant Parker was a God-fearing man and a strong believer, and he is with his Savior now." Steve looked into Kyle's eyes. "Would you like to spend some time alone now?"

"I'd like that, Steve. Thanks." Kyle looked gratefully at him and took Steve's hands in his and shook them warmly.

"I'll meet you back at the house." Steve nodded to the bereaved soldier and turned toward the house. "Father, please grant this man peace. Please heal him from the unseen wounds in his heart."

Kyle knelt next to Joe Parker's grave. He noticed the fresh greenery by his headstone and on the headstone next to Joe's. It read, 'Shadow—beloved companion and protector.' Kyle bowed his head in silence for a moment then looked up. "Hey, Staff Sergeant, it sure is great to be talking to you again. Tom came up to see Sandy to deliver your message and I sort of tagged along. I hope you don't mind. Naw, I didn't think you would."

Kyle paused then struggled on, "Staff Sergeant, I just need to know if you forgive me for what happened. I swear if I could trade places with you right now, I would. Please tell me you forgive me." Kyle bowed his head and wrapped his arms around himself and rocked gently forward and back and cried, "Lord, please forgive me for what I've done to Sandy and the boys. Please Lord, help me forgive myself."

There were no trumpets sounding or angels' choirs, just a subtle warmth and comfort that enveloped Kyle Johnson. A cool wind blew softly across his face, and he would swear that God kissed him that day.

Psalm 55:13 "But it is you, a man like myself, my companion, my close friend, with whom I once enjoyed sweet fellowship as we walked with the throng at the house of God."

CHAPTER 18

Steve came into the kitchen through the mudroom and went straight to the coffee pot. He poured out the last of the coffee and commenced to make another pot.

"Where's Kyle?" Tanya asked.

"He'll be here in minute." Steve said as he took a seat next to his wife. He smiled at Morgan, "Good morning."

"Good morning, Steve," she answered, more sociable after having her coffee.

"When Kyle gets back, I think it would be a good time for you to tell us your story, if you're up to it," Steve said, unaware that Sandy had just questioned her.

"Yeah, sure." Morgan took another sip of her coffee. She was in no hurry to dredge up the horrible memories of what happened, but it was too important not to. They had to know the danger that was coming.

Breakfast was just being served when Kyle walked into the kitchen, and the smell of the bacon and eggs woke his stomach to the fact that he was famished. He gave Steve a subtle nod and took a seat next to Morgan. "Good morning," he smiled at her.

Morgan studied Kyle's face. His eyes and nose were red, and she couldn't tell whether it was from the cold wind or whether he had been crying. She left it alone. It was obvious that a bond was being formed between Steve and Kyle. "Good morning yourself," she smiled back at him and got up to bring him a cup of coffee.

"Kyle, after breakfast Morgan is going to fill us in on what happened in her town," Steve said.

Kyle turned to her quickly, "Are you sure?"

"They have to know," she said quietly. She placed his coffee mug in front of him and sat down.

Kyle put his hand on her back and rubbed gently, knowing that this would be hard on her.

When everyone had finished their breakfast, Morgan sat back in her chair and re-told everything just as it happened. When she was through, Kyle and Tom exchanged glances; she had left out the part about the church.

Joe took his seat and surveyed the classroom. Judging by the laughter, he decided that the majority of his classmates were eager for the new system to take place. "Hey, Joe isn't this great! We'll be living in these great houses, and we can sleep as late as we want because we don't have to get up and go to school. We'll have school right at our house! Pretty cool stuff, don't you think?"

"Yeah, sure, that'll be great, Dave." Joe pretended to read his history book. He wanted to avoid the nonsense at all costs, especially the annoying boy behind him.

"Class, class. Everyone, please take your seat." The teacher walked to her desk and clapped her hands loudly. "Thank you. Now, I know you are all very excited about what is happening, but we must take care of a few things before tomorrow. First, you must turn in all your books. If you didn't bring them all this morning, please retrieve them after you finish filling these out." The teacher held a handful of five by seven cards; "The cards I am passing out must be filled out and turned in before you leave class today," she said. Joe hated filling out these types of forms. The amount of information requested was bad enough, but the part that pained him the most was the information needed about his father. He only wrote one word, 'deceased,' but he felt the pain all over again. Of course it had subsided over the past eight months, but it still hurt him to be reminded. Joe finished his card and went to his teacher. "I need to go get the rest of my books, ma'am."

"Of course, Joe, go ahead. I'm going to miss you, you know. Maybe we'll run into each other when we get settled in The City."

Joe smiled back at her. "Yes, ma'am." He turned and left the classroom quietly. He had hoped to see his brother Ben in the hallway, but as he approached his locker all he saw was Mr. Garrison turning the corner; the scent of his aftershave lingering heavily in the air. Joe shook his head with disgust. Every man he met he compared to his father or to Uncle Steve and every man always fell short of his expectations. It never surprised him though; he didn't believe there would ever be another man that would measure up to his father. He pulled the rest of his books from his locker, slammed it shut and returned to his classroom.

Ben, in the meantime, was doing his best not to be noticed. He watched the man with no name follow him to his locker, then to his classroom. Once he was seated and the class was settled, his teacher proceeded to give the same speech that Joe's teacher had given. The students filled out the same cards and Ben struggled with the same questions about his father. When the books were turned in, the teacher lined up Ben and his classmates to go to the auditorium for an all-school assembly. "Attendance is mandatory," she reminded them.

Once the entire student body was seated, the lights dimmed and the screen at the front of the auditorium lit up. Ben looked around for his brother but there were too many faces, happy, smiling, excited faces. Ben's stomach twisted into a knot, and he turned his attention back to the screen. He watched in dismay at the families in their new designer homes and dreaded what was to come. A voice boomed over the loudspeaker, "You are about to enter a place where all of your dreams will come true. Your dreams of a beautiful home, security, education, and good health will be realized at last. We are very anxious to welcome you into your new home and your new neighborhood."

The movie ran for forty-five minutes, flashing on families playing in meadows and on captivating seashores. It showed cityscapes of beautiful buildings that glowed at dawn's early light, and zoomed in on plush, newly furnished homes. As the background music played on, Ben looked around again and was shocked to see the kids gazing in awe at the screen. He finally spotted his big brother, but Joe didn't see him. He appeared to be watching someone else. Ben followed his brother's line of sight to see whom Joe was sneering at. His eyes came to rest on the man with no name who was staring right at Ben.

Ben felt his blood grow cold as he took in the man's scrutiny. Suddenly the man began moving toward Ben, but just as he made his approach, someone spoke to him and broke his focus on Ben. The twelve-year-old breathed a sigh of relief and slinked down in his seat. His eyes never left the screen.

The bus ride back home was the longest either boy had ever experienced. When they got on the bus and didn't recognize the bus driver, they made eye contact with each other, understanding that it would be best not to speak until they got home. Joe did not see Charlotte get on the bus and hoped that her parents had picked her up. Finally, they arrived at their stop and found their mom was waiting for them. She looked at the driver and realized that he was not the same one who had picked them up that morning. She hid her surprise and gave him a wave. He glared out the dirty window at her and sped away, kicking up gravel before the boys were even out of the road. Joe, with Ben in tow, walked quickly to the truck. "Mom, we need to talk."

"What happened today, Joe?" Sandy asked as she slid across into the passenger seat and Ben scooted in next to her.

Joe got behind the wheel and slammed the truck into first gear, "Just wait 'til we get home, Mom. Is everyone still here?" Joe prayed that Tom, Kyle, and Morgan had not left yet. He wasn't sure why, but their presence offered him comfort that he didn't understand.

"Yes, Joe, but I don't know how long they will stay. They may have to be moving on."

"I really hope they stay, Mom." Joe skidded to a stop in front of the house and grabbed his backpack from the bed of the truck. Sandy jumped from the passenger seat, reached for Ben's backpack, and tossed it to him as he hurried after his brother. The cold wind bit her bare ears as she followed her sons into the house and closed the door behind them. Joe quickly turned back to the door and locked it, then went to meet everyone in the living room. When he entered, all eyes turned to him and his brother.

Joe settled into the wingback chair next to Tom near the fireplace and let the warmth from the roaring flames wash over him. He rubbed his hands together and paused a few moments for the chill to leave him. While the boys were getting warmed by the fire, Sandy brought in a tray of coffee, hot chocolate and home-made oatmeal cookies and set it on the coffee table. Tanya poured the coffee for the adults while Sandy passed the chocolate and cookies to her sons. When everyone had been served, she settled on the floor in front of Joe and Tom. Ben sat next to his mom on the floor, and they all waited for Joe to speak.

Joe took a sip from his hot chocolate and set it down to cool, then proceeded to tell his audience what had happened at school. When he finished, he took a deep breath and settled back into the chair. He hadn't realized that while he was speaking, he had been sitting just on the edge of his seat. He took a bite of his cookie and looked at Ben. The twelve-year-old felt the butterflies gather in his stomach. It was his turn to speak. He was not just nervous about talking in front of all these people, but he didn't care to re-live what had occurred earlier. He included the incident where he saw the man with no name at the assembly, the man who had stood behind them at the meeting.

Joe looked surprised when Ben related how the man was watching him while Joe was watching the man. "I wondered who he was looking at, Ben. He didn't look very happy."

"Well, that stupid movie sure showed a lot of happy people. Good grief, Mom, it was ridiculous," Ben said. "Anyone could see right through it, but every one of those kids in the auditorium was, well, it was like they were hypnotized or something."

Steve stood up and ran his hands through his thick, wavy hair. "Tom? Kyle? Are you folks in a big hurry to leave?"

"No, not really," Tom answered. "We were discussing it earlier and we thought it might be a good idea to hang around for a while. We've really got nowhere else to go."

Relief washed over Sandy. For some reason she felt safer knowing that her new friends would be staying on. Joe breathed a sigh of relief too, and silently gave thanks to God.

Sandy looked over at her brother-in-law. "Steve, do you think you all should stay here at the ranch? I'd feel better knowing you, Tanya and the guys were closer."

"I think she's right, Steve," Tom said. "These people are not friendly. When it comes time to clear everyone out, they will not go about it quietly . . . or nicely. Those folks who leave should go without a fight, but from what we've seen, and you know what Morgan has witnessed, it would be wise to be out before they come through."

"Steve, I think we should go now before it gets dark and get what we need from the house." Tanya looked at her husband and knew what she was asking was a lot. Steve loved their home as much as she did.

"Okay, honey. You've got a point. But you stay here. Kyle, do you mind coming with me?"

"Not at all." Kyle patted Morgan's knee and got up. "I'll be back."

Sandy noticed how Morgan smiled back at him. "Ah, young love." She smiled to herself. "Perhaps some good would come out of this after all."

"Tanya, while we're gone, I think the rest of you should think about what supplies we will need. We'll get what we can from our house. Kyle, be thinking of anything we can use."

"You bet," Kyle said as he grabbed his coat on the way out the door.

Steve's truck ripped down the dirt driveway leaving a trail of dust and swirling leaves behind it. "Kyle, can we really expect everything you told us this morning? Do you think it will really get that violent?"

"Oh yes, it can and will get that violent, Steve. Morgan didn't tell you everything she saw. I'll tell you now, but I don't think you should say anything to Sandy or Tanya, at least not yet."

"What did she see, Kyle?" Steve asked.

"Folks went to the church thinking they'd be safe there, but these men bolted them inside and then torched the place; burned 'em all alive. Poor people, poor Morgan. She wasn't acting right when we found her. I think she was still in shock." Kyle shook his head, still finding the atrocity of it hard to believe.

"Kyle! No!" Steve's eyes went wide with horror, "Do you think they'll do the same thing here?"

"I wouldn't put it past them, Steve. I think they have a problem with religion or God in general."

Steve stepped on the gas and sped toward town. Traffic had already picked up with folks leaving town for the city twenty miles away. He stopped at the church and started for the entrance but stopped for a moment to gather his thoughts. What would they need if he were never to come back here again? His heart sank at the thought, but he realized time was short; he sprinted to the altar and took the Communion plate and Chalice from the cabinet. Before he left, he knelt at the altar to pray.

Steve had been gone for what seemed like an eternity as Kyle nervously watched the front door. He was anxious to be out of town and back to the safety of the ranch.

Moments later Steve came running from the back of the church. He had locked the front door from the inside and emerged through the back door locking the deadbolt behind him. As he climbed into the truck, he passed Kyle the silver Communion plate and Chalice. Kyle gave him an understanding nod and smiled.

"We'll need to make room for everyone, Tanya. You and Steve will sleep in my room, and I will hear no argument from you, do you understand?"

"Sandy! No!" Tanya began to protest, but knew it was futile when Sandy leveled a stare at her, daring her. "Fine," Tanya relented.

"It's only right, sis, and you know it. Morgan and I will take Ben's room and Kyle, Joe and Tom can bunk on the couch or in Joe's room. We've got the air mattress and plenty of sleeping bags."

"What about food, Sandy? There's going to be a lot more mouths to feed. Steve will bring back everything we have at the house, but do you think we should ask them to pick up a few things?"

"He needs to be careful, Tanya. It would be best if it didn't look like they were stockpiling." Sandy reminded her sister.

"Yeah, you're right. We just went to the grocery store the other day, so we should be fine," Tanya said. "Let's check with Morgan though."

Sandy pulled the last of the sleeping bags from the attic and handed it to her sister waiting at the bottom of the ladder. "That's a good idea."

Tanya called out, "Morgan! Can you come here a minute?"

Morgan, still holding the blanket she was using to make up the couch for the men, met them in the hallway. "What's up?"

"Morgan, can you think of anything we will need? Maybe something the guys will need to pick up while they are out?"

Morgan thought for a moment then said, "We'll be holed up here for a while, but eventually they'll turn off the power and unless you have a well, they'll be turning off the water too. We'll need the basics, food, water, and shelter. If you can get your hands on camping gear, that's the type of stuff we'll need. She looked steadily at Tanya and Sandy; her gentle countenance etched with worry. "Eventually we will be forced to leave."

Tanya and Sandy exchanged looks and turned their attention back to Morgan; neither woman wanted to think about the reality of what would eventually happen to the family.

Morgan cast her eyes down, not wanting them to realize her fear. "I'm sorry, you guys, but that's what will happen." Clutching the blanket closer to her, she went back to the living room to finish making up the couches. Having to think again about what had happened to her and the people she grew up with had petrified her; the long nights in the dark, men driving the streets and breaking windows, vandalizing shops and stealing anything they could get their hands on. She shook her head to clear that vision and turned her attention back to her work.

Meanwhile outside, Joe, Tom, and Ben started putting the horses up for the night. Joe walked them through the stable, opening the stalls they passed, "Ben, will you start filling the water buckets and feed troughs? Tom, there's a lead rope hanging by each stall. We need to bring them out to the pasture to bring in the horses. Once the first horse comes, they all usually follow." Tom noticed as they walked through the barn that there was a single patch of colored paint over each stall and a matching lead rope hanging on a nail next to it. He guessed it had been helpful when the boys were younger.

Joe and Tom walked together out to the pasture, turning their collars against the frigid wind that whipped around them and bit hungrily at their exposed skin.

"Just match up the lead rope with the same color halter; that'll help in figuring out who goes where," Joe instructed.

Pilgrim approached them and allowed Tom to attach the lead rope to his halter. Joe watched their interaction and gave his silent approval as Tom gently stroked the gelding and whispered softly. Joe could see that he was comfortable and confident around the horse and why his dad had been so fond of this man. He always used to say, 'If you can trust a man with your horses, you can trust him with your life.' "Once they're in the corral we can close the gate and bring them in one at a time," Joe said.

"They sure are fine horses Joe; you guys have done a great job taking care of them." Tom was glad to have a little quiet time with Joe; the boy was a lot like his father.

"Tom?"

"Yeah, Joe?"

"Did my dad talk much about us over there?" Joe was rubbing his horse's neck as they walked.

"He sure did," Tom said. "Whenever we had quiet times, which weren't often, he always broke out the pictures and told us stories about all of you. We all felt like we knew you." Tom slipped his hand underneath Pilgrim's mane savoring the warmth. "He was especially proud of you, Joe. He knew what a big job it was for you taking care of the family and running the ranch, but he also knew that you were up to it, and you'd do your very best. You know, these last couple of days I'd have to say that your dad was right; you've done a heck of a job keeping this place up. He'd be proud of you, Joe." Tom hesitated, "I'm proud of you."

"Thanks Tom," Joe rubbed Cheyenne's ear, "Do you think we can talk about my dad again sometime?"

"Anytime you like, Joe. He was a good soldier and a great friend." Tom led Pilgrim alongside Joe and Cheyenne. "He told me one time that you used to go to Chincoteague Island in the spring. It sure sounded like a good time. He also told me about your fishing pond. Is it still stocked with bass?"

"Oh, you bet," Joe, said. "There's a granddaddy bass in there that Ben and I tried to catch all summer, but he's pretty smart. We'll have to try again next year. Maybe if you guys are still here you can go fishing with us next year."

"I'd like that, Joe. I'd like that a lot." Tom followed Joe into the stable and took the horses to their appointed stalls. While Joe brought in the rest of the horses, Tom stayed behind with Ben to help him finish filling the water buckets and the troughs. When they had finally finished with the horses, the guys made their walk back to the house. Tom stopped and took in the beauty of the rolling pastures and mountains surrounding the property and watched as the evening sun dipped behind the western hills against a purple sky. He drew in a deep breath and filled his lungs with the cold, clean air. "Lord, you've given us so much beauty. Help us to remember where to look for it."

"Tom?" Joe was standing on the porch. "Are you coming in?"

"Be right there, Joe."

Amos 5:2 "He who forms the mountains, creates the wind, and reveals his thoughts to man, He who turns dawn to darkness and treads the high places of the earth—the Lord God Almighty is his name."

CHAPTER 19

STEVE AND KYLE RUSHED through the house grabbing whatever necessary items they thought they would need: Steve's shotgun, handgun, ammunition, food, water, blankets and pillows. When the banks were having so much trouble and closing down, Steve and Tanya had decided to transfer all their savings, money and gold to a small safe in the house. Steve eyeballed it carefully, "I never thought I'd have to lift this thing," he thought. He stooped low and lifted it carefully, minding his back. He staggered out to the truck with the safe leaning hard against his chest, then with a grunt he heaved it into the bed of his truck and hurried back into the house. After he and Kyle had finally transferred the last of the boxes of supplies out to the truck, they hustled back into the house for one last check.

Morgan tucked the sheet into the couch, but her mind was far away still wrestling with the memories that had been stirred up. She jumped when Sandy hurried into the living room. "I forgot to check the mail today, Morgan. Can you hold down the fort while I run to the mailbox?"

"Sure, but Sandy, I don't think you should go alone." Morgan protested.

"I'll be careful." Sandy pulled on her boots, grabbed her drover from the hook by the door, and pulled on her leather gloves. "Be right back." She turned up the collar on her drover as she trotted out the door and down the lane, relishing the cold, refreshing wind against her face. She kept up her pace down the lane until she crossed the cattle guard and entered the dense forest that bordered between the main road and her yard. She walked slowly, letting the quiet of the forest envelope her. She thought about what Morgan had told her. The news was sobering, frightening, but the chilly wind helped pull her back from her dark thoughts.

Sandy paused and turned around, taking in the colors of the quickly approaching sunset behind her. "Lord, thank you for your beautiful paintings." She turned back toward the road and quickened her pace. The mailbox was on the opposite side of the main road, and she wondered as she neared the edge of the woods, if she could cross before a truck came by. The moment the thought crossed her mind, a military Humvee sped by, throwing up dust and gravel where the driveway met the road. It had come up so fast she didn't have time to think. She ducked quickly behind a thick oak tree. When she was certain that it was safe, she darted across the pavement, grabbed the mail from her oversized mailbox, and sprinted back across the road. She was surprised that there was only one letter but didn't pause to open it until she was certain she was out of sight from any more vehicles speeding past. The return address on the envelope simply read, 'The City' and the letter was addressed to the 'Parker family and friends.' A chill raced down her spine as she ripped open the envelope.

Dear Mrs. Parker and friends,

Due to the large influx of residents arriving at the new housing facilities, the transfer date for your family will be December 31. Please be assured that we will be in contact with you before then to make the transition as smooth as possible."

"Thank God for small favors." Sandy shoved the letter deep into her pocket and hurried back to the house. A dread began stirring within her and she knew that all too soon she and her family would be forced to leave the ranch. Before panic took control, she drew a deep breath and let the late autumn air settle her. "Lord, we'll be needing some help here. Please guide us in the direction you would have us go." Sandy reached the border where the woods met the yard and saw Tom standing in the back yard gazing at the sunset. She watched him for a moment and then noticed him turning toward the house as though he were talking to someone. The light was fading quickly, and she wondered what she would feed her new houseguests. Remembering the truck and the letter, she hastened toward the house. When she entered, she was welcomed with warmth and the scintillating aroma of the supper preparations. She quickly hung her drover by the door and pulled out the letter to show the others. Passing by the living room, she glanced in and saw Morgan snuggled up on the couch with Ben and Lucky. They were looking through an old photo album of the first years on the ranch. She also noticed that the fire needed stoking. She made a quick stop to lay two more logs on and gave Ben a quick wink when he looked up from the album.

Sandy joined Tanya and the others in the kitchen. "Smells wonderful, Tanya." Sandy walked up to her sister and gave her a peck on the cheek. "Thanks."

"I thought spaghetti with salad and garlic bread would be good, so I pulled a couple jars of your canned tomatoes from the cellar. Tom, do you like spaghetti?"

"I sure do, Tanya," Tom's long legs were stretched out in front him as he sat at the far end of the kitchen table, sipping a cup of steaming coffee. He seemed perfectly content. "Sandy, can I get you a cup of coffee?"

Sandy smiled at him, "I've got it, Tom, thanks. How did it go with the horses?"

"Great," Tom said. He sat up in his chair and turned to face Sandy, "I don't have to tell you that Joe is a fine young man. His daddy would be real proud of him."

Sandy nodded in agreement, "He's done an amazing job with this ranch. I can honestly say I couldn't have done it without him and God's grace."

"Allow me to correct," Tanya called over her shoulder as she vigorously stirred the spaghetti sauce, "You have ALL done an amazing job with this ranch, thanks be to God."

"Amen to that." Tom said, raising his coffee cup.

"Oh, I almost forgot." Sandy handed the letter to Tom, "Look what came in the mail." She took a seat at the table. "Nothing else came; just that, no bills, no junk mail. It's peculiar because we always get junk mail." Sandy watched Tom's face as he read the letter. The harsh, unforgiving climate of the Iraq desert had taken its toll on his tan, weathered face, and tiny lines had formed around his eyes from years of squinting in the desert sun. As he studied the short letter, she continued her scrutiny. His brown hair had grown shaggy over the last few weeks and light stubble covered his jaw. "He must be growing a beard," she thought. When Tom had finished the letter, he lifted his eyes to meet hers but didn't say anything.

Unable to grasp what his eyes were implying, she asked, "Well, Tom, what do you think?"

He looked around the group and said simply, "We've got about a month and a half to figure out what we have to do."

2 Corinthian 1:10 "And our hope for you is firm, because we know that just as you share in our sufferings, so also you share in our comfort."

CHAPTER 20

Two weeks after the small group of survivors gathered at the Parker Ranch, Willow Creek lay completely deserted, with only a handful of people left on the outskirts of the quaint little town. Gasoline was non-existent and the stores stood abandoned and vandalized. The church that Steve loved and preached at for so many years was still standing, but now was vacant and locked. Although the power remained on at the Parker ranch, they expected to be in the dark any day.

"Morgan, can you help me inventory the cellar today?" Tanya asked as she finished washing the last of the breakfast dishes." I have a feeling that we are running low on a lot of things and with Thanksgiving coming up, we'll want to have something on the table."

"Sure, Tanya," Morgan said. "I can't believe it's almost here."

Morgan grew quiet for a moment and Tanya suspected she was remembering past Thanksgiving holidays with her family. She went to her and put an arm across her slender shoulders, "I know we could never take the place of your family, Morgan, but we do love you like family."

Morgan smiled at her, "I'm all right. I was just thinking back to last year. It's gone by so fast and so much has changed. I love y'all, too. I don't know what I'd have done if Tom and Kyle hadn't come when they did. I thank God every day for that." Morgan slipped her arm around Tanya and hugged her back. "Now, what shall we make for the upcoming feast?"

"Well, we could swing by the supermarket and pick up a turkey and all the fixins," Tanya giggled.

Both women burst into laughter at the audacity of Tanya's suggestion. While Tanya and Morgan joked about the food or lack thereof, Sandy was pulling Joe's old crossbow and arrows from the closet. "Here you go, Steve. Can you guys use this? It won't make as much noise as your shotgun."

Steve took the crossbow from Sandy and studied it carefully. "Sorry, Sandy. I'm not much for bow hunting," Steve said. "I prefer my shotgun." He passed the bow to Tom. "Here you go. Do you know how to use one of these things? I don't think Joe would mind."

Tom happily took the bow. "I first learned to hunt using one of these. Thanks, Steve." Tom turned to Sandy and smiled. "I'll take good care of it."

"I know you will." She smiled back. "Now let me go see what those two are up to in the kitchen. Are you going out now?"

"We thought we would," Steve said. "Why, is there something you need?"

"Oh no, I was going to ask if you wouldn't mind taking Ben and Joe."

"Not at all. Where are they?" Steve asked.

"Well, if they've finished their chores, they're probably down by the pond," Sandy replied over her shoulder as she went to the kitchen.

"We'll pick them up on the way out." Tom said. "Any requests for supper?"

Sandy popped her head around the corner and gave a mischievous smile. "Can you bag us a turkey for Thanksgiving?"

The men whooped with laughter and went out the door, all three sending up a silent prayer that the good Lord would provide.

Tying on her apron as she came into the kitchen, Sandy asked, "Now, what are you two laughing about?"

Morgan was first to get her silliness under control. "Tanya had the great idea that we would go to the supermarket and pick us up a turkey and all the 'fixins'." She burst into laughter again.

"You guys are too much," Sandy grinned, "Okay, first things first. Thanksgiving is just two days away and we're a little low on 'fixins'." Sandy took a pad and pencil from the kitchen drawer and began taking inventory of the cupboards.

"Morgan and I will go check the root cellar, Sandy." Tanya said, picking up another pad and pencil from the drawer.

"Okay, but no goofing off," Sandy joked. She continued to survey the kitchen cupboards and pantry. Their supply of food was getting very low indeed and she wondered whether there would be anything left in town. The garden had been productive, and she was able to can everything they hadn't given away, but even those items were getting low. She would know more when Tanya and Morgan finished their inventory of the root cellar. She thought for a moment, "Do I dare make a full menu for Thanksgiving?" Sandy smiled to herself, "The Lord will provide what we need."

"Okay, Tanya, here we go," Morgan began. "We've got two jars of carrots, one jar of green beans, a jar of peas, and about two dozen potatoes down here." Morgan dug a little deeper toward the back of the shelf. She pulled out a large jar filled with something she did not recognize. "What's this?" She held it up so Tanya could see it in the dim light.

"Those are apples, Morgan. How many jars are there?"

Morgan moved the jars around, looking to see if they were all apples. "It looks like there's three here."

"That's great! Sandy can make her apple pie." Tanya exclaimed.

"You mean the same pie you served when we first got here; do you remember that night?" Morgan said fondly.

Tanya smiled at the memory. "I sure do. We were so happy you had come and yes, that was Sandy's pie. Did you like it?"

"Oh, it was delicious." Morgan said.

"Well, at least we have enough for three more. Is that it for the veggies and fruit?"

Morgan gave one last glance, "Yes, that's it. How does it look?"

Tanya checked the list and clucked softly. "We're pretty low. I don't think we'll have enough to take us through the next four weeks." She looked sadly at Morgan. "But by then it'll be about time for us to leave." She sighed heavily. "I'm not looking forward to that. I don't know how Sandy will handle leaving this ranch. She and Joe had put so much of their heart and soul into it." Tanya grew quiet and took a deep breath. "Well, we'd best get this list upstairs and see how Sandy is doing with hers."

Sandy was right. When Steve, Tom, and Kyle checked the barn and didn't see the boys they headed toward the pond and found them skipping rocks into the frigid water.

"Hey, guys!" Steve hollered.

Both boys turned when they heard their uncle and waved at the three men approaching them. They had been talking about their father and still missed him terribly, but when they saw their Uncle Steve and their two new friends coming down the hill, their spirits lifted some. Joe saw Tom carrying his dad's crossbow and felt a pang of sorrow. "Hi, Uncle Steve. Where you headed?"

"We're going hunting," Steve said. "Why don't we split up and you guys come with us?"

"I'm going with Kyle and Uncle Steve," Ben blurted out and ran toward them.

"Okay, I'll go with Tom." Joe was more than happy to accompany Tom. The time he spent with him made him feel closer to his dad.

Steve and Kyle went with Ben to the eastern end of the woods while Tom and Joe headed west toward the foothills. Tom didn't miss the fact that Joe had looked sadly at the crossbow more than once. "Did your dad ever show you how to use this, Joe?"

"Yeah, we went hunting a few times, but I was pretty young then, so I never shot anything with it."

"Do you want to give it try today? I believe you're grown up enough now."

Joe looked up at Tom with hopeful eyes. "Yeah, sure."

Tom passed the crossbow to Joe and gave him a brief review on cocking and releasing it and then helped him with the quiver and arrows. "You're all set; now we just need to find a big fat turkey for your mom for Thanksgiving."

Joe laughed at the prospect. "Boy, wouldn't that be something if we found one out here."

Sandy checked her watch. It was after four. She was anxious because it was nearly dark, and her two boys were usually home by this time of day. Of course, they were in very capable hands, and she had heard Steve's shotgun go off twice, so she knew they were close, but still she worried. She chalked it up to her mothering nature and went out to bring in the horses. Tanya and Morgan had already started making supper, so she was happy to take advantage of some time outdoors in the fresh air. The deadline for leaving the ranch was growing closer and that had been weighing heavily on her mind. "Soon we will have to start making those preparations." The thought lingered as she made her way down the aisle in the barn, lifting the lead ropes from their nails.

When she reached the other end of the barn, she laughed softly. The horses were waiting for her at the corral gate. "Are my babies ready to come in?" She cooed. Sandy brought the horses into the corral and led them, two at a time into their stalls. She would swear that on their own these horses could put themselves to bed. When they were all inside, she commenced to feed and water them. Her concentration broke and she almost dropped a bucket of oats when she heard voices carrying from across the field. A sigh of relief escaped her, and she ran to the end of the barn and watched her sons coming over the hill with Steve, Kyle, and Tom. She was surprised to realize how genuinely happy she was to see Tom and Kyle. She had grown quite fond of them over the last two weeks, and she hoped that they would be able to remain a part of the family for a long time. She felt an uncanny connection to her husband with the two men, Tom especially. He possessed a quiet strength that comforted her, and she understood now why he and her husband were so close.

Steve pushed away from the table, content and very full. "Ladies, that was delicious."

"Thanks, hon'," Tanya replied. "Guys, did you get enough to eat?" She leaned in and picked up the empty plates from Ben and Joe.

"Oh, yeah," they said together.

"Mom, when was the last time you made rabbit like that?" Joe asked.

"I suppose it was the last time you and your dad went hunting, Joe. It's been a little while." She shot him a gentle smile and got up to help clear the table. "Who wants coffee?"

The adults raised their hands; Tanya made the rounds with the coffee pot as Morgan and Sandy began to wash and dry the dishes. When they had finished, they all sat back at the kitchen table. Sandy exchanged glances with Morgan and Tanya then gave her attention first to Tom, then to Steve and Kyle.

Tom cocked his head to the side and searched her eyes, trying to figure out what it was she was about to say. "What is it, Sandy?"

"Guys, we are running low on food supplies. If we are going to stay here for another four weeks, we'll have to find provisions somewhere; any suggestions?"

The men glanced around the table at one another. They decided that Steve, Tom, Kyle, and Joe would venture into town for more supplies.

"We'll go tomorrow night." Steve announced.

1 Chronicles 29:12 "Wealth and Honor come from you; you are the ruler of all things. In your hands are strength and power to exalt and give strength to all."

CHAPTER 21

SANDY AND BEN WAITED outside the barn for the men to come out. She was desperately trying to keep the worry in her heart from spilling out onto her sleeve as her oldest son prepared to go out on a potentially dangerous undertaking. As fearful as she was, she drew comfort in the fact that he was in the company of family and trusted friends. Joe and Tom were the first to emerge from the barn. Joe was riding Cheyenne and Tom was astride Pilgrim, a horse very particular about who rode him. Seeing Tom seated comfortably in the saddle, she grinned, not surprised that the horse had chosen Tom to ride him. She wondered whether Pilgrim had sensed the connection between his former master and this man. She went to them and turned to her son. She marveled, not for the first time, at how much he looked like his father, especially in his drover and his dad's cowboy hat. She let out a heavy sigh. "Joe, you stay close to the others, you hear?"

"Yes ma'am," Joe said.

Sandy rubbed Cheyenne beneath his thick mane. "And you take care of my boy." She placed a soft kiss on the horse's velvety muzzle. When the horse puckered up to kiss her back, a trick that Joe had taught him, she laughed, relaxing the tension that lay over them all. Joe gave Cheyenne a light kick and moved the quarter horse away from the group, to wait. Sandy looked up at Tom. "You take care too, Tom, okay? Look after Joe?"

"You bet," Tom said smiling. He studied her face and saw the bravery of this woman take over where worry should have been. His heart was moved by her smile, and he wondered whether his respect for her was beginning to grow into something more.

Inside the barn, Steve held Tanya tight in his arms. She hugged him back hard, not wanting to let go. "Be careful, okay? Don't be gone too long."

"I'll be careful, I promise." He kissed her softly and took the reins from her. "Keep the home fires burning, darlin'?" He smiled at his corny statement and swung into his saddle.

Tanya smiled up at him and led his horse outside to stand with the others.

Morgan and Kyle were the last to leave the barn. Already mounted, Kyle leaned down, stroked her flushed cheek, and smiled. "You gonna be okay?"

Morgan gazed up at him and laid her hand on his boot, then looked down again, and kicked at a piece of hay on the ground. Frustrated with her emotions, she swiped a tear from her cheek and turned her eyes back up to him, "Of course, why do you ask?"

"Hey now." Kyle placed his leather-gloved hand on the back of her neck and pulled her toward him. "We'll be back by daylight and then we'll have coffee together. Okay?"

"Okay." Morgan smiled back at him apologetically, "I don't mean to be such a baby; I really am stronger than this."

"I know that, Morgan. Don't worry, all right? You get some sleep tonight and we'll see you in the morning."

She stood on her tiptoes and giggled at his whiskers as he brushed her cheek with a light kiss. Savoring his closeness, she inhaled deeply, delighting in his scent. Holding hands, they exited the barn together.

Once everyone was outside, the group formed a circle and bowed their heads; the rustler's moon shone down on them as Steve led them in prayer. "Father, you are so gracious, thank you for our freedoms and for our family. We pray that, if it be your will, you bring us back safely from our journey tonight. I pray that we stay warm and that you will provide enough provisions to get us through the next few weeks. Please give comfort to those who wait for us and help us to be a light in this dark, dark world. It's in Jesus' name we pray. Amen"

The horses and riders picked their way quietly down the path that led deep into the thick woods that surrounded the ranch. The three-quarter moon offered just enough light to help them see as the chill wind nipped fiercely at them. They rode on, each man deliberating in his own mind what could possibly happen during the night. Kyle and Tom fully expected to find the town of Willow Creek destroyed, much like Morgan's town; Steve and Joe didn't know what to expect. After nearly three hours of riding, they finally arrived at the fence line on the edge of the main road. They rode along the fence row to a clearing.

"Okay, we'll stop here," Steve whispered.

The group dismounted and tied their horses off to the trees on the side of the clearing farthest from the road. As the men were preparing to cross into town, Joe went to Tom and Kyle's horses, checking the lead ropes to make certain they had tied their horses properly for a quick release if the trucks came by. Seeing that the ropes were less than satisfactory, he re-tied them and made a mental note to show Tom and Kyle how to tie the slipknot once they were safely back at the ranch.

Steve approached him. "Joe, you be sure to stay back in the trees and out of sight. If you see or hear anything, you whistle like Tom showed you."

"All right, Uncle Steve," Joe said quietly.

Steve could tell by the boy's muttered response that he did not want to stay behind with the horses. "Joe, listen, you're the best man for this job if the horses get spooked. Do you understand that?"

"Yeah, but are you sure mom didn't have anything to do with it?" Joe asked with just a touch of irritation.

"Maybe just a bit," Steve smiled and patted Joe's back. "We won't be long."

Tom and Kyle overheard the conversation and offered their own encouragement. "Stay sharp, Joe," Kyle said.

"Lay low, buddy. Is there anything you need from town?" Tom asked.

"Maybe you can find a box of Cheerios for Ben?" Joe suggested.

"I'll see what I can do." Tom grinned at the special request and followed Steve and Kyle toward the road. Once they cleared the split rail fence, the men eyed the road carefully checking both directions.

Then with their saddlebags slung over their shoulders, they sprinted across. The icy wind stung their eyes and the exposed skin on their faces, but the adrenaline surging through them pumped their energy level, and the cold ceased to matter with their heightened senses. Tom led the way, Steve was in the middle, and Kyle brought up the rear, his surveillance of the road continuing as he moved.

The first building they reached was the grocery store and, like the stores in Morgan's town, the Regulators or vandals had smashed out the front windows leaving glass strewn across the sidewalk and inside the store. Doing their best to keep out of sight, they pressed tightly against the cold brick and, keeping in the shadows, they cautiously moved around the building. They crept along the deserted sidewalk, checking every turn expecting the enemy at any time. The same adrenaline rush that had screamed through their veins in Iraq more than seven months ago was back with a vengeance; the only differences were, they were holding shotguns and nine millimeters instead of M16's, and the current temperature was about seventy degrees colder.

Tom motioned Kyle to move around the north side of the building while he and Steve advanced to the south. Steve followed closely behind Tom, marveling at the systematic way Tom checked the windows and doorways before they passed by. When they reached the back of the building, Kyle was just coming around the corner in the same manner. Seeing first-hand the soldiers in action, Steve's heart swelled with pride and a new respect for the American military man. He knew right away that they would be safe no matter what happened.

"Okay, we're clear on the outside," Tom whispered. "Kyle, when we go in, you go right. Steve and I will go left. Check each aisle and stay low. Got it?"

"Got it, Nelly."

Tom smiled to himself. Kyle had automatically reverted to calling him by his old handle as he did when they were in country. Once inside, Tom signaled Kyle to "move out." The soldier nodded his understanding, crouched low and disappeared around the corner. After a thorough search of the store and finding no resistance, the three of them reached the far end of the store and were finally able to look closer at the surroundings. They weren't surprised to see the store ransacked with dried foods, boxes and cans scattered everywhere.

"Let's split up," Tom suggested. The men separated and hurried down the aisles, quickly filling their saddle bags with whatever food and supplies they could find. Tom felt as though he had struck gold when he stumbled across some damaged bags of flour and sugar. He remembered Sandy saying how she'd like to bake a pie but was low on flour. Although some of the bags had split, he managed to get them into the saddlebag without losing very much. He made a mental note to grab some plastic bags on their way out.

When he had finished that aisle, just on a hunch, he headed down the breakfast food aisle and into a mangled mess. Strewn throughout the aisle were crushed and torn boxes of cereal; the flakes, puffs and tiny 'o's' crunched beneath Tom's heavy boots. Seeing the littered floor and empty shelves, he grew discouraged and turned to go to the next aisle. Just as he began to turn away, something caught the corner of his eye. A smile crept slowly across his face as he squatted down and withdrew a large undamaged box of Cheerios from beneath the bottom shelf. He nearly laughed aloud. "Thank you, Father." Tom grinned broadly, as he made room for the big, yellow box among the flour and sugar and other items already in his saddlebag. He was more excited about finding that box of cereal than he had been about anything in a long time. Once it was stowed safely, he went to find the others. He saw Steve in the canned fruits and vegetables aisle. "You about ready?"

Steve nearly jumped out of his skin when Tom's voice broke the silence. Although it was just a whisper, Steve's nerves were tight as piano wire, and he was anxious to be out of there. "Yes, I'm just about through." Whatever cans of fruits and vegetables he could find, Steve was shoveling into his bag. Although the pickings were slim, he was pleased with what he found. He and Tom went looking for Kyle and found him crawling along the floor in the dried foods aisle, loading his saddlebag with beans and pasta. If the choices were slim in the other aisles, they were non-existent here. He looked into his near-empty saddlebag and felt defeated. "There's not much here, guys. How'd you do?"

"We did all right," Tom said. "But you know a lot of folks went through here before we did. We shouldn't be too surprised." Tom took Kyle's saddlebag and draped it on the soldier's shoulder, "C'mon, the good Lord will provide all our needs."

Kyle looked at Steve and smiled, "Amen. Ain't he always right about those things?"

"He is." Steve replied. He was growing to love these men like his own brothers.

They left the grocery store in the same manner as when they arrived, keeping low and constantly watching. Tom motioned toward the hardware store, and they moved in that direction. For the remainder of the night, the two soldiers and the minister went from store to store, searching for supplies that would carry them and their loved ones for just a few more weeks. In some of the stores they were successful, but in others there was nothing left but empty shelves.

"Tom, do we have time to stop by the church?" Steve asked when they exited the last store.

"Yeah, but we'll need to hurry. I'm getting a bad feeling. We've been out here for too long."

"It won't take long," Steve reassured him.

"Kyle!" Tom spoke softly but his voice was laced with urgency, "We're making an unplanned stop. Stay sharp." With Kyle trailing, Steve led Tom in the direction of the church.

After Ben had gone to bed, the ladies decided to camp out in the front room. While Sandy stoked the fire in the fireplace, Morgan laid out the blankets, and Tanya busied herself in the kitchen brewing hot tea; it was all she could do to keep her mind from worrying herself sick over her husband. She thought Sandy was a strong woman when her husband went off to war, but Tanya never really understood the loss that her sister felt until now. Nevertheless, as much as she worried about Steve and the others, she knew there was nothing to do except pray for them.

"I'm glad the guys had a clear night to ride," Morgan said, as she fluffed a pillow and dropped it on the blankets at her feet.

"Me, too," Sandy said. "It's cold, but at least it's not snowing or worse, raining." Suddenly the lights flickered, and the house went black, leaving the living room bathed in the golden orange light from the fireplace.

"Well, that's it then," Sandy said. "They've turned off the power. I'm glad we spent the day getting everything in order. The good Lord must've compelled us to do it knowing what was coming. Tanya, you okay in there?"

As soon as the lights began to flicker, Tanya stopped what she was doing and collected some candles from the kitchen drawer. "I'm fine, Sandy, just bringing some candles in. Do you need anything else?"

"Not at the moment, the fire is giving us plenty of light for now." Sandy helped Morgan finish the pallets they'd be sleeping on and then plopped down on the one next to the stairs. "I'll stay here in case Ben wakes up."

Tanya walked into the living room, carrying a wooden tray laden with a steaming teapot, cups, sliced fresh bread and apple butter. Stepping carefully over the blankets and pillows, she made her way to the coffee table. The candle flame flickered as she gently placed the tray down. "Here we are," she said, and sat on the floor next to Morgan. "This would be nice if the circumstances were different."

"Isn't that the truth?" Morgan agreed.

In the darkness, the women talked softly of their current situation, the men who were away, and what they would do now that the power was off.

"Where do you suppose they are right now?" Morgan asked.

Sandy smiled. She knew Morgan was thinking of Kyle. "I would expect right now they are still on their way to the clearing by the road. It's a good two-hour ride, especially if they are trying to go quietly."

Morgan nodded but didn't say anything. She took a sip of her tea and then turned to Tanya. "How long has Steve been a minister, Tanya?"

Tanya thought for a moment, "Oh I'd say about thirteen years. He went to seminary school a little later than most, graduated, and came to Willow Creek after our last minister retired and moved to Florida."

"How did you meet him?" Morgan asked.

Tanya giggled at the memory, "When the folks in town heard that we were getting a new minister, all of Willow Creek buzzed and, of course, everyone showed up at church for his first service." Tanya broke into giggles as she recalled the event that Sunday. "Sandy, do you remember that day?"

Sandy laughed with her sister; "Like it was yesterday. Poor Steve was nervous already, but when we walked in and sat in the front row and he laid eyes on Tanya, that was it. He fell head over heels in love that day. For the rest of the service, he tried so hard not to stumble over his words, but every time he looked at Tanya, he lost his place in his notes." Sandy smiled warmly at her sister, "That was a good day."

Tanya continued the story. "Well, we didn't really date, we just sort of talked at church or other town gatherings. We moved very slowly. Him with a new town, a new church, and a pretty large flock to tend to, and I wasn't ready, to be honest. I thought my time had come and gone. I never expected to be married after I turned thirty." Tanya smiled softly. "He was well worth the wait, though."

"It wasn't until after Joe died that the relationship really blossomed," Sandy added. Not long after that they were married.

Tanya smiled, "What about you Morgan?" Tanya asked, "Did you have someone special where you used to live?"

"No. Not exactly; I spent most of my time at my Uncle Walt's house when I wasn't in school or working. To tell you the truth, the boys in my town weren't very interesting. I was happier helping my uncle with his horses."

"Well, that explains it." Sandy threw her hands up.

"Explains what?" Morgan questioned.

"Why you have such a way with the horses." Sandy answered.

"Oh, your horses are all sweethearts, Sandy," Morgan said. "I think it's Joe. He has a gift with those animals."

"I'll have to agree with you on that, Morgan," Sandy replied. "He does have a gift."

Tanya leaned over and whispered to Morgan, "Well, call me crazy, but it's pretty obvious that Kyle is sweet on you."

Morgan could feel her face grow warm. She looked down and gazed into her tea but couldn't keep the smile from spreading across her face, lighting her up. She looked hopeful.

"He's such a good man, Morgan," Tanya pressed. "I think you two make a good match."

"He really is a sweet guy," Morgan said quietly, "but I don't know."

Sandy was surprised, "Morgan, what's not to know? He likes you; you like him."

"Kyle talks to me about God sometimes, but I don't know that I believe like he does. I mean, I do believe, but I've never been baptized, and I just don't think I could measure up to him and his beliefs." Morgan glanced up at the two women.

Tanya moved closer into the circle, "Morgan, it's not about measuring up at all, but more like a journey together. As long as you have Jesus as the goal that you are both striving for, then you are on the right path. Think of it as a triangle where you and Kyle are at opposite sides of the base, and you are both working your way up the triangle to meet at the top where Jesus is waiting." Tanya drew an invisible triangle on the blanket she was sitting on so Morgan could grasp the idea. "And as far as baptism goes, it is just an outward expression of an inward belief. Kyle believes that Jesus is his Savior, and he was baptized to show that he believed. It doesn't prove anything, nor does it guarantee a ticket to Heaven like some believe."

"Okay, I see!" Morgan's excited expression told Tanya that she had just given Morgan hope for a possible future with Kyle.

"I have one more question that I'm not sure I know how to ask, but I feel like I need to say it."

Tanya and Sandy gazed patiently at the young woman. They were touched by the fact that she trusted them enough to be so open on such a personal level. They waited while she organized her thoughts.

"I want to talk to Steve about my salvation. I have a lot of questions."

Tanya leaned over and hugged Morgan warmly and then pulled away, "We'll talk to Steve in private tomorrow; okay?"

Morgan nodded, "That would be great."

A silence fell for just a moment until Lucky, evidently tired of the inattention, plopped himself in Morgan's lap and looked up at her with hopeful eyes. She rubbed his ears and snuggled him close.

Sandy let out a heavy sigh and put her teacup on the table, "Well, it has been a perfect evening with you both, but I'm whooped. If you don't mind, I'm going to turn in." She leaned over and hugged Morgan, then Tanya, and lastly kissed Lucky on the head. "Good night you guys."

"Good night, Sandy. I think I'm going to turn in too, Morgan." Tanya whispered and then buried herself deep into her blankets, wishing her husband were there with her.

Morgan lifted Lucky and tucked him beneath the blankets with her. She thought about the talk she had with Tanya and hoped she would have the courage to go forward with her decision. She prayed, "Jesus, you know me already and I so want to know you more and learn everything about you. Help me to be obedient to you."

After it had grown quiet, and all that could be heard was the soft steady breathing of the others, Sandy lay staring into the fire. What was to become of all of them? Again, there were so many questions with so few answers. Would her sons be strong enough to face what was sure to come? Would she be strong enough? She thanked God for sending Tom, Kyle, and Morgan. She took another deep breath and rolled over onto her back, and pondered some more until finally, she drifted off into a restless slumber.

Psalm 62:1 "My soul finds rest in God alone; my salvation comes from Him."

CHAPTER 22

JOE STOMPED HIS FEET and stood closer to Thunder, sharing in the warmth coming off the horse his Uncle Steve had ridden. The boy had to admit that he was angry about having to stay behind, but after considering what Steve had told him, he realized that he really was the only one for the job. He knew Steve wanted to check on the church and Tom and Kyle, well, they were soldiers, and this was what they did.

Joe knew that God blessed him with patience and a way with the animals; he just needed to be reminded of it. He decided he would apologize to his uncle when they returned. The silence of the forest was deafening, and Joe was grateful for the owl that hooted from time to time. Trying to stay alert, he changed his position and went to Cheyenne. It would do no good if he fell asleep when he was supposed to be on watch.

Suddenly he heard the low rumble of a truck far off in the distance. At first, he wasn't sure if it was real, but headlights piercing the dark and coming toward him confirmed it. The truck was a good two maybe three miles away, but the darkness made it difficult to tell how fast it was going. He had to take a chance and warn the others. He went to the fence and leaned in toward the road, hoping Steve and the other two would hear him. He cupped his hands around his mouth, let out a long, low whistle, and quickly stepped back into the shadows. He stepped forward again, leaned into the fence toward the road, and repeated the shrill warning, then slipped back into the shadows again. He considered whistling a third warning but decided against it. The truck was already too close. His heart raced with anticipation and fear for his companions. There was nothing more he could do but pray for them and hope that they would hear the truck as well.

He stood back in the trees and rubbed Cheyenne's ears and then went to each horse, rubbing and cooing softly to it. He knew they would spook if the truck came too close. The rumbling of the seven-ton grew louder as it approached the intersection where the church stood. Joe leaned his head against Pilgrim's massive neck. "Lord, please protect them." He peered through the darkness, desperately searching the buildings and streets for Steve, Tom, and Kyle.

Steve, Kyle, and Tom had just reached the church when Tom stopped abruptly. A low whistle cut through the night. Tom grabbed Steve by the arm. They froze where they stood -- then a second warning whistle! Steve spun around to see Tom put his finger to his lips. "We've got company," he whispered. "Get behind the building, quick!" Tom grabbed the front of Steve's coat and dragged him to the back of the Parish Hall. He suddenly realized that the truck was coming closer to them. They darted to the next building; a shed where Steve used to keep the lawn mower and other gardening tools.

The men edged deeper into the trees behind the shed. They waited and watched. They were well hidden when the truck pulled up in front of the church. The brakes screeched noisily in protest as the massive truck slowed to a stop. Steve hung his head and feared the worst. A strong hand rested on his shoulder, and he turned to see Tom's sorrowful eyes looking back at him. They all knew what was coming next. The seven-ton continued to idle for what seemed like forever. Heavy canvas covered the rear of the transport truck, concealing what was inside. They prayed that it was empty.

Steve looked expectantly at Tom. "What are they doing? Do you think they'll pass it by?" He whispered.

Tom continued assessing the situation and shook his head. "No, they'll follow through. Look." He lifted his chin toward the truck and the men who were emerging from the cab and from the back of the truck.

Steve felt a lump rise to his throat as two men carrying several red five-gallon gas cans approached the church. In the insanity of it all, he found himself wondering where on earth they had acquired the gasoline, but his thoughts immediately returned to his church. All the men wore black and gray camouflage with M-16's slung across their backs. The two who went toward the church circled it and splashed the gasoline up its exterior walls and around the foundation. The other two stood guard behind the truck. From time to time, one would speak, and they both would throw their heads back and laugh.

Steve's heart sank as he remembered the day he first walked the perimeter of the church. It was an architectural masterpiece with a high steeple and bell tower. Stained glass windows were on all sides of the church, and each depicted a story from the life of Christ. Steve wept as the men continued to make their way to the back of the church. When they arrived at the back door, one of them drew a handgun from under his coat and shot out the lock on the door. Once inside, they continued the saturation of the church as Steve, Tom, and Kyle watched in horror; helpless.

Joe hung back in the trees waiting for a sign that his Uncle Steve and the others were on their way back. When he heard the shot, he rushed to the fence but saw nothing. Suddenly an explosion rocked him to his knees. The ground beneath him shuddered from the violent percussion and the sky lit up with brilliant yellow and orange flames shooting high into the air. Startled by the unexpected explosion, the terrified horses whinnied and reared. They frantically pulled at their ropes in an attempt to get away.

Joe calmed the horses, surprised at his own composure. He watched as the flames licked hungrily at the black night sky, unaware of the tears streaming down his cheeks. "Oh Dad, what is happening?" He brushed the tears from his face and took a deep breath. Over the roar of the fire, he heard the rumble of the truck and ducked deeper into the shelter of the trees. The headlights of the truck split through the darkness in the woods and Joe held his breath as they barely missed Kyle's horse. When the truck turned onto the main road, the headlights panned across the woods creating a horrifying possibility of exposure.

The frightened sixteen-year-old watched the truck pull away. Then a sudden movement across the street startled him. With relief, he realized it was Tom leading Steve and Kyle across the road toward him.

Joe sprang into action and quickly untied the horses and fastened the lead ropes around the saddle horns. Even though he had a million questions, they had to wait. For the moment, he was grateful that they were all safe. With skilled hands, he tied the bulging saddlebags onto the back of the saddles. As soon as Tom and Kyle's backsides hit the saddles, Joe slapped the horses hard on the rump causing them to leap forward and bolt into the darkness toward home. Steve jerked Thunder's lead rope from the tree. Not bothering to tie it to the saddle horn, he threw it across the saddle, mounted his horse, and galloped after Tom and Kyle. With everyone safely on their way back to the ranch, Joe climbed aboard Cheyenne and kicked him hard. The gelding whinnied; surprised at the force his young master was using on him. They raced after the others, who were already far ahead as the fire in the sky masked the approaching red dawn.

Sandy awoke from her troubled sleep with a start. What woke her, she couldn't tell. The clock on the mantel read five-thirty. Struck by the freezing temperature in the house, she squirmed reluctantly from the depths of her sleeping bag and smiled when she saw Lucky still snuggled up with Morgan. His muzzle pressed against her cheek.

"What time is it?" Morgan mumbled sleepily. She cuddled closer to Lucky, not wanting to leave the comfort of her quilts.

"Five-thirty," Tanya offered and pulled her bathrobe tight around her. "I'll get the coffee on. The guys should be home soon."

Morgan crawled reluctantly from beneath her blankets as Lucky playfully licked the sleep from her face. "Okay, okay, Lucky. Hang on. I'll bet you won't want to stay out in the cold for long, you goofy, desert dog." Morgan laughed as she wrapped the quilt around her. "I'm putting Lucky out; be right back." Morgan shuffled out the back door after Lucky. What she saw when she stepped outside, took the breath right out of her. She screamed, "Tanya! Sandy! Come quick!"

Sandy and Tanya rushed to where Morgan was standing dumbstruck on the back porch. When she saw the northwestern sky ablaze with angry flames, Tanya cried, "What's happening, Morgan? What's burning?"

Morgan looked solemnly at Tanya, "I expect that's the church, Tanya. That's what they do. They move everyone out of town and then they set the churches on fire. I just don't understand why. I pray no one was inside." When she realized what she said, Morgan dropped her head and wept. Sandy was close to tears herself but knew that it was not the time for crying. She was confident that God would bring back all the men, her son included. She put a hand on Morgan and Tanya and gently pushed them back into the farmhouse. "Come on, you two. The guys will be home soon. We don't want them coming in to see us wallowing in tears, do we?" Sandy waited as Lucky scampered into the kitchen and then closed the door. She turned back to Tanya and Morgan, "We don't know what happened, so we must wait to find out the truth. I'll start up the woodstove. Tanya, will you please make the coffee? Morgan, I need you to pick up the front room, please? I'll be in to help in just a minute."

Tanya and Morgan did as they were told, no words, just silent compliance. Just as Morgan was finishing folding the last quilt, she heard the thunder of hooves coming from the woods, Ben, too, heard the riders coming in and dressed quickly to meet them. The men stormed into the side yard and pulled up hard on their horses. Cheyenne reared up pawing at the air with his mighty hooves. Joe spoke softly to him, then quickly dismounted, and led his horse to his stall. "Ben, get the rest of them; I've got Cheyenne!" He yelled. Once Ben removed the saddlebags, he took the reins from the riders and led the horses to their stalls. "You guys must be hungry," he said gently to Thunder.

Steve handed Tom his saddlebag, ran to Tanya, and fell into her arms. "They burned the church." Tanya held him tight, and they cried.

Suddenly Steve pulled away from her.

"What is it?" Tanya wiped the tears from her eyes and studied his face.

Steve took a deep breath and shook his head. "God just reminded me that the church was just a building. We can be thankful that no one was inside."

Tom asked Sandy, "Were you all okay last night?"

"Yeah, we were fine." Sandy looked down at the ground and shook her head. "I'm sorry Steve had to witness the burning of his church. That must have been absolutely devastating for him."

Tom shook his head. "It was pretty bad, Sandy."

As they talked, she was aware that Tom's gaze lingered on her. She turned her head sharply and motioned him toward the house. "Well, I guess we'd best get you guys inside for some hot coffee and a good breakfast."

Kyle had gone straight to Morgan and wrapped his arms around her. She sensed that the burning of the church had shaken him, and her heart broke for him, knowing how deep his faith was. She hugged him tightly.

Ben dumped oats into the feed trough and watched Joe cautiously, "What happened out there?"

"They had guns, Ben." Joe felt his throat tighten. "They had guns, and they burned down Uncle Steve's church!"

Ben's jaw dropped. "What?"

"I don't know what's going to happen, but I have a feeling that it's going to get a whole lot worse."

"I'm glad you got back all right, Joe. I was kinda scared for you," Ben admitted. He didn't like to let on to his big brother that he was afraid, but under the circumstances he knew Joe would understand.

"Truth be told, Ben, I was a little scared myself. C'mon, let's finish up, I'm starving."

1 Peter 5:8 "Be self-controlled and alert. Your enemy, the devil prowls around like a roaring lion looking for someone to devour. Resist him, standing firm in the faith, because you know that your brothers throughout the world are undergoing the same kind of sufferings."

CHAPTER 23

THREE WEEKS HAD PASSED since the church burned down and Christmas was right around the corner. Morgan made her decision for Christ and Steve performed the baptism in the ice-cold waters of the pond. Kyle and Tanya stood by with heavy quilts and once the ceremony was completed, they rushed down to wrap them in love and affection and then rushed them back to the warmth of the farmhouse.

Sandy sat on the couch, pouring over hundreds of pictures in the albums that she had collected over the years. "What to take; what to leave?" It was cruel that she had to choose; after all, these pictures told the story of not only her life, but also the life she had shared with her husband and their sons. It wasn't fair that she was being forced to leave the ranch she had loved for so many years to potentially let it fall into the hands of people who didn't know or care about its history. Sadness started to overcome her, so she put the albums aside. "I can't do this right now," she thought. She quickly wiped her eyes and looked up to see Kyle and Steve standing in the doorway, holding a large plastic bucket. Sandy cocked her head to the side and questioned them, "What are you two up to?"

Steve explained, "Sandy, we know we will have to be leaving soon, and we won't be able to take all of our belongings, but Kyle suggested we box up and hide the special things that we can't take with us. Then, when this is all over . . ." Steve hesitated for a moment, then his face brightened, and he turned to Kyle. "Well, personally, I think it's a great idea."

Sandy wondered why Steve hesitated. His countenance, normally bright and hopeful, appeared troubled and it concerned her. It was as though a shadow had passed over him then just as quickly had left. "Are you okay, Steve?"

"Yeah, yeah, I'm fine," Steve reassured her. "Like you, I don't want to leave the ranch. It was hard enough leaving our home, but the memories here, too . . . We have to trust that God will bring us back."

"You're right, Steve." Sandy rose from the couch, "I like your idea, Kyle."

"What idea?" Morgan asked as she entered the room. She looked warm and refreshed in her jeans and heavy cotton sweater. Her hair pulled back in a short ponytail, emphasized her almond shaped brown eyes. Kyle drank in her beauty and held out his free arm, welcoming her closer if she chose. She did and slipped in easily next to him.

"Kyle had the great idea to stash all of Sandy's photo albums that she can't take with her." Steve said.

"That is a great idea." Morgan exclaimed and reached up and kissed him on the cheek. She giggled at his whiskers and rubbed her nose. "You need a shave, soldier." She smiled sweetly and then turned to Sandy. "Do you have a sec?"

"Sure." Sandy left the albums with Steve and Kyle and walked with Morgan out to the kitchen. She was surprised to see Tanya waiting for them. "What's up?"

"Did you know that today is Tom's birthday?" Morgan asked indignantly.

"You're kidding." Sandy was amused by Morgan's tone, as though she were angry with Tom for having a birthday and not telling anyone.

"Nope, Kyle told me," Morgan said, still agitated.

"Sandy, why don't you bake a pie for him? He loves your apple pie especially, and there's plenty of apple filling for his pie and the Christmas pie, too." Tanya suggested.

"Great idea," Morgan said. "It's settled. We'll have it after supper."

"Hold on a minute, girls," Sandy exclaimed. "Who's going to keep him out of the kitchen? You know he likes to kick back at the kitchen table. Someone will have to keep him away for at least an hour and then I'll have to hide the darn thing until after supper."

"We've got it all under control, Sandy. You just worry about that pie. I'll go get one of the jars from the cellar now." Morgan went to the cellar, leaving Sandy with her mouth hanging open.

Tanya looked at her sister and laughed. "Sandy, close your mouth before someone sees you like that. I'm going to find Tom."

Sandy sputtered but gave up. She was perfectly happy baking Tom's birthday pie; she only hoped he would not find out about it.

"Mom?"

"In the kitchen, Ben!"

Ben burst into the kitchen sliding in his socks across the linoleum floor. "Mom, where's Tom?"

"I'm not sure. Aunt Tanya went to look for him. Why?"

"I just want to talk to him." Ben went to the mudroom to put on his boots, coat, hat, and gloves. "I'll be outside."

"Okay, but stay close to the house, please." Sandy watched Ben from the kitchen window as he approached Tanya and Tom. They were walking toward the house, and she hoped they wouldn't come into the kitchen. Although she hadn't begun the preparations yet, Tom was very keen and if he saw her, he would know she was up to something. She continued to watch them as they talked briefly, then Tom and Ben left together.

"It's all set," Tanya said coming into the kitchen. "Tom and Ben are going to collect a LOT of firewood. I told them we needed extra for Christmas dinner." Tanya said, satisfied with her ruse.

Ben and Tom had been collecting wood for nearly two hours and Tom was ready for some of Sandy's coffee. "Ben, are you about ready?" Tom called to the boy from across the pond. He smoothed Pilgrim's mane and whispered softly to him while Lucky bounced across the field chasing something that only he could see.

"Yep, I think I'm good now, Tom." Ben picked up one last piece of wood and carried it awkwardly back to Tom who was waiting for him beneath the tree.

He watched Ben coming toward him and chuckled. "Here, let me help with that." Tom took the larger piece of wood and tossed it up toward the front of the sled. "There we go. You did well, Ben. This ought to last quite a while." Tom patted him hard on the back, causing Ben to stumble forward.

"Let's go." Tom patted Pilgrim on the rump and the big gelding lurched forward and made for the house with Tom and Ben on either side of him. The sled was fashioned out of wood slats they had pulled from the top floor of the barn and then attached to an old plow harness.

When the electricity was turned off, the gas had been turned off at the same time, which left the wood stove and fireplace as their only means of cooking meals and heat.

Ben looked fondly up at the man on the other side of the horse, "Tom, how long are you staying with us?"

Tom smiled down at Ben, not sure how to answer the question. "Well, I don't know, partner. I guess it all depends on what will happen. We seem to be working pretty good together, don't you think?"

"Oh yeah, you bet. I'm glad you're here and I think Mom is too." Ben paused and Tom wondered what he meant by his last comment. Ben continued, "Sometimes at night I can hear her prayers. I know it's not right to listen and I don't mean to, but our house is a little crowded you know."

Tom smiled at Ben's statement but said nothing.

"Anyway," Ben went on, "she thanks God for you, Kyle, and Morgan every night. I do, too, Tom. You guys feel like family now."

The young man's remark moved Tom, and he had to clear his throat before he answered. "Thanks Ben. I'm grateful to God that we found you, too. I believe He wanted us all to be together for this. What do you think?"

"Yeah," Ben flashed a smile at his friend.

"Well, I don't expect we'll be going anywhere for a while. To tell you the truth, I don't think any of us have anywhere else to go. Looks like you're stuck with us."

While they walked and talked, a light snow began to fall. Tom lifted his face to the soft flakes. "Looks like we may have a white Christmas, Ben."

"Wow! That would be great!" Ben exclaimed.

Tom was already thinking of where they would put the Christmas tree.

Morgan and Tanya went down to the cellar to take inventory of the remaining food. Pickings were slim, but they estimated that there would still be enough to last through the end of the month, if they were careful. Tanya chewed on the end of the pencil she was holding. "We may have to send the guys out again for some fresh game and, hopefully, a goose for Christmas."

Morgan agreed. "We'll bring it up at supper tonight."

While the ladies were in the cellar, Steve, Joe, and Kyle were busy working at the kitchen table on the high frequency base radio that was brought from Morgan's uncle's house. They were hopeful that they would be able to hear some kind of news of what was going on outside their little world or at least to reach someone, anyone nearby. Sandy placed the finished pie to bake in the oven of the wood stove. She felt like taking a walk and realized that it had been a while since she checked the mailbox, so she shrugged into her drover, donned her leather hat and gloves, and walked out the door. After being in the toasty kitchen all day, the cold air refreshed her. Ever since they had received the last letter; there had been no other mail. She knew that the time for them to leave was drawing near and she grew more unsettled with each day. Everyone else felt it, too. A silent foreboding had fallen over the farmhouse and, although everyone was as close as family, a tension filled the air that no one could name. She pulled the collar of her drover closer around her neck and searched the sky. It was full of snow, and she wondered how much they would get and how soon it would come.

Sandy arrived at the main road, paused, and listened intently. Nothing; no trucks; no traffic, the eerie silence of the abandoned roadway was unnerving. She looked down the road and saw nothing. The coast was clear. She jogged across quickly. As she approached the oversized box, her steps slowed until she froze in her tracks. She felt her breath suddenly leave her and she struggled to catch it. The mailbox door was sitting halfway open! She had always closed the door completely in the past. She checked the road again; nothing there. It appeared safe. She slowly lowered the mailbox door. It creaked loudly on its rusty hinges, and she cautiously peered inside. There in the darkness lay a single letter. Her heart raced as she slowly slid her trembling hand into the mailbox and picked up the envelope.

Her attention was suddenly ripped from the letter she held in her hand by the distant growl of an approaching vehicle. She slammed the box closed and darted across the road, ran down her driveway, and ducked behind a large maple. She peered cautiously from behind the tree and watched as a Humvee drove slowly by. When it reached her driveway, the truck slowed to a stop. She panicked when she realized that the mailbox door lay open. She must have slammed it too hard. Keeping out of sight, Sandy pressed further behind the tree, held her breath, and waited. The man in the passenger seat stood up and pointed in the direction of the farm and then turned to the driver and said something. As hard as she strained to listen, Sandy could not hear the words above the loud rumble of the truck's engine as it idled in front of her driveway. The driver finally put the truck in gear and drove off, but not before the passenger pointed into the trees again, as though he saw something. "Oh, dear, God; please don't let them come yet." When she was certain that the truck was gone, she turned and raced down the driveway toward the house.

She charged into the house and stopped short in the foyer. After her mad dash to get to the safety of the house, once there, it seemed as though she had never left. Everyone was still busy with what they were doing when she had left. "Steve! Tanya!"

"Steve and Joe went out to the shed, Sandy," Kyle called from the kitchen, "and I think Tanya is still down in the cellar with Morgan." Surrounded by parts of the radio they were still working on, Kyle looked up from what he was doing, "Are you all right?"

"No, Kyle. I need everyone here. We got another letter today." She was afraid to say anymore.

"Hang on and I'll round everyone up." Kyle grabbed his coat from the hook by the back door, took a long stride off the porch, and trotted toward the shed. She heard him call out to Tom and Ben and watched as they hurried toward the house. Tanya and Morgan had run up from the cellar to find Sandy sitting at the kitchen table, with the single letter in her hand. Their hearts sank, knowing what was coming.

Finally, everyone had gathered. Unaware that she was still wearing her drover, hat, and gloves, Sandy looked around the table at the people she loved. Joe was sitting next to her with his arm across the back of her chair. The envelope lay unopened on the table daring someone to pick it up. Steve took the challenge and reached for it. He opened it carefully and read slowly,

"Dear Parker family and friends," he paused and glanced around the table at Tom, Kyle, and Morgan. Shaking his head, he continued, *"we have finally come to the time where we are able to bring in the remaining residents of Willow Creek. We hope you are as excited to be in your new home as we are to welcome you. We will be arriving at your home very soon to help you with the relocation."* Steve dropped the letter on the table and looked up at Sandy. "That's it. That's all there is."

"There's more." Sandy said shakily, "I think they saw me."

"What?" Tanya sat up in her chair. "Sandy, what happened?"

"I was across the road at the mailbox and just as I was reaching in to get the letter, I heard a truck coming. As soon as I heard it, I ran back across the road and hid behind a tree. When the truck drove by, the driver slowed down in front of the driveway as if he were looking for something. Sandy looked around the table, "I don't think they saw me, but . . ." Sandy said, trying to convince herself as well as the others, ". . . but one of them pointed in my direction so I don't know; they may have seen me. I'm so sorry." The pitch of her voice rose with her anguish. "If I'd known they were coming, I would never have crossed the road." Sandy held her face in her hands and cried, her long chestnut hair falling onto the table.

Joe removed her hat, put his arm around his mother's shoulder, and hugged her. "Mom, it's not your fault," he said. "They were probably looking for the house. They know it's back here somewhere, but they wouldn't know exactly where we are. I'm sure that's all they were doing. Right, Uncle Steve?"

"Absolutely," Steve assured her. "Sandy, I believe Joe is right. There is no way they could have seen you. Relax, it'll be all right. We need to concentrate on our next move."

"It'll have to be soon." Sandy raised her head, and the room fell silent as everyone directed their attention to the one who spoke. Tom searched the faces of those around him and then his gaze rested on Sandy. "Maybe they didn't see you, Sandy, but maybe they did. No one can say for sure. Who knows how long that letter sat in the mailbox? I'm thinking we need to leave, and we need to leave very soon."

Sandy could tell there was more on Tom's mind than he was letting on. She searched his face trying to understand; she had a feeling that no one would like what he was about to say.

Tom took a deep breath and continued. "I think we should split up."

"What do you mean, Tom?" Tanya asked.

Kyle nodded his head. Obviously, he and Tom had already discussed it, both agreeing that it was the best option.

"I'm thinking we need to put someone on the inside," Tom explained.

"Now wait a minute, Tom!" Steve stood up and began pacing the floor. "We need to stick together." He turned to face Tom, his eyes pleading with him.

Tom's voice remained calm and steady. Sandy could tell he had put a lot of thought into his plan. "How are we going to know what's going on if we stay out here? You know what they say, 'Keep your friends close, but your enemies closer.'"

Sandy shook her head, "Tom, I have to agree with Steve. It will be much too dangerous." She stared into his eyes, hoping to convince him to change his mind, but she knew that he had already made up his mind and would not waver.

"Tom's right." Everyone turned to see Joe looking at all of them. "He's right, someone needs to be inside and I'm going with him."

"Joe, No!" Sandy cried. Her eyes flashed at Joe then to Tom, "Tom! Did you talk to Joe about this before coming to me?"

"No, Mom," Joe said. He shifted his attention to Tom, "You'll need some sort of back up."

Tom was surprised. He hadn't expected Joe to speak up, but he was glad that he would have someone else inside. He nodded in agreement, "You're right, I could certainly use the help and the company. Are you sure this is what you want to do, Joe?"

"Yes sir."

Sandy felt helpless. She knew she would not be able to talk her son out of it or forbid him. Their country had changed, and her sons were changing with it.

After much debate, it was decided that they would pack and prepare in the morning, rest up and leave on horseback at dawn the following day. Tom, Joe, and Lucky would go to The City, while Sandy and the others would take whatever they could pack on horses and move northwest, away from The City, her ranch, and her son.

The group gathered after supper in the front room for pie and coffee, to pray, talk and spend their last few hours together. Conversations lingered on well into the night until one by one everyone drifted off to sleep. Sandy lay awake listening to the soft rhythmic breathing of the people she loved. She knew Joe's decision to go with Tom was the right one, but it didn't make it any easier to accept.

Psalm 143:8 "Let the morning bring me word of your unfailing love, for I have put my trust in you. Show me the way I should go, for to you I lift up my soul."

CHAPTER 24

Barbara Beechum closed her Bible and rubbed her old eyes. The dim light offered by the single lamp at her bedside table was barely enough to read the small print, but she was too stubborn to invest in the larger print. Besides, if she were to go out looking for a Bible now, she would not find one.

Her husband, Richard, lay in their bed. By all appearances, he could have been sleeping peacefully, except now his face was sallow, ashen and his breathing labored. She worried that he would not make it through the night. During this difficult time there would be no minister to comfort her, no doctor to advise her; only a nurse that came by daily to see to Richard's needs and replenish his dose of morphine. The building, known as the 'last stop' was where Barbara and Richard were housed along with a dozen other elderly folks who were either single, too sick, or too old to be bothered with. There was no hope in this cold, desolate, gray place, only despair and loneliness. The only hope she found was in the delicate pages of the book she held. Barbara knelt beside the bed and prayed softly to God, that He would be merciful and take her husband home while he slept.

Heavy footsteps from the night security echoed from down the hall intruding rudely on her prayers. As they drew closer, she heard the caustic voice of the officer shouting, "LIGHTS OUT!" Barbara rose as quickly as her arthritic knees would allow and reached for the lamp. She didn't want him banging on her door tonight, disturbing Richard. The room immediately went dark leaving only the glow of the bathroom nightlight to soften the shade. As the night guard's heavy footfalls passed by her door and the jangling of his keys faded down the corridor, she let out a sigh of relief. "Boy, wouldn't I love to teach him a few things about manners," she mumbled. Then, knowing he only made one pass at night, she defiantly turned the lamp back on. They were fools for assuming that just because the residents were old; it meant they were senile and easily manipulated. Barbara

Beechum had plenty to show them, but it had to wait. Some things she knew she couldn't do alone. "I'm waitin' on you, Lord. You just tell me when and where."

She missed the old farmhouse in Willow Creek that she and Richard had shared over the last fifty-five years, as she surveyed the little apartment. On the surface, it was beautiful with select pieces of fine antiques adorned with handmade lace and embroidery. Pictures of loved ones decorated the walls and the top of her bureau. However, beneath the top layer of hominess and comfort lay a diseased and smoldering monster that ate away at her sense of security, safety, and hope. She knew Richard would not live much longer, what with the cancer spreading and no treatment available to him, but she was grateful and safe in the fact that, when it was time for him to go home, Jesus would be waiting for him with open arms. She stroked his limp, unresponsive hand and thought about Joe Parker, a man she knew from Willow Creek. She believed with all her heart that Joe, too, would be waiting for Richard when his soul arrived in heaven.

When they received the news of Joe's death in Iraq, Richard had taken it very hard. He cried as though he had lost his own son. Barbara wiped a tear from her faded blue eyes remembering how brokenhearted, yet strong, Joe's wife had been. She paused in her reflections and gazed up at the white ceiling and beyond, "Joe, I'm counting on you to be there when Richard arrives."

Twelve hours later, at eight a.m., security passed by again, knocking on each door awakening the residents from their fitful night's slumber. The day security was just as threatening as the night security and Barbara, and the others were convinced that it was just another form of psychological torment. On this day, Christmas Eve, Barbara decided to keep with tradition and read the Christmas Story from the book of Luke. She lifted her Bible from her nightstand, and it suddenly occurred to her that it would be nice to have others join her. A mischievous smile spread from her lips to her eyes. "Why not invite a few of my neighbors over?" Knowing the phone operator listened in on the conversations, Barbara hurried down the hall and knocked quietly on a door.

Dorothy Stone opened the door slowly and peered down the dimly lit hallway before her gentle gray eyes rested on Barbara. Her deeply creased face wrinkled even more when she smiled. "Good morning, Barbara. Is everything all right?" She spoke softly.

"Oh yes," Barbara replied, "as well as can be expected of course."

"Indeed." The elderly woman smiled. "Won't you come in?" Dressed in her threadbare housedress of pink and blue polka dots on a yellow background, she was wearing a pair of pink scuffs with the soles worn to nearly nothing, Dorothy stepped back and opened the door just enough for her friend to slip in. "I can offer you some tea and toast, but not much more I'm afraid. After George died, they cut my monthly allowance by more than half." Dorothy shook her head causing her thin white hair to float gracefully about her delicate face. She directed Barbara to the kitchen. "We can talk in here."

Barbara noted the meager breakfast of tea and raisin toast that had been set on the kitchen counter and took a seat at the table. "Thank you, Dorothy, but I've already had my morning meal; please don't let me keep you from your breakfast."

Dorothy nodded her thanks and carefully moved her teacup and saucer and the small plate of toast back to the table where she daintily ate and listened.

Barbara began, choosing her words carefully. "The reason for my visit is to invite you and some others to my unit this evening. Since its Christmas Eve, I thought it would be nice to read the Christmas Story and talk about the real reason for Christmas." She watched her friend expectantly, certain that she would decline.

Dorothy dabbed at the corners of her mouth with her napkin before she answered. "Barbara, I would love to come, but you know I must be back in my room by quarter to eight. I don't want that discourteous security guard snooping around or banging on my door."

It was difficult for Barbara to contain her excitement as her heart leapt with joy, but her words were gentle and reassuring, "Of course, dear, we will be sure to finish before then and get you all safely back in your rooms." Dorothy's acceptance of her invitation encouraged Barbara to be on her way and invite others. More than that, she didn't want to spend too much time away from Richard. "Well, I'd better be on my way. I want to invite a few more of the residents. Why don't you come over around six?" Barbara stood to take her leave.

"I'll be there. Thank you, Barbara." Dorothy walked her friend to the door, "Oh, I didn't ask about Richard. How is he doing these days?"

"Not so good I'm afraid," Barbara replied. "Between the government's takeover and the Cancer, he just sort of gave up. I think he's waiting on the angels to come fetch him and take him to heaven."

Dorothy gave her friend a hug, "I understand, and if it's all right with you, I will pray to God to send His angels down for Richard."

"Thank you, Dorothy. You know, as much as I'll miss that old man, I hope he can be rescued soon from the pain he is in." Barbara gave Dorothy another quick hug. "I'll see you tonight."

Dorothy closed the door softly behind Barbara and prayed immediately for Richard Beechum that he would pass peacefully in his bed. She thought about her own husband of sixty years; neglected at the infirmary and left to die in a crowded hallway. She remembered the day vividly.

The emergency room doctor had diagnosed her husband George with only a cold when they admitted him to the infirmary. However, because his illness was not life threatening, they had pushed him aside while the doctors and nurses attended to the 'critical care patients.' After hours of waiting, the doctors finally went to treat him, but they were too late. The cold had actually been a severe case of the flu. Dorothy had spent weeks with Barbara after the incident, trying to find it in her heart to forgive them. She did, eventually, and now she just waited, impatiently at times, for the day that she could join her husband.

Barbara made her way down the stark corridor, her footsteps echoing off the concrete walls. Delighted that one more couple agreed to join her and Dorothy, she confidently knocked on the door of Mr. Harris's apartment. He was a grumpy widower when he arrived and had only grown more embittered as the weeks turned into months. He swung the door wide and scowled at the smiling Barbara. "What do you want?" He bellowed.

Taken aback by his aggressive assault, Barbara squared her shoulders and quickly regained her composure. "Good morning, Mr. Harris. I hope I didn't catch you at a bad time."

"In case you haven't noticed, old woman, we are all in bad times. Now, what is it that you want?"

Barbara stammered slightly, "Well, I . . . I was hoping you'd join a few others and me this evening to read the Christmas Story, it being Christmas Eve." She held her gaze on the angry man. "Lord, please help this man," she prayed silently.

"I'll have nothing to do with that nonsense and if you know what's good for you, you'll forget about the whole thing, Christmas and all!"

"I cannot do that, Mr. Harris," Barbara said sharply. "I'm sorry to have troubled you."

"Be grateful I don't call the Regulators on you!" With that, he slammed the door in her face; the percussion of its force blew her gray curls back from her face. Her heart pounded from the violent interaction with her neighbor and with every heartbeat, she could feel her enthusiasm for the evening plans diminish. She stood for a moment gathering her wits and allowing her nerves to settle. Slowly she began to feel better. Realizing that she had been gone longer than she'd planned, she worried that Richard would awaken, and she wouldn't be there. She hurried back to her unit.

When she got back to their room, she at once went to her husband's bedside. There sadly, but mercifully, lay Richard's lifeless body. She wept softly; saddened that she wasn't there to spend his last minutes with him. But as she cried, she was encouraged knowing that by inviting friends to read His Word, she had done exactly what God had bid her to do. She was comforted that now; finally, Richard was with Jesus, free from pain and sorrow. Barbara filled her lungs with a cleansing breath and wiped her tears before she picked up the phone and dialed the front desk. "This is Barbara Beechum in unit 10J. My husband has just passed away."

"I'm terribly sorry for your loss, Mrs. Beechum." Stephanie said. She remembered the elderly couple and nearly all the residents from when she worked at the bank in Willow Creek. "I'll send someone up right away."

"Thank you, Stephanie." Barbara hung up and went to the bathroom to wash her face before the men showed up to take Richard's body. There would be no funeral, no gathering of family and friends, and no flowers or food brought for the grieving widow. She didn't know where the bodies were taken, but at this point she didn't care. She knew Richard's soul was already being welcomed into Heaven.

Three hard bangs on the door startled her from her grooming. Tucking a stray gray curl behind her ear and smoothing her dress, she went to the door. Before she opened it, she took another deep breath and lifted her chin; she would remain strong and not allow anyone to see her grief.

When she opened the door, two men in their customary black suits and heavy overcoats were waiting with a gurney. "Where's the body, ma'am?" The man in front asked, not bothering to look at her.

"Through here." Barbara directed them to the bedroom and stepped aside as they loaded her husband's body for transport. She could feel the eyes of the second man on her while she waited. It was as though he were waiting for her to break. She stood firm and prayed continually until they were out of her apartment.

As they wheeled the body down the corridor, the first man commented, "She's a tough old bird."

"Yeah, she's one of those Christians," the other replied.

"Are they going to be a problem?"

"They could be."

In her grief, Barbara was still able to smile at the last remark, "Yes, the Christians, will be a problem."

Matthew 5:4-5 "Blessed are those who mourn, for they will be comforted. Blessed are the meek, for they will inherit the earth."

CHAPTER 25

Joe and Tom led their horses off the trail, deep into the woods. "We'll make camp here for the night," Tom said. "I want us to have some decent shut eye before we go in."

Joe looked uneasily through the trees to the east and the fading horizon. Somewhere beyond lay The City. He shuddered, not knowing whether it was from the cold or the thought of what waited for them. "How long before we get there?"

Tom gazed at the heavy boughs above them as though they held the answer to Joe's question. He turned his attention to the boy, "I expect it'll take the better part of the day. According to the map Steve drew up, it's a straight trail from here, so we can run the horses. We'll definitely get there tomorrow. Are you up for it?"

"Yeah," Joe lifted the saddle and blanket off Cheyenne and with a grunt, dropped them near an outcropping of boulders.

Tom saw the concern etched in the young man's face and for a brief moment, he questioned whether he had made the right decision in allowing Joe to come with him. "Joe, there are a few things I want to go over with you before we go in tomorrow." He hesitated. "Some things that need to be discussed may not be pleasant, but nonetheless need to be said."

"I'm okay, Tom; really. I wouldn't have come if I didn't think I could do it. Besides --" Joe felt his ears grow warm despite the cold.

"You got something you want to tell me, Joe?" Tom asked as he carried the saddle and blanket from his own horse over to the boulders.

"Well, you see, there's this girl," Joe began. Tom smiled knowingly and kept walking. "Do you remember our last day of school? It was the day after you, Kyle and Morgan arrived."

"Yeah, I remember," Tom thought wistfully. "That was a good day."

Joe returned to his horse to remove the rest of his tack, "Her name is Charlotte, and she used to ride my bus. On the last day of school, she was really scared, and

I sort of promised her that I would come find her." Joe kicked at the rocks with his boot and then turned to Tom. "Do you think I was a fool to say that?"

"You'd have been a fool not to, Joe." Tom said matter-of-factly. "She was scared; right?"

"Yeah."

"And she likes you?" Tom pressed.

"Yeah."

"You, her?" Tom smiled.

Joe grinned sheepishly. "Yeah."

"Well, then you have every good reason to go find this lady. She must be special for you to make this trip."

"Kinda like the trip you made to come find us. Isn't it, Tom?"

Tom sighed heavily, thinking of the people they left behind -- one person in particular. "Yes, I guess you're right." He looked evenly at Joe. "You were right to say what you did. You gave her hope, Joe, and that is one of the greatest gifts anyone can give."

Joe smiled at Tom but still appeared uncertain. "Thanks, Tom. I'll tend to the horses."

"Anytime, Joe. I'll get some firewood." Tom disappeared into the woods and realized the gratitude he felt at that moment. Was it because he was given a chance to have a sincere heart to heart talk with the son of the man he had admired and loved for years? He expected so.

When Joe had finished feeding and watering the horses, he checked their hooves, gave them a good rubdown, then went to the campsite where Tom had already started the cookfire and put on a pot of coffee. Joe waited for him. Leaning forward, he dug a heavy stick deep into the orange, glowing embers and stirred them up. He watched in quiet reflection as the sparks floated up, scattering in all directions and then melting into the cold blackness of the night sky. He thought about his mom and his little brother and wondered what they were doing at that moment. He and Tom had been travelling this bitterly cold trail for two days and even though he knew they were walking into certain danger Joe was anxious to get to The City.

Holding two tin mugs in his hand, Tom came and knelt next to him. He knew Joe was missing his family and his heart hurt for him. "Coffee about ready?"

Joe broke from his thoughts, "Sure smells like it," and accepted one of the mugs. He grasped the hot coffee pot handle with a rag and poured first for Tom, then for himself.

"Thanks, Joe."

Joe nodded and put the coffee pot back on a rock next to the fire pit. He enjoyed Tom's company and was as comfortable with him as he was with his own dad, not many words, but mutual respect and genuine love. He was glad he came on the trip if only because he was able to spend some one-on-one time with the man who knew his father best in the war.

Tom settled back against a large rock and waited for Joe to get comfortable. "Joe, I don't know what's going to happen once we get in there, but we need to be prepared. We'll most likely get separated."

Lucky came to Joe and curled up in his lap. The pup had grown considerably since Joe's dad had found him in Iraq. Now the dog weighed in at about fifty pounds, but still thought he was a lapdog. "Do you think we will be able to keep in touch?" Joe asked, trying to keep the anxiety out of his voice and Lucky out of his coffee.

"I don't know," Tom said. "But for now, I would say our main goal will be to find as many folks from town as we can. If we can communicate with them first, we should be able to gather enough information to figure out our next step."

Joe rubbed Lucky behind the ears as he contemplated his next question. "I was thinking about trying to work at the place where they keep the animals. I know Charlotte had a dog that was going to be kept there. If the dog is still there, she will be coming to see it. What do you think?"

"I think that's a great idea, Joe," Tom said. "Tell you what, then. Just to help you get there, you take Lucky in. He'll be your dog."

Joe looked up suddenly, "I couldn't, Tom. He's your pup!"

Tom's voice was firm, but not unkind. "He's our pup, Joe. He really belongs to all of us; and if having him with you will increase your chances of getting to where you need to be, then you must take him. It just makes sense, Joe. Don't you think?"

"Yeah, you're right," Joe agreed. "Have you thought about what job you might be doing?"

"As a matter of fact, I have." Tom smiled and reached for the coffee pot. He held it out to Joe to fill his cup then filled his own. "I'm thinking that security would be a good choice. With my being a former sniper, I figure they might be able to fit me in somewhere."

"And with that you will have access to weapons," Joe added.

"Exactly!" Tom smiled ruefully and raised his coffee mug.

Joe smiled back and raised his cup in return.

"There's one more thing, Joe. If you don't see me, say within a month, consider that they've taken me somewhere else, and make plans to go to your family in Berkley Springs. I'll find you all one way or another; okay?"

"No way," Joe argued. "I'm not leaving you behind."

"Joe, we don't know what we are walking into. If it becomes too dangerous for you, you must think of your family." Tom countered. "Believe me when I say, I will find you no matter what happens."

Joe stared into his coffee mug. He didn't like the part about leaving Tom behind. The thought of losing him, too, was more than he wanted to think about. He prayed that it wouldn't turn out that way but knew that it was a real possibility.

"Now for the weapons," Tom said, wanting to turn the conversation around. "They will no doubt search us and the horses before we go in, so we should leave all but one of our guns here. They'll get suspicious if they search us and don't find any firearms. I figure we can stow our weapons in this pile of rocks. When we leave The City, we can come back here and retrieve them."

"It's a good idea, Tom, but I can't shake these jitters about going in."

"That's normal for any soldier to feel a little anxious before going on a dangerous assignment, but just so you know, it's not your nerves that have you hyped up, Joe. It's adrenaline."

Joe appreciated the encouragement from his friend. "Thanks, Tom."

Tom clapped Joe on the shoulder. "Enough about this tonight; how about reading the Christmas Story while we eat?"

Joe relaxed some and smiled as he got up to begin making supper while Tom dug out Joe's tattered Bible from his saddlebag and went back to sit by the fire. Abruptly Joe paused with his food preparations.

"Tom?"

Tom looked up from Joe's Bible, "Yeah?"

"What do you think Mom and the rest of them are doing right now?" Joe asked.

The expression in Tom's eyes grew soft as he gazed sadly at Joe. He missed them, too. "I expect they're thinking about us, like we're thinking about them."

The two ate a meager supper of boiled potatoes and dried venison. Afterwards Tom read until he realized that Joe had drifted off to sleep. Quietly he stoked the fire and tucked Joe's sleeping bag tightly around him. He motioned to Lucky and together they crawled deep into his own sleeping bag. He thought again about those they had left behind and prayed that they were safe.

Hebrews 13:6 "So we say with confidence, 'The Lord is my helper; I will not be afraid. What can man do to me?'"

CHAPTER 26

Barbara Beechum closed the door after the last of her guests left, pleased with the success of her first Bible study group. They had fellowshipped and shared the sparse refreshments that everyone had brought and agreed to meet the following week. Although all had suggested that they postpone the reading because of Richard's passing, Barbara had insisted albeit tearfully, "Richard is with Jesus on His birthday. We have good reason to celebrate."

The following morning, she awoke feeling refreshed and hopeful. Taken by surprise at these unexpected, but welcome emotions after the loss of her husband, she knelt down and prayed with a grateful heart. She thanked God for her Christian friends, for keeping her strong, and for taking her husband to live with Jesus. A hard rap on the front door startled her, but she wasn't through with her prayers yet. The rude intruder would have to wait. When she was finished, she rose slowly from her painful knees. BANG! BANG! Two more hard knocks at her door. "I'm coming," she called, without bothering to hide the irritation in her voice. When she opened the door and found Nick Garrison, the head of the Regulators on her doorstep, her heart drummed fiercely.

He stood tall before her, a menacing smile exposing his perfectly straight, white teeth like a shark grinning at his prey before the attack. Nick was a man thick in mind and body, between forty and forty-five years old. His black hair, cut short around his ears and above his starched, white collar, was interspersed with silver at his temples. His strong features, muscular build and classic salt and pepper hair would have been attractive on any other man, but Garrison's cruel ways destroyed anything appealing about him. His dark eyes stabbed at her as he spoke, "Good morning, Mrs. Beechum. I hope I didn't wake you."

"No, you did not, Mr. Garrison; what can I do for you?"

He took a presumptuous step forward, "May I come in?" He smiled.

Barbara held her ground, bracing the door against her shoulder, "Sir, I am grieving the loss of my husband; I'd rather you didn't." She was stunned by his inappropriate request but considered the source and let it go.

Garrison glared at her. "Of course." He placed the palms of his hands together and bowed his head in mock apology. "I'm terribly sorry for your loss, ma'am. I really just came to check on you because, you see, our security cameras showed that yesterday morning you went to several units in your building and angered Mr. Harris. Then, later on, at approximately six p.m., several residents showed up at your unit and remained there until seven forty-five." He spoke softly, almost whispering. Anyone who heard him but did not see him would think that he was being sincere. However, as he spoke, Barbara studied his eyes and saw no evidence of caring there, just malicious brutality. "We just want to ensure that everything and everyone is all right."

"Everything and everyone is as well as can be expected, Mr. Garrison, given the circumstances. I was merely inviting people over for a visit. It was, after all, Christmas Eve." Barbara paused, expecting him to comment, but when he didn't, she continued, "Mr. Harris did not appreciate the intrusion or the season and told me to leave, so I apologized to him, and I left." Barbara's defenses were rising along with her heart rate. She was grateful that he at least respected her wishes and stood in the hallway; otherwise, he would have seen her trembling.

"Why, Mrs. Beechum, I'm surprised that you were able to entertain after losing your husband so suddenly," he said in exaggerated disbelief. Every expression that Nick Garrison conveyed was exaggerated and mocked.

"My husband has been on his deathbed for weeks, sir. I can assure you, it was not sudden. My friends, who were coming over anyway, came instead to comfort me in my grief. I don't believe that is against your rules, is it?"

Garrison could tell the old woman was beginning to lose her temper, and it pleased him. "Of course not, ma'am. All we ask is that you do not offend the other residents. We want everyone to get along now; don't we?"

Barbara's blood pressure peaked. Her husband used to say that she was 'fixin' for a fight' when she got this angry. "Mr. Garrison, as long as what I'm doing behind my door doesn't break God's law, I don't care whether the other residents are offended or not." She glared at him angrily.

Garrison looked away, down the long corridor, and then turned back to her, his smiling eyes now like hardened granite. He moved in closer and spoke through clenched teeth, "Mrs. Beechum, I am telling you this for your own good. Be careful and watch your step." His eyes continued to drill into hers as he nodded at the newly installed video camera pointing directly at her door. "You are being watched. Good day, Mrs. Beechum." He turned and marched loudly down the hallway and through the heavy metal door at the end, letting it slam behind him.

Barbara watched him storm off before turning her attention to the new camera perched across the hall from her door. She stared at it for a moment, tempted to make an obscene gesture at it, but thought better of it and closed her door. The exchange she had with Garrison agitated her, but encouraged her, too. She knew this whole situation would not end well for many of them, but she was confident that victory would be theirs. "Lord, please give us strength to move forward with whatever you have in mind for us."

Joe awoke to the smell of strong coffee and light snowflakes on his face. He peered over his sleeping bag and saw Tom bending over the fire, pouring coffee for himself. "Mornin,' Tom."

Tom turned and smiled broadly at him. "Mornin'." Tom picked up the other tin cup, poured coffee for Joe, and set it on a rock by the fire.

"How long have you been up?" Joe asked, crawling out of the bag and rushing to get his boots and drover on.

"Oh, 'bout a half hour or so," Tom said. "I'm afraid coffee is all we've got for breakfast."

"That sounds fine to me. Be right back." Joe grabbed his canteen and hurried into the woods to answer nature's call and brush his teeth. When he returned, he saw that Tom had all the weapons laid out.

"Hey, Joe, come take a look. What do you think we should take in?" Tom asked.

Joe picked up his cup of coffee and joined Tom. He studied the cache of weapons spread out before him and thought for a moment; two large hunting knives, Tom's Mossberg 500 12-gauge, a Winchester 30.06 rifle and a Smith and Wesson .357 Magnum handgun. All were fine weapons as far as he was concerned, but they had to consider that whatever they brought in would be confiscated. "Where are the night vision goggles and the Glock?"

"I gave them to Kyle," Tom said. "I figured that since your Uncle Steve only had a hunting rifle and a shotgun, they needed them more than we did."

Joe nodded in agreement. "Good call. Well, I'd say leave the knives, the hand-gun and the shotgun and bring in the rifle. Hopefully, we'll get it back."

"I was thinking the same thing," Tom grinned. "Okay then, it's settled. We'll put these in the duffle bag and stash them in the rocks. Then whenever you're ready, we'll make for The City."

Joe hesitated then went to his saddlebag. He dug deep until he found what he needed. Carefully he pulled out the tattered, American flag he'd brought from home. It had been a brand-new flag when his dad raised it the day he left for his last deployment and Sandy had flown it every day since. The day they all left the ranch, they had gathered around the flagpole and as Tom lowered Old Glory, a pang of sadness filled Joe. He had made a silent promise at that moment to himself and his family and friends that the flag would fly again when they returned. Joe brushed away the painful memory and carried the flag to Tom. "Here, put this in with the weapons. I'm afraid of what might happen to her inside."

Tom carefully and reverently took it from Joe and glanced back at the boy just in time to see him wipe a tear from his cheek. "Joe, are you sure you want to leave her behind?"

"I'm sure. She'll protect the weapons and one day she'll fly high and proud again."

"As long as you carry the flag in your heart she isn't going anywhere, son." Tom gripped Joe's shoulder and locked eyes with him, "God will guide us on this mission, Joe, and with His good graces we'll succeed."

Joe nodded. "I understand, Tom. I'll go get the horses ready."

The firearms, ammunition, and knives, all swaddled in the American flag, were put in the duffle bag, and pushed deep into a crevice in the rocks. When he was sure the bag was out of sight, Tom piled more heavy rocks on top of the opening and prayed it would stay safe and dry until needed.

Joe brought the horses around as Tom was putting out the fire with the last of the coffee. "Ready?"

"Just about." Tom put the coffee pot into his saddlebag, "You got the rifle?"

"It's in your scabbard." Joe said, passing the reins to his friend.

Pilgrim tossed his head and danced away as Tom slipped his boot into the stirrup, forcing him to hop on one foot after the spirited horse with his other foot still in the stirrup. "They can sense that something's up, can't they?" Tom asked, finally settled into the saddle, his warm breath coming out in clouds of white vapor.

"Yeah. I really hope I can get into the animal shelter. I dread the thought of someone else handling our horses and Lucky."

"Let's pray before we leave, Joe." Tom and Joe took off their hats and bowed their heads. The snow fell heavier now, and it quickly covered their heads with a pure white cap. Tom paused and sighed heavily before he began, "Father God, Creator of all things, thank you for bringing us this far in safety. We pray that You will continue to watch over us on our journey into The City. Help us to be a beacon of Your light to the people and please, Lord, put us in the places that will help us do Your Will. We also humbly ask that you watch over Sandy, Ben, Steve, Tanya, Kyle, and Morgan on their journey as well. Thank you, Father, for Your Son, our Savior, Jesus Christ. It's in His name that we pray. Amen"

They took the trail for the better part of the day until they finally reached the tree line where the woods ended, and an open field began. Just beyond the field they could see the road that led into The City. Joe pulled back on his reins, sat for a moment, and then looked over at Tom.

Tom looked at him without speaking.

"Merry Christmas, Tom," Joe said quietly.

A rush of emotions swept over them as they thought about their loved ones and this special day. Tom reached his hand over to Joe and they shook hands, "Merry Christmas, Joe."

They crossed the field without incident, but the instant they turned their horses onto the road, Tom and Joe braced themselves as two four wheelers left the main gate of The City and sped towards them, plumes of blue smoke billowing from behind. "Okay, Joe, here we go. You take care of yourself and God speed."

"I will, Tom. You, too."

Psalm 37:28 "For the Lord loves the just and will not forsake his faithful ones."

CHAPTER 27

THE FOUR WHEELERS SKIDDED to a halt in front of the horses, causing them to rear up. Joe spoke gently to them, calming them. Between the two horses, Lucky crouched with his hackles up and snarling. "Lucky! Down!" Joe ordered. Still growling deep in his chest, the dog reluctantly took a step back and sat down, the fur on his back still ridged as he watched the men approach. The older man had his M16 leveled on Tom; while the younger one kept his gun aimed at Lucky.

"Is that dog going to mind or are we going to have to shoot him?" The man with the M16 asked. He had about thirty years on the boy with him and managed himself and his rifle with confidence. The thing that Tom noticed first was the stare. His steely gray eyes squinted against the setting sun as he glared hard at the travelers, daring them to move. The kid next to him stood anxiously waiting for orders from his superior. It was obvious that the boy was nervous with his weapon, and looked as if he might shoot the first thing that moved.

Joe sized up the two strangers and cast a quick sideways glance at Tom who was apparently doing the same. "He does as he's told."

"Come on down from those horses and keep your hands where we can see them," the older man ordered. "Larry, go check 'em and, for cryin' out loud, don't screw this one up."

"Sure thing, boss." The boy, not sure at first what to do with his rifle, looked at the man for a hint, but the only thing the man offered was a nasty glare. The kid finally used the sling and moved it to his back as he approached them. "You got any weapons?"

"Just the rifle in the scabbard," Tom said, motioning with his thumb toward his horse.

The kid went to Pilgrim, slipped the Winchester out of its leather sheath, and tossed it to the senior man, who caught it without breaking his stare on Joe and Tom. He then ran both his hands over Tom, checking his pockets, his back, and around his ankles. Lucky continued his low growl and took a step toward Larry until Joe repeated his command.

Satisfied that Tom wasn't carrying any weapons, the kid went to Joe and repeated the frisking. "They're clean, Red."

The older man nodded and checked the confiscated rifle. "Is this all you've got?"

"Yep," Tom answered.

"You're travelin' pretty light for the uncertain times we're livin' in boys."

"All I need is one shot." Tom said.

"What are you, military?" Red questioned.

"U.S. Army Sniper."

"Humph. What about you, kid? You're pretty good with that dog. How are you with horses and livestock?"

"I used to live on a ranch. I can do all right." Joe answered.

"Well, looks like we may have a job for both of you, but you gotta answer a couple of questions first. Where are you going and where did you come from?" He held his aim on Tom and waited for an answer to his questions. "C'mon soldier, we ain't got all day."

Tom nodded toward Joe. "I met the kid and his dog when I was passing through that town about fifty miles west of here. He had nowhere else to go so I invited him along. We're just passing through, but if you have work, some food, and a hot shower we'd be much obliged. Times being as they are, there isn't much work in these parts."

Red threw his head back and roared with laughter. "Son, there ain't much work anywhere unless you join up with us. Kid, I expect you're just what's left of that poor little town back there. You have any ID?"

"In the saddle bags," Tom said.

"Well go on and get 'em. Daylights fadin,' and I haven't had my supper yet." After Tom handed over his military ID and Joe his driver's license, the men turned and went to their four-wheelers and waited for Tom and Joe to mount up then followed them to the heavily guarded front gates of The City. The wall surrounding The City was much bigger than it had appeared from a distance, and Tom realized that they would have to devise another way out. When they reached the checkpoint, two men, also armed with M16s, were waiting for them. They wore the same dark green jumpsuits with a red and gold emblem on the left breast pockets as the kid did.

"Dismount from your horses, please, and place your hands against the wall," the first man ordered. The second man stood by and eyed them suspiciously, his finger resting lightly on the trigger of his rifle. Tom and Joe did as instructed and leaned forward, placing their hands against the wall, and spreading their feet. A third man emerged from the small security office and frisked them thoroughly. Joe thought to himself, Larry could learn a lot from this guy. While they were being checked out, a kid Joe's age came from behind the security station with a dogcatcher's noose and two lead ropes. He wore a brown jumpsuit with the same emblem, "What's the dog's name?" he asked Tom.

Still leaning with his hands against the brick wall Tom nodded toward Joe, "It's his dog."

The kid looked at Joe and a glint of familiarity shadowed his eyes, but just as quickly it was gone. "Name?" he asked, impatiently.

"Lucky," Joe answered. He recognized Jason O'Malley from school but was careful not to acknowledge him.

"What about the horses?" Jason asked.

"The big red one is Cheyenne, and the bay is Pilgrim."

The kid nodded his thanks and slipped the noose easily over Lucky's head. Tom's and Joe's hearts broke as Lucky glanced forlornly at them before he was led away with the horses.

"Where are you taking them?" Joe asked.

"Don't worry, you'll see them soon enough," the older man who brought them in said. While the men were searching Joe and Tom, he had gone into the security office with their identification cards and appeared to be making several phone calls. When he came back out, he held a clipboard and had a pencil tucked behind his right ear. "You guys 'bout done playin' patty cake with these fellers? The boss wants to see them."

"They're clean; they can go." The man who frisked them went back into the security office while the two guards returned to their post.

"Gentlemen, if you will follow me, we'll take care of a little business, and you can get that hot shower you were asking about."

Exhausted, Tom and Joe followed the man down a sidewalk, past shuttered up storefronts. The night was growing colder, and the snow continued to fall. With the prospect that they might soon have a hot shower, warm bed, and hot food, their bodies cried out for them. After a brisk half-hour walk, they finally arrived at what was once a Hyatt Hotel. Two gunmen pulled open the heavy glass doors for them. As they passed through, the man muttered a greeting to the 'doormen' but kept walking.

"Can I ask a question?" Joe said.

"Make it quick kid. We're almost there and you'd do well not to speak in the elevator." He warned.

"Who's the boss?" Joe asked.

The man muttered something else inaudible, and then said, "You'll find out soon enough, kid."

"Yes, sir." Joe mumbled.

When they arrived at a bank of mirrored elevators, their guide pressed the 'up' button and stepped aside. Just before the elevator arrived, he looked squarely at Tom. "You've been assigned to where you can do some good."

Tom wasn't sure he heard him correctly, but the man's wink just before the elevator doors slid open told him they would have an ally on the inside. He said a silent prayer of thanksgiving and stepped into the elevator. Joe followed and their friend entered last.

Inside the mirrored cube, two grizzled men stared back at Tom and Joe. Tom knew that his hair had grown out considerably while at the ranch, but he wasn't expecting to see his hair falling down below his ears. His beard, too, was thick and shaggy. Joe examined himself as well and unconsciously pushed his hair behind his ears and rubbed his scruffy beard. He had not imagined it would grow out this much.

The man with them watched them, his eyes sparkling with amusement, "Don't worry, kid. The boss ain't going to care what you look like."

Joe hadn't realized that he was being watched and quickly thrust his hands deep into his drover pockets.

The elevator rose silently until it finally shuddered to a stop at the top floor. "Right this way, gentlemen." They followed him down the carpeted hallway to a set of double doors. The man looked one last time at Joe and Tom then knocked sharply on the heavy door.

Suddenly the doors swung wide and a man with a sinister grin greeted them. He wore the same black suit with a red carnation in the lapel as he did when Joe saw him the first time. He was one of the men from the school. As the man held the door, his suit jacket opened just enough for Tom and Joe to see a .45 semi-automatic pistol in his shoulder holster. The man who brought them there nodded to him, "Good evening, Mr. Smith."

"Good evening, Mr. Dalton. What have we here?" Smith glared at Joe. He also remembered him from Willow Creek.

"We found them out on the road. I've already spoken with the boss."

A loud voice called from a room in the back. "Mr. Smith, please stand aside and allow our guests to enter."

"Come right in, gentlemen," Smith bowed low and swept his hand dramatically to the side as the men passed in front of him. His laugh was low and nasty as Joe walked by.

The voice was frighteningly familiar to Joe as they walked toward the back office. Already certain that it was Garrison, Joe peered through the darkened room. The image that sat behind the desk validated his fears.

"Good evening, gentlemen. My name is Nick Garrison. Welcome to my City! Why, Joe Parker, I was wondering when you would grace us with your presence. How's the family?"

"I don't know, Mr. Garrison," Joe said quietly. Avoiding the eyes of the evil man, the boy stared at the pattern of heavy red and gold lines that swirled in hapless circles within the deep brown carpet.

"What do you mean, son? They skip out on you, or did you skip out on them?"

"I left them. I got tired of the farm and having to do without all the time," Joe said.

It killed Joe to say such things and Tom knew it. "I found the kid in the town west of here."

"Willow Creek." Garrison informed him.

"That's right," Tom continued. "He and the dog were just wandering around, not knowing where to go. I convinced him that we should come here and try to start over with your help. I didn't see anyone else nearby, so I figured he was an orphan."

"Well, that was a very wise decision on your part, Mr. Connelly, and I'm glad our young Mr. Parker had the good sense to come with you. Mr. Dalton tells me that you are a soldier."

"Yes, sir," Tom said.

"I beg your pardon?" Garrison asked, raising his eyebrows.

"Yes, sir, Mr. Garrison," Tom said louder.

"Of course you were a soldier, Mr. Connelly, but thanks to our Supreme Leader, we are not engaged in war anymore, are we? The United States is on its way to living in peaceful surrender forever. So, tell me, former soldier, are you a fair shot?"

"Yes sir. I am a sniper."

"Is it true that snipers only need one shot?" Garrison inquired.

"Yes sir," Tom said, growing tired of this question-and-answer game.

"And how are you under pressure?" Garrison continued. He could tell Tom was getting irritated, but he didn't care. "You seem to be a very cool-headed individual."

"I am. I had to be in my line of work, sir."

"Impressive." Nick Garrison turned his attention back to Joe. "And you, Mr. Parker, living on the ranch as you did, I assume you worked with livestock?"

"My dad taught me a lot."

"Did he teach you how to shoot?"

"Yes sir. If you live on a ranch, you have to know how to shoot."

"And why is that?" Garrison asked.

"Predators, sir." Joe explained. "From time to time we'd get a mountain lion or black bear coming around. We needed to protect our livestock."

"Of course!" Garrison threw his hands up at the revelation and rose from behind his desk. He strode toward Joe with his hand out. "We're glad to have you aboard, Mr. Parker. I believe a job in our stables would best suit you. What do you say to that?"

Unable to hide his joy, Joe's face split into a wide grin. "I'd like that a lot, Mr. Garrison." Joe did not want to take the man's hand, but knew he had to play the game now that he was inside. He grasped it firmly and shook. "Thank you, Mr. Garrison."

"You're welcome, son." Garrison turned to face Tom. "Mr. Connelly, we could sure use your sharp eye and cool head in our security division. Are you up to the job?"

"Yes sir." Tom said, equally happy.

The meeting with Garrison was brief, but still too long for Joe. He was glad that Garrison assigned him to the shelter, but being in the presence of these evil men made his skin crawl. He and Tom followed Mr. Dalton in silence out to the sidewalk now covered in a blanket of snow. As they passed through the front doors, the man again mumbled something to the armed guards; they nodded and watched the three men walk to a golf cart parked on the corner.

"We need to make a couple of stops before I take you to your quarters," he explained as he slid in behind the wheel. "Hop in." He checked his rearview mirror before he pulled the cart out onto the deserted street.

"Don't talk, just listen. There's a lot to say and a short time to say it. My name is Chuck Dalton, but you can call me 'Red' on account of I used to have red hair before it turned gray and fell out." Red laughed huskily and went on, "I am chief of security in this City. Most of the people you'll be working with are followers. Trust no one. I'll be at the security gate most of the time, but as far as you and I are concerned, we are all followers like the rest. Tom, I'll look after Joe as best I can."

"Red, how did you know we could be trusted?" Tom asked.

"I've come to realize that followers have a particular blank, 'deer in the head-light' look about them and," Red paused for a moment then glanced at Joe in the rearview mirror. "I thought I recognized Joe, and then when I checked his identification, I knew."

Joe leaned forward in his seat, alarmed. "Knew what? How do you know me?"

"Lean back, son, there's cameras all over the place. I actually knew your father and in case no one's ever told you, you're his spittin' image."

"H-how --?" Joe stammered.

"We used to go to the same fishin' hole. Oh, it was long before he ever met your ma, but I remember when he met her. I knew that my fishin' buddy was gone for good." Red laughed despite the bittersweet memory. "We never saw each other outside of that fishin' hole, but I remember before he went off to boot camp, he came one last time and told me of his plans. I served in the Army myself, you know, so I was right proud of him and told him. He was about fifteen years younger than me."

Red looked thoughtfully at Joe. "He was a good kid. I'd still see him in town from time to time when he was home from the war, and from what I'd heard over the years, he turned out to be a good soldier. I was sorry to hear that he was killed." Red shot another glance at Joe before he turned his attention back to the road. "Gettin' back to trust, you can trust me, but everyone else is a follower until I give the all clear. Understood?"

"Yes, sir," Joe said.

Red reached into his coat pocket, pulled out a plastic card, and checked it before he handed it to Tom. "This will be your identity from here on out. It has everything about you on it, your name, and location here in The City, your occupation, and a pre-determined number of credits for the month. You use the credits to buy your food and whatever else they think you need." Red pulled another card out of his pocket and handed it to Joe. "This one's for you. Keep it on you at all times." Joe took the card and held it in his grimy hands.

As they drove, Tom surveyed the empty street and the abandoned buildings that surrounded them. Snowflakes blew softly into his face. "Where are we going?" He asked.

"I'll take you to the Market first and then I want to show you something." They rode in silence until Red pulled up in front of a storefront with black iron bars stretched across the dirty plate glass. Several large posters covered the windows making it difficult to see inside. The posters depicted happy children gulping down glasses of a beverage with the words 'the healthy alternative to soft drinks' emblazoned across the tops of their heads. Another poster showed smiling children shoveling 'the better alternative to junk food' into their open mouths.

The men climbed out of the golf cart and stood in front of the store. Joe looked at the window coverings and grumbled, "From the looks of those posters, I doubt they'll have any soda pop in there will they, Red?"

"I'm afraid not, kiddo. Fruit juice, milk, and water, those are about the only choices you'll find. No, wait! I think I remember seeing some chocolate milk in there and some sports drinks."

Joe nodded and pulled on the front door to go in, but he was met with resistance. He looked at Tom and Red. "Are they closed?"

"Where's your card?" Red took the card from Joe and swiped it through a magnetic reader on the doorframe. "This card gets you into the store, into your unit, and gives you admittance into your place of work. It also serves as a timecard. Like I said, don't lose it. You do and you're up the creek with no paddle." Red paused before opening the door. "Just get what you'll need for tonight and tomorrow morning. You'll have time after work tomorrow to come back. Word of caution though, watch what you buy. The pricing is a little tricky." He winked and held the door open for them.

When they entered the store, a skinny clerk was waiting for them with two baskets. "Good evening, gentlemen, Mr. Dalton," he said in a high pitched, whiny voice. "The store will be closing in ten minutes. If you need any assistance, please don't hesitate to ask." He peered out through thick glasses, but still squinted as he handed the baskets to Tom and Joe. His smile revealed yellowed teeth and swollen gums.

"Evidently oral hygiene is not on his list of priorities." Tom thought to himself.

"We've got it, Ernie," Red said. "These boys came in this afternoon and just met with the boss. They only need to pick up a few things, then they'll be back tomorrow for the rest."

"Ah, very good." The clerk nodded and followed them, hunched over and wringing his bony hands as he went. "So, you saw the big boss, hunh? Isn't he the most wonderful man you've ever met?"

Tom caught Joe by the arm just as he was reeling around in response to the clerk's comment. When Joe looked up at him, Tom shook his head just enough for Joe to understand.

Because Ernie's focus was set on his shuffling feet and the dirty floor, he missed the interaction between Tom and Joe. Red did not, "Ernie, tell you what, why don't you go stand by the door in case anyone else comes in. I'll show these boys around and we'll be out of your hair before closing time."

"Very good idea, Mr. Dalton," Ernie bowed slightly to them and hurried to the front of the store.

"He's harmless, I think," Red whispered, "but I'd still keep an eye on him. He believes Garrison walks on water and that alone is cause for me to despise the little creep. Come on, let's get you guys set up."

Joe suddenly remembered the comment Red had made when they first met him, "Red, what about your supper?"

Red threw his head back and laughed. "Son, my supper isn't going anywhere. It's ready when I pull it out of the microwave. But thanks for your concern." He knew he was going to care too much for this kid, and it bothered him. In his experience, it was best not to get too attached to anyone.

While searching the shelves, Tom noticed some of his old favorites were not available, like salt and vinegar potato chips or spicy tortilla chips. He shook his head and settled for what was offered. He understood now what Red had said about the store having whatever 'they' thought he needed. He was grateful for the food, nonetheless. When they finished, they proceeded to the checkout. As Tom laid his items on the conveyor belt for Ernie to check out, the gnawing in his belly intensified, knowing that he would eat soon. Tom eyed Ernie carefully and handed over his identification card. He understood what Red had said about the 'followers' having that particular look about them. Nevertheless, Tom's instincts told him to watch this guy and watch him he would.

Ernie began to tremble and avoided Tom's penetrating stare by focusing on the grocery items, "Did you find everything all right, Mr. Connelly?"

"Yes, I did. Thank you, Ernie." Tom's eyes drilled into him.

"You're welcome, Mr. Connelly. Here is your card." Ernie continued to keep his eyes averted and handed Tom his identification card. "I look forward to seeing you tomorrow." Ernie lied. He did not ever want to encounter this man again. His watchful stare made him nervous.

Never taking his eyes off him, Tom took the card from Ernie's sweaty hand and slipped it into his wallet. "See you tomorrow, Ernie." Tom smiled, enjoying the effect he was having on the anxious clerk.

Joe bit his tongue trying to control the smile that began to creep across his face as he loaded his items to check out, but when he glanced at Red standing behind him, he saw that Red was making no effort to hide his amusement.

"Your card, please?" Ernie asked sharply, looking squarely at Joe.

Joe jumped and drew his attention away from Red when Ernie spoke, "Oh yeah, sure." Joe dug into his drover pocket and pulled out the card "Here you go."

Ernie snatched it from him, and Joe could only assume that Ernie had seen him smiling while Tom was tormenting him. Ernie continued ringing up Joe's items and handed the card back to Joe without looking at him. "Will there be anything else tonight, Mr. Dalton?"

"No, I think we're good for now." Red said still grinning from the encounter between Tom and Ernie. "But like I said, you'll probably see these fellas tomorrow."

"Good night then, gentlemen." Ernie walked them to the door and locked it behind them.

"Not a word until we get on the road," Red said before anyone could speak. He pulled the golf cart out onto the street and then burst into laughter. He turned to Tom. "Man, I thought I made that guy jumpy. What is it about you, soldier?"

Tom chuckled, "Don't know. He's a nervous little fella though, isn't he?"

"I don't think he liked me much," Joe said.

"Son don't worry 'bout that. He only treated you that way because you were the youngest and he figured he could get away with it. Just be careful, Joe. Remember there are cameras everywhere. Don't be afraid to push a little, just know your limit. That goes for you too, Tom. It's one thing to intimidate some of these people, but some may be part of the boss's little collection of minions. I honestly don't trust this one and wouldn't be surprised if he was one of 'em."

"We'll be careful." Tom turned and looked back at Joe and smiled.

Joe returned the smile, grateful that he would have Tom close enough and Red even closer. He almost felt ashamed of the excitement that was coming over him but remembered what Tom had said about adrenaline and chalked it up to that. He settled back into his seat and surveyed the surrounding buildings. It was barely past eight o'clock when he realized that not a single light was on in any of the buildings. "Red, is there a curfew?"

"You noticed." Red said, looking into the rearview mirror. "Yes, Joe, there is. Eight o'clock sharp. That may be what they start you doing, Tom. You will make your rounds in each building making sure everyone is in for the night and lights are out. At least, that's where I was put when I first got here. Things may have changed."

"How long have you been here, Red?" Joe asked.

"For too long. Here we are. This is what I wanted to show you." Red got out from behind the wheel of the golf cart and motioned for Joe and Tom to follow him. "There are cameras on every corner and believe me when I say they are watching. Do you remember seeing all those CCTV monitors behind Garrison's desk?"

Tom and Joe nodded and noted the cameras all around them.

"Tom, your quarters are right here," Red stopped in front of a black ten-story building. "But I also wanted you to take a look at something else." Red nodded toward a single-story building with glass block windows, "See down there, that square concrete building surrounded by the chain link fence and razor wire?"

Tom looked in the direction that Red was pointing, "Yeah, what building is that?"

"In that big concrete box is the whole security system for this entire city, from the identification cards to the monitors for every street, building, and even individual units of a few problem residents. They keep the munitions locked in there too. There are two levels in the building, with munitions on the basement level and all monitoring systems and administrative offices on the ground level. I don't know when, or if you'll have access, but I just wanted you to know it was there. The building just behind it is the power substation. Disable that and the whole city is paralyzed if you get my drift."

"I appreciate that, Red." Tom nodded toward a tall red brick building with thick, black smoke billowing from a fifty-foot smokestack. "What's that over there?"

"You can thank your lucky stars that we're up wind from it." Red said. "That, my friend, is where they take the dead and anything else that needs disposal. There is no such thing as funerals here. They take the bodies and cremate them. What they do with the ashes is anyone's guess. I know they don't return them to the family. The bottom floor of the building is where they bring in the trash and bodies to be burned, and the top floors are reserved for residents who have made the mistake of ticking off Garrison. I've heard it's the closest thing to Hell that you can get this side of eternity."

A shiver raced up and down Joe's spine. He prayed he would never have to experience the smokestack.

Red looked casually around then slapped Tom on his shoulder, "Oh, one more thing," He pointed to the top of Tom's building as though he were going to say something about it, but what he said had nothing to do with the building. "There is a way to communicate with the outside world. Where are your people?"

"Berkley Springs, West Virginia." Tom said excitedly.

"Fine, I'll get the word out that you are safe. Hopefully, someone there will get the message."

"Is it safe though, Red?" Tom said. His eyes wide with surprise at the unexpected news.

"Tom, first of all, don't look so shocked. Remember we are all being watched. And no, it's not completely safe, but we do what we can." Tom looked toward the top of the building, "Sorry, Red. I just didn't see that coming."

"No problem. Well, we'd better get going. Do you want to stay, Tom, or ride along with Joe? I don't mind bringing you back."

"That's all right, Red. I'll stay. It's late and I'm sure you want to get back to your unit too. Joe, I'll be in touch; okay." Tom gave a quick salute to the young man.

"Okay, Tom. I'll see you." Joe waved goodbye to his friend and climbed into the front seat of the golf cart. As Red pulled away from the curb, Joe looked back at the building where Tom would be. The black concrete walls and barred windows gave it a foreboding, evil appearance. Joe shuddered at the thought of what would happen if a fire ever broke out in the building. The thought frightened him as much as the smokestack and he quickly brushed the disturbing thought aside and continued his survey of the building.

There were no doormen with guns guarding this building, just barred, glass double doors marking the entrance. Joe watched Tom as he swiped his card, entered the building, and disappeared into the darkness.

"It's exactly ten blocks from here to the shelter, Joe." Red said. "It's not a far walk and as soon as I find out his hours, I'll let you know." Red clapped Joe on the shoulder, "You okay, son?"

"Yeah, I guess everything is just starting to catch up with me. I'll be all right." Joe looked at Red and gave him a tired smile. "I'm real glad that we'll have a friend on the inside."

"Me too, son. Just remember what I said, okay. As soon as they find out we're not followers, they'll separate us, and God only knows what will happen after that. The best advice I can give you is keep to yourself, don't talk unless spoken to, and don't make any friends unless I give you the go ahead. Do you understand?"

"Yes sir."

"Good. Like I told Tom, I'll get word out of your safe arrival, but there won't be any more communication after that, at least not for a while."

The two men rode in silence until Red pulled the cart up in front of the shelter and turned it off. "Here we are. It ain't home sweet home, but its shelter from the cold at any rate."

The familiar smell of manure drifting in from the field brought Joe back to the ranch and he breathed in the sweet memory and embraced it. "How close are my quarters to the shelter?"

"If you walk down this sidewalk and take a right at the corner," Red pointed to a long row of single-story concrete buildings, "that's where the shelter workers live. Your unit is the one on the far end. C'mon, I'll take you there."

Joe grabbed his sacks of food and followed Red to the place that would be his home. For how long -- he didn't know. As they walked, curious eyes peered from behind slightly drawn curtains then quickly faded into the darkness when Joe looked their way.

Tom followed the dimly lit hallway to a bank of elevators. He was still reeling from the comment Red had made about the radio when he suddenly realized that he didn't know where he was going. He turned quickly and watched as the golf cart disappeared around the street corner. He was alone. Again, he turned back to the elevators and spotted a magnetic card reader on the wall that separated the elevators, similar to the one at the grocery store. He shrugged his shoulders. On a whim, pulled his key card from his wallet, and slid it into the slot. The doors opened with a soft 'ding.' Tom stepped into the mirrored cube, spied another slot, and slipped his card in. The doors shut.

As the elevator rose smoothly, he surveyed the walls and ceiling of the elevator car and noticed a camera in the corner. "You guys aren't going to make this easy, are you?" he thought. The elevator shimmied to a stop on the sixth floor and the doors glided open with another 'ding.' Tom stepped out and found himself at the end of a dark, deserted hallway. With no choice of direction necessary, he turned to the right, and began walking, checking the doors. There were nameplates on the doors and as he walked, he thought, "It would be no surprise to find my name already on a door." He was almost at the end of the hall when he saw the name 'Connelly' stenciled on a gray metal door between two other doors. He chuckled to himself. He used his card to open the door and entered what would now be his home. God would tell him what he should do next.

The unit was modest. A single cot against the far wall to his left and a chest of drawers against the opposite wall. He placed his grocery sacks on the cot, went into the bathroom, and looked around. A shower stall, single stand sink and a commode filled the tiny space. He was glad to see a window in the apartment, even if it was in the bathroom. When he tried to open it, it didn't budge. "I may have to do something about that." He left the bathroom, collected his groceries, and crossed the sleeping area, into the kitchen. A telephone with no buttons or rotary dial hung on the wall to the right. Curious, Tom picked it up. "Good evening, Mr. Connelly. How can I help you?"

Tom stammered, "G-good evening, I'm sorry, I hadn't expected anyone to be on the other end."

"The City has its own operators twenty-four hours a day, so if you ever need to make a call, just pick up the phone, tell us who you'd like to reach, and we can connect you. We even have a wake-up service."

"Well, that's very nice," Tom said, still in shock, "but I'm fine for now. Thank you. H-have a good evening."

"You too, Mr. Connelly."

Tom gingerly hung up the phone. "So that's how they do it. They can monitor who comes and goes, who calls whom, and most likely they can listen in to all phone conversations." Tom shook his head and resumed his survey of the kitchen. The stainless-steel sink added to the coldness of the apartment. The refrigerator with its rusted corners, was probably older than Tom. He opened the door slowly, leery of what might have been inside, but was pleasantly surprised to see it clean and empty. Tom placed his food sacks on the small counter that was sandwiched between the sink and the refrigerator and put away the items he wouldn't need right away. The cabinets, both of them, were also empty except for two place settings, four glasses, eating utensils and a small assortment of saucepans and skillets. "It doesn't look like I'll be doing much entertaining." He smiled and continued his survey. An oven and two-burner stove were located against the adjoining wall next to the refrigerator—preventing him from opening the refrigerator door all the way. In the center of the tiny kitchen was a small, round table with two chairs.

Tom sighed. The day was finally catching up to him. Too tired to cook anything, he opened the cabinet and took down a bowl. Cream chipped beef on a cold night would certainly hit the spot. He dropped the package of frozen white gravy and beef into the bowl and placed it in the mini microwave oven sitting on the countertop. While his supper heated, he went back into the bathroom to unload his toiletries and examine the window more closely. He found that someone had pounded two nails flush into the jam just above the window. The nails would be difficult to remove, but not impossible. Going back to the kitchen, he passed the dresser and noticed a handwritten note. He grabbed it to read it while he ate.

Good evening Mr. Connelly,

I trust you arrived at your unit without incident. Please report to the security building at oh seven hundred sharp tomorrow morning. It is the one Red showed you behind your building.

Tom shuddered. "This is getting downright scary," he muttered to himself.

Your regular hours will be oh seven hundred to sixteen hundred hours, Tuesdays through Saturdays with Sundays, and Mondays off. However, you will be on call twenty-four hours on the days you are off. If you have any questions, bring them with you tomorrow morning. Gabe McCloud will be waiting for you.

Nick Garrison

Tom laid the paper on the kitchen table and finished his supper. "The only thing they got right so far is the military timetable," he thought.

"Well, son, this is where I'll leave you," Red said as they approached the door to Joe's unit.

"What about work tomorrow, Red?"

"Go on in and look around. They more than likely have already been here and left you instructions. If not, don't worry, they'll let you know." Red wanted to shake his hand but only nodded.

Joe watched his friend walk to the security office before swiping his card and entering the dark room. His idea of his first place was nothing like this, but he shrugged it off and went to the kitchen. He was famished and decided to eat one of the microwave all-vegetable pizzas he had bought and a tall glass of chocolate milk. He would rather have had pepperoni with extra cheese and an ice-cold root beer, but he was content with what he had and ate heartily. While he ate, he considered what Red had said about the radio. Joe hoped that he would be able to get through and wondered just how many people he had been in contact with on the outside.

When Joe finished his meal, he went to the other room and sat down on his cot while he drank the last of his milk. He looked around the room but did not see any notes or any sign that someone had left instructions for him. He thought about the phone in the kitchen and went to it. No sooner had he put his hand on it than it rang. Joe jumped and let it ring a second time to allow his pounding heart to slow down.

"Hello?" he said into the receiver.

"Good evening, Mr. Parker. I trust Red got you to your unit and you are settled in."

Joe recognized the voice of Nick Garrison, "Yes, sir. Everything seems to be fine."

"I'm glad to hear it," Garrison said. "I would have left you a note, but I thought a phone call would be more neighborly. I was sorry to hear that you had to leave your family, but it sounds like you had a very good reason. Will they be coming to see you?"

"No, sir." Joe said, wondering why he would ask. "As far as I know they are still at the ranch, but you would already know that, wouldn't you." Joe paused to determine exactly how much these people really knew about the goings on at the Ranch. He felt his ire begin to rise but held his tongue and waited for the response.

"You are right, Joe. We do know that, and we are watching them carefully. Now, about tomorrow."

Joe breathed a sigh of relief. "These people had no idea that his family had all left."

"Your hours of work will be oh six hundred to fifteen hundred Sunday through Thursday, with Fridays and Saturdays off, however, you will be on-call twenty-four seven on your days off. Tomorrow being Thursday, you will only have one day to train, but I don't think you'll have any problems, do you?"

"No sir. I'm pretty sure I can handle it," Joe said.

"Good. Be at the main entrance to the shelter tomorrow morning at oh six hundred and see a man named Silas Grey. He is the supervisor.

Do you have any questions?"

"No sir."

"Very well, if you think of anything, you can ask Mr. Grey tomorrow. We're glad to have you aboard, Joe."

"Thank you, Mr. Garrison. Good night."

Garrison hung up and Joe stayed by the phone, wondering how he would ever get up on time for work. Then, just on impulse he picked up the receiver.

The same friendly voice that greeted Tom, greeted Joe, "Good evening, Mr. Parker."

"Hi, I -- I need a wakeup call in the morning. Can you help me?"

"Of course, what time would like us to call?"

"Five a.m."

"Okay, no problem."

"Thanks." Joe hung up and hoped someone would remember. Meantime, he had been thinking all day about a long hot shower.

He stripped off the filthy clothes he had been wearing for the past three days and stood in the shower, letting the hot water run over his head and stream down his tired, aching body. It had been months since he had been able to do this. When they lost power at the ranch, they resorted to taking baths with water heated on the woodstove and during that time, he had gained an appreciation for the pioneers. Now he let all the days of riding and tension wash off him. He had bought razors at the market, but after a close inspection of his beard, he decided to let it grow out, and trimmed around it instead. His shock of dark hair had grown into wavy curls that rested just above his collar and his green eyes sparkled in bright contrast.

With the extra work on the farm and the limited diet, Joe was pleased to see that his shoulders and arms were still well muscled, but he was a lot leaner than he was in the months before the takeover started. He finished cleaning up, checked the front door, and then suddenly remembered what had been nagging at him since they arrived. His saddlebags had remained with the horses when they were taken away to the stables. His Bible, the one that belonged to his dad and now belonged to him, was in one of them.

Red Dalton locked his door behind him and went straight to the radio base station he kept hidden in his closet. After several attempts he was finally able to get through to someone. "This is Boss Daddy. Is anyone out there; over?"

"This is Devil Dog. We read you loud and clear, Boss Daddy. What can we do for you this fine evening; over?"

"Howdy, Devil Dog. Get the word out that we've got a couple of sheep in the pen; over."

"Ten-four, Boss Daddy. Any news yet; over?"

"Not as yet, but soon; over."

"We're standing by; over."

"Copy that; over and out."

2 Timothy 4:18 "The Lord will rescue me from every evil attack and will bring me safely to His Heavenly Kingdom. To him be glory forever and ever. Amen."

CHAPTER 28

THE SUN SHONE BRIGHTLY but did little to warm the chill morning air as Joe walked briskly toward the man leaning against the fence by the stable entrance. He wore a brown jumpsuit similar to what Joe was now wearing. He checked his watch when he saw Joe coming toward him. "Joe Parker?"

"Yes sir." Joe extended his hand, and the man took it and gave it a quick shake.

"Welcome, Joe. I'm Silas Grey. I'll be your supervisor. C'mon, let me show you around." Silas took Joe through the stables first. As they walked, Joe looked desperately for Pilgrim and Cheyenne. When he finally spotted them, they tossed their great heads and nickered softly.

"Are those your horses?"

Joe nodded and stroked Cheyenne's nose. "Yes, they are."

Silas reached inside the stall and pulled up two saddlebags, "These must be yours then. The kid that brought the horses in removed the saddlebags and just left them here. Security's already been through them; just don't forget to take them with you when you leave tonight."

"I'll do that, sir. Thanks," Joe said, looking carefully at them. He prayed his Bible was still there and unharmed.

"There isn't much to your job, and since you've worked around horses before, I expect you won't have any trouble. Feed and water the horses, groom them, and muck their stall, that's pretty much it." Silas continued his walk down the aisle until they reached the end. "The morning shift, that's you, turns the horses out into this field. The night shift gets to bring them back in again. We have twenty horses in here, so you'll have your work cut out for you." Silas continued his speech as they exited the stables and headed toward the equipment shed. "By the time you're done with your work, it'll be time for the next shift.

We were short on help before, and had the dog guy doubling up, taking care of the horses and the dogs. It's a good thing you came along when you did. Between the dog poop and horse manure, he was pretty ticked off." Silas chuckled at his last remark. "To get the horses first, you must have impressed Garrison. Normally the new guy gets to pick up after the dogs and believe me, we have a lot more dogs than we do horses."

Silas stopped in front of the shed, unlocked the padlock on the door, and pulled it open. When they stepped inside, Joe was hit by a wave of warmer air that smelled of dirt and fertilizer. "This is where we keep the lawn maintenance equipment, fertilizer, and some overflow from the tack room. Over there in the corner is the wheelbarrow. The compost pile is behind the barn." Silas grabbed a pitchfork from a row of rakes and shovels and handed it to Joe. "Any questions?"

Joe nodded, "No, sir. I think I'm good."

"I'll let you know how good you are, kid." Silas turned on his boot heel and left Joe standing in the shed.

Silas Grey was a man in his sixties, tall and lean, with a hooknose that stretched out over a bushy, gray moustache. He wore an old black Stetson hat, marked with stains from years of wear and his shoulder length gray hair flowed freely from beneath it. The stable supervisor appeared to Joe to be a throwback from the 1960s, combined with an old cowboy who was not quite ready to take up the rocking chair. He didn't care much for the Regulators, or what the government was doing. As far as his future or the future of the country was concerned, Silas didn't care one way or the other. He always made a point to take the days one at a time.

Joe watched the bowlegged old cowboy walk away, then his thoughts turned to Charlotte. He wondered how often she came to the shelter. No sooner did he start thinking of her than he began to wonder if he'd even see her at all. What if something happened to her dog and she didn't come to the animal shelter as she had said she would? What if something happened to Charlotte and he couldn't find her? Joe shook his head at his 'what ifs' and puzzled over the promise that he had made to find her. He was angry for making such a pledge. "It's done," he thought to himself. "There's nothing more I can do about it now. I'm leaving it to you, Father." Joe threw himself into his work and prayed that he would see Charlotte again.

Tom stood at the gate surrounding the security building and rang the buzzer. He waited for a response and estimated the fence, marking the height at about ten feet, with an additional two feet of razor wire.

"You're studying that fence awfully close, soldier." A gruff voice crackled from the speaker box. The gate began to open slowly, and Tom stepped through. Halfway across the yard, the door to the security building buzzed and Tom had to take two long strides to reach the door before the buzzer stopped. Once inside, he paused for a moment to allow his eyes to adjust to the dim lighting.

"Tom Connelly, I presume?" The same voice that spoke over the speaker outside was now addressing him from behind a metal desk. The man stood up and extended his hand. "I'm Gabe McCloud, but most people just call me 'Mac'."

"Good to meet you, Mac. About the fence, I was just checking out the workmanship." Tom said.

Mac chuckled, "Well if you had an eye for security fences, you'd see that there are plenty of weak spots in that one. You just gotta know where to look. C'mon, let me show you around."

Tom considered Mac's comment about the fence. 'You just have to know where to look.' It was good information. McCloud could prove to be very helpful. He followed him throughout the building, taking note of the security pass codes for the administrative and security monitoring wings and was surprised to discover that they were the same. He was beginning to realize what McCloud must already know. The people who planned this building, as well as its security system, were overconfident that they were going to be in total control. At the end of a hallway, they came to another door. McCloud positioned himself in front, as he keyed in the combination, shielding it from Tom. "This is where we keep the weapons, Connelly. I'll give you the combination when your probationary period is over."

"All right." Tom paused, "How long is that?"

"I'll let you know," McCloud said, not bothering to face him. "C'mon, we're running behind schedule."

Tom quickly followed Mac down a concrete stairwell to the bottom floor where the munitions were stored. McCloud opened a cupboard door where an assortment of labeled keys hung from small hooks. "This is where we keep the 'keys to kingdom' as they say," McCloud said. He picked one from its hook and then moved further down the hall to a wide metal cabinet. "The weapon of choice for Garrison is the M16, but we also have several that we have confiscated from the residents."

"No second amendment rights here." Tom thought.

McCloud unlocked the gun cabinet, withdrew an M16 rifle along with an extra magazine, and handed both to Tom.

Tom took the weapon from McCloud, while his eyes swept over the assortment of weapons in the cabinet. He spied the Winchester they had brought in the day before, and then turned his attention to the key to the gun safe. McCloud returned it to the hook and then slammed the door shut. Tom was amazed to see that the cabinet that held all the keys to The City did not lock.

McCloud wasn't aware of how closely Tom was watching him. He was too busy thinking of the procedures he needed to explain to his new recruit. "You're going to shadow me this week, Connelly." McCloud turned to face Tom, "but next week you're on your own. If they don't trust you to do the job right after the first week, you're out of here or worse. Got it?" Tom nodded.

Mac went on, "First thing you do each day, come here and pick up your weapon. There are five sections in your jurisdiction, and they're scattered all over the City, so you'll be assigned a golf cart. They don't move very fast, but around here we shoot first and ask questions later. Since you're an Army sniper, you shouldn't have any trouble with that. Am I right?"

"Sure. No trouble at all." Tom couldn't believe what he was hearing. He prayed he would never find himself in a position where he would have to shoot anyone except the Regulators or their bosses.

"The sections you are responsible for are the infirmary, the old folks' building, the grocery store, and the animal shelter where they keep the family pets. The fifth section is the southwest area of the City itself. We have security that patrols all sections of The City, including the full perimeter. At least two dozen security officers are always on the wall."

"Why so many?" Tom asked. "I'm no expert you said so yourself, but the wall is enormous. What is it, twenty feet high?"

"Twenty-five," McCloud said. "And believe, Connelly me people could get out if they really tried. As I said, this place isn't as secure as they would have you believe. Now that I've armed you with that knowledge, I expect you to keep it under your hat. If any of this information gets out, you'll wish you'd never been born. You got that?" McCloud snapped.

Tom was growing irritated with Mac. "Yeah, I got it. Don't worry, it's safe with me."

Mac nodded and headed toward the door, not saying another word until they were outside. "Our first stop will be the old folks building, or the 'Last Stop'." Mac chuckled at his play on words. "You are their wake-up call. Eight o'clock sharp every morning. If you ask me, I don't know why the boss wants to wake up the old geezers. Half the time they go back to sleep anyway. But, if that's what the boss wants, that's what the boss gets. Got it?"

Tom only nodded. McCloud was already getting on his nerves. "Lord, please help me hold my temper and not punch this guy in the mouth."

When they arrived at the building, McCloud nodded to the guard at the door and then asked Tom, "You got your card?"

Tom pulled it out of his pocket. "Right here." He swiped it through the reader on the door and waited for the buzz, then pulled the door open and allowed Mac to enter first.

"You go straight to the top and work your way down," Mac said as he entered the elevator and held the button for Tom. "There are ten floors to this building, with ten units on each floor. That's not to say that they are all occupied, mind you. We've lost quite a few since we opened. In fact, we just lost Mr. Beechum. Poor old guy died on Christmas Eve. I was kind of sad to learn that he died. He was a good guy but didn't last long once he got sick with Cancer."

As they rode the elevator up, Tom thought carefully about his next question. "Has the care for the elderly changed much since they came here? I only ask because I heard on the road that they don't get the same kind of care that the younger folks do."

"Well, you heard right. There's only so much that can be done and once people get to a certain age, they just sort of overstay their welcome, if you know what I mean. Now, don't get me wrong. I got nothing against them, but wouldn't it be better to use our limited supply of medicine and resources on those who can still contribute to our society?"

Tom's fury continued to mount, "Yeah, I suppose that's true." He thought about the old man at the pawnshop and shook his head.

The elevator jerked to a stop on the top floor and the doors slid open. "Well, here we are. There's nothing to it. All you gotta do is go down the hallway and bang on the doors to wake 'em up. Like I said, half the time they go back to sleep, but it's what the boss wants. If you ask me, I think he's got control issues." With that, Mac roared with laughter as he proceeded down the hall and banged on the first door. "Rise and shine, folks!"

When they arrived at Barbara Beechum's door, both men were startled when Barbara suddenly opened the door. "Mr. McCloud. Don't you people have anything better to do than pound on people's doors?"

Gabe smiled, "Mornin,' Mrs. Beechum. You nearly gave me a coronary. Is everything all right?"

"Everything is fine, Mr. McCloud. You didn't answer my question."

"Forgive me, Mrs. Beechum. In answer to your question, we do have better things to do, but as I told Officer Connelly, it's what the boss wants. And may I say, ma'am, I am very sorry for your loss."

Barbara ignored McCloud's remark and narrowed her eyes as she scrutinized Tom. "A new Regulator. Well, that's wonderful. Pleased to meet you, officer. I pray that you have better manners than some of your co-workers."

Tom stifled a smile and nodded his head. "Yes, ma'am," was all he could say. He looked directly in her eyes and held her there for a moment.

Barbara paused and nodded. "Good day, gentlemen." Then she slammed the door.

Mac tapped Tom's shoulder with the back of his hand and pointed to the camera aimed at Barbara's door. "She's one of our problem children. A feisty old bird, but I'm pretty sure she's harmless. She only just started after her husband died. She's just like the rest of them, they talk a lot, but there's not much bite anymore."

"Is she one to watch then?" Tom asked, still smiling.

"It can't hurt. C'mon, your turn." Tom committed Barbara Beechum's unit number to memory and decided to pay her a little visit once he was on his own. The men worked their way down the hall banging on the doors.

After McCloud and Tom were out of sight, Barbara hurried to Dorothy's unit and tapped gently on her door. Her friend answered and Barbara was stunned at the look of frustration on her face. "Dorothy, what's the matter?"

"I get so tired of their banging, Barbara. I honestly don't know how much more of it I can stand."

Barbara stepped into Dorothy's apartment and closed the door behind her. "Come into the kitchen, Dorothy." Barbara felt giddy after her encounter with McCloud and Tom.

"What is it? You're acting awfully strange." Dorothy said as Barbara gently pushed her toward the kitchen and set her down in a chair.

"I think I just saw the man who is going to help us get out of here." Barbara whispered, as she took the other chair at the table.

"What on earth would make you say that, Barbara? Certainly, you're not talking about Mr. McCloud! Wasn't that him that came by just before you arrived?"

"Yes, you're right. That was Mr. McCloud, but he had someone with him. There was something different about him, the way he looked at me." Barbara felt as if she would burst with joy. "I think God has finally sent us our rescuer." With that, Barbara stood and gathered Dorothy in her arms. "Oh, Dorothy, finally, finally, we will be away from this horrible place."

Psalm 91:11 "For he will command his angels concerning you to guard you in all your ways."

CHAPTER 29

A LIGHT SNOW DRIFTED softly on the six riders as they began their careful ascent up the rocky slopes of the Allegheny Mountains.

"Mom, what do you think Joe and Tom are doing right now?" Ben's attempts to pass the time with questions about his brother and their friend always fell short and only worsened the pangs of loneliness for him and his mother. The group had been riding since six a.m. with no breaks, and more than that, Ben's stomach was telling him it was getting close to lunchtime.

"I'm not sure, Ben. Are you warm enough, honey?" Sandy hated changing the subject every time Ben brought up his brother, but it was all she could do to cope with Joe's absence. She had worried about him constantly since they had said their goodbyes three days ago.

"Yeah, I'm fine. I'm getting hungry though, Mom."

"We'll be stopping soon. Can you hang on a little longer?" Sandy asked.

"Yeah, sure." He was disappointed that his mom didn't want to talk about Joe and leaned forward in the saddle, laying his head on Buck's neck. He relaxed into the steady rocking as they made their way up the trail. Unlike his mother, Ben was comforted to talk about his big brother. Hot tears began to fall, and he turned his head away from his mom. "Joe, I hope you are all right. God, please watch over my big brother. I miss him so much." Ben wiped his face and sat up in his saddle. He needed to be stronger. He wouldn't want Joe to know that he was crying for him. Pulling strength from a verse his dad had taught him years ago, Genesis 26:24 "Do not be afraid, for I am with you . . ." Ben squared his lean shoulders, turned up his collar and pulled down his hat to shield himself from the icy wind that bit hungrily at his moist cheeks. "I won't cry anymore." He kicked his horse up the steep embankment.

Once they all had reached the top, Kyle called to the group, "Break time!" and walked his horse to a clearing just north of the trail. He dismounted and tied his horse to a nearby maple tree, smiling as he recalled how Joe had taught him and Tom how to tie off a horse correctly. Brushing the bittersweet memory from his mind, he approached Morgan. "How are you doing?"

"I'm fine; a little hungry." She smiled at him as he slipped an arm around her, and they walked together to meet the others. "I miss Tom and Lucky," she finally said.

"You don't miss Joe?" Kyle asked, trying to lighten the mood.

"Of course I do, Kyle. You know what I mean." She gave a gentle shove to his ribs.

Kyle laughed softly, "I know what you mean, Morgan. I miss all of them too. But you know God is watching over them."

"Yeah, I know," Morgan smiled. "We can be grateful for that."

"Come on, let's get some lunch." Kyle said.

Kyle built a small campfire while Steve contemplated the gray sky. "The snow has stopped for the time being, but it looks like there may be more on the way. We need to find some decent shelter tonight."

"I'll keep my eyes open for a good spot," Kyle offered. He took a swig of water from his canteen and then passed it to Ben. "Here you go, buddy. How are you holdin' up?"

"I'm good. How long before we get to where we are going, Kyle?"

"Going by the map and the current weather, I'd say another three days."

"That's not so bad." Ben took another swallow of water and passed it back to Kyle.

The group ate a meager lunch of chicken broth, crackers, and dried fruit. After a good warm up around the fire, Kyle stood and stretched. "Time to go, folks!" They rode on for another hour with Kyle in the lead. He couldn't stop thinking about Berkley Springs and prayed that they would be able to stay there for a while. He could see the strain of this trip on everyone's faces, and his leg was aching horribly from the constant exposure to the cold. He heard a horse coming up from behind and turned in his saddle to find Steve trotting up beside him.

"Hey, Kyle, do you know what day it is?"

"It's Christmas Day," Kyle smiled.

"I think we should keep our eyes peeled for supper," Steve said, "and a decent place to spend the night."

Kyle beamed, then suddenly a shadow passed over his face and his smile faded. "I imagine it's going to be tough on Sandy. It's the first Christmas without Joe and with Joe Jr. being gone, too--"

"Yes, I'm afraid so." Steve patted his horse's neck and nodded. "It will be difficult indeed." Steve glanced back and saw that Tanya and Sandy were riding together, "I'm going to go walk with her and Tanya for a bit. Do you mind holding the lead until we stop?"

"No, I don't mind. Why don't you send Ben and Morgan up here to keep me company?"

"You got it." Steve grinned. "Let's try to make camp earlier so we'll have time to hunt."

"Good idea," Kyle said.

Steve gave Kyle a last glance, reined his horse around, and headed toward the back of the line where Morgan and Ben were walking their horses side by side. "Hey, you two, Kyle needs you up front."

Morgan's face lit up and with Ben right behind her, she kicked her horse, Skye, into a trot. The group rode on for another three hours when they came across an empty cave.

"This looks like a great place," Kyle said, dismounting from his horse. He tied his horse's reins loosely around a sapling while he went to investigate. "It's empty and it doesn't appear to be 'home' to anything or anyone!" He shouted to the group.

Relieved that they were finally stopping for the night, everyone else clambered down from their horses and began to make camp. Steve, Kyle, and Ben went hunting for supper, while Sandy worked on getting the campfire started.

"I've got the cooking box, Morgan," Tanya called out.

"And I'll get some firewood," Morgan said as she disappeared into the woods.

"Be sure to bring enough wood to last a while, Morgan!" Sandy said. "Hopefully the guys will bring back some fresh meat."

At the mention of fresh meat, Morgan's stomach growled, reminding her that she hadn't eaten anything substantial in days.

The men had been gone for over an hour when Sandy saw them coming toward the campsite through the trees. Her heart sank when she didn't see them carrying any game, but as they drew closer, draped across the front of Steve's saddle were two large rabbits.

After a hearty supper of roasted rabbit, boiled potatoes, with gravy that Sandy made from the last of the flour, and some dried fruit, everyone relaxed around the campfire. Some would say they got lucky, but this group knew that God had provided generously for them at every turn.

Within the shelter of the cave, Steve reached behind him and pulled his Bible from his saddlebag. He considered the group in front of him, and the snow falling softly behind them and began to read, "'In those days Caesar Augustus issued a decree that a census should be taken of the entire Roman world.'" After Steve finished reading the Christmas story he looked up from his Bible and smiled. "Praise be to God that we can still celebrate this most blessed season."

"Amen." Kyle cleared his throat and looked sheepishly around the group of friends, "I've got a couple of gifts I'd like to give, if that's all right?"

Steve cocked his head and gave Kyle a quizzical look.

"Just a couple of things I found that I'd like to pass on.' Kyle explained. "Hang on a sec." He rolled on his side and stretched up to dig through his saddlebag. "Here we go," he grunted and turned to Ben first. "I guess I should ask your mom first, Ben, but times bein' as they are and she bein' the sensible woman that she is--" Kyle winked at Sandy, then put his attention back to Ben. "A good friend of mine gave this to me while we were still in Iraq. I'd like you to have it." Kyle handed Ben a blade in a weathered leather sheath.

With wide eyes and a gaping mouth, Ben accepted the gift. He admired the object that he cradled in his hands and then looked to his mom for approval.

Sandy recognized the handle of the knife and nodded her consent. With great appreciation of the gift, she watched her son slide the knife carefully from its protective sheath. "It's beautiful, Ben," she whispered.

"Wow!" Ben gasped with his eyes glued to the weapon. He pulled his gaze from the knife and looked up at Kyle, "Thanks, Kyle." Ben laid the knife down gingerly, reached forward to hug Kyle's neck, and then picked up the blade again.

"It's a Ka-Bar," Kyle explained. "A buddy from Iraq, a Marine, gave it to me. We were in medical together after I got shot and he was being shipped home. Since I was going back out to the field, he thought I might need it."

"I love it, Kyle. I really do." Ben looked at his mom, "Can I keep it?"

"Of course you can keep it, Ben. Kyle, you will have to show him how to use it."

"Oh, you bet, Sandy." Kyle turned and looked at Morgan, his eyes softened, "I've got something else," he said softly.

Morgan fixed her gaze on Kyle and her heart fluttered gently. From the day she had met him, and each day after that, she realized that she was falling in love with him. His blue eyes searched hers as he reached into his coat pocket. When he found what he was fishing for, he smiled broadly and extended his hand slowly toward the woman in front of him, then opened it palm up for her to see. Morgan moved her gaze slowly from his scruffy, bearded face, down to what was lying in the palm of his gloved hand, a heavy gold ring with a ruby gem and deep engraving on either side. She recognized it right away as his Army Ring. "Kyle?" her voice cracked. She watched him guardedly; her eyes never leaving his. "Kyle?"

"Morgan, will you marry me?"

"Kyle! Oh my gosh!" She erupted into mingled giggles and weeping as she threw her arms around him and cried into his neck.

Steve laughed out loud and slapped Kyle on the back, "So, that's what you've been up to. I thought you had a little something up your sleeve today, but I couldn't put my finger on it! Congratulations to both of you!"

Sandy, Tanya, and Ben joined in the celebration until suddenly Kyle gently pushed Morgan back. "Wait!" He was puzzled.

"What?" she exclaimed, still giggling.

"You didn't answer me!" Kyle said.

Morgan laughed and wiped at the happy tears that streamed down her face, "Yes! Yes, Kyle. I would be honored to be your wife."

Kyle smiled broadly. "The ring is pretty big, but you can wear it around your neck until I can get you a proper engagement ring."

"It's perfect," Morgan leaned into him and kissed him, causing everyone to erupt into another cheer. When they had finished with their celebration, she turned to Steve. "When its time will you do the honors?"

"Absolutely," Steve smiled. "You name the day and we'll all be there."

"I think the spring," Morgan said. "Kyle? What do you think?"

"In the spring would be perfect," he said and kissed her softly again.

Sandy reached for her saddlebag, "Well, since we are exchanging gifts now," she burrowed deep into her bag until she finally produced a small box and an envelope. "Ben, you first. It's not much, but I believe your dad would have wanted you to have this." She passed the box to Ben and waited for him to open it.

Ben opened it carefully. His bright smile over Kyle and Morgan's good news turned melancholy. In the box were the Staff Sergeant stripes that his dad wore on his camos in Iraq. "Thanks, Mom. I love them.

Can you sew them on for me?"

"Absolutely, Ben. On your drover?"

Ben paused for a moment. "Yeah," he smiled.

"Sure," Sandy said.

"Thanks, Mom." Ben leaned over and kissed her cheek and gave her a strong hug. He held onto her for a long time before he finally let go.

Sandy gave him an encouraging smile and stroked his cheek. "You're welcome, sweetheart." When she addressed Kyle, her voice was still shaky from the emotional interlude with Ben, "Next." Sandy passed an envelope to him, "This fell out when I was going through the photo albums."

Kyle accepted the gift from her and after removing his gloves, slid a photograph from the tattered envelope. He found himself staring at a picture of Staff Sergeant Parker, Tom and himself, together in Iraq. "Sandy, where did you get this?" he whispered.

"Joe sent it to me not long after you got there. In case you hadn't noticed, he was particularly fond of you, Kyle."

"I love it, Sandy, really. Thank you very much." He smiled. "You know I remember the day this was taken." He chuckled softly and shook his head, "We had just returned to base camp from a sweep, where there was a good bit of action, but thankfully, we had all made it out. Next thing we know, Staff Sergeant is pulling his camera from his pack and got one of the guys to take this picture. 'Just a little something to remember the day,' he had said." Kyle gazed wistfully at the picture, "Funny how things change. Here, take a look." Kyle passed the picture around for everyone to look at.

When the picture came around to Ben he held onto it for a few seconds longer, and then passed it to his mother.

Sandy studied her husband's face then handed it quickly to Morgan who returned it to Kyle. He took another quick look and then tucked it inside his coat into the breast pocket of his shirt.

"I'm sorry, everyone, but that's all I have." Sandy shrugged, still struggling with her emotions.

"Let's remember the most wonderful gift of all," Steve said and then led the group in singing Silent Night. When they had finished, Sandy and Tanya left to clean up the supper dishes.

"Hey, you okay, kiddo?" Tanya put her arm around Sandy as they walked to the fire pit to fetch the hot water for the dishes.

"Yeah, I'm fine. It has been tough, that's for sure, but the circumstances make it a little easier to bear if you can understand that."

"I understand," Tanya answered. "There's a lot here to take your mind off things and being at the ranch would--" Tanya paused, uncertain of how she wanted to finish the sentence.

Sandy watched as Tanya struggled with her statement, "You're right, though. Being at the ranch would have stirred up so many memories. The memories are good, and I'll hold onto them, but right now, I just can't."

"I'm so proud of you, Sandy."

Sandy took a deep breath, "I've had my moments," she sighed. "And I know it'll get better. Of course, it would be a lot easier if Joe were here." Sandy smiled at her sister, "But I've got my Ben and all of you. Above all, Jesus is there to help me through just like he's there to watch over Joe and Tom." Sandy wiped out the pot they used to boil the potatoes and put it back in the cooking box.

"I wonder if they are getting any of this snow," Tanya said as she poured out the dishwater and looked up into the drifting snowflakes. "It doesn't look like it's going to stop any time soon."

Luke 2:10-11 "But the angel said to them, 'Do not be afraid. I bring you good news of great joy that will be for all the people. Today in the town of David a Savior has been born to you; he is Christ the Lord.'"

CHAPTER 30

IT HAD BEEN OVER a week since Richard Beechum's passing, and Barbara found herself facing the daunting task of sorting through his clothes and belongings and packing them away. Stephanie, the switchboard operator, and Garrison's 'go-to girl' provided Barbara with boxes for Richard's clothing and personal items. Now Barbara sat on the bed and stared at the boxes stacked in the corner, still waiting for her to fill them. She did not want to dispose of all her husband's things, but she had no choice. Stephanie would be coming soon to collect it all. It was the law in The City that clothing and personal items of the deceased be relinquished to the Regulators 'for dispersal to the greater good.'

Richard's clothes, along with his shoes, belts, and ball caps, lay neatly on the bed. Certain items she chose to keep; the cufflinks that he wore on special occasions and the bolo tie that he wore to church every Sunday. She didn't believe those items would be missed. How would they even know they existed? She checked her watch; she needed to get started. As she began to fill the first box, a flood of memories washed over her; overwhelming her with emotion. "Oh, Richard, I never could get you into anything but your dungarees and plaid shirts." Then she smiled and held up the tie, "except on Sundays." It hadn't felt like a final goodbye until now and she wept throughout the packing until she finally finished.

Looking around the bedroom, she saw that she still had one box left unfilled. "I'll just set it out with the rest of them," she thought. As she sealed the last box and lifted it off the bed to place it with the others, she noticed something fall to the floor and roll underneath the bed. With a heavy sigh at the prospect of having to get down on her already aching knees, she placed the box by the door and went back to the bedroom to investigate what had fallen.

Barbara slowly lowered herself down on her hands and knees and peered beneath the bed. "Oh, for Pete's sake," she mumbled. The light from the bedside table wasn't enough to see past the bed skirt. She reached into the nightstand drawer next to her and took out Richard's flashlight. She pressed the button, and when the light didn't come on, she gave it a hard smack. A bright light streaked across the room. Satisfied, she bent over, aimed the beam beneath the bed skirt, and discovered a button from one of Richard's shirts that had fallen. As she was struggling to get up, the light hit against the wall at the head of the bed on what appeared to be a small, shiny, rectangular box. She searched her memory for when Richard may have put it there. "I don't recall Richard ever putting anything under the bed." She was about to reach under the bed to pull it out when someone banged on the front door.

Painfully Barbara rose from the floor and hurried to the door. When she opened it, she saw Stephanie's smiling face. "Hello, Stephanie. I see you brought some help with you." Barbara eyed the two men who were standing behind Stephanie wearing green jumpsuits and holding their M-16's tight against their chest.

"Yes. Sorry, Mrs. Beechum. You know the rules. I have to bring security with me when I come to collect."

"And who's this?" Barbara asked looking up at the husky, bull-necked third man positioned at her door.

"This gentleman will relieve you of your boxes. That is, if you are through packing."

"Yes, I've just finished. They're right here. I haven't had time to put them out in the hall yet." Barbara stepped back just enough for the large man to reach in and pull the boxes out to the hall.

When he picked up the empty box he looked sharply at Barbara, then at Stephanie, "This box is empty." He tossed it to the floor.

Stephanie looked at Mrs. Beechum, surprised. "Really? Are you sure you packed everything?"

"For heaven's sake, Stephanie, what more do you people want? All I had left of Richard was his clothes and a few personal items which I kept."

"I'm sorry, Mrs. Beachum. It's just that I gave you three boxes, and we were expecting three full boxes back. Forgive me." Stephanie turned abruptly to the big man. "Just take what is there. Mrs. Beechum, again, we are all sorry for your loss." Stephanie gave her a quick, cold smile and looked back at the armed guards. "C'mon, let's go."

"Sorry, my foot," Barbara mumbled and slammed the door.

"Watch your temper, woman. All in God's good time." Richard's voice came to her.

"Yes, dear." Barbara lifted her tear-filled eyes to Heaven. "Oh, Richard, I miss 'us' so much." Then she remembered the box underneath the bed. In all the commotion with Stephanie she'd completely forgotten about it. Curious now, she hurried to the bedroom, grabbed the flashlight, and wiggled beneath the bed. She could just barely touch the box with the tips of her fingers, but when she tried to push it, she realized it was too heavy for her to move with just her fingers. "Well, for Heaven's sake, Richard! What have you stashed under here?" She wiggled her way back out from underneath the bed and went to the kitchen for the broom. "This should do it." With her last comment, Barbara suddenly realized that she had been talking out loud to herself, "I'd better keep quiet; someone may be listening." She snickered.

After twenty minutes of reaching and pushing, Barbara sat on the bed and stared at the mysterious metal box that her husband had hidden. There was a small combination lock on it and after exhausting every combination of numbers she could think of, she gave up. "Perhaps if I just walk away for a while." She lifted the box and carefully pushed it back under the bed, just in case some unexpected visitors stopped by.

Barbara went to the kitchen to make some tea, hoping it would clear her mind. While she waited for the water to boil, she took stock of the items she would need from the market the following day. When she had finished her list, she picked up the phone and waited for the operator to connect her. "Hello, Dorothy."

"Hello, Barbara. How are you holding up?" Dorothy asked.

"I'm doing all right. You know, good days and bad days. I was calling about tomorrow."

"That's right, it's our shopping day." Dorothy said excitedly.

"Yes, it is," Barbara smiled. "I'll come by your unit around eight thirty. Is that all right?"

"That will be fine," Dorothy said. "I'll see you then."

"See you tomorrow." Barbara hung up the phone and tore her grocery list off the pad. She tapped her pencil on the fresh piece of paper then began playing with different numbers that were important to her and Richard over the years. Suddenly she froze. "Of course!" She jumped from her chair, hurried into the bedroom, and slid open the drawer of the bedside table where she had found the flashlight. She dug furiously until she came up with what she was looking for.

There in her hands, she was certain, was the combination to the lock. Richard had always played the lottery, much to her annoyance. Of course, they never won, and he was good about purchasing only one ticket per week, but this time she was sure that these were the winning numbers. She placed the box carefully back on the bed and went to work. Finally, after many failed attempts, she tried the combination one more time. Her breath caught in her throat when the lock softly clicked open.

"Well, mercy me!" She said before she realized she was talking to herself again. "Okay, Richard, let's see what you've been keeping from me."

When Barbara lifted the lid to the metal box, she gasped when she saw stacks and stacks of gold and silver coins, a snub nose .357 revolver and four boxes of bullets. "Richard!" she exclaimed. Then almost as in answer to her, she spotted the corner of a piece of paper peeking out from beneath one of the stacks of gold coins. Carefully she lifted them out and laid them gently on the bed. God forbid anyone walking by would hear all the jingling. She would most certainly be arrested. She tugged lightly at the paper until it slipped out.

She opened it and read,

"Dearest Barbara,

I pray it is you reading this and not Garrison. I wish I could see your face right now. There should be enough here to help you along the way once you get out of here. I'm sorry for suggesting we come, but I guess at that time we were led astray like many of the others. Keep the gold and silver hidden somewhere beside the box just in case someone comes snooping and finds it. Keep the .357 close to you, but most of all, my dear, keep your eyes and ears open. God will be sending you an angel soon to lead you all out of there.

Stay strong, wife, and know that I've always loved you.

Richard.

Barbara wiped the tears from her face and folded the note but then thought better of it and ripped it into tiny pieces and flushed them down the toilet. She went back to the bed and sat down heavily, wondering what she would do with the treasure her husband left for her. She picked up the handgun and checked to see if it was loaded; it was. She carefully laid it in the drawer of the nightstand and put the bullets and coins back in the box. She would have to think about where to hide them, but for now, they'd be safe where she found them.

1 John 4:19 "We love because he first loved us."

CHAPTER 31

"STEVE, STEVE, TIME TO get up." Kyle shook Steve awake. It was barely dawn, but Kyle wanted to get an early start on the day and proceeded to wake the others. They expected to arrive in Berkley Springs, West Virginia that day, and he was more than a little anxious about what to expect. Once everyone was roused, Kyle returned to the fire for his coffee. When he saw Steve coming, he poured a cup for him.

"Hey, Kyle. Thanks." Steve gladly accepted the tin cup. "Mmm, smells great." He wrapped his cold fingers around the cup for warmth and sipped slowly, enjoying the heat as it coursed through him on this frigid, winter morning. "I think we'll arrive just in time. It's getting pretty darn cold."

"Boy, you can say that again." Kyle looked up to see that the women were stowing away the sleeping bags and pulling the cooking box out for the breakfast preparation. "Steve, before we all go in together, I think I should go scout it out first to check out the mood of the town. I sure wouldn't want to bring everyone into a hostile situation."

"That's a good idea, Kyle, I hadn't thought about that." Steve agreed.

"Hi, guys." Morgan dropped the box of cooking tools next to Kyle and proceeded to dig through it for the grill top and cast-iron fry pan. "Gosh, it's cold out here. It'll be nice to be in some kind of shelter, but I'm a little apprehensive about the whole idea, Kyle." Morgan admitted. When she looked up from the box and into Kyle's face, she saw the same concern etched into the tiny lines around his eyes.

Kyle knew she wouldn't like what he was about to say. "I was just telling Steve that I'm going in first to check the area. Hopefully, if anyone is there, they'll be friendlies and not the Regulators."

"I know I can't stop you, but just be careful, okay?" Morgan absently slipped the Army ring on her finger and slid it up and down the chain it was attached to around her neck. "Don't worry, babe. I'll be fine." Kyle smiled at her and handed her a cup of coffee. "Here you go. Warm yourself up."

Morgan smiled and took the cup and then continued with the meal preparation.

After they had finished breakfast and the dishes were cleaned, Steve led the group in prayer, before Kyle set off for town. "Lord, you are such an awesome, loving God; we thank you for the clear day and the food you have provided for us. Please grant your continued protection and watch over Kyle, Lord. Keep him alert to whatever may be waiting for him in Berkley Springs. We pray that the people of the town are friendly and that we can be a reflection of Your light and an example of Your love and kindness. We ask all this in Jesus' name. Amen."

Morgan walked with Kyle to his horse. "Are you sure you don't want someone to come with you?"

"Positive. Besides, if something should happen . . ."

Morgan gasped, "Don't say that."

"I'm not saying something will, but if by some chance something does go wrong, Steve and I didn't want you and the others to be left alone. Not to say that you couldn't take care of yourselves." Kyle smiled as he pulled her to him with his right hand and held the reins to his horse in the other.

"Good recovery, soldier. For a minute there I thought you were going to say that we needed a man around to take care of us." Morgan reached up and kissed him.

"The thought never crossed my mind," Kyle said and kissed her back. "Hopefully tonight we'll be breaking bread with other Christian believers." Still holding the reins, he slipped both arms around her and held her tight. As he held her, he felt her arms tighten around him and hoped that she wouldn't start crying.

Ben ran up to the couple with Steve, Tanya and Sandy trailing behind him. "Kyle! You weren't going to leave yet, were you?"

Kyle pulled himself slowly from Morgan's embrace and smiled at the twelve-year old. "Not yet, Ben; I wouldn't leave without saying 'see ya later.'"

Ben smiled, "Here, I'll watch Thunder." He took the reins from Kyle and walked the gelding to the creek for water while the adults talked. As Ben led the horse, he stroked its neck. "Hey, buddy, you take good care of Kyle, okay? It may be a little scary going in there, but God will be looking out for you. Okay?"

The gelding nickered softly and nuzzled Ben's shoulder.

Meanwhile, the others were saying their goodbyes to Kyle. Sandy reached up and gave him a kiss on the cheek. "You be careful now,

Kyle, and don't take any chances."

"Yes, ma'am," Kyle gave her a hug and turned to Tanya.

"Ditto, Kyle. Know we'll be praying for you." Tanya said.

"I appreciate that." Kyle smiled.

"God speed, Kyle." Steve shook his hand, "We'll be right here. If you're not back in a couple of hours, we'll be there in a jiffy."

"Thanks, Steve." Kyle took a deep breath and turned back to

Morgan. "Stay strong, lady. I'll be back before you know it."

Morgan nodded and smiled. "Just be careful."

"Ben!" Kyle yelled, "I'll be needing my horse back!"

Ben walked Thunder back to the group, "He's all watered and ready to go."

"Thanks, partner." Kyle ruffled Ben's hair and gave him a half hug with one arm. Once mounted, he turned his horse onto the path and trotted toward the town of Berkley Springs. He had no idea what he was riding into, but trusted that God would see him through it, no matter what.

A bright, but distant sun suspended in the cerulean sky offered no warmth for Kyle as he made his way to the town. The faint smell of wood smoke hung in the air. Someone somewhere had built a fire. Whether they were friend or foe was anyone's guess. As he approached the outskirts of the town, he was reminded of when he'd done this before, gone into a place unfamiliar and potentially dangerous. He thought about Tom and wished he was there for back-up. Kyle stopped to check his pistol and ammunition. He was set.

He pressed onward, until he came to the street that led into the small town. Kyle quietly dismounted and tied off his horse. Then using the shelter of an old oak tree, he scanned up the street and back. There was no sign of life and Kyle had the sinking feeling that this was just another town abandoned by its residents. He decided to walk through the woods that bordered the town on both sides. He would look into any building that offered a window at the rear, unsure whether he wanted to find anyone or not. If there were other believers, it would certainly be a blessing, but if the Regulators occupied the building, he and the others would have to make a wide detour. If it was just another abandoned town, it meant they would be alone in their fight, at least for now, and would have to push on to find someone, anyone, who would join them in standing against the corruption that had taken over their country.

He came upon a building with a rear window and approached it cautiously, his gun drawn. He stood just to the side of that window and tried to look in from a side angle, but he couldn't get a clear view. A movement from the other side of the room caught his eye. He ducked below the window and crossed to the other side. He peered inside. What he saw made him guardedly hopeful. An old woman, who looked to be in her ninety's lay on a mattress surrounded by what he could only assume were the remaining townspeople. Their ages ranged from very young to very old and it looked as if they were kneeling around the old woman, praying. Kyle left that window and moved to the next and the next, until he reached the end of the street. Finding no one else on this side of the street, he turned, counted the buildings, and returned to the building where the people were gathered. He looked through the dirty glass again. The group was milling about, and some were leaving. Kyle whispered a quick, but sincere, prayer and hurried back to his horse.

Kyle rode through the trees and stopped just short of the edge where the woods met the street. He holstered his pistol and let his hand rest lightly on the butt of his gun as he moved into the street. At first, the people who were leaving the building did not know how to respond to the stranger riding into their town. Two women, with four small children, pulled them close and ran back into the building. One man close to Kyle's age stood on the sidewalk with his hands in his pockets.

Kyle could only assume he was waiting for Kyle's next move. An older man emerged from the building holding a rifle on Kyle and walked to the younger man and spoke. The young man nodded and disappeared into a building across the street. When he came back out, three other men wielding assorted firearms were with him. Kyle's horse sensed the tension in the air and began lifting his hooves high and tossing its head. He backed away from the approaching men. "Whoa, Thunder, let's just wait right here for now." Kyle immediately held both hands up in the air and spoke loudly so everyone could hear him. "I don't mean any harm, folks!"

"Who are you and what's your business, young man?" The older man with the rifle shouted.

Kyle assumed that he was the one in charge. "I come from Willow Creek, Maryland. They came through the town and ran everyone out."

"Who are 'they'?" the same man questioned.

"I think you know," Kyle shouted, "Looks like they came through here, too."

"Stay where you are. We're coming to you." The man motioned to the others, and they followed him. Thunder tossed his head again as the men approached.

Kyle rubbed his neck to calm him. The leader of the group came to stand next to them, "Come on down from there, son."

Kyle studied the man carefully as he slowly dismounted. His heart raced and he felt for sure that at any moment they would shoot him. "I don't want any trouble here, guys. We'd just like some shelter from the cold."

"What's your name, stranger?" One of the other men asked.

"Kyle Johnson."

"How many are in your party, Mr. Johnson?" another man asked.

"Six, including myself; one is a child, a boy. They're waiting for me back in the woods about a half hour ride from here."

"Do you plan on staying or just passing through?" The man in charge questioned. He was a tall, heavyset man with a handlebar moustache and bushy, gray eyebrows. He spoke gruffly and his handling of his rifle and his men convinced Kyle that this man had to be former military and most likely a man of authority.

"We'd like to stay on a few days if that's all right. We've been on the trail for nearly a week now." By the looks he was getting, Kyle felt sure they were going to run him out of town.

"You travelin' with any weapons?" The younger man asked.

Kyle looked at him, irritated, "Well, yeah, I got this revolver here. These days it'd be stupid not to."

The man chuckled at Kyle's response, "No need to get uppity, Mr. Johnson, we're just being cautious. And for crying out loud, Anders, let me do the talkin'. Every time you open your mouth you show your backside."

Kyle was growing impatient, and the cold was causing his leg to ache. "Look, like I said, we're just looking for a little shelter and a decent night's sleep."

The gruff man finally lowered his rifle, "All right, Mr. Johnson, I believe we can trust you. Do you need any help gathering your people?"

Relieved, Kyle couldn't wait to get back to camp to tell the others, "No, we'll be fine. Do you have stables or a barn for our horses?"

"Sure do," the head man replied. He nodded toward the younger man he called Anders, "He'll show you where you can put up your horses."

Kyle acknowledged Anders with a nod and hoisted himself up on Thunder. "I'll be back in about an hour. We really do appreciate your hospitality."

The man in charge nodded to Kyle and turned back toward town waving to the others to follow and leave the traveler alone.

Kyle was bursting with gratitude as he galloped down the street and into the woods.

Ben, waiting with the horses, was the first to see him come charging through the trees. He ran to him and grabbed the reins that Kyle tossed to him. The grin on the soldier's face told him everything. Ben quickly tied off Thunder and ran to join Kyle and the others.

"Good news!" Kyle announced. "There are a few folks in the town, and they seem to be somewhat friendly, but mostly just cautious. They said we could come in and spend a few days."

"Oh, that is good news, Kyle!" Steve exclaimed.

They quickly gathered their gear and rode off for Berkley Springs. As he led the way down the main street, Kyle could feel the eyes of the townspeople on them. He scanned the empty buildings as they trotted through and was pleasantly surprised when the more curious folks stepped out of the homes . . . smiling. Before the group moved closer, Kyle raised a fist indicating a stop to the riders behind him. Anders was walking out to the street to meet them. He and Anders spoke briefly, and then Kyle turned in his saddle and motioned for them to follow him.

They merged off the main street onto a side road lined with large apple trees and Sandy thought to herself, "How beautiful this road must have been in the spring and fall."

Soon after they turned from the main street, they arrived at the stables. It was nearly midday, and the sun had climbed high in the sky. Anders showed them the empty stalls for their horses and proceeded to fill the water buckets from a well behind the building. Sandy noticed that it had been covered with a large black tarp and even larger tree branches. "May I ask why you keep the well covered?"

Anders looked at her blankly and replied, "It's our only source of water, ma'am. We don't want anyone finding it and poisoning it."

"I see." Sandy's heart sank as she was reminded of the bitter times they were living in. She went back to removing Annie's bridle and bit.

"Anders!" Kyle hollered.

"Yes sir!" Anders hadn't liked Kyle from the first moment he had seen him. He had enough trouble with Sheriff Dixon always on his back, and now this new guy had made him look like a fool in front of everyone.

"Is there a building nearby where we could stay close to the horses? I don't want to leave them clear out here with no one watching them."

Anders sneered at Kyle and pointed with his chin to a two-story house about twenty-five yards from the stables. "No one's staying in that house; you guys can bunk in there."

"Thanks, man. Let me ask you something else."

Anders rolled his eyes and leveled an impatient stare on Kyle.

It was obvious that the guy wanted as little conversation as possible with this stranger, but Kyle had questions, and he needed answers. "Where are the horses? You have stables and it looks like they'd been put to good use at one time."

"The thieving government men stole 'em." Anders lowered his head and kicked a rock hard into the wood plank wall of the stable. "Is there anything else I can do for you, Mr. Johnson?"

"No. Thanks, that'll do for now, Anders. I'm sorry about your horses, man." Kyle winced and rubbed his left leg.

Anders didn't miss it and asked him, "You hurt?"

"Just an old war wound. It always acts up in the cold."

Anders nodded his leave-taking and strode down the road toward town.

While he waited for the others to join him, Kyle slung his saddlebags over his shoulder and wondered what Anders' story was.

With the horses put up, the group was finally getting settled into their new surroundings. Sandy hoped they would be able to stay for more than a few days. She didn't want to think about getting back on the trail any time soon. Right now, all she wanted was a warm bath, some food and a soft bed. She went to the kitchen sink and prayed that this house used well water like the farm. She turned the cold-water knob, and, after some sputtering and spitting, the faucet brought forth clear, ice-cold water. Sandy closed her eyes. "Thank you, Lord. You always provide."

Tanya came behind her and hugged her. "God is good!"

Sandy looked over her shoulder and smiled. "Yes, He is. Come on; let's see what we can find for lunch. I'm famished."

After a quick inspection of the cabinets, they found several cans of soup, vegetables, and beef stew. "Jackpot!" Sandy exclaimed. "Where's Ben?"

"Right here, Mom." Ben strolled into the kitchen from the front living area.

"Honey, we're going to need some firewood for the fireplace and woodstove."

"Okay, Mom." Ben ran out the back door but didn't get far before his mom called him back inside.

"Ben, wait!"

The boy sighed and turned back, dragging his feet. "Yes, ma'am?" "Don't wander too far," Sandy said, smiling.

"Okay, Mom." Ben turned around and bolted out of the house.

Tanya had searched the pantry and discovered a tub of shortening, a container of salt, and a half bag of flour in the pantry. She quickly mixed up a pan of biscuits. While Sandy and Tanya busied themselves in the kitchen, Morgan was upstairs checking on the sleeping quarters. She found four bedrooms, two overlooking the stables and the other two overlooking the street. "Oh, these will do nicely."

While she was turning down the bed sheets, she glanced out the window towards the street and saw a man crossing the road, coming toward the house. She ran out of the room and down the stairs. "Kyle! Steve! Someone is coming!" She found them checking out the fireplace in the living room. Both men got to their feet and strode quickly to the front door, opening it before the man even had a chance to knock.

He smiled warmly at them. "Afternoon, folks. My name's Gus Wilkerson. I live just over there." He pointed to a house two doors down on the opposite side of the street. "I saw you comin' in earlier and wanted to welcome you and bring you a message from the sheriff."

"Come on in, Mr. Wilkerson." Steve stepped aside to allow him to enter. By now, Sandy and Tanya heard the unfamiliar voice and came to join them. After they introduced themselves, the man continued, "There's not many of us left in town so we usually have our evening meal together. You folks are welcome to join us. Normally, we ask that everyone bring something, but seeing as how you just arrived, we'll let you slide for tonight." He winked a bright blue eye at Morgan and smiled.

"We certainly appreciate the invitation, Mr. Wilkerson." Steve looked around at the group, "Are you all up to it tonight?"

Everyone nodded and Tanya spoke for all of them. "That sounds good, Steve," she said as she wiped the flour from her hands onto a kitchen towel.

"Thank you, Mr. Wilkerson," Steve said.

"Supper starts at six-thirty, and we meet over at the firehouse. Come early if you like. It'll give you a chance to meet everyone."

"We'll be there." Steve shook the man's calloused hand, "Thank you."

"Sure thing." The man smiled, then turned and left them.

Sandy woke with a start and realized that the room had grown considerably darker. After lunch they had all decided to grab a little shut eye, but in their exhaustion had nearly slept through supper. She rolled quickly out of the soft feather bed and hurried down the hall to Steve and Tanya's room and knocked sharply. After some commotion, the door opened and a bleary-eyed Steve came stumbling out, with Tanya holding onto the back of his shirt. "I guess we slept a little later than we planned," Sandy said.

Steve went to rouse Kyle and hoped he wouldn't have another episode like he did the first time he had tried to wake him up. He knocked on the door before he entered and spoke softly, "Ben? Kyle? Get up, you, guys. It's late."

Kyle lay on his stomach and lifted his head from his pillow. "Man, I haven't slept this good in months." He turned to Ben. "Hey, partner, rise and shine." Kyle gave Ben a shove before he went to find Morgan.

It was nearly six o'clock, by the time everyone gathered in the front foyer. Steve took their flashlight and led the way down the street toward the fire station. When they walked in, warm smiles greeted them along with a few cautious stares. Gus Wilkerson approached them, and they shook hands, "Glad you all could make it. You look like you got some rest."

"We sure did," Steve answered. "We nearly slept through dinner."

"Come on over here, I want you to meet the Sheriff." Gus guided them through a group of people to the man who had greeted Kyle when he first arrived. Kyle recognized him and smiled.

Suddenly to Kyle's surprise, Morgan loosened her grip on his hand, ran to the Sheriff, and threw her arms around his neck and wept.

Kyle started after her until he realized that the Sheriff had to be her Uncle Walt. He watched the reunion and gave a heavy sigh of relief.

Sandy went to Kyle, "Who is that?"

"I'm not positive, but I believe Morgan just found her Uncle. You remember? She told you about him when we first arrived at the ranch."

Sandy nodded and smiled as Morgan and the Sheriff walked toward them.

Kyle put his hand out at once, "Sir, it's a pleasure to meet you again."

Puzzled, Morgan looked at Kyle, then back at her uncle. "Again? Have you met before?"

Walt grinned broadly. "I'd considered shootin' him earlier today, but I'm sure glad I thought better of it. It's good to see you again, Mr. Johnson."

"Call me Kyle, sir."

After they made the rest of the introductions, the Sheriff pulled Kyle aside. "I thought you should know; we have had radio contact with some folks inside The City. You got anyone in there?"

Kyle's eyes grew wide, and he reached for Sandy. "Sandy, come here a second."

Sandy turned and smiled at him. "What is it, Kyle?"

"Sheriff says they've had radio contact with someone inside The City."

It was Sandy's turn to be surprised, "Have you talked to anyone lately?"

"As a matter of fact, I have." Walt answered. People had begun to crowd around them, so he took Sandy and Kyle by the arm and pulled them closer. "A few days ago, I was told that they just got 'two new sheep for the pen.' That's their way of saying that two new people came in."

Sandy wanted to explode with joy, but she kept her composure. "Thank you, Sheriff. You have no idea what a weight I've carried by not knowing."

"So, you have family in there?" he asked.

"Yes, sir; my son and Kyle's good friend." Sandy looked up at Kyle and smiled.

Kyle gave her a quick hug. "That's good news."

"Yes, it is. How often do you speak with them, Sheriff?" Sandy asked.

"Well, it's not like picking up the phone, I can tell you that. They only call when someone new comes in or when something is happening that we should know about. It's been fairly quiet, so I was pretty surprised to get the message. Oh, and just so you know, this radio business, strictly confidential. Only a couple of us here know about it and we'd like to keep it that way. Get my drift?"

"Sure," Kyle said. "Thanks for letting us know, Walt."

"My pleasure," Walt said. "Now, let's have some supper."

After the meal, Kyle pulled Walt aside. "Sheriff, I thought you should know; I've asked Morgan to marry me, and she said 'yes'. I would have asked her dad, but . . . Well, you know the story."

Walter beamed, "Well, congratulations, son! You have my blessing. It's unfortunate about her parents, my sister and her husband, but God willing, we'll find them one day." He shook Kyle's hand firmly and smiled. "I can tell you're a good man, Kyle, so this old Marine won't hold it against you being Army."

"Thank you, Walt." Kyle's attention drifted over to Morgan, but he suddenly remembered something and put his attention back to Walt, "Sir, I have to ask. Earlier this morning when I was scouting out the town, I was around back and looked through a window. I saw several people praying over an old woman. May I ask what happened to her?"

"She was one of the first residents of Berkley Springs and this afternoon she went on to be with the Lord."

"I'm sorry." Kyle said, saddened by the news.

Walt smiled warmly, "Don't be, Kyle. She is resting in Jesus' arms now. This is no world for her. We should celebrate. He turned around and whistled sharply, drawing irritated gawks. "Can I have your attention please? I've just been told that this fine young man has asked my niece, Morgan, to marry him!"

"What'd she say?" someone yelled.

"She said, yes! How about a little music, Leroy?" Walt shouted.

A gentleman who looked to be in his eighties picked up the fiddle laying across his lap and drew his bow across the strings into a lively old bluegrass tune. As the snow fell outside, the people of Berkley Springs danced into the night, putting out of their minds, at least temporarily, the world that was falling apart.

Kyle and Morgan cuddled on the couch and stared into the hypnotic flames in the fireplace. "I was glad to meet your Uncle Walt tonight. He's a good man," Kyle said.

Morgan smiled, "Yeah, he's the best. I didn't think I'd ever see him again."

"How did he manage to become sheriff of the town? Did he say?"

"He told me that he rode in right after the Regulators left. When the towns-people saw him riding in, they slowly began to come out of the woods. He said they were so frightened that they didn't know what to do. They were just sort of . . . lost. Of course, Uncle Walt, being the man that he is, took control. He set up committees to oversee the food and water situation and put the town back in order. When they realized his fairness in settling disputes, they named him sheriff."

"Did he say anything about your folks; where they are?" Kyle asked as gently as he could.

Morgan shook her head solemnly. "He doesn't know where they were taken. He thought I had gone with them but left the note just in case." Morgan smiled up at her fiancée, "That's just like Uncle Walt. Hope for the best, then prepare, and pray for the rest."

Sandy sat at the kitchen table with a cup of tea and her Bible. The long nap she had taken earlier now robbed her of any sleep for the rest of the night, leaving her mind to wander to The City where Joe was. Lost in thought, she didn't hear Morgan and Kyle come into the kitchen.

"Hey, Sandy. What are you still doing up?" Morgan asked.

Sandy closed her Bible and smiled tiredly up at the couple, "I can't sleep." She bit her lip and nodded her head as tears stung her eyes and spilled down her cheeks. "It was such a good day, but I still can't stop thinking about him," she cried.

Morgan pulled a chair up next to her and wrapped her arms around Sandy. "Go ahead and cry. You're just missing your boy. You know he's gonna be fine, though. Tom will look after him, won't he, Kyle?"

"Like he was his own son, Sandy. Try not to worry. Joe's a lot stronger than you might think. You still see him as a little boy, but I tell you what, when they left, I saw a strong, confident young man. He'll be fine, you just wait and see."

Sandy wiped the tears from her face and looked up at Kyle. "You're right, Kyle. You're both right. I'll be fine. Kyle, if you're tired, I can take the first watch."

Kyle grinned and patted her shoulder. "All right, I'll take you up on that, Sandy. Thanks."

Sandy watched the couple leave, and then turned back to her tea. When the house had grown quiet again, she decided to go outside for some fresh air. Stepping off the back porch, she gazed up into the sky and watched the clouds as they broke, revealing the full moon behind them. She paused for a moment and wondered if anyone in the City was looking at the moon at that very same time.

Philippians 4:6 "Do not be anxious about anything, but in everything, by prayer and petition with thanksgiving, present your requests to God."

CHAPTER 32

THREE MONTHS HAD PASSED since their arrival in Berkley Springs and, although Sandy and the others had become active members of the town, she was growing restless. Soon it would be time to leave. She sat in the kitchen and stared into her coffee cup, trying to think of a way to break the news to the others. Kyle and Morgan had begun making wedding plans and Steve and Tanya had started the church up again. A few other folks had come into town during the winter and the folks of Berkley Springs welcomed them graciously. Sandy decided to get some fresh air and went out to check on the horses. When she came to the last stall, she was surprised to see Ben sitting in the corner. "Hey, honey. What are you doing out here?"

"Hi, Mom, nothing really. I just wanted to sit and talk with Buck for a while. What are you doing?"

"Same thing I suppose. I wanted to come and check on the horses, clear my head."

"Are you thinking about leaving, Mom?"

Sandy looked at her son, not quite surprised at his question. "Yes, I am." She answered.

"I am, too. I was going to talk to you about it tomorrow, if you didn't bring it up soon. I think we should leave after Morgan and Kyle get married."

Sandy took a deep breath and let it out slowly. "Ben, I'm so glad you agree with me. I was having a hard time trying to figure out how to tell the others. It seems as though they've settled in here and the past has been forgotten. They don't even talk much about Tom and Joe anymore."

"I've heard Kyle and Morgan talking, Mom, and they haven't forgotten. I'm pretty sure they'll be ready to go when it's time."

"Well, I'm glad to hear that," Sandy said. "Can I come in or would you rather be alone?"

"No, come on in. Like I said, I'm just sitting here. I don't think Buck will mind."

"Thanks, Buck." Sandy stroked his neck as she made her way around him. His hair was still thick with the winter coat, and he nickered softly at her touch. Sandy sat next to Ben and picked up a piece of straw before she spoke. "You've been thinking a lot about Joe, haven't you?"

Ben nodded, "And Tom. I know they are all right, but I just miss both of them."

Sandy put her arm around her son and hugged him. "I miss them too, Ben. So, what do you suggest? Should we make our way towards The City or head back to Willow Creek to see what's happened there?"

Ben thought for a moment, "I know Tom said they would come back here, but I just have this feeling that we need to go back to Willow Creek. We would only be about three days ride to The City if they need us."

"You're right, Ben," Sandy said. "Let's tell the others tonight during dinner."

Ben nodded his head. "Okay."

Mother and son sat for a little while longer, both of them just enjoying the other's company and missing their loved ones. The light outside began to grow soft. "I've got to get supper, Ben. Do you want me to call you when it's ready?

"Naw, I just have to feed and water the horses and I'll be right in."

"Okay. I'm glad we had our talk, Ben." Sandy gave him a hug.

"Me too, Mom." Ben watched her leave the stable, then went to the well to draw some water. It had become habit, to look carefully through the heavily wooded area before he removed the tarp and branches covering the well. Somewhere behind him, the brush suddenly moved.

His heart jumped and he quickly ducked down. Watching from behind the large branches he had just pulled off the well, he spotted a young woman slipping through the trees, heading away from town. He considered calling out to her but decided against it. She was one of the newcomers who had arrived just two weeks ago. She had come in the company of two older men. According to her, they were her brother and her uncle. Very few people believed her, but they could not prove otherwise. The Sheriff decided to offer them the house next door to his own so he could keep an eye on them. They joined in the meals at the firehouse and attended church with the others but kept mostly to themselves. Ben watched as the young woman made her way deeper into the woods until he could no longer see her. He scanned the area for the two men but saw no sign of them. When he was sure she was gone, he quickly watered and fed the horses and then ran back to the house.

"Mom!"

"What's up, Ben?" Steve was at the kitchen table peeling potatoes for their supper.

"Uncle Steve, I saw that woman from town that came in a couple weeks ago with those two men. She was sneaking through the woods."

"Perhaps she was just going for a walk, Ben," Steve suggested.

"No, she kept looking all around and she crouched down like she was trying to hide. I think she was running away, Uncle Steve."

"Who was running away?" Sandy asked, coming into the kitchen and tying on an apron left by the former residents.

"That young woman who came to town a couple of weeks ago; you remember, she was with those two men," Steve said.

"Oh, yeah, I remember her." Sandy said looking out the back door at nothing in particular.

"I was just telling Uncle Steve, that I was getting water for the horses when I spotted her sneaking through the woods."

"Hunh. There was always something about those folks that didn't set well with me." Sandy said. She placed a large pot into the sink and began filling it with water.

"Do you think she heard us talking, Mom?" Ben asked.

"I don't know." Sandy looked at Steve. "Ben and I were talking about leaving; when and where we should go."

Steve laid the knife and the potato on the table and looked up at Sandy. "Funny you should mention that, Sandy. Tanya and I were talking just this morning about when a good time would be to leave. As far as that woman is concerned, I wouldn't be surprised if she was a spy, along with the men that came with her."

Sandy was relieved that Steve and her sister were discussing the prospects of leaving, but at the same time, she was concerned about what the woman might have heard. She lifted the heavy pot of water from the sink and placed it on the hot stove then crossed the kitchen and took a seat next to Steve. "If she is a spy, should we be worried?"

"Naw, I don't think so, but we do need to be cautious. I'm afraid we've gotten a little lax. We haven't been standing watch anymore and I can't remember the last time I fired my pistol. I think we need to practice in all areas before we take our leave of this place. Kyle and I will talk to Walt in the morning." Steve said. He patted Sandy's hand and smiled.

She returned his smile, grateful that the weight that had been on her had finally lifted. Steve didn't miss it, "Feel better?"

Sandy stood up, leaned across the table, and kissed him lightly on the cheek, "Yes, I do. Thank you, Steve."

"Should we start taking watches again, Uncle Steve?" Ben asked.

"Yes, I think we should, beginning tonight." Steve answered. "Are you up to it?"

Sandy turned sharply to her brother-in-law, but Steve knew what her reaction would be and kept his focus on Ben.

"Yeah, I'll take the first watch," Ben said with more eagerness than Sandy liked.

"Good. Then I'll take the second and we'll let Kyle have the last, since he's not here to debate it."

Both Ben and Steve chuckled at Steve's remark and Sandy realized that her young son was growing up before her eyes. She smiled with them; happy . . . proud that Ben was becoming a fine young man like his brother, but also a little sad. Too soon, her baby would be gone . . . grown into adulthood in these hard times.

Joe and Tom had acclimated well to The City during the past three months. Joe had seen no sign of Tom or Charlotte, but he did find Sasha and every day during his lunch break, he made it a point to spend some time with the dog. Joe recalled Tom's order to get himself out if he hadn't heard from Tom after a month, but Joe couldn't. He wouldn't leave Tom and Charlotte behind.

"You keep feeding those dogs your lunch and your mom won't recognize your skinny self!"

Joe swung around and wanted to throw his arms around the man, but Tom took a step back and stuck out his hand. "Keep it low profile, Joe. Remember the cameras."

Joe grasped Tom's hand and shook it vigorously.

Tom grinned, "It's great to see you, Joe. You look good. Your beard's growing out nice."

Joe absently rubbed his jaw. "Thanks, Tom. How've you been?"

Tom smiled and bent down to give Lucky a good head rub, "Doing well. Looks like you're taking good care of Lucky here; how you doin' boy?" Tom hugged the dog and gave him a kiss on the head before he straightened up and adjusted his M16. "I can't stay; just making my rounds. You haven't seen me before now because they've been moving me around a lot, and I've been training other security officers. Have you been all right, Joe?"

"Yeah, I've been doing all right." Joe contemplated his next thought and then looked seriously at his friend. "Tom, I've been thinking. We need to get these people out of here. I think we need to plan a rescue."

"You're right, Joe. I've been thinking the same thing. Keep your ears and eyes open okay, pal? Have you found your lady yet?"

Joe hung his head. "No, not yet, but her dog is still here."

"I'm sure if she were able, she'd be here, Joe. Hang in there, son." Tom put a reassuring hand on Joe's shoulder, "You take care of yourself, you hear?"

Joe smiled weakly at his friend. He had hoped to spend more time with Tom, "Yes, sir."

"Think spring." Tom said with a smile.

"See ya, Tom." They shook hands again and Joe nodded then went back to work, missing Tom, but feeling more motivated than he had in a long time. "Think spring. So, Tom had been considering a rescue, too." Joe would be 'thinking spring' every day until then. When his shift was over, he went into the tack room to punch out. When he came out, who would be standing there waiting for him, but Charlotte! He felt his face grow suddenly warm and was grateful for the low lighting in the stable. "Charlotte!" was all he could say.

"Hello, Joe." Charlotte looked down shyly at her worn boots, self-conscious of her shoddy appearance. Joe's heart broke for her. When they were in school, she was always the girl in class who wore matching ribbons, clean shoes and kept her silken hair combed and neatly coiffed. Now, her frayed jeans dragged beneath her boots and her honey gold hair hung loosely in a ponytail. The coat she wore appeared to be two sizes too big; she had obviously lost a lot of weight. Joe noticed that the sparkle had left her eyes, but they were still as blue as a clear autumn sky. He found his voice and went to her. "I was wondering when I'd see you. How are you?"

"I'm okay," she replied, but she didn't fool him. "I've missed Sasha," Charlotte explained, "but my dad's been sick, so mom and I have been busy trying to keep up with his work."

"What kind of work is it?" Joe asked, noticing her rough calloused hands. He thought of his mom.

"He was working over at the incinerator. They burn everything here, Joe. It's so gross." She crinkled her slightly turned up nose. "When I heard that some new people came in and that one of them was working with the animals, I hoped it was you." She looked up at him and smiled.

Joe's heart melted and he took her hand. "C'mon. When was the last time you saw Sasha?"

"Oh, it's been months. Is she all right?"

"Yeah, she's fine. I have lunch with her and Lucky every day."

"Who's Lucky?"

"My dog. He's not as big as Sasha, but he's a good dog."

When they arrived at Sasha's pen, the dog whimpered joyfully when she saw her mistress. Sasha put her large paws on the top of the gate that separated them and eagerly licked Charlotte's face. Charlotte giggled and allowed Sasha to love on her and then reached over, took the dog's head in her arms, and buried her face in Sasha's thick scruff. Joe noticed Charlotte's slight shoulders quivering as she cried. Not knowing what else to do, he turned his attention to Lucky. When Charlotte looked up, her eyes were red rimmed and wet. "I'm sorry, Joe. I try not to cry, but it's so depressing here. And with dad being so sick, mom and I don't know what's going to happen to us."

"Try not to worry, okay? I know it's hard not to, but really try, all right?" Joe said.

She smiled, "Okay, Joe. Can I come see you again?"

Joe shrugged, but inside he was doing handsprings. "Sure. I'm off tomorrow and Saturday, but I'll see you around."

"Thanks, Joe." Charlotte said. She took his hand, "I'm glad you're here."

"Me, too," Joe said as he gazed into her eyes.

Charlotte released his hand. "I'd better get going. Mom wanted me back before dark." She slowly turned and began to walk away.

"Can I walk you home?" Joe blurted out before he realized what he was saying.

Charlotte turned a shy smile at him, "I'd like that," and let him take her hand. While they strolled down the sidewalk, Joe was nervous. He had wanted to do this very thing for a long time and now that he was actually able to walk her home, their situation was nothing as he had imagined. He wanted to talk to her; to find out how things were when she first arrived, and what had been happening since then, but he didn't want to bombard her with too many questions. He figured with their first meeting, he'd keep it simple and just enjoy her company.

When they reached her house, he was surprised. "It's nothing like what they showed us at school that day, is it?" he said.

"No. Not at all," Charlotte said. "They really tricked a lot of people, and I don't think anyone is happy about it. If folks could, they'd leave this place and never come back. But I don't know if we can ever get out of here."

"Like I said, Charlotte, don't worry about it right now." Joe watched the fading night sky. "I'd better get going. I'll see you soon, okay?"

"Okay, Joe. Thanks for walking me home." The young woman smiled sweetly.

Joe nodded, "Anytime." As he hurried back to his unit, there were only two words on his mind, "Think Spring."

Red Dalton hung up the phone and radioed Tom. "Connelly!"

"What's up, Red?"

"Garrison wants you to start training some new recruits. He's taking a dozen of your trained officers and making them Regulators." Red barked into the mic," We need to discuss this, so come by the office after work."

Three hours later, Tom finished his rounds and took a golf cart to the front security office. "I'm here, Red. What do you want to discuss?" Tom said as he went straight for the coffee pot in the security office.

Red leaned back in his chair with his booted feet propped up on the corner of his desk. "Garrison is sending out more Regulators in the spring. Evidently, Baroam isn't happy with Garrison's numbers. Too many are still on the outside."

"Well, where does he plan on putting them?" Tom asked.

"Your guess is as good as mine," Red replied.

"You know, Red, I was talking with Joe earlier and we both think that the best thing would be to --"

"Get these people out of here." Red finished his sentence.

Tom grinned, "Yeah."

"I've been thinking about it for months, Tom, but it wasn't until you and Joe showed up that I realized that it was even a possibility." He stood up from his chair and clapped Tom on the shoulder. "I'll get on the radio a little later and call Berkley Springs."

That night, "This is Boss Daddy calling Devil Dog, do you copy; over?"

"Devil Dog here. What have you got, Boss Daddy; over?"

"Investigative assignment will now be a rescue operation. I repeat; investigative assignment has turned into a rescue operation. We'll be in touch. Get prepared; over and out."

At their initial meeting, Tom knew that Barbara Beechum would be a great ally on the inside, but after speaking with Joe and Red, he decided that she should play a part in the rescue as well. She would be very useful in organizing the elderly in her building. "Good morning, Mrs. Beechum," he said when he spotted her coming down the sidewalk with Dorothy.

Conditioned to fear the men in the jumpsuits, panic washed over Barbara when she saw Tom, but when she recognized him, she relaxed and greeted him. "Good morning, Officer. I see you and your fellow Regulators still haven't learned any manners. You still bang on our doors every morning."

Tom wasn't sure, but he thought he saw a glint of humor in her eyes. "Yes, ma'am, I have to do what I'm told." Tom towered over the women by at least a foot and with his black coveralls and M-16, he was a fearsome sight to Dorothy. But his voice was gentle as he continued, "I wonder if I could have a word with you, Mrs. Beechum." He paused, "In private."

"Officer Connelly, whatever you have to say to me you can say to my friend." Barbara turned to face Dorothy. "Darling, this is the gentleman I told you about. Do you remember?"

Dorothy took a small step towards him and looked up, "Yes, I do remember you mentioning him. I believe you were quite pleased to see him, weren't you?" Dorothy paused for a moment and whispered, "He is quite handsome, Barbara."

Barbara squeezed her friend's hand gently and smiled. "Yes, but we mustn't say that out here. Do you understand?"

Dorothy put her hand to her mouth, "Oh dear. I do understand. I'm terribly sorry, Barbara, Officer Connelly."

Tom nodded, "No harm done, but we do need to be careful. Can we talk after the prayer meeting tomorrow night?

"Yes, of course," Barbara replied.

"By the way, it will have to be at eighteen hundred hours They are changing the curfew to eighteen hundred hours instead of twenty hundred hours." All of a sudden, Tom spotted McCloud coming toward the women from behind. In a harsh voice he nearly shouted, "Now be on your way, ladies and don't forget what I told you."

Barbara threw her shoulders back at his sudden rudeness and was about to scold him, when she heard McCloud's voice behind her.

"Are these ladies giving you a hard time, Officer Connelly?" He walked past Barbara and Dorothy and turned to stand next to Tom.

"No, they're fine. I was just reminding them that curfew will be at eighteen hundred hours instead of twenty hundred hours."

Barbara didn't miss a beat, "In English, Officer."

"You'll have to excuse him, Mrs. Beechum, he's a soldier and they sometimes forget they are living in the civilian world. Allow me to translate. Curfew will be at 6:00 p.m. tonight and tomorrow instead of the usual 8:00 p.m. We will go back to our regular time on Thursday."

Barbara turned an angry glare to Tom. "And why would you be restricting our freedoms even more? Isn't 8:00 early enough?"

"Just routine training, ma'am," Tom smiled.

"Fine then, thank you for that important piece of information." Barbara nodded to the men and took Dorothy's hand, "Come along, Dorothy. We're done, here," and with that she marched down the sidewalk toward the grocery store.

McCloud threw his head back and laughed. "Connelly, you sure have a way of making people mad. Why is that?" He patted Tom on his back and continued chuckling. "C'mon. I need to show you something."

Tom followed McCloud across the street to the security office to pick up a golf cart. They rode toward the south wall of The City where a dozen or more security guards were gathered. Tom's adrenaline began to rush, "What's going on, Mac?"

"Someone tried to escape," McCloud said quietly.

"Who?"

"Don't know, they got away, but they left something behind. That's what I wanted to show you."

Ephesians 6:12 "For our struggle is not against flesh and blood, but against the rulers, against the authorities, against the powers of this dark world, and against the spiritual forces of evil in the heavenly realms."

CHAPTER 33

"MAY I HAVE YOUR attention please?!" Walt rapped sharply with a ball peen hammer on the metal desk, but everyone in the hall continued to chatter. He pounded again, but the talking continued. He glanced over at Kyle sitting next to him and shook his head. "They're not going to like this," and let out a piercing whistle that caused everyone to put their hands over their ears. "Will everyone take their seats, please?" He shouted. Finally, the crowd settled down and Walt laid down the hammer, "I suppose you are all wondering why we called a town meeting." The statement brought nods of agreement and started more chatter from the crowd. "Quiet, please!" Walt shouted again. "You all know our minister, Steve Barnes, his wife, Tanya, and the rest of the family. When they came to us this past winter, they had come from a town in Maryland called Willow Creek. Like my town and here in Berkley Springs, the Regulators came to Willow Creek and destroyed it, taking loved ones and neighbors back to the place they call 'The City.' Without going into any more detail, we are here to tell you that we have word from inside The City that an earlier assignment to gather information about The City and the people in control has been changed to a rescue mission." Obviously stirred by this information, the people began their muttering again.

Walt picked up the hammer and pounded on the desk again and shouted, "You should know that we have been able to communicate with someone on the inside who can confirm this."

"What does any of this have to do with us?" Someone shouted.

Kyle recognized him as one of the men who had come in with the woman who had stolen away weeks ago. "It has everything to do with people everywhere who want to live free again and to those who have family and loved ones on the inside," Kyle said, clearly irritated. "Do you think it will stop here? The Regulators know there are still survivors on the outside. Eventually they will come back for them. The people on the inside are sick and some are dying. Is it fair to leave them there?"

The man muttered something and sat back down in his chair.

"Kyle is right, people," Walt continued. "The information we have is legit, but you must realize that when they do come back, they won't be any nicer."

"They weren't very nice before!" Someone shouted.

"My point exactly," Walt said. "If they know a rescue is being planned, believe me, they aren't going to take it lying down." "So, what's the plan?" Anders asked.

"I'm turning the floor over to Kyle Johnson. He'll give you a brief explanation of what we're thinking on doing." Walt answered.

"Thanks, Walt." Kyle stood up and looked around the room. Fear stared back at him, yet there were some determined to be a part of whatever was going to happen. Those, Anders being one of them, were the ones he wanted to speak to. "The plan is to leave Berkley Springs on horseback and make a stop somewhere outside The City to re-group. We'll rest up a couple of days before we head in. With the communication with the people we have on the inside, we should be able to coordinate a plan of attack from the outside."

The man in the back spoke up again, "How on earth are you going to do that when there are only six of you! Not to mention that three of you are women and one is a boy."

Sandy bristled and stood up to speak, but Ben touched her hand, and she sat back in her chair. Kyle spoke for her, "Sir, I don't know when the last time you fired a gun was, but I can tell you that these women and this young man can beat the best shooters here. They are not to be reckoned with. Now, getting back to what I was talking about. Anyone who cares to join us is welcome, but the road is hard, and it will be dangerous. Some of you may not come back. If you do choose to join us, we will have a separate meeting to go into more detail. That is all we are going to say about it right now. There is a sign-up sheet here on the desk. Come on up, sign your name, and stick around. Anyone who decides not to come, we will not hold it against you. As I said, it will be dangerous and a very, very hard journey."

Except for Anders, no one stirred. Kyle knew he would be the first one up and shook his hand after he had signed his name. "Thanks, Anders."

Anders nodded back. "I want my horses back and I want to teach the people who took 'em, a little something about horse thieving."

"You'll definitely have your chance, my friend." Kyle laughed.

Anders stood next to Sandy and the rest of the group as others came forward to sign up. He watched her disappointment when more people were leaving than were staying.

Ben noticed it, too, and took her hand when he saw her expression. "Mom, isn't it better that we have a few strong ones, than a lot of weaker ones?"

Sandy nodded but didn't say anything. She watched the people come up to sign their names, and she shook their hands as they came to stand with her. Fifteen brave souls had made the choice to fight.

Walt skimmed over the signatures and then studied the faces of the people who remained. "Lord, help us," he thought. "Well, folks this is good. Not too many and not too few. Steve, before we get started would you mind leading us in prayer?"

"Sure, Walt. Will everyone bow their heads, please?" Steve paused for a moment and took a deep breath before he began. "All glory to you, Almighty Father. Thank you for your blessings these past months in Berkley Springs and for the new friends we have made. We beseech you, Father, to be our ultimate Leader and to guide us on this mission to rescue those who are imprisoned and to put an end to the evil that has moved across our great country. We ask for your protection for Joe, Tom, and everyone who will be a part of this dangerous undertaking, and for those who are unable to protect themselves. We ask this in Jesus' name. Amen."

After the prayer, everyone found a seat except Walt and Kyle, who remained at the front of the room. Walt began, "Since I arrived in Berkley Springs, I have come to know each of you here and I have to admit, I'm not surprised that you have made the decision to fight, and I thank you. For security purposes I think we should keep our little group as tightly knit as possible, so I suggest we all move into the firehouse until it's time for us to leave. There's plenty of room there and we can take shifts watching the horses. What do you all think?" The others nodded in agreement.

"Good. We'll make the move to the firehouse tomorrow. Kyle, you have the floor."

Kyle stood up "Thanks, Walt. Beginning tomorrow after we settle into the firehouse, I want us to start training, not only physically, but also with weapons. We don't know what we're going to encounter, and I want everyone to be ready for whatever comes." Kyle looked around the room, anticipating the mention of weapons would be a problem for some. He was right. Nancy Davis and Joann

Watson glanced at each other, worries written all over their faces. "Is there some-thing wrong, ladies?"

"We weren't expecting to use any weapons, Kyle." Nancy said.

Her husband, Herb looked at her as though she had broccoli growing out of her ears. "Honey, what did you think we were going to do, waltz in there and talk nice to them?"

She cocked her head as though considering the suggestion, "Well, yes. Can't we try a civilized form of communication first?"

"With all due respect, Nancy," Morgan interrupted, "I saw firsthand what these people do, and they are not interested in any form of civilized communica-tion. They take what they want, and they have no problem murdering to get it."

"Did you see them murder anyone?" Nancy asked with just a hint of inso-lence—hurt that Morgan would speak to her in such a gruff tone.

"I saw them burn down a church full of people," Morgan spat. "Talking doesn't work." She turned in her chair away from Nancy and the others.

Kyle saw her wipe a tear from her cheek and understood the harsh nightmares she still endured whenever anyone brought up the Regulators. "Nancy, if either you or Joann have any reservations about carrying this out, I urge you to think about it and pray on it. Whoever joins will need to be with us 110 percent."

Walt folded his arms and leaned against the table, toward his audience. "Tell you what, Nancy, you, Herb, Joann, and David go home tonight, talk it over, pray together, and let us know at the next meeting; Fair enough?"

Nancy nodded reluctantly, not daring to look at the confusion on her hus-band's face.

"All right then, we'll close the meeting now and take it up again next week." Walt said.

The guards dispersed when they saw McCloud and Tom approaching from across the field. The first time Tom had seen this area, he knew it would not be a good place to attempt an escape. It was wide open, with spotlights that blazed down from atop the twenty-five-foot towers positioned along its perimeter. He couldn't think of anyone who would try to escape from this area, mainly because those he met were either too afraid or too old to attempt it by themselves.

McCloud climbed out of the golf cart and strode quickly over to a site where everyone was standing. "All right, gentlemen, break it up. Tom, come take a look at this, will you?"

Tom moved in next to McCloud and was shocked at what he saw when the other men stepped aside. Laying in the grass next to a fresh mound of dirt was a shovel and a hay-baling hook with a heavy rope attached.

"What do you make of it, Connelly?" McCloud queried.

Tom hunkered down next to the hole and picked up the rope to examine it more closely. "Looks to me like they'd been planning it for a while. They must have buried this hook shortly after they arrived, judging by the amount of dirt in this rope and the grass that has grown over top of the whole mess. And here, look at this." He handed the rope over to McCloud.

"Whoever they are, they shouldn't be hard to find." McCloud said, handing the rope back. "There's blood all over it."

Tom continued his examination of the rope and then looked up at the guard closest to him, "How deep would you say that hole is?"

"About four feet, sir." He was young, inexperienced, and scared.

Still crouched next to the hole, Tom's eyes squinted against the afternoon sun as he questioned the young man, "Who was first on the scene?"

"I was, sir. I got the call from Garr -- I mean Mr. Garrison and came right away. I didn't see a soul around, just this stuff." The young guard pointed with his rifle but kept his focus on Tom. "Am I in trouble, sir?"

Tom straightened up, looked hard at the officer, and checked the nametape on his uniform, "No, Officer Wesley, you aren't in trouble. Try to make it to the scene a little quicker next time. And don't be afraid to use your weapon if you observe any suspicious behavior."

Officer Wesley dropped his head, ashamed that he had disappointed his superior officer. "Yes sir."

It wasn't like Tom to be so rough, but he had to keep up the image of a hardnosed soldier from the war. Because of his past, Garrison had promoted him to Commanding Officer of the new officers coming in. He drilled them and trained them hard, yet he was always fair with them and had earned not only their respect but also that of McCloud and Garrison. Smith, on the other hand, was a different story. Smith neither liked nor trusted Tom and with Tom, the sentiment was mutual.

"Has anyone notified Mr. Dalton yet?" Tom asked.

"He's on the way," Someone answered from behind the group.

Tom turned to the sound of Smith's voice and saw him storming through the crowd. "Don't you people have anything better to do than stand around looking at a hole in the ground?"

Obviously afraid of Smith, McCloud stammered, "We, we were just questioning the guards, Mr. Smith. You know, to find out whether they saw anything else."

Smith cocked his head slightly, "And . . .?" he questioned impatiently.

"No one saw anything, Smith," Tom said. "You officers, get back to work now!" He shouted at his underlings, and they scattered. Tom locked a hard stare on Smith.

"Was one of your soldiers responsible for this, Connelly?" Smith glared back and waited for an answer. He used to be Garrison's right-hand man, but since Tom came along, Garrison leaned more on him, than on Smith for his security issues. Although he preferred to call on Smith to do his dirty work, Smith still hated the fact that someone shared his spotlight. "There'll be hell to pay if any of them were lax in their duties."

"How 'bout we let security investigate this before we start pointing fingers, Smith," Tom growled. "If this was done as long ago as it appears; it happened on your watch, not mine, or my guards." Tom narrowed his eyes, daring Smith to respond.

Smith's face went crimson with rage, but he stayed silent. He turned with a grunt and stormed back across the field.

"Connelly, where do you come off talking to him like that? Not that I blame you; he can be a jerk most of the time and I personally don't like him, but good grief." McCloud shook his head. "I'm glad I'm on your side."

Tom abruptly turned and looked squarely at McCloud. "Are you, Mac?"

The man's smile shifted to confusion, "Well, yeah. I thought I was. Am I, Tom?"

"You'll have to make that decision on your own." Tom slung his M16 on his shoulder and by habit checked the Ka-bar at his side, then he strode toward Red and the two other security officers coming toward him.

"Whatcha got, Connelly?" Red asked, not bothering to slow his pace.

Tom joined Red and walked with him to where Mac still stood, "Looks like someone tried to make a break for it." Tom shook his head "What they were thinking?"

Red examined the hay-baling hook and rope that Mac handed to him. Talking more to himself, he mumbled, "Hmm, blood on the hook, some on the rope."

He handed it to one of the guards with him. "Get this stuff bagged and bring it back to the office. Officer Connelly and I need to see Garrison." Red turned back to Tom, "They must have decided that the rope was too far gone to support their weight and just left it. Not to mention from the amount of blood . . . someone got a pretty nasty wound." Red hollered at McCloud, "Hey, Mac! Give us ride to Garrison's, will ya?"

"Sure, Red. No problem." Gabe McCloud met them at the golf cart. Still puzzled by Tom's last words to him, Mac always noted the manner in which Tom treated the residents of The City and how he responded to them. Mac knew that Tom was not in support of The City or of the motives of those behind it.

The golf cart quietly put down the street toward the building that Garrison and Smith occupied. As they rode, Tom watched the people walking by. A man coming out of the grocery store nodded to him and Tom recognized him as one of those he knew he could count on when the time came to make the escape. He nodded back.

When they arrived at Garrison's building, Red and Tom got out of the cart while McCloud remained seated behind the wheel. "I'll just wait for you guys here," he said.

Red shook his head, "Not a chance, my friend. I'm sure Garrison will want a word with you, too."

McCloud reluctantly slid out from behind the wheel and joined Tom and Red.

"What happened, Connelly? I thought you had these officers trained!" Garrison yelled.

Connelly's voice remained calm, but firm. "Those officers are just kids, Garrison. The oldest one is twenty years old, with no military training. You can't expect them to be highly trained officers in a matter of months. Besides, by the time my guys got there, the perpetrator was gone."

Garrison swung around to Red, "Well? What do you have to offer?"

Red was not intimidated by Garrison. "Whoever it was, buried the hay-baling hook and rope at least six or seven months ago. It had to be before winter set in, before the ground froze. The hole was about four feet deep, and the grass had grown over top of it. I'd venture to say that it was done not long after this place started filling up." With that remark, Red turned to Smith and waited for him to defend himself.

Garrison spoke through clenched teeth; his voice trembled with rage, "Mr. Smith, I am going to leave this problem with you. I don't want you to rest until you find out who the perpetrator was and bring them to me, personally. Do you understand?"

"Yes, sir." Smith bowed his head and waited for further instructions from his boss.

"Now, get out of here! All of you!" Garrison flailed his arms in the air, and then swung around toward the window. He knew he would have to call Baroam about this. The last time the Supreme Leader was disappointed in him, The City was just getting started, and they were behind schedule. The mental anguish he went through was bad enough, but this time -- this time Garrison knew that the punishment would be more than psychological. He made up his mind that he would wait until he heard back from Red Dalton. Garrison jumped when the phone suddenly rang. He didn't have to guess who was calling. He picked up the receiver, "Hello?"

"Mr. Garrison, I just received some disturbing news, and I had expected that you would have called me about it by now." Baroam's voice was particularly whiney.

"Good afternoon, Commander Baroam. Yes, sir. We did have an incident earlier, but I had hoped to learn more from my security people before I called you. The only thing I can tell you is that someone tried to escape, but they failed and was injured in the attempt."

"Mr. Garrison, do you know what will happen if we allow these people to do as they wish? We must maintain control. Our Supreme Leader will tolerate nothing less. Do you understand?"

"Yes, Commander, I understand." Garrison said weakly.

"When you find this person, I presume you will make an example of him for all The City to see. If you do not, I will make you the example." The phone went dead.

Red, Smith, and Tom remained silent until they were in the elevator, then Red patted Smith on the back. "I'll get you the findings of the investigation as soon as I can, Mr. Smith."

"Thanks, Red." Smith exited the elevator without saying another word. Then, just as the doors were sliding shut, he quickly put his hand against one of them, holding it open. "Red, what kind of hook did you say that was?"

"A hay-baling hook—the kind that's used when moving or baling hay." Red said.

Smith nodded his head. "Interesting. Thanks." He withdrew his hand allowing the doors to slide shut.

"I've never seen Garrison go off like that before!" McCloud exclaimed, as he climbed into the golf cart.

"Only one other time I've seen him like that," Red said. "And I have a feeling it's going to be happening a lot more often."

"Why's that?" Mac asked.

"He's losing control and the man who's pulling his strings knows it. Whoever is really in control of things is starting to bear down on him and he's feeling the pressure. They are all losing control."

"Losing control of what?" Mac asked, obviously confused.

Tom remained quiet while Red attempted to enlighten McCloud of what was going to happen in the next few weeks.

Red waved his arm towards the buildings they passed by, "This, McCloud. They are losing control of this. Can't you feel it?"

McCloud shook his head. It was starting to ache. Too much was happening too fast. "I'll admit I've been feeling something in the air . . . tension, anticipation maybe, I can't quite put my finger on it." McCloud pulled the cart over in front of the security office.

Before Red got out, he looked directly at McCloud. "I'm going to be frank with you, Mac. I like you and I believe you know the difference between right and wrong, but right now, you're on the fence about it. You need to pick a side, my friend. I just hope it's the right one. Connelly, come on. I need you to have another look at the evidence. I'll talk to you tomorrow, Mac. Thanks for the ride."

McCloud's mind reeled at Red's remark. Not two hours ago, Tom had told him the same thing He stammered, "Yeah, you -- you bet. See you, Connelly."

Tom turned and nodded. "See you, Mac."

Gabe McCloud pulled the golf cart away from the curb and headed back toward the security bunker on the other side of town. He was being convicted and the more he examined himself, the more fearful he became. Suddenly he needed to talk to Tom.

Red turned off the light in the front office and led Tom through to his private unit attached to the back of the office. Once in the bedroom, he opened the closet door and pushed the boxes aside, revealing the high frequency base radio. Tom's heart leapt to his throat. There was only one person he wanted to talk to, and he hoped Red would be able to get through. "Tom, I think it's about that time, don't you?"

"Yeah, I do. You gonna put the word out?"

"Yep." And with that, Red sat on a box in front of the radio and began, "This is Boss Daddy. Anyone out there tonight; over?"

"Evenin,' Boss Daddy. Devil Dog, here; over." Walt answered from Berkley Springs.

"Get the word out, Devil Dog. The sheep are getting restless; over."

"You got it. Any word on the two that arrived a few months ago; over?"

Red laughed, "As a matter of fact, I'm having mutton for supper right now. What about you; over?"

"Yeah, we're having the same thing. Standby; over." Walt pushed away from his desk and as fast as his big gut allowed, hurried out to the fire station's main room where the others were playing cards, and talking. "Sandy, Kyle can I see you for a minute, please?"

Kyle led the way to the back room where Walt was waiting in front of the radio. He pointed toward two chairs on the other side of his desk. "Have a seat." Once they had settled around the desk, Walt got back on the radio. "Boss Daddy requests confirmation on that; over."

Red grinned and turned to Tom. "They're there; your people. Do you want to say anything?"

Tom's adrenaline spiked so much he had to catch his breath. He wished that Joe could be there, but there was no time to get him. He sprang from his chair and in one long stride was next to Red.

"I expect you used something similar in the war, so I don't need to explain to you how to use it." Red said.

Tom grinned at his friend then put his mouth to the microphone, "This is Nelly. You out there, Sandman; over?"

Recognizing his old handle from when they were in Iraq together, Kyle reached for the radio, "Nelly, we're all here; over."

Tom took a deep breath and smiled over at Red. He didn't realize how much he missed his old Army buddy. "It's so good to hear you; over."

"It's good to hear from you too, Nelly; over." Kyle grinned.

Sandy went to stand behind Kyle and laid her hands on his shoulders, "Please, Kyle, can you somehow find out how Joe is?"

Kyle glanced up at her and then leaned into the radio, "You got a sitrep on the little lamb; over?"

"Little lamb is strong and healthy; ready for slaughter; over."

Aghast at what Tom said, Sandy nearly shouted, "What on earth does that mean?" She turned to Walt.

"Don't worry, Sandy." Walt laughed. "We have to use code words. I would expect that 'ready for slaughter' means he's ready for the fight. It looks like we're going to see some action soon, folks."

Tom couldn't stand it. He had to hear Sandy's voice and gave her the only handle he could think of on such short notice. "Sandman, can you put Lady Blue on, please; over?"

Sandy suddenly felt happy tears sting her eyes as she took the chair Kyle offered her. The expression on his face was soft, gentle. He knew his best friend was missing her too.

Sandy pressed on the mic button and spoke into it. "Hello, Nelly; over." Embarrassed that that was all she could think of saying, she looked up at Kyle and shrugged.

"Evening, ma'am," Tom said, "It's good to hear you. All is well. I'll send wishes to the young un; over."

Sandy couldn't hide the relief she felt. "Thank you, Nelly. I'm glad you are well, too. It's good to hear your voice; over."

Red was getting nervous and motioned to Tom that he needed to cut the call short.

Tom nodded his head. "Time is short, Lady Blue. All the best to everyone; over."

Red got back on the radio, "Devil Dog, we'll be in touch; over and out."

Sandy stepped away from the desk and emotional overload kicked in as she burst into tears. She turned to Walt. "Thank you so much!" And she threw her arms around his neck.

Walt hugged her back. "Well, you're very welcome, little lady. I'm glad you had the chance to talk to him and learn about your boy. But remember, not a word of this to anyone. We still don't know who's loyal to whom."

Kyle shook his hand. "You have our word, Walt. Thank you." He looked at Sandy, "Gosh it was good to hear his voice. I hadn't realized how much I missed him until now."

Sandy looked up at both men, "Well, now what? From the sound of it, they're ready to move. I think we should start soon, don't you?"

Kyle and Walt exchanged glances and shrugged. "No time like the present," Kyle said. "Walt?"

Walt's expression was resolute. "The Davis's and Watson's have had nearly a week to think about what they want to do. We'll call a meeting tomorrow night."

Tom sat on the bed with his head in his hands. For a moment, Red thought he was angry because he had to cut the call short, but when Tom looked up at him, he was wearing a huge smile, "Red, thanks. You have no idea how much I needed that. Somehow, I'll let Joe know, but I promise I'll be very careful." Tom stood up and shook Red's hand. "I guess I'd better get going. No doubt McCloud will be wondering where I'm at if I don't turn this in." Tom patted his rifle.

"All right, Tom. I'll talk to you tomorrow. If you happen to see Garrison or Smith on your way back, tell 'em I'll give 'em a call in the a.m. I'm going to take a look around the stables tonight and see what I can find out. The suspect shouldn't be too hard to find with that injury. Then I may stroll on over to the infirmary."

Tom took his leave and walked down the street, enjoying the smells from the stables and the spring blossoms that filled the evening air. Thankfully, the wind sent the stench of the smokestack to the far end of the City. His walk took him past the building where Garrison and Smith lived, and he hoped he wouldn't run into them again. He was still enjoying the high he felt from talking with Kyle and Sandy and didn't want to ruin it. His hopes evaporated when he cleared the building and nearly ran into Smith. He shouldered his rifle and looked directly at the man. "Smith, for what it's worth, I don't think Garrison was fair in what he said."

"I don't need your sympathy, Connelly. I'll find out who was trying to escape and one way or another, you're gonna end up in the middle of it. Mark my words."

"What do you mean by that?" Tom asked.

"I mean I'm convinced you had something to do with it, along with that kid you came in with, and I'm going to see you both hang for it."

Tom shook his head. "Smith, you do what you have to. You won't find anything on me or the kid." Tom turned to leave, then as an afterthought, he looked back at Smith. "Oh, and Red said he'd give you a call tomorrow morning. Good night." Tom turned and grasped his rifle again. Some things the muscles never forget, like how to hold an M16 on patrol. Close to the body, the trigger finger flat against the trigger guard, eyes alert and always on the move. When he arrived at the security bunker, McCloud was waiting for him at the front desk. Everyone else had already left except for the night watch down the hall. "Hey, Mac. Sorry I'm late. I don't think Red will have much trouble finding out who it was." Tom cocked his head and took a closer look at the man staring back at him. "You okay, Mac?"

Gabe McCloud looked intently at Tom with an expression Tom couldn't identify -- relief, defeat? He stepped closer and swung his rifle around to his back. "What's going on, Mac?"

"I'm picking a side, Connelly."

Joshua 24:15 "Then choose for yourselves this day whom you will serve. . . but for me and my household, we will serve the Lord."

CHAPTER 34

WALT CALLED THE MEETING to order at seven o'clock. "Okay, before we get started, we need to find out from you folks whether you want to stay in or not. Remember, no one will hold it against you if you decide not to be a part of this." Walt turned to Herb and Nancy Davis first. "Herb, have you and Nancy talked it over?"

Herb stood up with his hands in his pockets, looking like an awkward fifth grader about to give his first oral report in front of the class. "Walt, everyone." He nodded to the others around the room. "Nancy and I have decided that she will stay behind, but I will go with you." He turned and smiled at his wife, understanding her fear, then faced the group, bowed his head slightly and quietly took his seat next to his wife, who clasped his hand in both of hers.

"Thank you, Herb," Walt said. "We can appreciate what a difficult decision that was to make for you and Nancy." Walt turned to David and Joann Watson. "David, what have you and Joann decided?"

"We are both going." David said without standing. "Now, that being said, we will need some intense training in certain areas, if you know what I mean." He made eye contact with Kyle, Walt, and Sandy as if to say he expected them to make certain that he and wife would be ready for the fight.

"Thank you all for your honesty and courage to speak. I've said it several times and I'll say it again. Just because someone is staying behind doesn't make them a coward. We need folks back here to hold down the fort. Nancy, since you still have a dog in this fight, or should I say a husband," Walt laughed from deep down in his belly, "how about we make you our radio woman? We'll get you set up after the meeting. That way you will still be a part of the team."

Nancy beamed, thankful that she would still be included. "Thanks, Walt. I really do want to help."

"And that you will. I'm going to turn the floor over to Kyle, since he will be heading up the training program."

Kyle stood up to address the group. "Okay everyone, since we've got folks of all different ages and physical abilities, it will be your responsibility to let me know how you are doing. The training will be tough, and you all know your limitations, I do not. Everyone hear me on that?"

They all bobbed their heads in agreement. "Now, that doesn't mean I want you to wimp out on me." Kyle's blue eyes danced when he smiled. "We'll start with running every morning before breakfast. After breakfast, we'll do some strength training, break for lunch and then after lunch we'll take a run to the range. We only have two, maybe three weeks at best to train, and we'll be going at it hard, so you will be sore and tired. That's the normal stuff. Anything other than that, tell someone. Now," Kyle clapped his hands together and turned his attention on Sandy and Morgan, "these lovely ladies will be training on the gun range. If anyone has a weapon and ammunition, bring it. Our little group is limited, but I'm pretty sure, once we get inside The City, there will be plenty more ammo we can get our hands on. If you're already familiar with your weapon and just need practice, then have at it. The ladies will help only if you need it. Gus, how's your supply of re-loading materials?"

Gus Wilkerson stood up, "I've got plenty of shotgun shells. They're pretty cheap, so I stocked up on them, but I'm low on casings and firing pins for the handguns and rifles."

"Do you think you can put your hands on some more?" Kyle asked.

"Yeah, sure. The place where I used to pick up my supplies is only about five miles up the mountain. I can ride over first thing in the morning." Gus replied.

"I don't want anyone going anywhere by themselves." Walt interrupted.

"I'll go with him." Steve offered. "We'll leave right after breakfast."

Walt nodded his approval. "Bring as much as you can carry."

Gus chuckled. "The place is abandoned; I'll clean it out if I can."

Kyle looked around the room. "Does anyone have any questions?" The team looked at one another and shook their heads. "Not yet." David Watson said.

"Well, if anyone does come up with a question or concern, don't hesitate to say something. Okay then, we'll see everyone bright and early at oh six hundred tomorrow."

Walt went to Herb and Nancy right after the meeting ended, "Nancy, you and Herb come with me for a minute. I want to show you what you'll be doing."

They followed Walt to the back room while the others gathered at the coffee pot or mingled in the main room.

Joann Davis filled her cup with coffee and went to stand with Morgan. "Hey, Morgan."

"Hi, Joann," Morgan said with a smile. "I'm glad you and David decided to come."

Joann appeared nervous. "I am, too, but Morgan, I'm going to need some individual help on the range tomorrow. Can you help me?" "Of course," Morgan said, "have you ever fired a gun before?" "No, not unless you consider a BB gun a real gun." Joann joked.

"It is a real gun," Morgan assured her. "The gun you'll be firing will have a good bit more kick to it and it won't bode so well for the bad guy on the receiving end. As long as you know the basics of gun ownership, you'll be fine. One thing Uncle Walt always told me, never point a gun at anything unless you intend to kill them. That's the single most important thing I can tell you."

"Thanks, Morgan. This is kind of exciting, isn't it?"

Morgan took a sip of her coffee, "Yeah, it is. But I can't stress enough how vicious these people are, Joann. They mean business and they don't hesitate to kill. We'll talk more about it on the range tomorrow. Will you excuse me, please?"

"Sure, Morgan," Joann turned to her husband. "David, am I taking this too lightly? I mean, Morgan was a witness to their evil. We only saw what came in their aftermath."

"We'll see soon enough, but I think we should expect the very worst from the Regulators. C'mon, I want to say 'hello' to the rest of the team and then I think we should get some sleep." David put his arm around his wife and led her toward Sandy, Ben and the others.

While the small group gathered to visit, Kyle and Alan Anders left the firehouse to check on the horses. Although their first meeting did not go well, as the months went by, Anders had gained a great respect for all of them, especially for Kyle. He had always wanted to join the military, but for health reasons he couldn't and was resentful about it for years. When Kyle found this out, he tried a little harder to understand and make friends with the man.

Anders shoved his hands into his jean's pockets. The early spring night was unseasonably chilly. "Kyle, I've been thinking."

"Uh oh," Kyle laughed. "Just kidding, Anders. What's up?"

"How many people do we have coming along?"

Kyle sighed and turned his eyes toward the sky as he counted people in his head, "Let me see, we've got twelve. Why?"

"How many horses do we have?" Anders asked, knowing no one else had considered it until now.

Kyle's eyes grew wide at the realization. "Not enough, that's for sure!" Kyle exclaimed. "Good thinking, Anders. What do you suggest?" "How many more horses do we need?" Anders questioned.

Kyle considered for a moment, "Well, Walt has the two he brought when he came, we've got the ones we rode in on plus the pack horse, but that still leaves us short by three." "I have an idea," Anders offered.

Kyle raised his eyebrows in question but didn't say anything.

"When Gus and Steve go after the supplies tomorrow morning, there are a couple of farms along the way. They could always check there. I know that sometimes when owners turn their horses loose, the horse will usually come back to the place where they are most familiar. It could be the owners turned them loose and the horses came back." Anders shrugged, waiting for Kyle's response.

"Sounds like a plan, Anders. We'll tell them about it when we get back." When they arrived at the stables, Kyle stopped short and held his hand up signaling Anders to stop. He reached for his handgun and moved cautiously in; Anders followed close behind him. They crept ever so quietly down the aisle between the stalls. All of a sudden, Kyle spotted someone slipping out of the back of the barn. "Freeze!"

The trespasser fled into the darkness of the woods, with Anders charging behind him.

"Anders, wait!" Kyle shouted, but Anders was already out of the stable and into the woods. "Alan!"

Anders charged through the trees. The brush slapped fiercely at him as he ran. He paused and leaned against a tree to catch his breath, when all of a sudden, a shot pierced the night and a bullet whistled by him, just barely missing his cheek. He decided against the pursuit and jogged back to the stable.

When Alan took off after the man, Kyle bolted out the back of the stable and peered into the woods, trying desperately to see his friend. At last, he spotted Anders stumbling back to the stable. As he staggered toward him, Kyle quickly ran his eyes up and down the young man, praying he wouldn't see any blood. Aside from a few scratches, there was no blood and Kyle thanked God for that.

"Anders, I admire your courage for running after him, but don't ever do that again, do you hear me!"

Anders bent over at the waist with his hands on his knees, gasping to catch his breath. "I almost had him," he huffed. "Thankfully, he's a lousy shot and it was dark. Are the horses all right?"

"Yeah, but who had watch tonight?" Kyle asked.

Anders thought for a moment. "We were all in the meeting. I think we need to recruit someone to guard the horses while we are training, don't you?"

By this time, the others had heard the shot and poured out of the firehouse running into the street and toward the stables. The rest of the people in town ran out to the street, curious to see what was happening.

"Back inside, folks," Walt shouted to them as he hurried down the street. "You're safer inside. I'll let you know what happened."

Morgan knew that Kyle had gone out to the stables with Anders, and now fearing for his safety, she raced ahead. "Kyle! Alan!"

Kyle held his hand out to her. "We're okay. There was someone in the stables when we got here, but he ran off. Anders tried to catch him, but whoever it was shot at him and got away."

"Were the horses unattended while we were in the meeting?" Walt asked.

"I'm afraid so, Walt. We're going to have to enlist someone to keep an eye on them while we train and when we hold the meetings, someone outside the rescue team, but someone we can trust." Kyle said. Steve looked around at everyone and spoke up, "I'll do it."

Sandy was stunned, "Steve, what do you mean?"

"I mean, someone needs to stay here to protect those that are staying behind and besides, who would lead the church service? Tanya and I have been talking about it and praying on it, and we feel that God wants us to stay. I'm sorry to be springing this on you so suddenly."

Gus Wilkerson agreed, "I think he's right. We'll need an able-bodied man to keep things running back here and I think it'd be best if he were from the original party, if you know what I mean."

Tanya turned to Sandy and took her hand. "You understand, don't you, Sandy?"

"Of course I do, Sis." Sandy gave Tanya a hug and stepped back. She studied her sister's face and wondered whether there was another reason why Steve and her sister would stay behind.

"We'll need to be on watch through the night, Walt. I'll take the first quarter," Kyle said, walking with Walt and the others to the front of the stable.

"Sounds good," Walt said. "I'll come relieve you around midnight." The men shook hands. "Anything comes up, or if that clown comes back, shoot first and we'll ask questions later."

"You can count on that," Kyle said grinning.

Morgan stayed behind after the others had left and walked the aisle with Kyle, stopping at each stall to rub the nose or stroke the shedding winter coat of the horses there. "Kyle, why do you think Steve and Tanya want to stay behind?"

"I don't know. What are you thinking?"

A playful smile crept across her lips as she turned into his arms and looked up at him, "I'd rather not say. At least, not yet. We'll wait until Sandy talks with Tanya, and then I'll tell you what I think."

Kyle smiled at Morgan and kissed her softly, "Come on, you'd better get back to the fire station. It's getting cold out here, and you don't have a coat on."

They turned and walked together, "Be careful, Kyle. Are you tired?"

"I'll put on a pot of coffee," Kyle assured her. "I'll be fine." He wrapped his arms around her and held onto her until she started to giggle. "What's so funny," he asked, pushing her back to look at her beautiful face.

"You, silly. You tell me to go, and then you hold me for so long that you make it nearly impossible to leave."

Kyle wrapped her up in his arms again and chuckled. "Sorry, Morgan, it just feels so good to hold you. He gave her one last squeeze and released her, "Okay, now you really do need to go. I'll try not to wake anyone when I come in."

"Good night, Kyle." Morgan whispered.

"Good night, babe." Kyle went to the tack room and started a pot of strong coffee. While he waited for it to brew, he pulled out the lawn chair they used when they kept watch, and a couple of horse blankets to ward off the cool night air. Then he again checked each of the horses, their feed buckets, and the water buckets. Satisfied that the intruder hadn't poisoned them, he went back to the chair. With cup in hand, he made himself comfortable and opened the Bible that was kept in the tack room next to the coffee pot.

The man stopped to rest. He didn't think he had hit Anders but was glad that at least he had stopped him from chasing him. Now he had to get back to The City to report to Garrison what they were planning to do. He had no way of knowing if the woman had made it back to The City. She had slipped away, but according to their instructions, he would not know until he arrived there himself.

Malachi 4:1 "Surely the day is coming; it will burn like a furnace. All the arrogant and every evildoer will be stubble, and that day that is coming will set them on fire."

CHAPTER 35

Nick Garrison poured himself a tall scotch and went to stand by the window that overlooked the back lot where the attempted escape took place. The night sky had faded into soft purples and reds, and the wall had melted into the darkness. "If it was not for the searchlight and the fact that I already know the wall is there, I wouldn't even know it existed," he mumbled. "I need to bump up security." He snatched up his radio from the table. "Connelly, this is Garrison. Do you copy?"

Tom heard Garrison over the radio but ignored him. McCloud was showing him how he could manipulate the cameras and the timers that were in place around The City. "You see this?" Mac pointed to a camera view of Barbara Beechum's stairwell. "I can record the empty stairwell from the day before and play it back while the residents are being evacuated. It will appear to Garrison and anyone else watching, that the stairwell is empty."

Tom clapped Mac on the back, "You're a genius, Mac. I think this will work. I'd better get a move on, though; no doubt Garrison will be trying my unit any minute." Tom shook McCloud's hand firmly. "I'm awfully glad you picked our side, Mac. I really am."

McCloud smiled. "Yeah, me too, Connelly. I'll see you tomorrow."

Garrison grunted at the non-responsive radio, drained his glass, and setting both the glass and the radio on the table by the window, he went over to his desk and picked up the phone. "Hello, Stephanie."

"Good evening, Mr. Garrison. How may I help you?" "Get me the security bunker, please," he said flatly.

"Of course; hold on please." The phone went silent, followed by a series of clicks while Stephanie attempted the connection.

"Hello?"

"Mr. McCloud, please hold for Mr. Garrison." Stephanie hung up immediately, not waiting for Garrison's response, if any. He frightened her, especially when his temper was up, and tonight it was the worst she had heard.

"Mr. Garrison, what can I do for you tonight?" McCloud asked.

"I'm looking for Connelly. Have you seen him?"

"Yes, sir. He just left. Because of the escape attempt, I am implementing some new security procedures, and I wanted to explain them to him."

"I tried him on his radio, but he didn't answer." Garrison snapped.

"That must have been when we went down to the lower level, sir. He left his radio on the counter." McCloud lied. "You can probably reach him at his unit in a few minutes. Is there anything else I can do for you, Mr. Garrison?"

Garrison didn't bother saying 'good-bye'. He cradled the receiver and picked it up again. "Stephanie, try Officer Connelly's unit."

Frustrated that Garrison kept bothering her, Stephanie sighed heavily and tried Connelly's unit. Just as before, silence, then clicks as Stephanie attempted the connection, but this time she was unsuccessful. She took the call back and tried desperately to shield the fear in her voice, "I'm terribly sorry, Mr. Garrison, but he's not answering."

Garrison could feel his blood pressure peaking, "Smith, please," he growled through gritted teeth.

Silence, then clicks, then, "This is Smith."

Stephanie breathed a sigh of relief before she disconnected herself from the call.

"Mr. Smith, how are you progressing in your investigation?"

"Actually, I just got back from meeting Red Dalton at the infirmary. According to Dr. White, he's the doctor on call, no one came in with the type of injury that would have come from a baling hook, only sick kids and old people. You know how that goes."

"Yeah, I know. Listen, you know that old woman, Beechum, the one who holds those weekly meetings at her unit?"

"Yeah, Connelly's been going there for about a month now. Hasn't he been reporting to you?"

"Yes, he has been reporting to me, but nothing significant."

Smith's jaw clenched, "Sir, I'm not so sure about that guy. I can't quite put my finger on it, but I just don't trust him." Smith waited for Garrison's wrath.

Garrison's blood pressure was nearly back to its normal level, so he let this irritation go. "I am well aware of your dislike for Connelly. I need to talk to him tonight. I called his unit, but he didn't answer, and I can't reach him on the radio. Why don't you take a walk, Smith, and see if he is home? If he is, bring him here. I want to find out once and for all what that old bird is up to."

"Of course, sir, I'll head out now." Smith answered, already putting his overcoat on. "Is there anything else, boss?"

"Yes, while you're in the area, check in on the security bunker."

"Shouldn't it be locked up by now?" The second Smith said it, he wished he hadn't.

Garrison didn't let this remark slide. "Smith, this whole breakout attempt occurred on your watch. Do not question me!"

Before Smith could reply, Garrison slammed the phone down and spun around, looking for something to throw, but instead grasped the bottle of scotch and not bothering with the glass tipped it to his lips.

John Smith shuddered and laid the receiver back in its cradle. He had seen Garrison's temper flair many times, but lately it was getting out of control. Stepping outside, he turned up his collar against the cold north wind and headed down the sidewalk. Although spring had just arrived, the nights still carried a fierce chill. He passed by the grocery store and spotted Ernie. He stopped and went in. "Good evening, Ernie."

Ernie looked up from the magazine he was reading and nearly dropped it, "Good -- good evening, Mr. Smith. What – what can I do for you?" The power Smith wielded over Ernie made the clerk uncomfortable and Smith knew it and took advantage of it. If he needed information, he could always count on good old Ernie to provide it. "You been busy tonight, Ern?"

"No, sir. Are you looking for anything--" Ernie moved in a little closer and whispered, "--or anyone in particular?"

Smith grinned wickedly, "As a matter of fact, I am. Have you seen Officer Connelly or Mr. McCloud around lately?"

Ernie thought for a moment, absently picking at a pimple on his neck, "No, not since this morning. Officer Connelly was making his rounds when I saw him speaking with that Beechum woman. You know who I'm talking about." Ernie nodded knowingly, thrilled that he was able to give such vital information to one of the big bosses.

"Yeah, I know. Did you hear what they were discussing?" Smith sat on the counter. Judging by the way that Ernie began his story, Smith knew it was going to take a while.

"Well, no, because they were outside, you see, and I was inside. But they talked for a little bit, and now that I think of it, they did smile at each other for just a second, and then she shook her finger at him like she always does. After that Mr. McCloud came to talk to them and he left with Officer Connelly and the ladies came into the store." Ernie gazed at Smith, hoping for some sort of credit or recognition for his outstanding observation skills.

Smith ignored him and continued his questioning, "You said, 'ladies.' Who was the other lady with Mrs. Beechum?"

Ernie's disappointment passed. He knew Smith would always come to him for help, and he would always come through for his boss. "Oh, that would be Dorothy; you know, I can never remember her last name."

"That's okay, Ernie, neither can I. Can you think of anything else? Did you hear Mrs. Beechum and Miss Dorothy talking?"

Ernie went back to picking the pimple while he searched his memory. "Hmm, nope, they just went about their business and didn't say anything to me when they checked out."

"Do you remember what they bought?" Smith asked, getting tired of the questioning and of Ernie.

"Mrs. Beechum bought some pasta, a couple of bananas, a bag of frozen peas and a first aid kit."

At the last item, Smith's interest piqued. "A first aid kit?"

Unaware of its significance, Ernie nodded and continued, "Yes, and Miss Dorothy bought pasta, too, and a loaf of raisin bread, tea bags and a small carton of milk."

Smith rubbed the stubble on his chin and nodded. "Thanks, Ernie," and turned and walked quickly out the door. By the time he arrived at Tom's building it was completely dark. He took a look around the corner of the building to see if anyone was still at the security bunker. Just as he had suspected, a shadow passed across the glass block window that glowed with the soft blue lights from the security monitors of the night watch. He pulled his key card from his pocket and slid it through the slot next to the door of Tom's building. The door clicked and he quickly pulled on it, slipping quietly inside. He would love to catch Connelly doing something he shouldn't be doing, but knew the guy was too smart for that. Not wanting to alert anyone to his arrival, he took the stairs up and strode confidently down the carpeted corridor to Connelly's door. He paused before knocking, put his ear to the door, and heard the sound of running water. He pounded on the door "If he's in the shower that ought to get his attention."

Tom heard the pounding on the door and quickly rinsed off. Wrapping a towel around his waist, he walked to the door. "Who is it?" he shouted.

"It's Smith. Garrison asked me to stop by."

Tom opened the door and allowed him in. "We can talk in the kitchen, just give me a minute to get some clothes on," Tom said. Not waiting for a response, he grabbed a pair of jeans and headed to the bathroom.

John Smith took a seat at the kitchen table. He had to admit the room was terribly small, with barely enough room to open the refrigerator, and yet he never once heard Tom complain about the cramped quarters. John continued his survey of the kitchen and noticed a small skillet sitting on the stove with link sausages and eggs in it. The smell of sausage hung heavy in the air.

"Breakfast for supper has always been a favorite of mine," Tom said startling his guest.

Smith turned toward him, "Yeah, I have to agree, but I sure miss the pork sausage."

Tom laughed softly, "Yeah, turkey sausage and turkey bacon don't quite cut it. Have you eaten yet, Smith?"

Surprised at the question, it took Smith a minute to respond, "Uh, no, but thanks anyway."

"Fair enough." Tom put a lid on the skillet and pushed it to the back of the stove. "Coffee?"

"Yeah, sure, I'll take a cup." John Smith wasn't used to this type of treatment, respectful, almost kind. And he really didn't know how to respond to it. He accepted the cup of coffee that Tom handed him. "Thanks, Connelly."

Tom took a seat across the table from him. "I'm sorry for the cramped quarters. I don't do much entertaining." Both men smiled, but Tom could see that Smith was uncomfortable. "So, what is it that Garrison wants?"

"You know that old woman, Barbara Beechum that you've been spying on?" John tasted his coffee and set it on the table.

Tom grinned. "Yeah, she's a pistol, but I don't think she's much of a threat. Why?"

"Garrison has some concerns about her. He wants to talk to you, tonight."

Tom shrugged. "All right. Is that why you're here; to escort me over?"

"Yeah, you can say that. With the breakout attempt, he's gotten a lot more anxious. I think Baroam is coming down hard on him. Anyway, he thinks there may be more to her than anyone suspects."

The idea that Garrison suspected Barbara kept the grin on Tom's face as he took another sip from his coffee, "Does Garrison really believe she is somehow involved with this breakout?"

Smith didn't answer. He drained his coffee cup and stood up. "You about ready?"

"Yeah, hang on," Tom rose, strode to the dresser and pulled out a tee shirt. The coveralls he normally wore over his clothes hid the well-tuned machine underneath.

Smith watched as Tom pulled the tee shirt over his muscled shoulders and chest and made a note to himself never to get into a fistfight with the guy. "Garrison said he tried to reach you on the radio and at your unit, Connelly. Where've you been?"

Tom looked around the corner into the kitchen, "I was in the security bunker with McCloud for about a half hour, then I walked back to my unit. He must have just missed me."

The men stood at the door to leave when Smith leaned toward Tom and eyed him suspiciously. "You know we have cameras around, Connelly. We can easily check your story."

Tom shook his head in obvious frustration. "For crying out loud, Smith, go ahead and check the cameras."

Smith turned away, not saying anything else as they strode down the hall. Connelly could be as kind as Mother Theresa, but he still didn't trust him. He would check the cameras, and he would find him out.

When they arrived at Garrison's door, Smith finally spoke. "Mark my words, Connelly. I know you're up to something and I'll find out one way or another." He rapped sharply on Garrison's door.

"Enter!" Garrison turned from the bank of monitors on his wall when Smith and Connelly entered the room. "Thank you, Mr. Smith. That will be all for tonight."

John Smith nodded and gave Tom one last leer before he turned and left.

Tom took a step forward, "What can I do for you, Mr. Garrison."

Garrison's mood had lightened up, after a couple of glasses of scotch. "Tom, do you remember the first time we met?"

"Yes, sir. I had just arrived here and was mighty grateful for the room and work."

"Red Dalton had recommended that you be put in our security division. Were you aware of that?"

Tom shook his head. "No, but like I said, I was sure glad to get the job. Has my performance been satisfactory?"

"Oh, your performance has been exemplary, Officer Connelly. You've been quite an asset to our cause. The reason I called you here was to ask you one more time, can I trust you?"

Tom was fully aware of where Garrison was going with his questioning, but he had to continue the game for a little while longer. Tom's eyes narrowed, "Yes, sir. I've always been upfront with you about everything."

"And I'm going to be straight up with you, Connelly. If Mrs. Beechum is somehow involved with this breakout attempt, she will pay dearly."

Tom didn't like Garrison threatening his friend. He squared his shoulders, "Sir, I can assure you, Mrs. Beechum is one fiery old woman, but I seriously doubt she is involved in this. Is that what Smith is telling you?

"Yes, as a matter of fact. Can you prove to me otherwise?" Garrison challenged.

"No, sir, I don't know how I could prove it to you. You'll just have to take me at my word."

"With all due respect, Officer Connelly, taking a man at his word is a thing of the past. I have another idea. I'm calling a meeting tomorrow night of all the stable workers, infirmary workers, and security. After that, you and I are going to pay a little visit to your friend. How does that sound.?"

Tom nodded. "No problem, Mr. Garrison." Tom turned to leave.

"Oh, one more thing, Officer. I wonder if you wouldn't mind taking a look at this?"

Tom stopped suddenly and slowly turned around. Garrison tapped a few keys on his laptop, and a single photograph filled all the monitors on his wall. The picture was grainy, but there was no mistaking who the individual was in the picture.

Psalm 27:11 "Teach me your way, O Lord; lead me in a straight path because of my oppressors."

CHAPTER 36

JOE WAS JUST FINISHING his shift at the stables when he heard someone call his name. "Hey, Joe!" Jason O'Malley called out.

"Over here, Jason," Joe said, sticking his head out from behind the horse he was grooming.

Jason followed his voice and leaned over the stall gate, breathless. "Joe, what are you doing after work tonight?"

Joe continued grooming Pilgrim. "I'm having dinner with Carlotte and her mom. Why?"

Jason moved in closer and lowered his voice, "Old man Garrison is calling a meeting tonight for all the stable workers, security, and infirmary workers." The boy couldn't hid the anxiety on his face or in his voice. Seeing the disappointment in Joe's expression, he continued, "I'm sorry, man. I know you'd rather spend time with your girl. You've been seeing her a lot."

"Every chance I get," Joe replied. He proceeded to pick Pilgrim's hooves.

"I know it's not the same, but would you want to come to my unit for dinner before the meeting?"

Joe looked up, surprised. He had been wanting to talk to Jason in private ever since he found his father's Bible at his front door. A suspicious knock came at his door late at night the day after he arrived. When Joe went to the door, no one was there, but wrapped in burlap lay his Bible. He had always had a suspicion that it was Jason, but didn't want to ask until he was sure of where his loyalties lay. God was giving him the opportunity to speak with him. "Yeah, that sounds good, Jason. I just need to call Charlotte and tell her I won't be able to make it."

Jason grinned, "Great! I'll wait for you at my place."

"Where's the meeting?" Joe asked, coming around Pilgrim, patting him on the rump. Joe's focus rested on Jason's hand until Jason lowered it out of Joe's sight.

"In the lobby of Garrison's hotel. I hear security is going to be real tight." Jason looked quickly over his shoulder, then back at Joe. "Something must have gone down, don't you think, Joe?"

"I would expect so," Joe said. He had grown fond of Jason and judging by the way he'd seen Jason look at him, Joe was convinced that Jason had wanted to talk to him too but was not sure how to go about it either. "What time does the meeting start?"

"Twenty hundred hours," Jason said, checking his watch.

"All right, I'm going to get cleaned up and I'll meet you at your place at say eighteen thirty."

"Sounds good, Joe, and it'll be my treat tonight."

"Thanks, Jason. See you in a bit." Joe walked to his unit, curious about what Jason had to say; wondering whether it had anything to do with his Bible that Jason had found. He had no clue. All he knew right now was that he was about to disappoint Charlotte, something he didn't want to do but had no choice. He picked up his receiver. "Hi, Stephanie. Can you get me Charlotte, please?" "Sure, Joe, hold on." Stephanie chirped.

"Hello?" It was Charlotte.

"Hang on, Charlotte. Thanks, Stephanie," Joe said, knowing that Stephanie was in the habit of listening in on private conversations.

Stephanie stammered, "Oh, you're, you're welcome, Joe. Bye, Charlotte."

"Bye, Stephanie," Charlotte giggled. "Wow. What nerve."

"Don't hold it against her, Charlotte. I think she gets compensated for information she can dig up on people. How was your day today?"

"Not bad. They had me in the emergency wing of the infirmary. It's a far cry from the days of working at the incinerator. Since daddy died, I guess the people in charge got it through their heads that we weren't able to do as good a job as daddy. How about you?"

"Not a bad day. You know any day I can spend with horses is a good day."

"And dogs?" Charlotte teased.

Joe laughed. "Yes. And dogs. Sasha missed you today." Joe hesitated, "I missed you."

Charlotte's cheeks blushed. "I'm sorry, Joe. I really wanted to come see you at lunch, but things got a little crazy at the infirmary. A story was going around that late last night some guy came in with his hands all bloody, but he wouldn't talk to anyone except Dr. White. Since Dr. White was with another patient, someone else offered to help him, but the guy ran off. He left the place a mess, from what everyone said, and they told us not to speak a word of it. Isn't that strange, Joe?"

Joe thought for a moment, "Yeah that is strange." He fell silent as he recalled Jason's bandaged hand when he had seen him earlier. Joe made a mental note to ask him about it.

"Joe?" Charlotte asked.

"Listen, Charlotte, the reason I'm calling is that Garrison called a meeting tonight, so I'm not going to be able to come to supper. I'm sorry."

"I understand." She tried to hide her disappointment, but Joe noticed it at once.

"I'll make it up to you. I promise."

"I know you will," Charlotte said playfully. "Be careful."

"I will." Joe hung up the phone and pulled the Bible from beneath his mattress. He needed strength and focus for the night, and he knew just where to find it.

Stephanie quietly disconnected her line, a trick she'd learned early on, and rang Nick Garrison's room. "Mr. Garrison?"

"Yes, Stephanie?"

"There's something you should know."

While Joe was reading his Bible, Jason O'Malley was busy tidying up his unit. He felt nervous that Joe was coming over, but more than that, he was anxious about what he wanted to talk to Joe about. He knew that if anyone else had found the Bible, it would have been confiscated, and Joe would have been put on the watch list and not been given such a good job. Most likely, he would have ended up at the smokestack, or under the thumb of Garrison himself, or even worse, John Smith.

No, Jason had always liked Joe while they attended school and thought, at the least, he owed it to Joe for the kindness he had always received from him. Jason also fretted because he knew Joe would ask him about his injury and he struggled with the decision of whether to tell him the truth. Jason jumped when he heard a knock at the door. Peeking out of the small window, he saw Joe waiting and opened the door. "Hey Joe, C'mon in."

Joe entered the unit and saw that it was no different from his quarters. "Thanks for inviting me over, Jason. Are you sure you have enough food? I know they allow us only so much."

"Naw, I've got plenty, Joe. I've been saving it up." Jason directed Joe into the kitchen. "Have a seat, man. Can I get you something to drink?"

"Sure, what do you have?" Joe said, sitting down at the kitchen table.

Jason ducked into the small refrigerator and called out, "Milk, chocolate milk, apple juice or Gatorade."

"Apple juice sounds good," Joe said. He would have preferred chocolate milk, but he knew from his own experience that chocolate milk was expensive and sometimes difficult to come by. "So, what did you want to talk about, Jason? Is everything all right with you?"

"Oh yeah, everything is fine. The pizza should be ready in about ten minutes." Jason took a seat across from Joe. The young man took a deep breath and looked directly at Joe. "You know I'm the one who found your Bible, Joe."

Joe nodded, "Yes, I know. And I thank you for taking such good care of it. It belonged to my dad."

Jason stared at his injured hand while he considered his next words. "Joe, I want you to teach me what you know about the Bible. I mean, I've heard other people talk about Jesus and him being a Savior, but I want to know more. Can you help me?"

Joe lifted his gaze up to meet Jason and smiled. "I would be happy to Jason. You know it will be dangerous, though?"

"I don't care. I want to know Him, and I want to have that same peace that you seem to have."

Joe pulled the tattered Bible from his back pocket and handed it to Jason. "We'll start with the Book of Acts, but first I need to know what happened to your hand."

Jason's eyes dropped shamefully, and he sighed. "I did something stupid, Joe. I stole a baling hook from the shelter and hid it when I first got here. I buried it out by the wall, beneath some bushes, thinking that if things didn't settle down and get better; I could climb the wall and get out of here." Jason looked at Joe for some kind of acknowledgement or understanding.

When he didn't receive it, he continued, "Last night I slipped out. I was able to avoid being seen by security, but I just couldn't get the hook to go high enough over the wall. On my last throw, I missed the wall again and the hook came down and gouged my hand. I bled like a stuck pig, Joe. That's when I gave up. I tried to go to the infirmary, but the only one there I know, and trust is Dr. White. He was with another patient and couldn't see me right away, so I split and came back here. I called my grandma, and she came over this morning and bandaged me up.

She made me swear not to tell anyone." Jason's eyes filled with tears. "I'm so sorry I did it now, Joe. Do you think they'll find me out?"

Joe looked at his friend. "You reckon that's what the meeting is going to be about, Jason? I do. Who's your grandma? Do you think there's a chance that they'll find her out?"

"Her name's Barbara Beechum. She's not really my grandma, but she's been close to my family for years and she's always looked after me." Jason had his arms crossed on the table and now laid his head on them, "What have I done?"

At seventeen hundred hours, Tom knocked lightly on Barbara Beechum's door. This would be his fifth visit to her Bible Study meeting. The group had grown from four, including Mrs. Beechum, to nine with Tom attending. Barbara opened the door and greeted him warmly, taking his hand, "Good evening, Tom. I'm so glad you could come."

Tom smiled back at her. "It's good to be here, Mrs. Beechum."

"Please, Tom, call me Barbara. After all, you've been coming here all this time. We needn't be so formal."

"Yes ma'am." Tom smiled and entered the small living area of the apartment, greeted the other guests and took a seat. As they were about to get started, another knock at the door startled them.

"Are you expecting anyone else, Barbara?" Tom asked, getting up.

"No but let me just have a look." Barbara went to the door and with Tom standing behind her, she opened the door slightly and peered through. When she saw the man standing there, her face lit up, and she swung the door open, "Mr. Harris, what a wonderful surprise!"

Tom turned to the others in the room and examined their faces for any signs of recognition of the name, but they only shook their heads in denial.

Barbara stepped back to allow her new guest in. "Please, come in."

He put his hand out and shook with Barbara, then Tom. He recognized Tom and smiled halfheartedly. "It's good to meet you all. Barbara, first, may I please apologize for the way I treated you a few months ago? I was not very neighborly, and I was downright mean. Please forgive me."

Barbara took his hand again. "I forgive you, Mr. Harris. Please, come in." Barbara made the introductions. "Everyone, this is Mr. Bob Harris. He has been a neighbor on my floor since the day Richard and I arrived. Isn't that right, Mr. Harris?"

Bob noticed that she left out the incident when he had slammed the door in her face. "That's correct, Mrs. Beechum." He smiled at the rest of the group seated around the room, "It's nice to meet you all."

"You've joined us just in time, Mr. Harris. We were about to begin a new study on the book of Revelation."

"That's great. I've always been fascinated by that book," Mr. Harris said, taking the Bible offered to him.

"Would you like to start off then?" Barbara asked.

"I would love to. Thank you." Bob turned to the last chapter in the Bible and began "'Prologue, Chapter One. The revelation of Jesus Christ, which God gave to him to show his servants what must soon take place.'" They continued their study until it was nearly eight o'clock. After the closing prayer, Bob looked around the room, "I wonder if I could say something."

The others in the room nodded, acknowledging Bob's request.

"For months now I've been watching every week as all of you come to this unit to meet. The number of you has grown, and Officer Connelly has started coming too. You can understand how I might be intrigued."

The group laughed nervously. Bob continued, "I knew you were meeting to read God's Word, but something has crossed my mind, and I have to know."

The others waited; Tom had already suspected what he was about to say.

"Has anyone ever given any thought as to how to escape this horrific place?" He paused and waited for a response.

At his question, everyone fell silent, anxiously averting his or her eyes from him, everyone except Tom, Barbara, and Dorothy. They looked cautiously at one another but didn't speak. Harris took note of them and continued, "I see that only a few of you have considered it. Let me just say if, and hopefully when, you do decide to make a run for it, that you will include me."

Tom sensed the angst in the room, "Mr. Harris, I hope you will excuse me, but how can we be sure you aren't going to go back and tell Garrison or Smith about any plans we would make?"

"How can WE be sure YOU won't?" Bob Harris retorted, "After all, you are one of them."

Dorothy bristled. "Mr. Harris! You should know that Officer Connelly is not at all like the others. He is a kind, gentle, God-fearing man."

"Forgive me, Dorothy. I did not mean to insult anyone. I just think that it is about time something was done and, since it appears we have a friend on the inside," he nodded congenially to Tom, "then we should get started. Officer Connelly, do you agree?"

"I do, Mr. Harris." Tom looked around the room. "Is anyone else willing to take the chance to get out of here?"

The others hesitated and exchanged glances, and then slowly, one by one, they nodded their heads. "Yes, we want to leave," one said. Another spoke louder, "You just tell us what to do and we'll do it, right, everyone?" The room went electric as the people felt their first real hope in months.

"Then it's settled!" Barbara declared. "We will begin discussion of an escape plan next week. Will that be all right, Tom?"

"That'll be fine, Barbara. If anything comes up between now and then, I'll let you know." Tom stood up and turned to Barbara. "I wonder if I could have a word with you privately, Barbara."

"Well, of course, Tom. Come. We can talk in the kitchen."

The other guests stood to leave, but Tom stopped them. "If you don't mind, would you wait for just a moment? The camera on Barbara's door is sure to be watched and I don't want Garrison to see that I did not leave with the rest of you. He is already growing very suspicious."

The others agreed and sat back down to continue their own conversation of the upcoming escape. Tom followed Barbara into the kitchen. "What is it, Tom?"

"What can you tell me about the first aid kit you bought?" Tom asked, his eyes drilling into hers.

Barbara's eyes narrowed and she shook her head in disgust. "That little weasel! I knew he was a spy for them. Something told me not to make the purchase, but Jason was hurt, and I needed to tend to him. Does Garrison know anything more than that?"

"I don't know, but I have a feeling that more will be revealed at the meeting tonight."

"What meeting?"

"Garrison is holding a meeting tonight, but I expect it will be more of an inquisition. That's all I can say for now, Barbara, but I must warn you, Garrison and I will be coming afterwards to talk to you. I just wanted to give you fair warning." He drew her closer into the kitchen, "I want you and Dorothy to pack a bag and be ready to run the minute you get the word, okay? It may be sooner than we expect."

The certainty of the escape was beginning to sink in for Barbara, and Tom observed a wave of anxiety wash over her face. However, just as quickly it left her. She squared her shoulders, lifted her chin, and nodded her head. That small simple movement at once brought Sandy to the forefront of his mind and his expression softened at her memory. Barbara didn't miss it. "You are in love with her, Tom," she said gently.

Tom snapped back to reality and struggled to cover the surprise on his face. "Beg your pardon?"

"That look that just crossed your face; you were having a memory of someone you cared for very deeply, weren't you?"

Tom bowed his head, embarrassed and ashamed that his feelings for his best friend's widow were so obvious.

Barbara patted his strong forearm, "You hang in there, dear. You'll see her again. We'll all see our loved ones again."

Tom bent and wrapped his arms around her, "Yes, ma'am."

A dark figure slipped quietly through the rear gate of The City and made its way to Nick Garrison's building. Arriving at Garrison's place, he knocked softly on the door, hoping no one else would hear him.

Garrison peered through the peephole and then opened the door wide. "The prodigal son comes home! Come on in, Clifford." As the man moved past him, a wave of rancid body odor followed. Garrison pinched his nose and scrunched his face. "After your report, please go take a bath. Did you not have running water where you were?"

Clifford had all week to think about what he was going to say to Garrison, but now that the time had come, he had completely lost his nerve. "As a matter of fact, no. There was no running water or electricity. I've been on the run for over a week, Garrison. What do you expect?"

Garrison waved his hand through the air and walked toward the bar, "Look, forget about it. What can you tell me?'

"Willow Creek is still abandoned. It doesn't appear that anyone has come back. I also checked out the Parker ranch like you wanted and that was deserted. I can tell you that the folks who were at Willow Creek have found their way to Berkley Springs and are planning something in the very near future. They were secretive about it, but they did have a meeting to decide who would go. My best guess is they have, maybe, ten people."

Garrison burst into laughter, "Ten!" Ten people are coming to my city to break everyone out?" He continued in loud guffaws, leaning over and holding his stomach. "Is that all they could pull together?"

Clifford said nothing. He hated Garrison, but at the same time, didn't care for the folks in Berkely Springs either. Garrison poured Clifford two fingers of bourbon and handed him the glass. "Here, it's the least I can do. Take the room three doors down on the right. There's a meeting tonight at twenty hundred hours, and I want you to be there."

Clifford swallowed the amber liquid in one gulp and headed toward the door without saying a word. When he walked into his room, he found clean clothes hanging in his closet and clean linen on the bed. This is certainly a far cry from what the folks in West Virginia have to live with. He called room service and ordered the biggest bacon cheeseburger they could make with steak fries and a tall bottle of ice-cold beer. He had earned this meal. While he waited for his dinner, he turned on the shower as hot as he could stand it and stepped in, letting the last two months wash off him.

Isaiah 5:20 "Woe to those who call evil good and good evil, who put darkness for light and light for darkness, who put bitter for sweet and sweet for bitter."

CHAPTER 37

THE FRONT LOBBY OF Garrison's hotel filled quickly with security officers, stable workers, and infirmary doctors, nurses, and their assistants. Joe and Jason walked in together and took seats toward the back. In the short hour and a half that Jason spent with Joe he had tried to learn as much as he could from him, but there was still so much that he wanted to know. He glanced around nervously, fearful that others would notice his bandaged hand. Joe nudged him. "Stop fidgeting, Jason. You look nervous."

"I am," Jason replied. "Hey, Joe, there's Charlotte. I didn't know she had to come to this."

Joe quickly turned to find where Jason was looking and saw Charlotte with her mother and others from the infirmary. He watched her until he caught her eye. She shrugged her slender shoulders ever so slightly as if to say, "I don't know either," and turned back to her mother. "I don't like the looks of this," Joe said. He searched the crowd for Tom or Red and was relieved to see them walking in together. He stood to make sure they saw him, and they came toward him.

Tom, as always, carried his M16. "Hey Joe, Jason." he nodded.

Jason was never comfortable around the security officers, especially Tom and Red, and quickly tucked his injured hand between his knees and nodded back. "Officer Connelly, Mr. Dalton."

Joe smiled to himself, knowing Jason's uneasiness around Tom, even more so now that he had something to hide. If Jason only knew what a good man Tom was, he wouldn't worry so much. "Can you sit with us?" Joe asked.

Jason shot his friend a glance, shocked that he would extend such an invitation.

Joe ignored him and focused on Tom.

"Not a good idea tonight, son," Tom answered. "I'll be in touch." He nodded quickly and walked off with Red.

Visibly disappointed, Joe sat back down in his chair.

Jason couldn't understand how Joe could be so comfortable around Officer Connelly. Obviously, they knew each other well enough for Tom to call Joe, 'son.' He would have to ask him about it another time.

Garrison, followed by a man that Tom did not recognize, approached the podium at the front of the hall. He eyed the heavyset man carefully. His appearance was sloppy, and his face was puffy and unshaven. Garrison turned to the man and whispered something, then turned back toward his audience and held the hay bale hook up high for everyone to see. The man took a step back while Garrison surveyed the room, looking for any sign of recognition, uneasiness, or acknowledgement. "I have my security officers posted at every exit to this room. They are watching you. If any of you know anything about this, anything at all they will know." He continued to scan the room until his eyes rested on Charlotte. Joe watched in horror as he followed Garrison's line of sight to his girlfriend. She sat frozen with fear; her face went pale.

Garrison knew! Somehow, he knew what happened at the infirmary. He motioned to one of his guards. "Seize that young woman!"

Charlotte's mom screamed and reached for her daughter, but the men grabbed them both and hauled them away. During the altercation, Joe had jumped to his feet, but three officers next to him leveled their guns at him, daring him to make a move. Jason tugged at his arm and pleaded, "Joe, now's not the time. C'mon man, sit down. Please," he whispered.

Joe watched helplessly as the guards dragged the women away. Dread washed over him, and his chest tightened as though someone was grabbing him from behind, but he knew Jason was right. He sat back down in his seat, powerless. He grasped his knees to keep his hands from trembling and turned his stricken face to Tom. He knew Tom could not acknowledge him now. Not now. Joe shifted his attention back to Garrison. How would he get Charlotte out of the hands of Garrison and Smith? His stomach wrenched, but he forced himself to pay attention.

"I know there are others of you who know about this, and it will not be long before we search you out." Garrison shouted. "Turn yourselves in now and the punishment will not be as severe." The room remained silent. He continued, "I have also been made aware that some folks are planning a breakout." He paused and looked around the room, nothing. He grew agitated, but continued, "And that a group will be on its way here to assist with that breakout." He paused again. Tom's eyes searched the room and rested on Joe and, for a brief moment, Joe felt hope coming back and prayed that the ones coming were his family. Garrison continued his rant, and everyone kept their attention on him. "If you thought security was tight before, you are all in for a rude awakening," he shouted. "Beginning tonight, there will be an armed guard posted at each building twenty-four hours a day, seven days a week.

A young man stood up, "You already have us under surveillance twenty-four seven. What else can you do?"

Garrison shouted, "Guards, we have another one!"

The young man pulled his arm away from the grip of an officer. "Hey, let go of me! I didn't do anything!"

"Officer, please escort the young man to the lockup with the others. He obviously doesn't know the limits of my power." Garrison yelled.

When the officer grabbed the young man again, he continued to resist. The officer growled, "Hands behind your back!" Realizing that the boy would not go quietly, the guard lifted his rifle and slammed the butt against the back of the boy's head, and he crumpled to the floor like a rag doll. The room erupted into shouts of objections and gasps of horror. Suddenly a single shot echoed throughout the auditorium causing everyone to scream and crouch to the floor. Garrison, still holding the smoking revolver high, shouted, "Ladies and gentlemen, remember who is in control here!" The people in the room slowly took their seats again. Many of them were crying and all of them trembled with fear. The truth was finally confirmed. Garrison was invigorated at the sight of the weeping, frightened people before him, "Everyone in The City is hereby sentenced to house arrest!"

***

Ten riders set out from Berkley Springs, West Virginia toward Willow Creek, Maryland. The first leg of their trip remained a secret between only them and the rest of the team that had stayed behind. After the incident at the stable, they weren't sure who could be trusted. Three weeks of hard training every day left them in the best physical shape they had ever been in, and they were confident that the rescue would be a success. They had been on the trail for three days. Kyle had taken the point position, with Walt riding in the middle and Sandy bringing up the rear. Breaks were few and when they did stop, it was for no more than ten minutes. Time was growing short, and they all sensed it. Kyle pulled up on his horse and dismounted.

"Are we taking a break, Kyle?" Gus asked.

"Just a short one," Kyle said, as he tossed his reins to Gus and hurried toward Walt. Whatever he wanted to talk about seemed important. Gus turned in his saddle and lifted his fist, signaling a break, and then dismounted to tie off both horses.

"What's going on, Gus?" Herb asked, concerned.

"Don't know," Gus said. He had just finished with the horses and took a look around the group as they gathered. He could feel the tension in the air all around him and saw it on the faces of Kyle, Sandy, Morgan, and even Ben. "We must be getting close to Willow Creek. Keep your eyes open and your ears perked."

Herb nodded and quickly scanned the woods around him. He had never witnessed the maliciousness of the men that ravaged the town, but he certainly felt it whenever the others talked about it.

"Hey, Walt," Kyle said.

"You don't have to say it, son. We're getting close, aren't we?"

Kyle nodded and looked for Sandy, Ben, and Morgan. When he spotted them, they were already watching him. He nodded to them to come over and walked further into the woods with Walt. Once they had gathered, he spoke quietly, "Same as before." He looked gently at Morgan, knowing she wouldn't like it, "I'm going in first to scope it out."

He felt Morgan's grip tighten on his arm. "No, Kyle. Not again."

He leveled his eyes on her. "I'll bring someone with me, Morgan, but you know we can't just ride in blind."

"I know. I just wish it didn't have to be you all the time." She sighed and laid her head against his shoulder.

"Take a look around, babe. Who else are we going to send in?"

Morgan didn't have to look. She knew Kyle was the only man for the job. "You're right again, babe. I'm just being selfish."

"You should take Anders with you, Kyle. He's able and a fair shot these days," Walt said.

"If it were any other town, I'd agree, Walt, but I need someone who's familiar with Willow Creek." Kyle turned to Sandy, "You up for it?"

Sandy was relieved that he wasn't going to ask Ben and immediately agreed, "Yeah. Sure. We're about three miles out. If we follow this trail, it'll take us to the south side of town."

"Is there enough cover there, or should we approach from another angle?" Kyle asked.

Sandy scanned the woods as she searched her memory for the layout of the small town, "We should be fine. Two miles from here, we'll come to the Beechum's ranch first, and then another mile will take us to the feed store. That'll give us a pretty good vantage point to see if there is any activity in town. There are plenty of places to find cover there."

Kyle nodded. "What about the road to the feed store from the Beechum's? Is it exposed or wooded?"

"It's not heavily wooded like this, but there is some cover. We could always leave the horses at the Beechum's and walk in."

Kyle nodded, "Okay." He gave Morgan a squeeze and a quick kiss,"
You and Walt hold down the fort here?"

"Of course," Morgan answered, smiling.

With Sandy leading, they took off at a gallop through the trees toward the Beechum's. When they were close, she drew up on her reins. "Let me just take a look around before we go any further," she said quietly.

Kyle followed Sandy as she slowly rode the perimeter of the house, keeping her horse just at the wood's edge. "It certainly looks abandoned," she whispered. "What do you think?"

"I think we're good. C'mon." Kyle pulled his rifle from his saddle holster and kicked his horse. They trotted into the yard and made their way toward the barn. As they passed through the barn, the smell of rotten hay lay heavy in the air. "What a shame," Kyle said as they rode past the bales. "So much waste."

"Mr. Beechum had just brought that in before he and Barbara left," Sandy explained. "He told me that their kids were going to come and pick it up, so they left the barn opened. I guess the kids never made it. We can put our horses over here," she said, and she walked her horse to the small paddock just on the other side of the barn. It was well hidden from the road and had patches of fresh spring grass and a water pump.

Kyle went into the barn and brought out two large buckets. He filled them with water before they left. "Check your weapon, Sandy."

Sandy pulled her pistol and checked it. Then reached into her pockets confirming the extra rounds she brought with her and quickened her pace to catch up with Kyle. It only took them fifteen minutes to reach the feed store. They looked around inside and found several bags of oats and two twenty-five-foot lengths of rope. "We'll pick these up on the way back," Kyle said.

After a thorough search of the town, they found no one there and no sign that anyone had come back. When they reached the church, they both paused and prayed silently. It was better that Steve and Tanya didn't come, Sandy thought. They didn't need to see this again. On their return trip to the Beechum's, they stopped for the supplies at the feed store. "Once we get settled back at the ranch for a day, we should probably come back here and see what else we can scrounge up." Sandy said, hoisting the ropes onto her shoulder.

Kyle shouldered the bags of oats, "Good idea."

They were back on the trail with the others within the hour. Kyle remembered this route. He, Morgan, and Tom had taken the same one a year ago. He couldn't believe it had been that long. Morgan must have been thinking the same thing because when he looked at her, she quickly wiped a tear from her eye. He smiled at her knowingly.

All of a sudden, Sandy saw the fence line of their property and she took off, crashing through the trees, passing Kyle and the others. Ben was close behind her.

Anders galloped up behind them, with his weapon drawn, "Sandy! Ben! Wait!"

Stunned by Sandy and Ben's sudden departure from the group, Kyle and Morgan kicked their horses into a run. "Sandy! Wait! You don't know what's there!" Kyle yelled.

The other riders followed but stopped short at the wood's edge where they found Sandy still on her horse, gazing out at what was left of her ranch.

Ben trotted over beside her—a big smile crossing his face. "It doesn't look as bad as I'd expected, Mom."

"No, it doesn't, does it?" Sandy turned in her saddle toward the others. "I'm sorry, everyone. I was just so anxious to see it."

"Sandy, you scared the daylights out of us," Kyle scolded her. "You know better than that." He softened and smiled at her and Ben. "It's been a long time. Let Anders and me ride in and scope it out. Wait for the 'all clear.' Okay?"

"Fair enough, Kyle. Thanks." Sandy stroked Annie's mane, resigning herself to waiting just a little while longer.

Anders and Kyle trotted alongside one another into the yard. From what they could tell, the place was definitely abandoned. The grass around the house had grown almost as tall as the porch and wildflowers bloomed all across the yard and in the small family cemetery up on the hill, the flowers' sweet aroma filled the air. Hay left over from the previous year lay matted in the field. The men rode to the barn first and saw that the roof had partially caved in, but the rest of the building was intact. "It looks like there's still enough room for the horses, if we clear it and double up a few of them in the stalls," Kyle observed. They left the barn and trotted up to the house. Kyle dismounted, pulled his rifle from its saddle holster and handed his reins to Anders. "Be right back," he whispered. He stepped quietly up the front porch steps and checked the front door. "Still locked." he thought to himself. "That's a good sign." He signaled to his partner to follow him around to the back of the house. "Doesn't look like anyone came after all," Kyle said, peering through the tall windows. "The kitchen looks just as we left it."

"Do you think there's more bark than bite to these people, Kyle?" Anders asked. "They made all kinds of threats, but it doesn't look like they followed through on any of them."

"I think you're right, Anders. Go ahead and give the signal. I know Sandy and Ben are anxious to come home."

Anders smiled broadly, rode out to the center of the yard so everyone could see him, held his rifle high, waved all clear.

Psalm 18:2 "The Lord is my rock, my fortress and my deliverer; my God is my rock in whom I take refuge. He is my shield and the horn of my salvation, my stronghold."

CHAPTER 38

TOM JOINED THE OTHER officers in rounding up the people and escorting them outside. He fought his way through the crowd until he was next to Joe and Jason. "Go straight to your unit and wait for me or Red. Do you understand?" He spoke low without looking at them.

"Understood," Joe replied. He took Jason by the arm, and they made their way quickly to the stables and back to his room. When they arrived, Joe sat Jason down at the kitchen table and looked squarely at his friend. "Jason, I need to know something, and you have to be completely honest with me."

Jason stared back at Joe, his eyes filled with terror, "Joe, I already told you everything."

Joe continued, "Do you know anything about the rescue?"

"No! I don't know anything about a rescue," Jason replied. "Why did they take Charlotte and her mom?"

"Garrison must have found out about the incident at the infirmary," Joe answered.

"But how?" Jason asked, still confused and frightened.

Joe gave Jason a look of disbelief, "Really, Jason? It was Stephanie. You do know that she listens to the phone conversations. She must have stayed on the line when I was talking to Charlotte and when she heard about the person showing up at the hospital, she called Garrison." Joe stood quickly, glanced out the small window, and saw two security officers hurrying toward Jason's unit, "Jason, I need to know right now where your loyalty is? Is it with Garrison or is it with the people?"

Jason looked down at the kitchen table and shook his head, trying to comprehend what his friend was saying. After the failed breakout attempt, he had surrendered to the fact that his future was in The City and there was no escaping it. Now that there was a possibility that he could be free, he felt frightened, unsure. He looked up at Joe. "I don't know, Joe. I hate it here, but where would we go, what would we do?"

Joe checked out the window again. The officers had left Jason's unit and were now coming to his. He turned back to Jason. "Security is coming, Jason. If you want to come with me and get out of here, follow my lead. This is it, Jason. It's time for you to pick which side you're on."

Just as Jason opened his mouth to speak, the door swung wide, and the two security officers rushed in. Jason jumped back from the table, but before he could get any further, the men grabbed him and Joe by the back of the neck and dragged them out into the night.

Sandy peered through one of the large kitchen windows and sighed, "Just as we left it." She reached up to the top of the door jamb and ran her fingers along the rough wood until they came to what she was looking for. A small crack concealed the key to the door. She smiled when she felt it and slipped it out from its hiding place. As she slid the key into the keyhole and turned it, she held her breath, feeling the tumblers fall into place. At the final stroke, she opened the door and stepped in. The faint smell of wood smoke greeted her, enveloped her. A lump formed in her throat. Oh, how she missed the old house.

Ben joined her and then, one by one, the others came in behind him. They murmured softly, delighted and surprised that the house was still intact. Sandy went down to the cellar on the slim chance that they had left any food behind, while Morgan and Joann Watson went upstairs to see about the sleeping arrangements. As they climbed the stairs, Joann noticed the empty walls where only the ghosts of pictures stared back at her. "Sandy has a beautiful home," Joann said.

"Yes, it was even more beautiful when Tom, Kyle and I arrived." Morgan said.

"It must have been difficult for her to come back here." Joann queried.

Morgan turned to look at Joann, "I can't even imagine."

"What about her other son has anyone heard from him or Tom?"

Sandy had told Morgan about the radio transmission back in Berkley Springs, but they had not told anyone else. They would reveal those details in good time.

"We'll discuss things tonight," Morgan replied. Coming up to the first bedroom, she went in. "Let's get started." The subject of Tom and Joe was delicate. Sandy and Kyle thought it best not to discuss them in open company while they were in Berkley Spring. Now that they were off the road and in a secure environment, Morgan felt sure that information about Tom and Joe would be more forthcoming. Once all the beds were turned and clean linens put down,

Morgan and Joann met up with Ben who was downstairs lighting the fires in the fireplace and wood stove. "Ben, when you finish there, would you mind taking care of your mom's room?"

Ben looked up at Morgan and smiled. "It's next on my list, Morgan."

"Thanks, buddy."

Joann smiled at the interaction. "He's a good kid. Sandy sure did a good job raising him.

Morgan smiled back, "She's got a heart for the Lord, that's for sure, and you can see it in her family. She would tell you that God was responsible for the way her sons turned out."

Just then Sandy came up from the cellar with two jars in her hand, "Well, we've got a jar of green beans and a jar of corn. Not much to feed everyone on. What do you think Morgan; is there still enough daylight left to go to town and see if anything is left?"

Morgan stole a glance outside, "Yeah, it could be another two or three hours before the sun sets. I'll go check with Kyle and Walt." Morgan went out the back door toward the stables, leaving Sandy and Joann in the kitchen. "Did Morgan show you the rest of the house, Joann?"

"She did and it's beautiful, Sandy." Afraid of dredging up old, sad memories, Joann was hesitant about saying anything more.

"I was going to take a walk to the mailbox. Do you want to come along?" Sandy asked.

"I'd love to," Joann said.

As the two women walked the leaf-strewn drive and into the woods, neither one spoke, each enjoying the company of the other and of the soft spring smells that drifted in from the thick trees on either side of them. "It must be difficult for you, being here again." Joann spoke gently.

Sandy turned to her, and Joann could see that her eyes were wet from memories. "It is. I love this ranch so much, but the memories . . ." Sandy's voice trailed off, then she began again ". . . so many beautiful memories and others, bittersweet." Sandy took a long breath. "I lost my husband, but God sent some pretty amazing people to help me through it." Through her tears, Sandy smiled at her friend.

Joann reached out and squeezed her hand. "You're an amazing woman, Sandy."

Sandy shook her head, "Naw, just blessed." Sandy saw that they were coming up near the end of the driveway. "Here, stay back for a minute, Joann," she said, putting her arm in front of the woman. "I want to check the road." Joann waited by an old oak while Sandy trotted up to the gate and peered over it, down the road. After checking both directions and sure that no one was there, she motioned for her friend to come up. "Sorry about that; it's just that the last time I was here, one of their trucks almost spotted me and I guess I'm a little gun shy."

"No apology needed," Joann said. "You know more about these people than any of us."

"You have no idea," Sandy assured her, "but I am surprised that they've left the ranch alone."

"Why are you surprised?" Joann asked.

The women were crossing the road now. "They just seemed particularly interested in it while we were here. I thought for sure they'd be here or at least would have come and trashed it."

Joann wondered, "Do you think there was something here that they wanted, that you or your husband was not aware of?"

Sandy paused with her hand on the door of the mailbox, a look of uncertainty on her face. She turned to Joann, "That thought never crossed my mind. What I believed was that they were going to use the ranch as some sort of communal compound. You know, to grow food and raise livestock for everyone housed in the surrounding areas."

"Yes, that would make sense," Joann agreed.

Sandy smiled at her friend and opened the mailbox. She peered in, her heart barely beating. Afraid of what she might find, she did not realize she was holding her breath. For a moment, she thought she saw an envelope lying in the shadow, but it was just that, a shadow. Letting out a heavy sigh, she looked at Joann. "I never thought checking the mail would be so stressful." They both giggled nervously and turned back toward the house. When they arrived back at the ranch Kyle and Anders were mounted and just leaving. Sandy gave them a wave and ran up to them. "Hey, you guys going into town?"

Kyle answered, "Yes ma'am. Can you think of anything you need?"

Sandy shook her head, "No, whatever you can find will be enough."

The men tugged on their reins, turned their horses toward the woods, and kicked them into a gallop.

Sandy went to Morgan, "Are you okay?"

Morgan nodded, "Yeah, I'm kind of getting used to this."

Sandy smiled and put an arm around her. "C'mon, you can have first dibs on the tub."

Morgan's face brightened, "Now you're talking."

Hebrews 4:16 "Let us then approach the throne of grace with confidence, so that we may receive mercy and find grace to help us in our time of need."

CHAPTER 39

Joe crashed headfirst into the metal sink and slid to the floor of his ten foot by ten-foot cell. "Smith will be down to see you directly," the guard snarled, as he slammed the cell door, and pushed Jason down the corridor. "It's the interrogation room for you, my friend."

Joe gingerly touched his head and groaned when his fingers came back bloody. He gently shook his head and stood up carefully. Things were not going well, and he prayed that Charlotte and her mom were safe. All he could hope for now was that Tom had not been found out. A single bulb, suspended from a power cord three cells down, offered little light to the dark corridor. He tried to peer down the dim hallway to the next cell, but all he could see were shadows. "Hello?" he whispered.

"Hello?" A hoarse whisper came from the cell next to him. "Who's there?"

"My name's Joe. Joe Parker. Who are you?"

"I'm Doctor White."

Joe shuddered. "Are you all right, Dr. White?"

"I'll be okay. They beat me up pretty good, though. I saw them bring in Charlotte. I'm afraid they roughed her up pretty badly."

Joe's adrenaline spiked. "Did you see where they took her, Dr. White? Was she with her mom?"

"No, Joe, I didn't see her mom. I can't be sure, but she's probably in one of these cells. Shh, someone's coming."

Joe took a step back from the bars, sat on his bunk and waited for the heavy footsteps and jangling keys coming his way. It was too early to fight his way out and even if he did get free, he had no idea where to go. All he could do now was wait to see what would happen next, and of course, pray. A dark figure stopped in front of his cell, but the poor lighting made it impossible for him to see who it was. It wasn't until the man spoke that he realized whom he'd be dealing with.

"Good evening, Mr. Parker. It seems that your girlfriend has gotten herself in a little hot water. You really should watch the company you keep. Because of your connection to her, you, too, are guilty by association."

"Guilty of what, Smith?"

"Treason, son; you, your little girlfriend, and the good doctor," Smith gloated. "How are you feeling, doc?"

Doctor White fought to keep the pain from his voice, "Just fine, Smith."

John Smith bristled, "You ready for another go round then?"

"Whenever you're ready. Do you think that beating up an old man and young girl will make you look better in Garrison's eyes, or Baroam's? I got news for you, Smith, you're losing it. All of you." White forced a laugh, sending Smith over the edge.

"Shut up, White! Or I swear, I'll kill you!"

"Smith!"

John Smith swung around, "Mr. Garrison." His eyes narrowed when he saw Tom Connelly was with him, "Officer Connelly."

A rush of relief came over Joe, "Thank you, Father. Thank you."

"Mr. Smith, I appreciate the passion you have toward our cause, but please don't make death threats, especially when there are witnesses. Right, Joe?"

Joe turned a hateful look on Garrison but didn't speak.

"So, tell me, Joe, how did you come to meet Officer Connelly?"

Joe knew what Garrison was up to, furthermore, he knew how to play the game. "You already know the answer to that question."

"Remind me," Garrison whispered, as he pressed his evil, grinning face against the bars that separated them.

Joe glared at Tom, then Garrison, as he retold the story, he and Tom had rehearsed repeatedly all those months ago while they were on the trail.

"And you have no idea where the rest of your family went?" Garrison growled.

"No, sir, I left in the middle of the night while they were sleeping. Just like I said," Joe spat.

Garrison reached through the bars and grabbed Joe by the front of his shirt and hissed, "Mark my words, Parker, I WILL get to the bottom of this and if I find you anywhere near it, you'll be sorry."

Tom eyed the matted blood on Joe's head and fought hard to keep from shoving Garrison away from him. They had to play out their parts just a little while longer. He knew Smith would be watching him closely and they couldn't afford any slip ups, now that they were so close to escaping. "Do you want him in interrogation?" Tom asked, still watching Joe.

Smith perked up at the request, hoping he would be the one to do the 'questioning.' "Boss, you want me to take him?"

Garrison pushed Joe across the cell, forcing him hard, once again, into the metal sink. "Not now. Where's the other kid they brought in? Let's see what he has to say." He knew Joe's loyalty to his friends. He had been watching the boy for months. Something about Joe, something Garrison could not name, threatened him, and he didn't like not knowing why. He made his way down the corridor to Jason's cell. When he saw the boy on his knees, praying, he whooped loudly. "You fool! Do you think your god is going to save you from me?" Garrison looked closer at the boy through the low lighting, "I see you've already had him in interrogation, Smith," Garrison said, scrutinizing the boy's beaten and bloody face. "What did you do to your hand, boy?" Jason ignored him, continuing his prayer.

"Smith! Get over here and open this door!"

Taking advantage of the distraction, Tom glanced into the cell next to Jason's and saw Dr. White's bloodied face. He winced, just imagining the pain the man must be suffering. Tom looked directly into the doctor's eyes and winked ever so slightly.

The doctor let out a sigh, bowed his head and smiled. There was hope after all and it came in the form of an Army sniper, turned spy. He heard Jason cry out suddenly and he moved over to the bars to peer down the darkened hallway. "What's wrong with you people that you have to pick on old men and children!"

"White! If you don't shut your mouth, I'll shut it for you, permanently!" Garrison yelled.

This was it. The violence was escalating, and Tom knew they would show no mercy to Jason. He wasn't ready for the consequences, but he couldn't stand by and watch them torture the boy. "Garrison!"

Garrison and Smith both turned at Tom's sudden outburst and saw his M16 pointed at them.

"That's enough," Tom growled. "This is not how it's done!"

"Well, then enlighten us, Connelly. How did you do it in the big war?" Smith snarled.

"Follow me." Tom said, turning around not waiting for them.

The two men looked at one another and shoved Jason to the floor. After locking the cell, they followed Tom to the end of the hallway, near the entrance.

"What's with you, Connelly?" Garrison asked. The short walk had calmed him, but Smith was still ready for a fight. "You got a problem with interrogating witnesses?"

"No, but I do have a problem with torturing kids and old men. These aren't the ones you want. They're just the little fish in a bigger pond. You need to turn them loose."

"Are you out of your mind?" Smith hissed. "How is that going to help? The kid tried to escape, and I'd bet anything Parker had something to do with it. I know for a fact that old lady Beechum knows about it."

Jason's stomach turned and he thought he would vomit, "You leave her out of this! She knew nothing about it!" He shouted from his cell.

"They're just kids, Garrison. So, what if one of them wanted to get out? What teenager have you ever known who didn't want to run away? All I'm saying is, they have nothing to do with the planned escape. Think about it, Garrison. You said Stephanie told you about the conversation between Joe and Charlotte, but did she say anything about who the perpetrator was?"

"No," Garrison said.

"Then what makes you think that Joe would know something about it? I know you've both been watching him. So have I and I have not seen anything that would indicate that he was planning or was part of an escape." Tom asserted.

Garrison saw the logic and turned his rage to Smith, "Smith, if I turn these prisoners loose, it's going to be your job to watch every move they make. Do you understand? And put your spies out there. Who's that creepy little guy at the market, Arnold?"

"Ernie, boss. I'll get right on it. What about the others? That old woman, Beechum, remember what I told you about her? She has to be involved somehow. She bought the first aid kit, and I'd bet anything she used it on the kid." The animosity that John Smith felt toward Barbara Beechum and the others was like nothing he'd ever felt before. If he could just have a few minutes alone with any one of them, he would be able to satisfy the urge for violence that was eating away at him.

Garrison knew it too. He did not like the people any more than Smith did, but he had enough to handle and was not about to turn Smith loose on them. After what he did to Dr. White, Garrison knew that Smith was one step away from committing murder. "Tom, she's your problem now. I want you to put your best man on that building and watch it morning, noon and night. We will revamp the entire security system in The City if we have to. Baroam is going to demand some answers and what am I supposed to tell him?" Garrison's expression was tense as he ran his hands through his thick hair. He was getting a headache.

"Tell him you've got a suspect and you're interrogating him," Tom suggested.

Garrison let out a deep breath and shook his head, a look of defeat on his face. "All right. It's worth a try." Garrison looked at John Smith, "Release them, except O'Malley. Connelly, you'd better be right. I've trusted you so far."

"What about Beechum?" Smith asked again.

"Tom, get your guy on duty tonight. I'll deal with her in the morning. Garrison left them and walked tiredly back to his room. The words that Dr. White had said to Smith kept coming back to him, "You're losing it. You are all losing it!"

***

Kyle and Alan approached the main road from the same path Kyle had taken with Tom and Steve just a few months earlier. Aside from the few abandoned cars that littered the road, the street was deserted. "It doesn't look like much has changed, Alan. C'mon, we'll have to take it slow. The grocery store is just over there," Kyle pointed across the road, "opposite the bank." The men kicked their horses and rode over the main road to maneuver quickly behind the store for cover.

Anders dismounted and checked his gun. "I don't understand why they have to trash everything, Kyle. What's the point?"

"That's just their way. The back door is over here. Like I said, take it slow."

Anders nodded and followed Kyle, ducking below windows and peering around corners before moving forward. When they were finally inside the store, he sighed. "Wow, what a mess!"

Kyle shook his head at the destruction and waste. "I'll take this aisle, you take the other side of the store, and we'll meet in the middle." "Sounds good," Anders replied.

After a full hour of careful scavenging, they had their saddle bags filled with dry and canned goods. Kyle checked the cereal aisle; hoping he would find one last box of Cheerios, but he had no luck this time. They made their way quickly back to the horses. Kyle tied down his saddlebag, got back on his horse and spoke quietly, "I want to swing by the church and check on it."

"You're the boss." Anders said. He turned his horse and followed Kyle down the back alley toward Steve's church. When they turned the corner, he could not believe what he saw. "Are you serious, Kyle? Why would they burn down a church?" Anders hung his head and sighed. "Kyle, what can we do about them? There's so few of us and so many of them?"

Kyle smiled. "Romans 8:31. What then, shall we say in response to this --

"If God is for us, who can be against us?" Anders grinned back.

"Ah, so you are familiar with that verse." Kyle said dismounting.

"Yeah, I've heard it before. Didn't Steve talk about it in one of his sermons back in Berkley Springs?"

"I believe he did," Kyle whispered. I'm going to have a look around. Do you mind staying with the horses?"

"No, go ahead. I'll keep watch." Anders dismounted, took the reins from Kyle, and scanned the area, the anger steadily building inside of him. It always happened when he saw what they had done or when he remembered how they stole his beloved horses. He was just turning to see where Kyle had gone when he heard the slow click of a revolver's hammer behind him.

Isaiah 42:16 "I will lead the blind by the ways they have not known, along unfamiliar paths I will guide them; I will turn the darkness into light before them and make the rough places smooth."

CHAPTER 40

ALAN SLOWLY RAISED HIS hands, keeping his back turned. "We mean no harm. We're just looking for food."

"Who's 'we'?" a shaky voice asked.

"My buddy and me. If you're hungry, we can feed you," Anders said cautiously, but sincerely.

"I don't recognize you. You're not from around here."

"No, sir. We come from Berkley Springs, West Virginia."

"How many are with you?" The voice sounded more hopeful, less scared at this last question.

"Before I answer that, friend, I need to know who you are. Times are dangerous," Anders reminded the stranger.

"Go ahead and turn around then, but no funny business," the voice said.

Anders slowly turned and found himself face to face with a tall, lanky young man of about fifteen. The boy's curly, red hair sprang out from beneath a wide cowboy hat that shielded his freckled face from the sun. Anders' expression relaxed when he realized that the kid was no threat. "I give you my word. We're not here to hurt anyone. We're just here picking up some food. Are you alone?"

The young man slowly lowered the gun and turned toward the building behind him. He lifted his arm and waved. The door suddenly opened, and a group of eight people filed out of the store. He seemed to be the youngest of the group.

Still holding the gun in his wobbly right hand, the boy watched as his companions came forward and then turned to Anders. "We've been in hiding for months now, but when we intercepted a radio transmission that some folks were coming here to Willow Creek, we came back. Are you the ones that they were talking about?"

Anders put his palms out, pushing the question back to the kid. "Hold on now. What do you mean, you picked up a radio transmission? Have you been listening in on our frequency? And more than that, how did you know which frequency?"

Surprised by the gathering of people, Kyle's heart swelled with joy. "Father, You always provide, don't You?" He hurried back to Anders and approached him from behind. When the kid aimed his revolver at him, he raised his hands. "I'm with him, folks. We're all friends here; right?"

A man, who appeared to be in his late thirties, moved from within the crowd and stood beside the teenager, "Here, let me take that off your hands," he said. He had a strong, intense face with jet-black hair trimmed short and clean. His brown eyes, shot with flecks of green, were kind and gentle.

The kid gladly handed the man the gun. "My name's Chris Larsen. This is Ronnie Sykes."

Kyle stepped forward, introduced himself and Anders and the four of them shook hands. "Chris, Ronnie, we're glad to meet you." Kyle looked past Chris to the people behind him, "So how many are in your group?"

"There are ten of us, including the kid and me. My man, Ronnie here, was on patrol and I guess with the town being abandoned, we became a little slack in our caution."

"Are all of you from Willow Creek?" Kyle asked.

"Ron, go on back and stand with the others. I'll be along directly." Chris patted the kid on the shoulder and then put his attention back to Kyle and Alan. "We come from a little town not far from here. If you're familiar with this area, you'll know that there are a lot of little townships scattered around these hills. Well, somehow, they found us and tried to gather us up to take us to The City." "Who's 'they'?" Kyle interrupted.

Chris cocked his head, "Beg your pardon?"

"You said 'they' found you. Are you talking about the Regulators?"

"I've heard them called 'Regulators and 'Control Officers'" Chris answered.

"Okay then, go on with your story," Kyle said. "I'm sorry I interrupted."

Chris nodded and continued, "Anyway, they were able to get a few of the town folk, including Ronnie's parents, but the rest of us took to the woods." Chris chuckled. "City folk don't like to go into the woods at night; that was to our advantage. By daybreak, they had given up looking for us."

Anders looked at Kyle. "The kid told me they picked up a radio transmission saying that folks were coming back to Willow Creek. He wanted to know if we were the ones everyone has been talking about." Still surprised at what the kid had said, Anders gave a hard inquiring look to Kyle.

Kyle watched Chris cautiously. "You want to fill me in on what he's talking about?"

Once we knew it was safe to come back to town, we acquired a high frequency radio, set it up, and started hearing transmissions between 'The City' and Berkley Springs, among other places. There was talk about a group of riders coming this way to overthrow The City in Willowdale and rescue the folks inside. We wanted to help, so here we are. The more able-bodied came along while the others stayed back in town. We've been waiting for you for about a week now. To be honest with you, I saw you earlier with a woman but figured since it was just the two of you; you couldn't be the ones we were expecting."

It took Kyle a few moments to digest what Chris had just told him. "How many other people do you think have been on our frequency?"

Chris shook his head, "I'm afraid I couldn't tell you. I just don't know, but believe me when I say, there are a lot more people planning the same thing. Americans are angry and they want their families back," Chris paused, "and their country. You know what I don't get, though?"

Kyle shrugged. "What?"

"How is it that most of the people that we've met on the outside, have been Christians?"

Kyle smiled. "I think it is because they already have someone to follow; the others didn't. But I'm pretty sure there are a few good Christians on the inside, too."

"I'm sure you're right." Chris scanned the sky, "The sun is setting; we should be going. So, what do you say? Can you use our help?"

"Absolutely," Kyle said. "What about food, weapons, horses? Do you have any?"

"Yes sir, we have all of that and then some. The horses are just beyond the tree line." Chris pointed up the street. "Wherever you're headed, we can meet you there."

"I'm not sure if you'd find it, Chris." Kyle said. "We'll wait."

"Very well." Chris turned and hurried back to the group and gave instructions. The people scattered and within ten minutes everyone was mounted and ready to go. They rode single file across the road, heading deep into the woods. Anders, who was bringing up the rear, suddenly stopped and turned quickly in his saddle toward the town. He knew he heard something, and what he saw confirmed it. A Humvee drove slowly by, stopping in front of the area where they had just crossed. Anders heart stopped. Afraid to move, he froze, but then he thought, "The others may get too far ahead and then what?" His mind raced, "What if I am captured?" He navigated his horse as carefully as he could behind a thick stand of saplings and waited. The truck remained idling, as though the driver was waiting or possibly looking for someone or something. Finally, the truck slowly began to pull away and Anders kicked his horse into a run. As he galloped through the woods he prayed, "Please, Lord, don't let them come. Not now." He passed the other riders, drawing confused and frightened looks from them, and rode straight to the front. "Kyle! Kyle!"

Kyle spun around. "Anders! What is it?"

"Kyle, they're here! I saw one of their trucks. It was passing through town just after we cleared the road! Then it stopped right where we crossed. I don't know if they saw us or not."

Kyle drew in a deep breath, "We may have gotten out of there just in time." He pulled hard on his reins, bringing his horse back onto the trail, "Bring up the rear, Alan and on your way back tell the others that we're picking up the pace."

"You got it."

Gus Wilkerson, Joann, and David Watson sat at the kitchen table with a two-way radio and tried to make contact with the friends they left behind. Since their arrival, they had been unable to reach Berkley Springs, and they hoped that nothing had gone wrong. Gus suddenly froze, his fingertips resting on the dials of the radio.

"What is it, Gus?" David asked.

"Kill the lights!" Gus ordered.

Joann, frightened, quickly blew out the oil lamp, and looked at her husband.

"Someone's coming." Gus quickly rose from the kitchen table and peered out the window.

"Maybe it's Kyle and Alan." David whispered, joining him at the window. Both men squinted through the glass, trying to focus in on the dark woods that stood just fifty yards from the porch.

"No, there's too many." Then Gus pointed excitedly toward the trees, "Look!" No sooner did he speak than Kyle burst through the trees at a dead gallop. Behind him rode ten more riders with Alan bringing up the rear.

Sandy, Morgan, and Ben were in the stable putting the horses up for the night when they heard the thundering hooves. They quickly secured the horses and ran out into the yard just as Kyle and the others rushed in. Kyle's face lit up when he saw Morgan. "Hey babe, we've got company!" He said breathlessly and dismounted. He tossed his reins to Ben and went straight to Morgan taking her in his arms.

Stunned by all the riders, Sandy went to Alan. "Where did all these people come from?"

"There's a lot to tell, Sandy." Alan turned and looked for Chris in the crowd. "Hey, Chris! Come on over here. There's someone I want you to meet."

Sandy's shocked expression remained as she took in the scene of riders and horses scattered in her side yard. When she turned to see who Anders was talking to, she saw a tall, lean man approaching her. By the way he carried himself, she was certain that he, too, was former military. The smile on his face was curious, but genuine.

Anders introduced them and Sandy stepped forward to take Chris' hand. "I'm pleased to meet you, Chris." She returned his smile, but cocked her head, puzzled. "Why are you looking at me that way?" she asked.

"You're 'Lady Blue.'" he smiled back, still gripping her hand.

Alan turned suddenly to Chris. "How did you know that?"

"It's just as I told you in town, Alan. There is talk all over the airwaves about Lady Blue, Sandman, Nelly, Preacher, and the little lamb. I'm Birdman. I don't mean to frighten you folks, but you really don't know what is being said out there, do you? It started not long after you left Berkley Springs, so of course you haven't heard anything."

Confused, Sandy shook her head and turned to Kyle and Walt, who were just joining them. "Is it still safe to be on the radio, you guys?"

"I think at this stage of the game we're all right." Walt stepped forward and shook hands with Chris. "Chris, I'm Walter, but folks just call me Walt, or you'll know me on the radio as 'Devil Dog'."

"Of course!" Chris's face split into a wide grin as he shook Walt's hand fiercely. "Were you in the Corps?"

"Affirmative; you?"

"You bet. Semper Fi, Devil Dog."

Walt let out a hearty laugh. "It looks like we've got a lot to talk about. How about we get you folks squared away and we'll discuss things inside; over supper?"

"That sounds like a great idea," someone yelled from the back.

Sandy turned to Ben, "Honey, will you show them where to put the horses?"

"Sure, Mom." Ben had already put Kyle's horse in his stall and now went around to the others, taking the lead ropes from some of the strangers. Ronnie and a few others followed him into the barn. Ben turned to the teenager next to him. "My name's Ben." "It's good to meet you. I'm Ronnie. Is this your ranch?"

"Yeah." Ben said.

"It's nice!" Ronnie exclaimed.

"Thanks." Ben smiled. He loved the ranch and always felt good when other people appreciated it too. "Where are you from?"

"A little township up the ridge, I lived with my mom and dad." Ronnie said.

Ben nodded as he led a horse to the rear paddock. "Are your folks with you?"

Ronnie lowered his eyes. "They were taken," he said quietly. "They saw the men coming in the truck and sent me into the woods to hide."

Ben waited before he asked the next question unsure whether he should. "Why didn't they go with you?"

"Mom was really sick, and dad couldn't leave her. She wouldn't have survived long without medical care, so when the Regulators came, dad gave me his shotgun and told me to take the horses and go stay in the woods until they were all gone." Ronnie let out a heavy sigh. "I haven't seen or heard from them since."

The boys finished up with the horses and followed the other people back to the house. The evening breeze was blowing light and fragrant, lifting everyone's spirits. An air of anticipation and excited urgency enveloped them as they climbed the porch steps and walked into the kitchen.

"Okay, let's everyone find a seat, or at least a place to stand. We need to run through a few things while the ladies prepare our meal." Walt smiled at Sandy, Morgan, and Joann who with the two women from the new group were busy at the other end of the kitchen.

Sandy was not sure there would be enough food to go around, then she recalled the story of when Jesus fed the five thousand with just a few fish and loaves of bread, and she became overwhelmed with gratitude.

Walt continued speaking, "I'd like to say on behalf of everyone in our group, we are glad you're here and with all this extra help, I know we will be able to devise a plan to get into The City and rescue our loved ones."

The people responded, "All right! Now you're talking!"

"Now, with that being said, we still won't be out of the woods." Walt warned them, "There's still the corrupt government to consider, but we'll have to save that for a later time. With so many people here, sleeping arrangements will be wherever you can find a comfortable space. I would only ask that you allow the lady of the house and her family to have first dibs on the bedrooms." Everyone nodded in agreement. Someone shouted, "Walt, all I'll need is a little piece of floor, out of the elements, and I'll be happy." This brought a rush of laughter from the group.

"That's good to hear," Walt said. "Now, I want to give the floor to Chris, and he can make the introductions."

By the time the introductions were done, supper was ready and spread out across the table. Sandy took a step back to survey the setting. "Well, I guess we'll have to picnic where we can, folks. I don't have enough place settings or chairs," She added. "Thank you all for your donations. We have a feast fit for royalty."

"Speaking of which," Kyle said, "before we dig in, let's join hands, and give thanks." The group joined hands, bowed their heads, and Kyle began, "Heavenly Father, thank You for sending reinforcements and friends to help us in the mission we are about to begin. We ask that You strengthen us and grant us courage and wisdom to carry out what You would have us do. I pray that You will grace those on the inside with courage as well as encouragement. Bless this food to our bodies, Lord, and bless those who prepared it. It's in Jesus name we pray. Amen."

Wherever they had found a place to sit or stand, the group ate hungrily and talked among themselves. Most of their chatter concerned getting to know one another, but eventually the talk turned to the rescue operation. When the meal was finished, Sandy and the other women collected the dishes and went about cleaning up, while the men grouped around the kitchen table. "Chris, what else do you have in the way of communications and weapons?" Kyle asked.

"Well, right now we've got the high frequency radio system I told you about earlier. For power, we're using a car battery we lifted from one of the multitudes of abandoned cars scattered around." Chris grinned. "I guess at some point, when the owner comes home, we'll have to return it. The radio works pretty well for the most part . . . when we can get a clear signal. This place is ideal, though. With the wide-open spaces and the tall trees, we should be able to mount the antennae on the roof of the house or, better yet, on the barn."

"I hope you have good luck with yours, Chris. We've tried all day but haven't been able to raise anyone in Berkley Springs or The City," Walt said.

"When the ladies are finished, let's give it a try," Kyle suggested, wanting Sandy and the others to be involved.

"Sounds good," Walt, replied. "What else do you have with you, Chris? What we need to do is pool everything together, to give us an idea of what we have to work with."

"Ronnie, where did we put all the ammo and weapons?" Chris asked the boy sitting next to him.

"Everyone pretty much has their own guns, but the rest of the ammunition and weapons are in a box in the mudroom." Ronnie answered.

"Good, why don't you and Ben get the box and bring it in here. Except for the C-4; just leave it where it is, all right?"

"You got that right." Ronnie said, throwing a cautious smirk at Ben.

Walt, Kyle, and Alan stared at each other, and then at Chris, "You have C-4?"

Chris grinned like the proverbial cat that swallowed the canary. "Yeah, along with the fuses and blasting caps; there are quite a few mining towns between here and West Virginia and we didn't think anyone would mind. For the cause, you know."

"Well, all right then!" Kyle said. "Between us I think we'll be a pretty formidable force against The City and its Regulators."

"What'd we miss?" Morgan asked, taking a seat next to Kyle.

"We have C-4." Kyle said.

"No kidding!" she said, surprised. "What are we going to do with C-4?"

"We haven't figured that out yet." Kyle answered.

"What about you folks?" Chris asked.

"We've got rifles, handguns, and reloading equipment. We also have a couple of handheld UHF radios. They should keep us connected to the ranch, or to The City, once we get close enough," Kyle said.

"What about radio range?" Chris asked.

"About five miles," Kyle answered. "We won't be in range of everyone all the time, but they'll work fine once we get to where we're going."

Chris leaned back in his chair and turned a smiling face to the group, "Gentlemen, ladies" -- he nodded politely to Sandy and the other women, "I believe we will be well prepared to take on the City. Now all we need is a plan."

Ephesians 6:16 "In addition to all this, take up the shield of faith, with which you can extinguish all the flaming arrows of the evil one. Take the helmet of salvation and the sword of the spirit, which is the word of God."

CHAPTER 41

AFTER THE ENCOUNTER WITH Garrison in the holding cells, Tom hurried back to Barbara Beechum's building. He gave a quick nod to the guard out front. "How you doin' tonight, Sam?"

"Never better, Tom. You going up?"

"Yep," Tom replied. "Can you get MAC on the radio?"

"Yeah, sure, hang on." The guard switched channels to the secure line and pressed the talk button on the radio attached to his collar. "Hey, Mac. Do you copy?"

"Whatcha got, Sam?" McCloud answered.

"Can you give me a five-second freeze frame on the old lady in thirty?" Sam said.

"You got it, Sam."

Sam looked up from his microphone to Tom. "You've got thirty seconds, partner. Make 'em count."

"Thanks, Sam." Tom nodded to the guard and slipped quickly through the blacked out double doors.

Meanwhile, John Smith stood outside the building to cool off after the tongue-lashing he received from Garrison, then he took the elevator down to the basement for another visit with the prisoners. As he approached Joe Parker's cell, he fished his radio out of his pocket. "Red, do you copy?"

"Right here, Smith. What can I do for you?" Red answered.

"I need a security transport to take some suspects back to their units. You'll need a cart." Smith said.

"Copy that. I'll be there shortly." Red switched channels on his radio and called Tom, "Connelly, you copy?" "Loud and clear, Red." Tom answered.

"I need to make a security run from the hotel to various units around The City. I'll need your help."

"That's fine; I'm on the North side. I can meet you at the hotel in fifteen." Tom whispered, not wanting to wake any of the residents as he hurried quietly down the hall."

"Sounds good, I'm out."

Tom knocked softly on Mrs. Beechum's door. He heard the soft shuffle of feet on the other side, then the door opened quietly, and he slipped in, unnoticed. Once inside, he turned in one swift movement, locked the door, then took her arm gently and walked her into the kitchen, "They have Jason," he said softly.

Barbara flushed and reached for the chair. "Oh no! Is he all right?"

Tom pulled out the chair for her and waited for her to sit. "He's fine for now. Garrison had Dr. White, Joe, Charlotte and her mom locked up, but I was able to convince him to release them. He wouldn't release Jason, though. He knows Barbara. Garrison knows that Jason is the one who attempted the escape."

Barbara grew frantic, "Tom, what are we going to do? How do we get him out?"

This was the first time Tom had ever seen Barbara at a loss, and it unsettled him. He counted on her to be the strong one, to be an example for the other residents in the building. He took a seat next to her. "Don't worry about Jason, Barbara. I'll look after him. I need you to be strong for the people here. Can you do that?"

Barbara filled her lungs with a deep breath and reached for Tom's calloused hands, "Yes, I can. Forgive me for being fearful. I know that Jason is in good hands and that God will be watching over him, as he watches over all of us."

Tom squeezed her frail hands. "That's right. The time to leave is coming soon, Barbara. Are you up for it?"

"Absolutely! You just say the word." Barbara exclaimed.

"Good." Tom said. He leaned down and gave her a warm hug. "Get some sleep, Barbara. I have to go meet Red Dalton. Expect to see Mr. Smith and me tomorrow morning. With Baroam breathing down Garrison's neck, and with Garrison all over Smith, he will no doubt hit you with some pretty tough questions."

Barbara hugged him back. "I will be fine, dear. You be very careful."

"Yes ma'am." Tom opened her door slightly and peered out at the single eye of the camera lens staring blankly back at him, and he prayed, "Lord, please turn Garrison away from the cameras for just a moment." Tom quickly slipped out the door, passed the camera and made his way down the hall. If Garrison had seen him, he'd find out soon enough.

After Tom left her, Barbara went to her room, reached underneath her bed, and pulled out the box she had found months earlier. When she opened it, it was just as she had left it; stacks of gold and silver coins, cash, and fifty rounds of bullets. She reached up into her closet and pulled down a backpack that Jason had given her and began filling it. Then she went into the kitchen and filled the pack with crackers, water, and the first aid kit. She lifted it with a small grunt. "Well, I think I can manage, but I'd better not put any more in here," she said to no one.

Since he returned from the meeting, Nick Garrison had been watching the monitors that lined his wall. He was especially interested in Barbara Beechum's unit and focused mainly on it. He turned away for just a moment to check another screen, and when he turned back to Beechum's monitor, he noticed the door to her unit just closing. He quickly found the camera on Beechum's floor, but by then the heavy metal door to the stairwell was just shutting as well. Someone was walking the halls, and he did not know who. He immediately grabbed the radio from his desk. "This is Garrison! Who's got the old folks building tonight?"

"Officer Sam Valdez, sir. What can I do for you?"

"Who just left the building?" Garrison barked.

"No one, sir." Sam lied.

"I just saw Beechum's door close, and then the door to the stairwell. Someone had to have been there!" Garrison yelled.

"Do you want me to go check on her, Mr. Garrison?"

"Yes! And call me when you get to her door!"

"Yes, sir."

The guard gave a sideways glance to Tom Connelly and grinned. "You better get a move on, Connelly. Stay in touch."

Tom grinned back and nodded. "I'll swing by when I'm through with Red. It'll be soon, Sam."

Sam smiled back and pulled open the doors, hurried up the stairs to Beechum's unit, and banged on her door.

Garrison watched the monitor carefully and when no one came to the door he began moving away from the monitor toward his door. "I'll go there myself and so help me, if she's not there –" he grumbled. Before he could finish his sentence, the door to Barbara Beechum's unit opened just a crack revealing her scowling face.

"What is it, officer?" She asked.

Sam held his index finger up to silence the woman, "Mr. Garrison, she's here. What would you like me to do?"

"Search the unit!" Garrison yelled into the radio, "She's up to something, and I want to know what it is."

"Yes, sir." Officer Valdez shrugged his shoulders and looked apologetic. "I'm sorry, ma'am. Boss says I have to search the place."

Sam took a step forward, but Barbara stood firm. "What is it you expect to find, Officer?"

"Honestly, I'm not sure, Mrs. Beechum. Mr. Garrison says he saw your door closing and wanted me to make sure you were still here. Curfew and all," Sam tried again to enter, and she finally stepped back and allowed him in.

"I can assure you, Officer, there is no one here." Barbara said firmly.

"I'm sure there isn't, but I still need to check." Sam insisted.

Barbara waited while Officer Valdez did a quick sweep of the unit. While he walked through the small area, he spoke quickly, "Mrs. Beechum, I know Officer Connelly was just up here and when it's time, you can count on me to help you. Do you understand?"

"I'm still not sure whether I can trust you people," Barbara said.

"You can trust me, ma'am." The doubtful look on Barbara's face made him smile, "You have my word, Mrs. Beechum. You should also know that there are others you can trust who may surprise you even more than I."

"Humph!" Barbara grumbled and followed the officer back to the door. "Thank you, officer."

"You're welcome, Mrs. Beechum." Officer Valdez held his finger up again while he checked back with Garrison, "Mr. Garrison, everything is clear here. She did tell me she opened her door to shoo out a spider." Sam winked at Barbara.

Garrison sighed. "That still leaves the stairwell door. I don't believe her, but there's nothing more to do tonight. Remind her that Connelly and Smith will be by in the morning."

"Yes, sir." Sam smiled down at Barbara, "Did you get that?"

Barbara returned his smile, "Yes, thank you. I'll put on a pot of coffee for them."

Sam threw his head back and roared with laughter. He was a young man, well-muscled and clean-shaven, including his head, a formidable opponent to anyone who did not know him, but a solid friend to those who did. His black eyes danced as he smiled at her. "You be careful, ma'am. I've heard things about you." Sam left, making sure to slam the door behind him.

Ephesians 6:14-15 "Stand firm then, with the belt of truth buckled around your waist, with the breastplate of righteousness in place, and with your feet fitted with the readiness that comes from the gospel of peace."

CHAPTER 42

EVERYONE HUDDLED AROUND THE radio at the kitchen table. With a little help from Chris and many prayers, Ben and Ronnie were able to climb up onto the barn roof and carefully mounted the radio antenna. Now everyone was waiting anxiously for a response . . . any response from their friends in Berkley Springs or in The City. Chris sat in front of the microphone and spoke clearly, "This is Birdman. Does anyone read me; over?" He paused and raised his eyes towards Sandy, Kyle, and Ben. The silence broken only by the chirp of crickets and night bugs that floated in through the open door and windows. Chris turned back to the radio. He couldn't stand to see the mixed expressions of hope and anxiety on their faces. "This is Birdman. Is anyone out there; over?" He paused again and realized that he was holding his breath. Finally, a thin voice, barely audible, came from the speaker. Everyone in the room began to whisper excitedly. "Shh!" Chris said as he held up his palm and leaned into the microphone. "Birdman calling. Say again, please; over." Chris looked up and smiled back at the happy faces.

Again, the thin, tinny voice came from deep within the radio, "This is Apple Blossom; over."

A loud whoop erupted from the crowd in the kitchen as Chris reached forward and adjusted the dials on the radio. "Hello, Apple Blossom. It's good to hear from you; over."

"It's good to hear from you, too, Birdman. What is your situation; over?"

"You'll be happy to know that we ran into some friends of yours. We are at a central location approximately twenty miles from The City. Everyone is well and ready to see some action; over."

Sandy and the others could hear the joy in the voices chattering in the background.

In Berkley Springs, Steve and Tanya stood at the radio with Nancy Davis. "That is wonderful news, Birdman. We've been worried. Everyone here is well and ready

for whatever comes up. Tell Sandman that Preacher is training us hard; over."
Nancy turned to Steve.

"Preacher, do you want to say anything?"

Steve didn't hesitate. "Yes, I do. Thank you, Nancy." Steve exchanged places
with Nancy and took Tanya by the hand. "This is Preacher and Preacher's Wife.
We're glad you are all well, Lady Blue and Lamb Two."

Chris stood and offered his chair to Sandy. She smiled at him as she wiped a tear
from her cheek, "Thanks, Chris." She pressed the mic button and spoke into it,
"Hey, Preacher and Preacher's Wife, we'll be with you soon enough. Please give
our love to everyone there, yourselves especially; over." Sandy looked up at Ben
and offered him the microphone, but he backed away slightly and only smiled. He
was so relieved to hear from his uncle and aunt that he was too moved to speak,
embarrassed that everyone might hear the emotion in his voice.

Sandy rose from the chair and moved so Chris could sit back down. "Thanks,
Chris."

"You're welcome, Sandy." Chris turned to the radio. "Preacher, have you been
able to raise anyone else in the last few days; over?"

"That's an affirmative. We spoke with Boss Daddy just a short while ago. It
sounds like things are heating up; over."

Chris covered the microphone with his hand and spoke quietly to Walt and
Kyle. "We need to get that plan squared away tonight.

"Preacher, we're going to back out of here and give them a try; over."

"Understood. We're out."

Chris closed his eyes and inhaled deeply, then looked up at the crowd around
him. "No time like the present. Let's give The City a try, shall we?"

Everyone nodded and moved closer. Sandy's heart rate picked up and she took
deep breaths to slow it down. Morgan saw her discomfort, covered her hand with
her own free one, and smiled. "It won't be long now, Sandy."

Sandy looked apprehensive, "Yes, and I think that's why I'm so anxious."

Chris tapped the microphone and leaned toward it, "Birdman calling Boss
Daddy. Do you read; over?" The radio crackled and hissed until Chris turned the
squelch down and tried again, speaking louder, "Birdman calling Boss Daddy do
you copy; over?"

Finally, a voice came faintly over the speakers, and then it grew louder. "This is
Boss Daddy. We read you loud and clear; over."

A chuckle of relief escaped Chris. "It's good to hear from you, Boss Daddy. What's the situation there; over?"

"Situation is under control for now, but it could get dicey pretty quick. What's your twenty; over?"

"We arrived at a temporary destination and have connected with Lady Blue, Sandman, and company; over."

Red let out a rebel yell. "Well, that's the best news I've heard in a long, long time! I've got company coming in three. Can we radio back; over?"

Chris turned a smiling face to Sandy and Kyle, "You may have a chance to speak to your loved ones on the inside."

Sandy beamed. "Oh, that would be so wonderful."

"We'll be standing by; Birdman, out." Chris stood up from the table and smiled at Sandy. "I can't imagine how you must be feeling. I'm glad we were able to get through."

"Me, too," Sandy agreed. She reached down and put her arm around Ben, pulling him to her. "I hope we'll be able to talk to Joe."

Ben was quiet and smiled back. "I do, too, Mom. I'm going to go check on the horses. I'll be back." He reached up and gave her a peck on her check.

Sandy watched Ben leave out the back door and smiled to herself. She shook her head in disbelief and sighed. He had grown up so much over the last year.

"He's a good kid," Chris said watching Sandy.

Sandy lowered her gaze. "Yes, he really is." She still felt Chris's eyes on her and stepped away, "Well, let's see. It's about twenty-one hundred hours, now, so they should be calling around midnight, correct?"

"That sounds about right," Walt said. "In the meantime, I suggest we put our heads together and formulate a plan, so we can have something to tell them when they do call." Walt scanned the room until he found the boy he was looking for. "Ronnie, go on out and help Ben, then both of you skedaddle on back here so we can get started."

"Sure thing, Walt." It only took two strides of his long legs before Ronnie was out the door.

Proverbs 16:3 "Commit to the Lord whatever you do, and your plans will succeed."

CHAPTER 43

RED ARRIVED AT THE hotel, still grinning from the news he had just received. He was anxious to tell Tom and Joe, but it had to wait. "Howdy, Smith. What do you have for me tonight?"

"We've got three prisoners on house arrest. That means a guard at each door. Do you have the men for that?"

"I've always got men for that. Gotta keep these sheep under control, right?"

Smith smirked, "You got that right." He liked Red Dalton. Unlike Tom Connelly, who was trouble from the day he arrived, Red had never given him any trouble. Smith pulled Red aside before they entered the building. "There's something you should know, Red."

Red raised a bushy eyebrow, "Oh, yeah? What's that?"

"When we took the girl and her mom, the mother tried to resist, and we had to shoot her."

Red felt as though someone had just punched him in the gut. He had seen Joe go to Charlotte's house many times and believed they were a good match. Red had wanted to tell the mother how much he appreciated her looking after the boy, but he never had the opportunity. Red shook his head. "Well, that's a real shame. Which one of our incompetent officers couldn't handle a hundred-pound woman? I'll have him sent to the smokestack."

John Smith cleared his throat, embarrassed by his guilt. "It was me, Red. It happened too quickly. I was sorry it happened."

Red couldn't hide his irritation. "Tell that to the girl who lost both her mother and father to The City, Smith. Where'd you put her body?"

"We transported it over to the incinerator," Smith sheepishly said.

"You didn't waste any time with that did you, boy?" Red Dalton knew his ire was showing more than usual and checked himself when he saw that Smith was eyeing him suspiciously. He quickly changed his tone. "I'm sorry, John; it's been a long night."

"That's all right, Red. It has been a long night. I'll go wait for Connelly at the front door. You got this?"

"Yeah, I got it. I'll radio for officers to meet us at the units. Thanks." Red patted Smith on the back and moved down the darkened hallway where the prisoners were waiting quietly in their cells. The first cell he stopped at was Joe's. "Hey, kid. How are you holdin' up?" He hated that he would have to tell Joe about Charlotte's mom. Did Charlotte even know? He would have to ask Smith. The last thing he wanted to do was to break the news to the girl.

Joe was holding his head in his hands, but looked up when he heard Red. "Hey, Red, I'm doing all right, I guess."

"I see they knocked you around a bit," Red said tapping his own forehead in the same area where Joe's wound was apparent.

Joe touched his forehead lightly and winced, "Yeah, I got into a fight with the sink. It won."

Red chuckled. "Tom should be here shortly and then we'll bring you, Dr. White, and Charlotte home." The second Red had finished his statement, he realized the mistake he had just made, and he dreaded the next question.

Joe narrowed his eyes and looked hard at Red. "What about Charlotte's mom? She was brought down here with Charlotte."

Tom made his way down the sidewalk toward the hotel where Joe and the others were housed. When he arrived, he found John Smith waiting for him by the door. "It took you long enough. Red called you quite a while ago."

Tom was getting tired of Smith and his constant nitpicking. "It's only been about fifteen minutes, Smith. Isn't that what I told Red?"

"Where have you been, Connelly?"

"Check the cameras. Then you'll know." Tom snapped back, not bothering to hold the door for Smith. "Is Red here yet?"

Smith followed Tom inside. "Yeah, he's waiting for you downstairs."

Tom took the concrete steps down into the basement two at a time and swung the heavy metal door wide. When he saw Red, he smiled cautiously. The expression Red wore made Tom want to turn around and leave. He knew he was walking into some very bad news.

"Connelly, glad you could make it." Red growled.

Tom cocked his head slightly and gave Red a questioning look, "What is it, Red? What's happened?"

Red stared hard at him. "I've got some good news and some bad news."

Psalm 68:5 "A father to the fatherless, a defender of widows, is God in his holy dwelling."

CHAPTER 44

ONCE EVERYONE FOUND THEIR seat around the heavy, oak table in Sandy's kitchen, Walt pounded on the table and the room fell silent. "Okay, folks, we've got about three hours to rough out a plan to break our people out of The City and, hopefully, shut the place down for good. When we talk to our friends on the inside, we can smooth it out, if we have to. I'm wide open for suggestions."

Someone at the far end of the room shouted, "Do we know how many allies we have on the inside?"

Walt looked at Sandy to answer the question.

"Through previous dispatches, we found out that there are at least twelve, maybe more. Some are in positions that will prove to be very, very useful."

Kyle motioned toward the back of the room. "Gus, Ben, Alan, I need you guys to move in a little closer." Kyle turned back to Chris. "Do we know how many entrances there are to The City?"

Chris took one of the placemats and set it in the middle of the table so the others could see. "There is the main entrance here and an entrance here, on the northwest wall, a secret door that no one is supposed to know about." Chris placed the salt and pepper shakers at the two areas he pointed out. "I would expect that your friend, Tom, would be privy to that information since he is head of security and, of course, Big Daddy would also know about it. The distance from one gate to the other is at least three hundred yards, with several buildings in between. It's going to be a good hike for whoever we send."

With his forefinger, Chris drew an invisible line around the placemat. "Along the perimeter of the wall is a hedge that stands about five feet high, so it will provide ample coverage for the rear gate. Now that being said, the gate is not your average gate. It's actually a small, circular opening, no bigger than three feet in diameter. Whoever enters by way of the back gate, will have to be small enough to get through it." Chris's eyes drifted directly to Sandy and Morgan. "While I don't care for the idea of either of you ladies going, in the first place, I think you two would be the best candidates."

"Is the gate locked?" Sandy asked.

"Yes." Chris answered. "It's locked from the inside." "Does anyone have a key?" Sandy asked.

"Tom should have a key or at least be able to get his hands on one." Chris replied.

"Yeah, but how do we know it will be Tom on the other side of the door?" Sandy asked.

Suddenly Kyle sat upright in the chair. "Challenge and pass!" he shouted.

"What's that?" Joann asked.

"Challenge and pass." Kyle pulled his chair closer to the table and leaned forward. "In Iraq when security was tight and we were going into a place where we knew we had one of our own waiting on the inside but wanted to make sure we were communicating with him and not the enemy, we used a challenge and pass -- two related words known only to the users. For example, 'lion and lamb;' most of us are familiar with those words used together, but others may not be. Do you follow? Sandy on one side of the gate will call out 'lion' and the person on the other side will call out 'lamb.' If it's anyone besides our allies they won't know the matching word, and we will know that the guy on the other side of the gate is not our friend."

Chris's face brightened, "Brilliant!"

Walt spoke up, "Great idea, Kyle. Sandy, will you and Morgan be up to planting the C4?"

Sandy looked over at Morgan, "Yeah, someone will definitely have to show us, but we can handle it. Right, Morgan?"

Morgan nodded. "Not a problem."

"Okay, good," Walt said. "We're going to have to talk to Tom and Red about the best place to plant the C-4."

Once you two are inside with Tom, head to the power substation and fuel station, and plant the C4. Be sure to get it right near the pumps at the fuel station. At the power substation, plant the C4 right next to the power lines. That will disable the power station and will be a distraction. The blast can also serve as the signal to start the evacuation."

"As far as the rest of us getting in," Kyle went on, "I'm recalling a mission Tom, and I were on in Iraq. Our unit had to clear out some suspected Taliban that were hiding in this sheik's abandoned mansion, but there was only one entrance. Before we went in, we set up a 360-degree cordon around the house for security, and then he and I kicked the door down and rushed in. Needless to say, we caught the bad guys completely off guard." Kyle chuckled and shared a grin with Anders. "It was like shooting fish in a barrel."

Ronnie gazed at Kyle, stunned. "You mean you killed them?"

"Well, yeah, we had to. It was them or us. That's war, son. Now, that's not to say that we have to go in and do the same thing in The City. Our goal is to remove the ones held captive. Does everyone understand that?" Kyle stood up and made sure everyone heard him. "We aren't going in to shoot up the place; this is strictly a rescue mission. What I'm saying is you have to protect yourself and the people you are charged with."

Walt agreed, "He's right. The element of surprise is always a good plan, Kyle, but this will have to be on a much bigger scale. We don't have enough riders to surround The City."

Chris interrupted, "That won't be a problem, Walt. There are only two vulnerable areas in the wall that surrounds The City. The main gate and the rear entrance. We will send someone with Sandy and Morgan to cover the rear entrance and the rest of us can focus on the main gate and provide security for those going in."

Walt seemed satisfied with Chris' suggestion and moved his attention back to Kyle. "Will your friend, Tom, remember that particular mission?"

Kyle smiled broadly, "Yeah, he should. That's when he made me his squad leader."

Anders gave Kyle a nudge. "I don't want folks to think that I don't value human life, because I do, but what about the livestock, the horses."

Complete realization fell across Kyle's face, "Lucky is in there!"

"And Pilgrim and Cheyenne," Sandy added.

Kyle patted Anders on the back. "Thanks, Anders. How could we forget them?" Kyle looked around the table. "In my group I think the best one for the job is my man, Ben. Sandy what do you think?"

Sandy agreed, "You're right, Kyle, and you, too, Alan, but how will Ben get to the animal shelter? He'll obviously need some help. He won't know anything about the layout of the place."

"That will just have to be one more thing to discuss with Tom when they call. Now, who do we send in and how many?" Chris asked.

Kyle looked squarely at Walt. "I know who I want. No offense to anyone else here, but you get used to the people you ride with. Along with Morgan, Sandy, and Ben, my picks are Anders, Gus, and of course you, Walt." Kyle faced the couple across the table from him, "Joann, David, we'll need someone here to maintain communication with Berkley Springs. Would you mind taking care of that end of it?"

Both Joann and David looked relieved. Joann wasn't sure about going in but wanted to remain a part of the team. Her husband read it in her face, "I think that would be the best position for us, don't you, honey?"

Joann smiled shyly, "Yes."

Walt laughed low and soft. "Okay, we've got your team set up, Kyle. What about you, Chris? Who in your group is prepared to go in?"

Chris looked around the room. "My men can serve as security for those going in and at the entrances. Ronnie can help Ben with the animals."

Ronnie's face lit up. Not only did he want to be involved somehow, but also, he had grown fond of Ben and could relate to his losses. The boys nodded to one another. Each of them felt the fear just beneath the surface, but at the same time, they were relieved that they would be working together.

Kyle moved on with the plan. "I think we should split the security detail up to cover as much as we possibly can. Sandy and Morgan, you two will have Tom to cover you while you set the C-4." Sandy and Morgan nodded their understanding.

Kyle continued, "I would suggest bringing in two from Chris's team for the infirmary. Whoever will be working to get those people out, will be occupied loading, attending to the sick, and to the injured. They won't have time to watch their backs, too. We also need to send one in to back up Ben and Ronnie. They'll be too busy with horses, dogs, et cetera to keep looking over their shoulders. The remaining people we leave at the front gate or move them after we are there to wherever they'll be needed. Again, we'll know more after we talk to Tom and Boss Daddy."

After nearly two hours of suggestions, questions and brainstorming, they had finalized the plan. They would get a good night's sleep, prepare the horses, munitions, and food the next day and then, at dawn on the following day, they would leave for The City. Soon their loved ones would be released from the hell they had been living in for the past year and Sandy and the others would be reunited with them.

***

Red motioned for Tom to follow him away from Joe's cell and back to the metal doors. "Be right back, kid."

Joe rushed to the cell door and shouted, "Red! What's going on?"

Red ignored Joe's plea and leaned against the door while he talked to Tom. "I spoke with one of the groups on the outside a little while ago. They've met up with your people and are at a temporary location, working up a plan. I'm going to try and raise them again around midnight. Do you think you can be at the security office by then?"

Overjoyed, Tom grasped Red by the shoulders, "Red, that is good news! I'll be there, absolutely! Is everyone all right?"

"Oh, yeah, everyone is fine. I think we're all getting a little antsy though. We need to coordinate the escape plan when we call."

"Good idea." Tom agreed. "I spoke with Barbara Beechum just a little while ago and she is ready. Sam in security will help the people in her building to get out, and I have McCloud on the cameras in the security bunker. We just need to set the date and time and make sure everyone is on the same page."

"What was the bad news, Red? I didn't like the look on your face when I came down."

"Charlotte's mother is dead." Red said.

Tom's eyes grew dark with anger, and he punched the metal door making it echo down the hallway. "How? Who?"

"I'll give you three guesses, but you'll probably only need one," Red said flatly.

Tom turned and bolted toward the door. He had had enough of John Smith.

"Now, where do you think you're going, soldier?" Red questioned, as he grabbed Tom by the bicep.

"Give me just five minutes with him, Red."

"Can't do it and you know it, Connelly. We've got bigger fish to fry right now. Come on, we've got to get these kids out of here." Red turned the angry man toward the hallway and gave him a push. Tom reluctantly led the way. His stomach wrenched in knots at the thought of having to tell Joe and Charlotte about her mother.

When they stopped at Joe's cell, he was grasping the bars so hard his knuckles had gone white. Anger and fear melded together on his bearded face. He ignored Tom, "What is going on, Red? You have to tell me!" He demanded.

Red opened the cell door and he and Tom each took Joe by the arm. "It's about Charlotte's mom, Joe," Red said waiting for the young man to piece it together.

Joe's mind raced, organizing the events of the last four hours. Suddenly the realization of what happened crashed through his mind and he charged toward the open cell door. "I heard a gunshot! Was it her? Did that monster kill her?"

Red released him and went to Dr. White's cell while Tom kept a tight hold on Joe. Joe fought, but Tom was much stronger. When he realized he could not break away, Joe relaxed and turned to face his friend and agonized, "Why, Tom? Why her? She was no threat; why would Smith do that?" He cried.

"Because, Joe, he is a coward; plain and simple. Come on, I don't know if Charlotte knows or not, but we need to tell her and then get you all out of here." Still holding tight to Joe's arm, Tom hurried him out of the cell and spoke quickly. "Once we get you to your units, a guard will be posted at each of your doors. Hopefully, some of them will be allies." They stopped in front of Dr. White's cell. "How are you feeling, doc?" Tom asked.

Dr. White chuckled. "Like I've been put through a meat grinder, but I'll be all right." The doctor put a trembling hand on Joe's shoulder. "I'm sorry, son. I wish there was something I could have done to stop Smith."

Joe shook his head, "There's nothing anyone could have done, Doctor White."

They followed Red to Jason's cell. When they found him, Jason was leaning over the stainless-steel sink, trying his best to clean up his injuries. His face was beaten and bloody and the wound on his hand had re-opened from the interrogation at the hands of John Smith. When he heard Joe and the others at his cell door, he turned around. When he saw Joe, a smile crossed his face, "Hey, man, I'm glad to see you're all right. I was just trying to make myself a little more presentable." He laughed, then winced and quickly put a hand to his side. "I think one of my ribs is cracked."

"Red, let me just take a quick look," the doctor said.

Red opened the cell door and stood back. "Make it fast, doc. We don't want Smith coming back down here to find you in there."

"I won't be long." The doctor motioned for Jason to lie on the cot. He methodically checked him over and finished cleaning his wounds as best he could.

When he pressed lightly on Jason's right side, Jason howled and sprang from his bed, "I take it that hurts a bit?"

"Yeah, doc, just a bit," the boy groaned.

"Without an x-ray I can't tell whether it's broken, bruised, or cracked. It's too painful to be only bruised, so let's hope it is just cracked. If it were broken, it would be way too dangerous to move you."

"Haven't you heard, doc? I'm not going anywhere; orders from the big boss himself."

Red tapped the bars with his keys. "Let's get a move on, folks. Jason, you sit tight. We'll be back for you. Just get as much rest as you can. You're going to need every ounce of energy you can muster."

"You can count on me, Red. I'll be ready."

Joe nodded to his friend as they left and Jason smiled back, splitting his lip open again, "See ya, Joe."

Charlotte's cell was further down the hall from the others. Why? Red could not tell. Perhaps it was because Smith was afraid that someone would find out about her mom and tell her. As they drew closer, he could hear her softly weeping. A lump grew in his throat, and he swallowed hard. For such a gruff man, he had always had a soft spot for young people; especially the ones whose parents raised them right and did their best to do the right thing. He turned around to Joe. "Maybe it's best that you tell her."

Telling Charlotte that her mother had been murdered was the last thing Joe wanted to do, but he didn't want anyone else to tell her, either. He took the lead and slowly approached her cell. He called out to her softly, "Charlotte?"

She rose from her cot and crossed her cell to the bars, "Joe? Is that you?"

Joe hurried to her cell and waited impatiently while Red unlocked the cell door. When it finally opened, Joe rushed into her waiting arms. "I'm here, Charlotte." They embraced for a moment, and then slowly he pulled away from her and strained to see her face in the dim lighting. What he saw enraged him all over again, but he quickly suppressed it. He did not want her to see him that way, not in her condition. He had to be strong for her. Steady. He took her chin and gently turned her head from one side to the other and studied her bruised face. Her left eye was blackened, and her lips were cut and bleeding. "Oh, baby, I'm so sorry I couldn't stop this." He kissed her softly on her cheek and lips.

Charlotte put her finger to Joe's injury on his head, "It looks like they got hold of you, too. Don't be sorry, Joe. There's nothing you could have done. I don't know where they took Mom, and I heard a gunshot. What do you think happened, Joe?"

By now, Tom had come into her cell while Red kept watch down the hallway, "We need to get going."

Joe took a deep breath and held Charlotte's hands to his lips and kissed them. "Charlotte, something happened."

Charlotte went stiff for just a moment and then she drew away from him, shaking her head violently. "No! Don't you dare tell me she's dead! Don't you dare, Joe!"

"I'm so sorry, Charlotte." He took her in his arms, but she fought him, trying to free herself. She wanted to run from him, from the painful news of her mom, from The City and all the people in it.

Desperation gripped her, but Joe held her tighter, accepting the slap she landed across his face more than once. He didn't let her go. Finally, she stopped and collapsed in his arms. Heavy sobs rose from deep in her soul and she clung to him. Joe held her close, stroked her hair, and kissed her, talking softly to her until she finally relaxed. She pulled away from him and took a deep, sobbing breath, "I'm sorry, Joe."

"Shh, don't be." Joe whispered.

Charlotte turned to Tom. "Officer Connelly, who was it that killed my mom? Was it that Smith guy?" she demanded.

Tom touched her gently on her shoulder, "It doesn't matter right now. We'll all be out of The City soon, but right now we need to leave."

Her anger reignited and she spun around and lashed out at Joe, "It was him, wasn't it?" she screamed through her tears.

Joe just shook his head in disgust, thinking of Charlotte's sweet mom and the monster Smith, "Come on, Charlotte." He put his arm across her shoulders to lead her out of her cell.

Charlotte tried to pull away from Joe one last time, but her need for his comforting embrace was stronger, and she reluctantly submitted and went with him.

Red led them back down the hallway. Before they entered the stairwell to the upstairs, he paused and looked at Tom. "We'll need to restrain them, Connelly."

Tom nodded his understanding. "Joe, Charlotte, we need to put these tie bands on you, just until you get to your units. All right? Joe, I'd probably put them on you anyway, knowing how you'd react to Smith when you see him." Tom drew Joe's arms behind him. "That too tight?"

"No, that's fine, Tom. And you're right about Smith." Joe said looking back at him.

Tom turned to Charlotte, "Let me know if these are too tight."

"They're fine, Officer Connelly. Thanks," Charlotte said quietly. Tom took Joe by his hands behind his back while Red grasped Charlotte and Dr. White and led them up the stairs.

"Okay, kids, doctor, eyes in front. Don't waste your breath on Smith. No doubt he's waiting out front to taunt you." Walt said.

You hear that, Joe?" Tom said squeezing Joe's hands.

"Yes, sir."

It was just as Walt had said. John Smith stood at the double doors smirking when the others came up from the basement holding cells. "Do you know what happens to people who commit treason in The City, boy?"

Joe kept his eyes averted, staring at the swirled patterns on the carpet in front of him. He recalled the day they had arrived and how he had kept his focus on the carpet then, too, when he had met up with Garrison again. His blood boiled now, as it did then, and he was grateful for Tom's firm grip on him.

"We hang them, Mr. Parker, and then we send the bodies to the furnaces."

"That's enough, Smith," Tom ordered. "Get the door or move out of our way."

"No need for all that, Smith. We're done here." Red Dalton bore his steely eyes into the antagonist, sending a shiver up the man's spine. John Smith pushed open both doors with a growl and stormed out. He would get them. He would get all of them, especially Connelly and Parker.

Proverbs 17:11 "An evil man is bent only on rebellion; a merciless official will be sent against him."

CHAPTER 45

RED DROVE THROUGH THE deserted streets of The City; the hum of the golf cart mingling with the symphony of crickets and cicadas on the warm summer night. He and Tom rode in silence until they reached the outer area of the housing units. Red glanced in the rearview mirror at Charlotte and Dr. White. "The time is coming when we make the escape. Are you all up to it?"

Charlotte had been crying softly into Joe's shoulder but looked up when Red spoke. "I'm up to it. You just say the word, Officer Dalton," she said, pulling her hair back into a loose ponytail.

Joe smiled at her; he admired her strength. "We'll be ready." "Is there a plan in place yet?" Doctor White asked.

Tom turned to face the group. "We'll be hearing from our contacts on the outside later tonight so as soon as we get the plan finalized, we'll let you know, somehow. Doc, will you be well enough to run and possibly fight your way out of here?"

"The good Lord willing, I'll be ready or die trying, Officer Connelly."

"That's the spirit." Tom smiled at the older man."

Joe looked up at Tom, his face beaming. "You mean you'll be talking to mom?"

Tom smiled at Joe. "I mean just that."

Red spoke up, "Joe, the man I will have posted at your door tonight is one of us, so you shouldn't have any trouble getting to the security office. When we drop you off at your unit, wait for the guard to knock on your door twice and then leave immediately. Since your unit is on the end, just go around to the back of the building and be sure to hug the wall. If you stay in the shadows, the cameras won't be able to spot you. We should be ready by the time you get there."

Joe was ecstatic at the possibility of talking to his mom and little brother. He tried to recall the last time he heard her voice but couldn't. It had been months.

"Okay, folks, here we are." Red stopped the cart and got out. "I'll escort Dr. White to his unit; you guys just stand by." Red walked the doctor up the sidewalk and nodded to the security officer already waiting out front, "I'll be right out."

The guard only nodded and eyed Dr. White cautiously. "He doesn't look like much of a threat," the officer said before he turned and unlocked the door.

"He's not, now that Smith had a couple of rounds with him. Keep an eye on the prisoners in the cart. I'll be right out."

"Yes, sir." The security guard turned and stood at attention facing the golf cart resting his right hand on his pistol, hoping, daring any of them to try and escape.

Joe scrutinized the guard carefully. "I don't think he's one of us, Tom. Do you?"

Tom stared hard at the man, "No, Joe, you're right. He's definitely not one of us."

Red led the doctor into his living room and released the bands around his wrists, "Okay, doc. Sit tight and get some rest; you'll be needing it."

Doctor White massaged his wrists where the bands had cut into him, "You just fill me in on the details, Mr. Dalton, and I'll be ready."

Red stepped back onto the front porch where the guard was still standing and clapped him on the shoulder. "Thanks, officer. I'll send someone by to relieve you at . . ." Red checked his watch, "oh nine hundred."

"Sounds good, sir."

Red strolled back down the sidewalk to the golf cart, slid in behind the wheel, and turned toward Charlotte's house. "When it's time, I'll be sure to vet the relief officers. Tom, when you take Charlotte up, let the guard know he'll be relieved at oh nine hundred."

"You got it." Tom walked Charlotte up to her front steps and the guard opened the door without saying a word. His look was enough to show that he was not one to be trusted either. Tom nodded to him as they climbed the concrete steps. "Evening, officer."

Again, the man did not speak but nodded his acknowledgement. When Tom and Charlotte had cleared the door, he closed it behind them. Standing in the tiny foyer, Tom gently removed the bands from Charlotte's delicate wrists. "I'm sorry about everything that's happened tonight, Charlotte, but I promise you, it will get better."

Charlotte turned to face him, "Thanks, Officer Connelly," I don't know what I'd do if I didn't have Joe, and now I come to find out that you and Mr. Dalton

are good guys. Well . . ." Her voice trailed off and her smile faded. She quickly turned away from him so he wouldn't see her tears.

Tom drew his nine-millimeter, "I'm going to take a quick look around, okay?"

"Yeah, sure, I'll be in the kitchen." Her voice was weak with exhaustion.

Tom went to the kitchen first and checked the pantry and laundry closet, then moved on through the rest of the house. After he was satisfied that the unit was empty, he found Charlotte fixing a pot of hot water for tea. "Everything checks out, so I'm going to leave. You try to get some sleep. Okay, Charlotte? If you need anything you know how to reach me."

Charlotte nodded. "Thanks, Tom. I'll be all right. I hope Joe gets to talk to his family tonight."

"Soon you will all be together," Tom said, lightly touching her cheek. "We'll be in touch." He turned quickly and left. When he was out the door, he saw that the guard was still staring Joe and Red down. "Your relief will be coming at oh-nine hundred," Tom spoke loudly, jolting the man from whatever evil thoughts that were going through his mind.

"Yes, sir. Have a good night, sir," the guard said without as much as a turn of his head.

Tom nodded and stepped off the porch, skipping the stairs. When he was back in the cart, he turned around to Joe, knowing what he was going to ask even before the young man had a chance to say anything,

"She'll be all right, Joe."

"Thanks, Tom." Joe smiled at his friend's intuition.

Red checked Joe in the rear-view mirror. "Are you clear on your instructions, son?"

"I'm clear, Red, but what about the camera that focuses along the sidewalk? Won't Garrison see me coming out of my unit?"

"They won't if you're careful, Joe. The cameras in The City are constantly moving on a swivel. When the camera that's fixed on your unit is turned away, that's when the guard will knock on your door twice. You will only have a second or two, so make them count."

Joe settled back into the seat and thought about Charlotte, all alone at her house. His heart ached for her, and he wanted to be with her, but there were things that had to happen first. He was anxious to get started and his mind wandered to his mom and little brother.

Slowly sipping her tea, Charlotte walked silently through her empty house. Her head was beginning to ache from exhaustion and sorrow. "A shower would be good right about now," she thought. She went into her room to get her pajamas when the phone rang. Not expecting a call, Charlotte jumped. Her heart skipped thinking it must be Joe, but when she looked at the clock, she realized he couldn't be back already. It had only been a few minutes since they had left. The phone rang again but she was hesitant, fearful. "What if it's Garrison or Smith?" Fear gripped her; dread overwhelmed her. She took a deep breath and expecting the worst, answered on the third ring, "Hello?"

***

Two soft knocks signaled to Joe that it was time. He quickly slipped out the door, hugging the wall just as instructed, and made his way to the edge of the building. He slipped around the corner and disappeared into the darkness. His adrenaline surged as he hurried along the back wall toward the security building, anxious to talk to his mom and little brother.

Just as he was about to cross to the other side of the stable, he spotted Silas Grey coming toward him. Joe quickly ducked into the tack room and squatted behind a rack of saddles and blankets. He peered over his cover and watched as Silas poked his head into the security office where Red and Tom were discussing new security procedures. "The stable's all locked down, Officer Connelly, Mr. Dalton. Is there anything else?"

Tom looked up and nodded his thanks. "No, that'll do for tonight, Silas. Thanks for staying late. We've got it from here."

"Good night, then." Silas turned and left. When he passed by the tack room, he noticed the door standing open and pushed it shut. "I don't remember opening that." He chuckled to himself, "I must be getting old," and he moved on.

Joe held his breath, afraid that Silas would hear him, and then exhaled slowly as the sound of his supervisor's footsteps faded into the night. Joe emerged cautiously from the tack room and entered the security office. When the door opened, both men looked up. "Sorry I'm late; Silas nearly spotted me."

"I was afraid that was going to happen," Red said. "C'mon, kid, we've got some folks waiting for us." Red led Joe and Tom to his unit in the back and went through the ritual of bringing up the others on his base radio. "This is Boss Daddy calling Birdman. Do you copy; over?"

Back at the Parker ranch, a shriek of excitement exploded from the kitchen and Chris had to wave his hands to quiet everyone so he could hear. "Boss Daddy, you're coming in fine. It's good to hear from you all.

How are the sheep holding up; over?"

Red chuckled. "They are restless, but all is well. I've got a sheep and little lamb here who would love to hear from some of their own kind. Is that possible; over?"

"Absolutely," Chris answered. "Standby please; over." He looked up from the radio toward Sandy, Ben, and Kyle. "Okay you three, you're on." Chris stood and allowed Sandy to sit, while Ben stood close to her.

She pressed her fingers to the microphone, remembering the last time she had done it in Berkley Springs. Joe and Tom had just arrived in The City and the same butterflies as before still battled in her. Her hands began to tremble. "This is Lady Blue and Lamb Two; over."

Tom's heart skipped, but it was only fair that she talked to her son first, so he gently pushed Joe toward the radio. "No names, Joe, you're the Little Lamb, your mom is Lady Blue, I'm Nelly, and I'm guessing that Lamb Two is Ben."

Joe raised his eyebrows, not pleased with his handle, "Little Lamb? Really, Tom?"

Red let out a hoarse chuckle, "Sorry, kid. That was my doing. I had to come up with a name quick when you two arrived and that's all I could think of at that moment. Go ahead, Little Lamb, your mamma's waiting," he laughed.

Joe shook his head and just smiled at Red and Tom. He sat in front of the radio and spoke, "Greetings, Lady Blue and Lamb Two, this is Little Lamb back at you; over."

Sandy nearly jumped out of her chair with joy, "Little Lamb, it's so good to hear from you. Everyone here is just fine. How are you; over?"

"We're hanging in here, Lady Blue, about ready to be moving along, if you know what I mean; over."

"We copy that. Lamb Two is here; over."

Joe grinned, "Hey, Lamb Two, it's good to know you're there, looking after things; over."

Ben smiled and leaned toward the microphone, "Little Lamb, we're waiting on you; over." Ben made a point to emphasize 'Little Lamb,' bringing a round of laughter from the group that surrounded him.

"We copy that, Lamb Two. I'm turning this over to Nelly; over."

Sandy knew that Tom was anxious to talk to Kyle, "Little Lamb, know that He is looking after all of us and that there is protection through Him. Do you copy: over?"

"We read you loud and clear, Lady Blue. Standby; over." Joe stood up from the radio and made room for Tom to step in.

After hearing Sandy's voice, Tom Connelly couldn't keep the smile from his face. He sat in front of the radio and spoke into the mic, "Lady Blue, so good to hear you. We've got things to work out. Is everyone ready; over?"

"Everyone is ready, Nelly. It's good to hear you, too; over."

"Lady Blue, there are things that I want to say, but that are better said in person. I look forward to that time; over."

Sandy felt her face grow warm. "Soon, Nelly; over." Sandy kept her head down as she rose from where she sat, allowing her long hair to hide the blush on her cheeks from the others. Kyle moved in next to her to take her chair and kissed her softly on the top of her head. He knew Tom had feelings for her yet understood the turmoil that Sandy must have been going through. She still clung to her husband's memory not ready to let go, but her feelings toward Tom had also changed. He could see it every time they spoke of him or when they spoke with him on the radio, as they were now.

Chris saw it too. During his conversation with Kyle at dinner, he had learned of Sandy's husband and the relationship he had with Nelly. The story saddened Chris and he prayed that she would one day find peace and maybe even love again.

Morgan patted Sandy's hand and gave her a hug as Kyle spoke to his friend, "Nelly, this is Sandman; over."

Tom couldn't hide the joy in his voice, "Sandman, I never thought I'd say it, but I sure miss you, man; over."

Kyle laughed, "Feelings mutual, buddy. We've been making plans on this end and should be at your door in approximately seventy-two hours, but we have some questions. Where are you with yours; over?"

"When you're ready, we'll be good to go. What are your questions; over?"

"Do you remember our first mission where you made me your squad leader; over?"

Tom smiled to himself. "Very clearly. Is that the gist of the plan; over?

"10-4. We'll be working with a secondary door. Do you know the one; over?"

"Intimately," Tom said. "How many in; over?"

"Two; over."

"Understood. Challenge and pass; over?"

"Our Savior has many names," Kyle said. "Lady Blue will call out one and you will know the one that goes with it; over."

"I'm clear on that. What other questions do you have; over?" Tom leaned back in the chair and smiled his thanks when Red brought him a cup of hot coffee.

Kyle studied the map Chris had made on the table with the salt and pepper shakers, "How far is the infirmary from the front gate and from the rear gate? Those sheep will have to be transported. We'll also need some help for Lamb Two in the stables; over."

"We'll have someone ready and waiting. The infirmary is approximately a half a klick from the main and a little over a half klick from the rear. The sheep within will be ready to follow orders from Nelly and others; over."

While Tom gave the information over the radio, Kyle positioned the salt and pepper shakers on the table to show the others the approximate distance they would be working with. "That sounds good, Nelly. What about the security system; over?"

"The security system is taken care of. The cameras will go on automatic at twenty-three fifty-five; over."

Kyle covered the microphone, thought for a moment, and turned to Walt. "That'll be cutting it awfully close for Sandy and Morgan to make their way to the fuel station and the power substation, and then find their way to the infirmary."

Walt shook his head; concern etched in face. "We'll need at least three additional minutes to make sure they can get to their next stop without the additional ground security being released. Remember, they will be coming from the rear gate, and they'll be right smack in the middle of The City by then. Plus, we need to know how far it is from the front gate to the motor pool."

"Nelly, we need more time. How far from the front gate to the motor pool; over?"

Tom glanced at Red and covered the mike, "Can we get them three more minutes?"

Red's eyebrows drew together in concentration, "I don't know how. We'll just have to pray that God can find it for us."

Tom sighed heavily, "The front gate to the motor pool is almost two klicks, Sandman. I'll have someone waiting for you at the gate with transportation and someone to assist with the trucks. They'll be prepped for you when you arrive.

That should also save you some time; over. We can't promise anything on the extra time; over."

"No problem, Nelly. How many trucks and will there be enough to handle all the old sheep and those at the infirmary; over?"

"Three altogether. There will be plenty; over."

Kyle looked around the table. "I think we're set, any more questions or suggestions?" Those gathered around the table looked at one another and shook their heads. Kyle got back on the radio, "Nelly, it looks like we're set. We'll be in touch once we get mobile; over."

"Very good. Take care everyone. We'll see you soon. Nelly, out."

Kyle withdrew from the microphone and surveyed the room. Surrounding him were faces filled with hope and determination. "Okay, folks, looks like we're set. We'll get a good night's sleep tonight, and then we ride out in the morning."

Ephesians 6:11 "Put on the full armor of God, so that you can take stand against the devil's schemes."

CHAPTER 46

CHARLOTTE'S KNEES BUCKLED AND she grabbed the table edge to steady herself, when she heard the soft, familiar voice on the phone, "Charlotte? It's me, Stephanie." Charlotte dropped into the chair next to her, her mouth agape. She searched her mind . . . her heart for words, but none came.

"Charlotte, are you there?" Stephanie asked. When there was no response she continued, "Look, I can't even imagine what you must be feeling right now, but I just wanted to call and tell you I was sorry. I'm sorry for everything that has happened."

Charlotte finally found her voice, "Sorry! You call me to tell me you're sorry when you were the one who started the whole thing in the first place! Who called Garrison after listening in on my conversation with Joe? Who has always been the one who spied on conversations and faced the people with a smile, but then turned around and did Garrison's or Smith's bidding? How could you, Stephanie? We used to be friends back in Willow Creek." Charlotte sobbed. "I really don't feel like talking to you right now!"

Stephanie's voice cracked, as though she were about to cry. "I don't blame you, Charlotte. I wouldn't want to talk to me, either. You're right about everything. I can't take back what I've done, but I want to make things right with you, Joe, and everyone else that I've hurt. Most of all, Charlotte, I hope that one day I can be forgiven."

"I'm not convinced, Stephanie," Charlotte said emphatically. "Why should I trust you now? For all I know, this is another one of your tricks, or Garrison or Smith could be listening in on the other line. I'm sorry, Stephanie, but whatever you have to say to me will have to be done to my face. Then I will be able to tell whether you are sincere or not."

"Fine, then I'll come over." Stephanie said with finality.

"Not now, Stephanie. I'm exhausted and my head hurts. Besides I'm under house arrest and I doubt they will let you in."

"I understand that you're not feeling up to company, but I would still like to come over. How about tomorrow morning? I'll bring the coffee." Stephanie was hopeful.

Charlotte was growing frustrated, "Like I said, I doubt they will let you see me, but, if you want to waste your time, that's fine with me."

"It won't be a waste of time to me. Thank you, Charlotte. I'll see you in the morning."

Charlotte wanted to talk to Tom or Joe, but because Stephanie was on the switchboard, she knew that she would be the one to connect them, and then what? Would she listen in on that conversation, too? She was even more exhausted now, mentally and physically. Charlotte prepared herself another cup of chamomile tea and went for the thing she needed the most—a long, hot bath.

The phone rang four times before she was able to pick it up,

"Hello?"

"Charlotte? It's Joe."

Her heart leapt, "Joe, I'm so glad you called!"

"Are you all right? I got worried when you didn't answer."

"Yes, everything is fine; I just fell asleep in the tub. You know what happens when I have too much tea." Charlotte giggled softly, but then was saddened at the memory of her and her mom sharing teatime in the afternoon on their days off. "Joe, Stephanie called me. I don't know if she is listening in now, but she apologized for everything that happened and wanted to be forgiven. She wants to come over tomorrow morning and I don't know what to do." Charlotte took a breath after her rant and waited for Joe to respond. When he didn't, she grew worried, "Joe, are you there?"

"Yes, sorry, I'm here. When did she call?"

"Not long after you dropped me off. Why?" Charlotte questioned.

"Because I just got off the phone with her and she told me basically the same thing."

"Do you think she means it?" Charlotte asked. "I want to believe her, but I just don't know. It's too soon."

"Yes, I know. I'm working tomorrow, so I'll talk to Walt. If she is up to something, he'll find it out, believe me." Joe knew that if Stephanie was, in fact, listening in, those last words would cause her to think twice about calling

Garrison. Although she answered to Garrison and Smith, they both frightened her. Walt, on the other hand, was always kind to her and Joe knew that any deceit she put toward him would feel like she was doing it to her own father. "Try to get some sleep, okay? Don't worry about it right now."

"You're right, Joe. I'll be fine. Get some sleep, yourself. I love you."

Joe's heart melted into his boots, and he smiled. "I love you too. I'll talk to you tomorrow. Good night."

"Good night, Joe."

Joe was still smiling when he hung up the phone. He knew that, somehow, he would have to talk to Tom or Walt the following day.

***

Nick Garrison, not ready to sleep yet, paced across the floor of his suite. The whole day had been difficult, to say the least, and now Baroam was on his way to see him. "I shall be there within seventy-two hours," he had said. "I will expect a full explanation, Mr. Garrison." Garrison knew that no explanation would ever satisfy the Commander and that his days were numbered. No one could save him from Baroam's wrath.

After lifting his bottle of bourbon and finding it empty, he pulled another bottle from the bar and opened it. "Maybe if I get good and drunk, it won't hurt so bad," he thought, contemplating Baroam's visit. Just as he raised the fresh bottle to his lips, there was a knock on the door. Garrison peered through the peephole and felt some relief. He opened the door wide. "Clifford, it's good to see you again. I have another assignment for you."

The big, burly man walked in and immediately snatched the bottle of bourbon from Garrison's hand. "What is it now, Garrison? I hear you've been looking for me. If I have to spend another night in the woods, it's going to cost you." He went to the bar and took a glass from the mirrored shelf.

Garrison let him keep the whiskey, knowing it would loosen the man up before the news he was about to deliver, "Oh come on, Clifford, it's summer. This is great camping weather."

Clifford looked at Garrison flatly. "I don't camp," and he proceeded to fill his glass.

Garrison held up an index finger, "Noted. This time around, I only need you to take a little trip outside the gates to comb the woods for a day or two. We have company coming and I need eyes out there. Besides, you're the only one here who would know what they look like. Take someone with you, if you think you'll need help." Garrison knew that last remark would get Clifford's ire up. He was a loner and had been more than insulted when Garrison sent the woman and other man to Berkley Springs with him.

Clifford emptied the shot glass in one gulp and proceeded to fill it again. "You know what happened the last time you sent 'helpers' with me, Garrison?"

"Refresh my memory, Clifford. What happened to your travel companions?"

"The woman got lost, as most women do out in the woods, and the other man, who claimed to be with us, stayed in Berkley Springs. I'd call him a traitor, plain and simple."

"Well, at least I know I can count on you." Garrison clapped the big man on the shoulder and poured himself a drink. "Go solo; I don't care, as long as you stop those people from getting here."

"Let me ask you something, Garrison. What do you have against the Christians, anyway? It seems to me that you're hell-bent on getting rid of them."

"The orders come from Baroam, not from me. Feel free to ask him when he gets here." Garrison watched Clifford squirm. For such a large, intimidating man, he was visibly nervous at even the mention of Baroam.

"Can you give me a heading? Are they coming from Berkley Springs, then?" Clifford grunted, ignoring the last remark.

"According to what you reported, they would have left Berkley several days ago. By now, they should be in or very near the town of Willow Creek. If you go in that direction, I'd wager you'll run right into them."

"That's what I want to avoid, Garrison. The element of surprise has always worked well for me." Clifford downed his drink in one swallow, "I'll leave in the morning."

After Clifford left him, Garrison went back to the monitors and watched them for a moment. Just watching the deserted streets and hallways soothed his jagged nerves. That, compounded with the bourbon and the conversation he just had, calmed him enough that he was now able to rest.

***

Gabe McCloud was waiting for just the right moment when Garrison's lights went out; he then began the procedure of recording and copying the video feeds that ran throughout The City. He didn't want any interruptions, and Garrison was notorious for those. In seventy-two hours, he would play back the uneventful feed of this night while Tom and the others assumed their positions throughout The City.

While he monitored the recording, he reflected on the last two weeks. That was when he felt God convicting him and it helped him to realize that what he was doing was wrong. Of course, he was still putting on the face of one of Garrison's Regulators, but his heart was no longer in it as it was before. He smiled to himself and thanked God for sending Tom Connelly. Tom had shown him that it was okay to be tough, as long as that toughness was pointed in the right direction. The good people he had met during his time here didn't deserve the cruel treatment he had shown them. At that moment, he made a covenant with God to do whatever he could to make things right with them.

After the tape had been running for nearly an hour, he switched off the recorder and locked it in a cabinet until it was time to use it. He chuckled to himself, "Those guys won't know what hit them." Suddenly his phone rang. He checked his watch. "It's nearly oh one hundred. Who on earth would be calling now?" He picked it up, "Mac here."

"Mr. McCloud, its Stephanie."

"Stephanie, it's late. Are you okay?" and then bit his tongue; the old Gabe McCloud would have made an inappropriate remark or asked her out for a nightcap.

"I'm fine, Mr. McCloud, I just saw your light on, and you know it gets a little lonely during the midnight shift."

"Why are you on this shift? I thought you worked days?" He already knew Garrison would have had something to do with it.

"Mr. Garrison asked me to pick up a few nights because the girl that normally works is 'under the weather,' and since I could always use a few extra tokens on my card, I agreed. So, how have you been?" Stephanie wasn't sure where to take the conversation; she only knew that she needed to keep him talking; John Smith's orders.

John Smith lounged on his king size bed and nursed a snifter of brandy while he listened intently to the exchange between Stephanie and Mac. He had a feeling Mac was in on something as well. He noticed a change in the man, but again couldn't quite put his finger on it. He was convinced that Tom Connelly was every bit as responsible for that as he was everything else that was beginning to happen in The City.

Gabe McCloud grew more uncomfortable with each question until he finally decided to put a stop to it. "Listen, Stephanie, unless there is a security issue you need me to handle, I'm beat. Can this wait for some other time?"

Stephanie was clearly disappointed, not just because the conversation was ending, but because she knew Smith didn't hear what he wanted to hear, and she would be blamed for it. "Well, all right. I can understand you must be tired. It has been a crazy week, hasn't it?" She made one last attempt to manipulate him into saying something about the sequence of events of the last few days, but McCloud saw through it.

"Yes, it has. Good night, Stephanie." Gabe hung up and made a mental note to let Tom and Red know in the morning. He settled back into the big recliner they used during the night shifts and closed his eyes.

Meanwhile, with trembling hands, Stephanie disconnected the call and dialed Smith's number. "I'm sorry, Mr. Smith," she implored. "I tried, but it seemed like he was trying to avoid me."

"Don't worry about it, Stephanie. Just keep me posted on all conversations between the people I told you about."

"Yes, Mr. Smith. Good night."

Smith hung up the phone and checked the bedside clock. It was after one in the morning, and he had to rise early. He had a date with Mrs. Beechum and Tom Connelly in a few hours, and he didn't want to be late.

Matthew 6:15 –16 "Watch out for false prophets. They come to you in sheep's clothing, but inwardly they are ferocious wolves."

CHAPTER 47

The morning dew lay thick on the grass as the sun crested the horizon. Sandy stood on the front porch, closed her eyes, and breathed deep the intoxicating smells of the early morning. This was her favorite time, when the day was still brand new, just barely unwrapped. The heavy, musky scent of the woods called to her. They would be leaving very soon, and the idea both thrilled her and unnerved her. It meant she would see her son, but at what cost? She had been watching Ben, and his uneasiness did not go unnoticed by her, Kyle, or Morgan. She was contemplating their departure when Walt approached her from behind. "Good morning."

"Good morning, Walt. How was your breakfast?"

Walt chuckled. "A lot like yours, young lady. You didn't eat much. Feeling a little anxious, are we?"

"Yeah, I suppose so," Sandy said, looking down at her boots and biting her lip absentmindedly. "I'm excited that I will see Joe again, but it's going to be dangerous. I just hope I can do the job and not drop the ball."

"You'll do fine. Kyle is a great teacher, even if he is Army. And believe me, that's tough to say for this old Marine. Besides, the One who's really in control," he looked at her expectantly, knowing that Sandy already knew what he was going to say, "will never drop the ball. Am I right?"

She smiled, "Yes, you are."

They watched as the sun inched higher into the sky, then Walt looked at her thoughtfully, "We'd best get going, don't you think?" Sandy took a deep breath, "Let's do it."

The group stood outside the barn, just as they had when they first parted, but instead of Steve leading them in prayer, it was Kyle. "Heavenly Father, thank you for the beautiful day and the friends and family we have with us today. Father, you know the tasks that lay before us and only You know the outcome. We ask you now, Lord, for Your protection, strength, and guidance as we move forward on this mission. We pray, Lord, that You also be with those on the inside. Hold them in Your mighty hands and strengthen them, Lord. We would also ask, Father, that Your light of salvation might shine through us, so that others could witness Your grace and forgiveness. Amen."

The group mounted in silence and picked their way down the trail that, in three days, would bring them to The City. Joe and Tom had taken the same trail six months earlier and Sandy wondered, or rather hoped, that they might find something . . . anything that the two may have dropped or left behind that would help her to feel closer to them. The group was quiet; even Ben didn't have anything to say. Each of them occupied with thoughts, expectations, and anticipations of what was coming. Once the trail cleared, they kicked their horses into a run. They had a lot of ground to cover in a short amount of time. After nearly an hour of hard riding, Kyle pulled up on his reins and stopped. "Let's take a break," he said to Morgan.

"Good idea." Morgan turned back and saw that the group had stopped and was dismounting. With the sun high in the sky now, it had grown considerably warmer. Many of the riders had shed their jackets and were tying them down to their saddles or stuffing them in their saddlebags.

Sandy met up with Walt and they went to join Kyle and Morgan. When Kyle saw them, he held up the hand-held radio. "I want to do a radio check. These things are good for about five miles, but at some point, we'll be in a dead zone, and I want to check in with the ranch before we lose them."

"Understood," Walt said. "When we're done here, I think another three hours of fast riding and then we should make camp. It'll take some time to get everyone settled and the horses put down for the night."

Kyle nodded then set the radio to channel nine and spoke, "Sandman to base, do you copy; over?"

Joann called out to her husband, "David! They're calling in!" Then she answered Kyle, "Base here, we read you loud and clear, Sandman; over."

"Very good," Kyle said, "I'm just checking out the communications. We'll be going into a 'dead zone' shortly, so you won't be hearing from us again until we get closer to our final destination; over."

"Affirmative, Sandman," David had joined his wife. "The prayer warriors will be putting in some overtime for the next few days. God speed, my friend; over."

"We appreciate all we can get. We'll hit our knees for you as well. Keep your ears open. We're out."

David looked up at Joann, immediately took her hands, and prayed. When they had finished, they radioed Berkley Springs, "Base two to base one. Do you read; over?"

"Good afternoon, base two. What's the good word; over?" Steve answered.

"Word is our party is entering a 'dead zone.' We've heard the last of them until they are within range of their destination; over." David called back.

"Understood, base two; we'll keep our ears up for any news. As soon as we hear it, so will you; over."

"And we'll do the same, Preacher. Give our best to the others, out." David got up from the radio and paced the kitchen floor. He was tense; it wasn't like him to be this tense. He went out and sat on the back porch while Joann prepared the afternoon meal. The familiar way she worked in the kitchen, with the sounds of pots being stirred and the kitchen faucet running distracted him from his troubled thoughts and calmed him. Again, he prayed.

Steve took Tanya by the hand and walked out to where the others had gathered in the fire house. It had become the meeting place for everyone in the small town now. The usual faces and gentle laughter brought comfort to everyone there. "We have word!" Steve shouted above the voices that echoed in the great room.

The people surrounded him, anxious to hear what he had to say. "Is it good news?" someone asked.

"They're about two days out from The City, but in the next few hours they'll be going into a 'dead zone'."

"What's a 'dead zone'?" another person questioned.

"A 'dead zone' is when they are out of range from the base in Willow Creek, but they are not quite in range of the base in The City yet."

"Is it dangerous?" the same person asked.

"I expect so. But remember who's out there and more importantly, who's watching over them," Steve said.

"Amen!"

Steve and Tanya retreated to the office they used for their own quiet time and Bible reading. He knew his wife was growing more concerned as the time drew nearer for the rescue. She had never been so far away from her sister and nephews, and she wore the concern on her face. He put his hand on the small of her back and led her to the loveseat in the office. "You're worried; I can see it all over your beautiful face."

Tanya smiled softly at her husband. "Just a bit. There's something else I've been thinking about that I wonder if anyone else has."

"What is it?" he asked, pushing a strand of hair away from her face.

"What happens once everyone is rescued? It's not like we can all just go back to our normal lives. That life is gone, isn't it?"

Steve's expression was sad, wistful. "You're right, it is. But you know, maybe that wasn't what God had intended for us. Maybe He needs us to get back to the roots of our lives and slow down. Maybe He needs us, all of us, to once and for all start relying on Him instead of the latest, greatest gadget." Steve put his arms around her and held her. "I have a good feeling about this, Tanya. We just need to trust God and let Him lead us."

Tanya tightened her hold on her husband, "You're right, Steve. Thanks."

He pulled away, "Anytime," he smiled and kissed her softly.

Hoping to avoid Silas, Clifford left the stables near dawn on a borrowed horse. However, he was too late in leaving. "Where are you going?" Silas asked.

"That's my own business," Clifford told him. He didn't like questions, and he liked Silas even less.

Silas shook his head as he watched Clifford ride off. He knew that the big man took orders only from Garrison, which meant that he was probably up to no good.

Clifford kicked his horse into a trot, wanting to put as much distance between himself and Silas Grey as he possibly could. His disdain for Silas couldn't be explained; it was a lot like the bitterness he felt toward the people in Berkley Springs. Clifford was not good with most civilized people. In fact, there wasn't anyone he could really call a friend. The longest conversations he'd had since arriving at The City were with Garrison, so he guessed he could be counted at least as an acquaintance.

He rode until noon, stopped for lunch, then continued until dusk started to settle. Spotting a big oak tree, he made camp beneath it for the night. By his calculations, the group coming from Willow Creek would take three days to get to The City. If they left when Garrison had said, he would come up on them late the next day, perhaps even after they'd settled in for the night. Surprising them would be effortless, especially once it got dark. He could take them out one by one. Clifford chuckled to himself as he stirred his stew over the fire, "This will be too easy."

He settled back against a log, sipped his coffee, and thought about things to come. Once this job is done, then what? Would Garrison have another job for him, maybe an assassination? Clifford could think of any number of people Garrison wanted gone, Baroam being one of them—not out of dislike for the man—but more out of fear. If Garrison had Baroam removed from the picture, there would be no telling how far he could go. However, that would require a huge undertaking; he was, after all, the man who answered to the 'Supreme Leader' himself. Clifford tossed his coffee into the fire and pulled his blanket up over him. That was too much to think about for the time being. Right now, all he needed to think about was getting up at dawn and finding the riders that were coming his way.

Right about the time Clifford left the stables, Tom was preparing to meet with Smith and Mrs. Beechum. He was not looking forward to the meeting and knew that Smith would go out of his way to be cruel to her. Before he left his unit for the security bunker, Tom prayed for his friend and for the meeting. When he arrived at the security bunker, he didn't see anyone inside and called out, "Hey, Mac!"

"I'm in the back, Connelly."

Tom followed Mac's voice to the wall of security monitors that glowed blue in the darkened room. Just beyond Mac, he noticed the door to the lower level was open. "You've been busy, my friend."

"Yes, I have, and I'll fill you in on it in a minute, but first I have to tell you about a call I received last night."

Tom's eyebrows rose in curiosity, "Oh yeah?"

"Stephanie called me last night, or should I say this morning, around oh-one hundred. I knew she was up to something, because she kept trying to turn the conversation to what happened with the breakout."

Tom frowned, while he considered what Mac had told him, "She's fishing."

"You can say that again. I can't be sure, but I had a suspicion that Smith was listening in on the other end."

Tom shook his head in disgust. "That wouldn't surprise me at all. So, tell me what you've been up to. I have to go meet Smith and Mrs. Beechum in a few minutes."

"This won't take long; the recording is taken care of, but I wanted to show you something else. Mac led Tom downstairs to the lower level where the rifles were kept and opened the safe. "The rifles are loaded, so they'll be ready when its time. You shouldn't have a problem getting them to your people. I'll keep the safe unlocked, so all you need to do is pull it open."

"Sounds good, Mac. Thanks."

Gabe pocketed the key to the safe, just in case some Good Samaritan found it open and locked it. He started back up the stairs. "Where are the trucks stopping?"

"The infirmary, the 'Last Stop,' and the third truck will go to the back of The City. It will take some time getting the patients out of the infirmary, but I've got Dr. White, Joe, and Charlotte helping with that. Those who are able bodied enough can help themselves and the others."

Tom studied Mac's face for a moment. "Am I forgetting something?"

Mac paused and then shook his head. "No, I think you've got it covered. Who's setting off the C-4?"

"I've got two friends coming in the back gate. When they've finished there, they will go help at the infirmary." Tom checked his watch. "I've got to run, Mac."

"All right, Tom, but do me a favor and warn Mrs. Beechum that I'll be driving the truck for her building. She may not get in if she sees me."

"I'll tell her." Tom laughed and left the bunker. When he arrived at Mrs. Beechum's building, he nodded to the officer on duty, "Mornin.' Is Smith here yet?"

"Good morning, Officer Connelly. Negative, sir."

"Get me on the radio when he is on his way up, will you?"

"Yes sir."

Tom took the stairs two at a time and in four great strides was in front of Barbara's door. She must have been watching for him, because no sooner did his knuckles knock at the door than it swung open. He entered quickly and closed it behind him. "Have you heard from Smith yet?"

Barbara looked relieved. "No. I was afraid it was him when I heard you coming down the hall. I'm glad you arrived before he did. I wasn't looking forward to having him in here, alone." She walked into the kitchen to start the coffee.

Tom followed her. "I don't blame you there. He's going to question you about Jason, Barbara. He already knows you helped him, so there's no point in covering it up. Just tell the truth and you'll be fine. Where is the gun that Richard left and your other belongings?"

Barbara motioned toward her bedroom. "They are in a backpack in my closet. I put them there last night so I could get to them easier."

"That was good thinking," Tom said. "At midnight tomorrow we make the escape. Sam, the guard, will come to your unit and help you gather the folks from your floor and bring them down in the elevator. While you're doing that, Mr. Harris is going to round up the others and bring them down the stairwell to the front doors. Do not go outside until Sam gives the all clear, Barbara. Do you understand?"

"Yes, Tom, I understand," Barbara said. She could not hide the tremble in her voice and her hands shook as she prepared the coffee pot.

Tom continued, "One of the trucks will pick you and the others up." Suddenly Tom took her by the shoulders, startling her, and turned her around to face him. He fixed his eyes on her and didn't waver, "Gabe McCloud will be driving the truck, Barbara. He is on our side, now."

Mrs. Beechum's eyes grew wide, "Tom, are you sure? I don't know if I trust him."

"You have my word," Tom assured her. "He's a good man and wants to help."

She was still skeptical and shook her head, "How could he change so quickly?"

Tom reproached her gently, "Barbara, I'm surprised at you, Christian woman that you are. You are familiar with the concept of forgiveness aren't you? Gabe saw the error of his ways, talked to me about it, and wants to make things right, starting with you and the folks in this building."

Suddenly Tom's radio crackled, "Officer Connelly, Smith is on his way up."

Tom pressed on his mike, "Thanks." He regarded her carefully, "Ready?"

Barbara gave him a quick nod and went to her room. "I'll be right back, Tom. Would you mind letting him in?"

Smith pounded on the door with his fist, not caring if others were awake or not. He hoped that Tom hadn't arrived yet and was irritated with himself that he didn't check with the guard. His question was answered when Tom opened the door, smiling. "Good morning, Smith."

John Smith's eyes narrowed, "Connelly. Is she awake yet?"

"Oh yeah, and I believe I smell fresh coffee brewing. Would you like a cup?"

Smith recalled the last cup of coffee he had shared with Tom Connelly and grew more agitated, "No, thanks."

Barbara emerged from the bedroom with her hair combed and fresh lipstick applied, "Good morning, Mr. Smith. I trust you slept well."

"I slept just fine, Mrs. Beechum. I have some questions for you and your answers will determine the future of Jason O'Malley."

Barbara glared at him. He knew just what buttons to push. "I will answer your questions the only way I know how, Mr. Smith; truthfully."

Tom took her by the elbow. "Let's move to the kitchen; this may take a while."

Barbara went to the coffee pot, "Officer Connelly, would you like some coffee?"

"Yes, thank you."

"Mr. Smith?"

"No thank you, Mrs. Beechum."

Barbara prepared two cups of coffee, brought the steaming cups to the kitchen table, and then took a seat next to Tom.

Smith pulled out a chair that was crammed between the table and the wall and slid into it. "I need you to tell me everything you know about Jason."

Barbara laughed. "Mr. Smith, this is absurd. You know he was a very close friend of my late husband's and of mine. Jason is like a grandson to me."

"What can you tell me about the escape?"

"He was unhappy here and he wanted to get away, as most young men do at his age. When he hurt himself, he asked me for help.

"Why would he ask you?" Smith retorted.

"Because I'm his only family, Mr. Smith. Ever since he was a little boy, he would come to me when he was hurt." Barbara turned to Tom. "He even came to me with his first broken heart. He's such a sweet young man."

She put her attention back to Smith, "He's a good boy, Mr. Smith. Jason would never do anything to hurt anyone. What you're doing is making a mountain out of a mole hill."

Were you aware of the escape before he attempted it?"

"No, I was not." Barbara quipped.

"Listen, Mrs. Beechum. I'm doing what Garrison told me to do and if he doesn't trust you or Jason, then I don't either."

"Mr. Smith, you're not even man enough to think for yourself," Barbara scolded.

"Just answer the questions, please," Tom said. He was worried that her bitterness for Smith would get her into more trouble than she already was.

"I'm sorry. Go ahead, Mr. Smith." Barbara took a sip from her coffee and rested her light blue eyes on Smith.

He took an agitated breath and continued, "Do you know of the relationship between Joe Parker and Jason?"

Barbara suddenly looked worried. She wasn't prepared to talk about Joe. Before the men arrived, she had rehearsed what she was going to say about Jason, but the inclusion of Joe threw her. She did not want to say anything that would incriminate him. "No. I mean, I know they work together at the shelter, and Jason is fond of Joe. He is a very kind, hardworking boy. I seriously doubt that Joe would have anything to do with this."

"So, you can be certain that Jason acted on his own accord and that there were no other parties involved." Smith pressed.

"I'm very certain, yes," Barbara insisted.

Smith had wedged himself between the chair and the table and now struggled to pry himself out. When he was finally free, he left the kitchen. "Connelly, can I have a word, please?" Once they were out of earshot, he glared at Tom, "She's either lying or she really doesn't know anything else about the escape. I guess that blows your whole theory out the window, about bigger fish being involved."

Tom tried not to laugh, "What did you think? She was the big fish I was talking about?"

Smith kept a hard stare fixed on Tom, "Well, then, what was all that talk about letting them go?"

Tom threw his hands in the air. "Just what you said, John; it was a theory. Look, we thought we had a lead, and it fell flat; that kind of thing happens all the time. It looks like you found the underlying cause of this after all. I was wrong, the kid acted alone." Tom almost felt sorry for Smith. After all, he was only acting on orders from Garrison. Barbara was right; he probably had not had an original thought in a long time. "So, are we done here?"

"Yeah, we're done . . . for now." John Smith stormed out without saying goodbye and let the door slam behind him.

Tom went immediately back into the kitchen. "Barbara, you did very well but please don't let your temper get the best of you like that. It will get you into an awful lot of trouble one day."

"I'm sorry, Tom. You know, my husband always used to tell me the same thing. I guess I didn't listen to him very well, did I?"

"I think it's over for now, but just be aware. How's Dorothy doing?"

"She's fine. She gets a little nervous when she starts to think about the rescue, but I just tell her that she will have lots of help."

"That's good. I've got to get going or Garrison will wonder why I'm hanging around after Smith left. I'll talk to you soon." He leaned down and gave her a kiss on the cheek.

Barbara smiled. "Thank you, Tom."

Stephanie bounced up the stairs to Charlotte's front door, "Good morning, Officer. Can I see Charlotte?"

"I don't know that she's even awake yet, Stephanie. Did you try to call her?" The guard eyed Stephanie up and down. He was a Regulator and had heard that she was in tight with Garrison and Smith, and although they were on the same side, he still didn't trust her. Without moving from his position, he reached back and knocked on the door. "If she's up, she'll answer. You have ten minutes."

"Ten minutes? I was coming to visit for a while. Can't you make it a little longer?" Stephanie did her best to charm another few minutes out of the guard, but he wasn't in the mood. He had been on watch all night and was anxious for his replacement to arrive. "Ten minutes, take it or leave it. Garrison's orders, not mine."

Stephanie opened her mouth to continue the argument but stopped when the door slowly opened. Immediately her scowl toward the guard was replaced by a smile that Charlotte saw right through. "Good morning, Charlotte, I told you I'd come by. I brought coffee." Stephanie held up the paper cup, to entice Charlotte into allowing her inside.

Charlotte stood in the doorway blocking Stephanie's view into her unit. She studied her face carefully and then slowly shook her head. "No, I don't think so, Stephanie. I just lost my mother; let me have my time alone. Besides, I just don't trust your motives." Charlotte watched Stephanie's face as she spoke and noticed a flicker of rage behind the young woman's eyes. "Good-bye, Stephanie." With that, Charlotte shut the door and leaned against it, closing her eyes, listening. She was sure that Stephanie would say something to the guard, and she was right.

"Tough luck, kid," the guard smirked. "Now you don't have anything to report to Garrison and Smith."

Stephanie tossed her head and stepped off the porch, "Who says I don't?" She lied. She had nothing to bring Garrison or Smith, and she was afraid. Her orders were to grill Charlotte as best she could and bring the information back to Garrison himself. She tossed the full coffee container into the street and trudged dejectedly down the sidewalk toward his hotel. Dread filled her, but she had no choice. She couldn't run and she certainly couldn't hide. There was no one she could turn to for help, because she had alienated everyone she knew from Willow Creek. For just a moment, Sandy Parker crossed her mind. She wondered what Sandy was doing and whether she would ever see her again. The last time she saw Sandy, she was making a large withdrawal from the bank, and Stephanie had reported it to Garrison.

Her deceit had begun long ago. She took a long breath and entered Garrison's hotel. She would face whatever she had coming; she had no other choice.

Garrison turned from the monitors when he saw Stephanie exit the elevator on his floor. He picked up the phone and called for two guards to come to his suite then went to the door and opened it just as Stephanie was reaching out to knock. "Good morning, Stephanie. Can I offer you some coffee?" His voice was thick with mock courtesy.

"No thank you, Mr. Garrison." Stephanie entered the room and took the seat that Garrison offered. Her heart was pounding, and she was sure that her boss could hear it. Her palms began to sweat in the anticipation of telling him the bad news and she wiped her hands absently on her jeans. She tried to think of something, anything she could share with him in order to appease him, but she came up empty. She watched Garrison casually walk around his desk to the leather chair behind it. She could hear the cleaning crew running the vacuum down the hall and the light laughter coming from the workers. They were clueless about her presence there or her situation. Stephanie waited for Garrison to speak.

He enjoyed this part of the game, watching his detainees awaiting their fate... squirming. He was still in control, and it felt good. He waited until he was seated comfortably behind his desk before he spoke. *"Why rush the final blow?"* he thought. *"Better to let her enjoy her freedom for just a little while longer."* Resting his elbows on the desk, he pressed his fingertips together in the form of a pyramid and smiled. His black eyes drilled into hers. "So, how did your visit with Charlotte go?" Garrison knew she had nothing to offer; he could see it in her pale face and frightened eyes. The eyes that were once lustful and captivating were welling with tears. Her voice went up an octave as she explained.

"Mr. Garrison, the guard would only give me ten minutes with her. I wouldn't have been able to get much, if any, information out of her in that short period of time."

"So, you were able to at least enter her unit, then." Garrison leaned back in his chair, weaving his fingers behind his head; the devilish grin never left his face.

Stephanie looked down at her folded hands in her lap. "No sir, I didn't. She wouldn't let me in." Tears began to spill onto her hands, and she made no attempt to wipe them. She hoped that Garrison would take pity on her.

Garrison stood and leaned across the desk toward her. "Don't waste your tears on me, Stephanie. They will not move me or deter me from rendering your punishment., Baroam is coming tomorrow, and I need to have something to show for the damage that has been done. Because of your failure to serve me and the City as a whole, you are sentenced to the smokestacks until I see fit that you should leave."

"Mr. Garrison, please! Can't I have just one more chance?" Stephanie cried.

Garrison clapped his hands once, and in an instant, two armed guards burst into the office and grabbed Stephanie, one at each arm. "Escort this woman to the smokestacks and be sure she is secured with cuffs and shackles. I don't want any more escape attempts!" Garrison turned back to the monitors, dismissing them and sealing Stephanie's fate.

Stephanie tried to pull away, but her efforts were futile. Her future now lay within the stench and darkness of the smokestacks of the City.

Isaiah 24:16 -17 "Woe to me! The treacherous betray! With treachery the treacherous betray! Terror and pit and snare await you, people of earth."

CHAPTER 48

THEIR FIRST DAY WAS rapidly ending when Kyle turned in his saddle to Morgan. "Send word back that we'll stop once we get clear of this narrow passage."

Morgan nodded and glanced behind her. "We're stopping after the switch-backs, Gus. Pass it on." Gus relayed the message as Morgan re-focused on the trail and the sweet fragrance of the mountain laurels that filled the air. However, intermingled with their gentle aroma was the scent of rain, which meant a difficult ride lay ahead. She knew the others could smell it coming, too, and prayed that it would hold off long enough for them to clear the treacherous trail ahead.

When they were at last upon the switchbacks, the riders fell back, leaving extra space between themselves and the horse in front, allowing for more room in case a horse slipped. The mountainside rose nearly vertically on their right and fell away just as steeply on their left. The horses picked their way carefully, their hooves scraping the shale rock that covered the trail. Morgan held loosely onto the reins, allowing the horse her head for balance, and spoke softly to her, encouraging her as he climbed the dangerous hairpin turns.

Finally, after a half hour and much prayer, they cleared the perilous trail and were able to stretch their legs and cover up before the rain. Morgan gave her horse, Skye, a good rub on the neck and then went to find Sandy. Her friend's face had been drawn and pale all day. "Hey, Sandy, how are you holding up? You've ridden much tougher trails than that haven't you?"

Sandy gave Morgan a half a smile, "I'm doing all right." She shook her head and laughed. "It's not the trail, Morgan. I don't know whether it's me feeding off Ben's intuition or if it's my own, but I've got a bad feeling about things. I know I need to be faithful, and I know it is in God's hands, not mine, but... I just don't know."

Morgan studied Sandy's face and could see her eyes begin to water. She took a deep breath and reached for her friend's hand. "You stay strong, Sandy. You've held together this long and there are lots of folks here who have no idea what they're walking into. We can't let the fear show."

Sandy quickly wiped her eyes. "You're right, Morgan. The last thing they need to see is one of us losing it. I'm sorry."

"No need to apologize," Morgan said. "Come on; let's go see what the guys are up to." They trekked through the brush, passing the others and saying "hello" as they went by. When they were well past them, Morgan nudged her friend, "I take back what I said, Sandy. They all look just as scared as you do."

Kyle smiled when he saw the women coming. "Hey ladies, I'm sorry we rode for so long, but I wanted to put some distance between us and the ranch on the first day. Tomorrow should go a little better." He lifted his head and inhaled deeply. "Do you smell that?"

"Rain," Morgan said. "How long do you think we have before it starts?"

"An hour max," Walt interrupted. "We may have to cut this next leg of the trip short, Kyle. It's going to be hard enough getting these folks settled in the dark, but add some rain, thunder and lightning, and it could get ugly."

"Okay, Walt." Kyle looked around the area where they had stopped, "How about we stop here? There's some pretty good coverage from the trees and the area is flat enough. And over there is a nice patch of grass for the horses."

Walt looked around. "Yep, this'll do nicely. I'll spread the word."

After Walt left, Morgan took Kyle by the hand. "Kyle, I've looked around and everybody looks scared. They're going to need some strong encouragement from the Bible reading tonight."

"Yes, I've noticed it, too. Perhaps a nice long read from Isaiah or Psalms." Kyle looked thoughtfully at Sandy. "You're feeling it, too, aren't you?"

"Yes, but I'll be all right." Sandy said.

"Of course you will," Kyle said. "Okay then, let's get settled."

Ben and Ronnie had gathered plenty of firewood and hoped there would be enough left over for the next morning. Then just as they were putting up the last tent, the rain finally came. Sandy and Ben slept fitfully as their first day on the trail came to a close. Something or someone was coming.

Day 2

Morning broke fresh and new. It was Clifford's second day on the trail, and he was confident that he would find them by nightfall. Find them and do away with them; then he could go back to The City and back to the comfort of his room. He didn't waste time for coffee or breakfast; he just wanted to move on.

Kyle conferred with his key riders. "Let's keep the group tighter today, folks. Anders, you ride with Chris and Gus flanking both sides, while Sandy and Morgan bring up the rear. Stay sharp. More than one of us is feeling a little restless today." They all nodded and after a group prayer, everyone mounted and pushed on. Just on a whim, Kyle tried the radio, hoping that they might be close enough for someone to pick them up; but they were still too far away from both bases. They were, in fact, deep in the 'dead zone' with no communication. If something were to happen, they would have to ride nearly twenty miles further toward The City to find a signal and even that would be sketchy.

They had been on the trail for more than three hours, as they continued their quick pace. Kyle was getting the same sense of apprehension. Could this be what Staff Sergeant Parker felt when they were on their last patrol together? It seemed like a lifetime ago and, in all actuality, it was. Life then and life now were completely different. Kyle had to snap himself back to the reality of the moment. He was thinking of Staff Sergeant Parker, Tom, and even Lucky. Suddenly, a report from a rifle shattered the calming silence as something whizzed by his head. The group scattered for cover away from the shots. Kyle kicked his horse into a gallop, running toward where the shot came from. Anders drew his rifle from its scabbard and followed behind Kyle.

Kyle's eyes searched frantically through the trees for the shooter, but the foliage was just too thick to see anyone. A second shot caught him in the arm, and he leaned down close to his horse's neck, making himself a smaller target. Anders spotted Clifford first and whistled to Kyle. "Thirty yards, your ten o'clock, Johnson! I'm circling around!" Without breaking stride, Anders turned his horse hard, heading away from Kyle.

Clifford grinned behind his rifle holding his sight on Kyle. He didn't see Anders circling around. He pulled the hammer back. He began to squeeze the trigger, then suddenly he heard thunderous hooves approaching from behind. Clifford didn't have time to even think or look behind him, before Anders slammed his horse into Clifford's. Clifford's horse reared up, sending him tumbling off its back. The assailant's rifle flew high into the air and fired when it hit the ground. When Clifford's head finally cleared from the fall, he groaned in agony as he watched his horse bolt through the trees. He quickly realized that something didn't feel right. Something broke. He had heard it snap. When he tried to move, he realized it was his left arm. A shock of pain ripped through him, and he cried out. When he looked up, he saw the barrel of Anders's rifle staring down at him.

"Give me one good reason why I shouldn't shoot you," Anders growled.

Despite the pain that was searing up his arm, Clifford laughed hoarsely, holding his right arm up in the air. His left arm lay helplessly at his side. He searched for his rifle, but it had fallen too far away for him to reach, especially now. "I never thought I'd see you folks again," he said.

"You're a liar," Anders snapped, "Get up."

"In case you hadn't noticed, I've broken my arm," Clifford pointed out.

"Your right arm still works. Get up." Anders stepped closer.

Clifford knew this man would shoot him if he didn't do as he was ordered. He moaned again and struggled to get up, crying out when he bumped his broken arm against the tree he was leaning on. "What are you going to do with me?" he whimpered still recovering from when he bumped the tree.

"If it were up to me, I'd shoot you where you stand," Anders answered, "but fortunately for you, it's not." He looked past Clifford and saw Kyle coming towards them and shouted, "What should we do with him?"

Anders saw that Kyle had made a tourniquet for his wounded arm and was leading the horse that ran away, "The first thing I want to know is where you got this horse?"

Clifford cradled his arm as he leaned against a tree, "I got him from the stables in The City. Why?"

"Because I know this horse and I would bet that you've got quite a few other horses there, don't you?"

Anders scowled at their prisoner, "Why do you people steal horses?"

"Don't you get it, kid?" Clifford spat, "It doesn't matter to them what they take; they just take."

Anders pleaded with Kyle, "C'mon, man, just once in the foot."

Kyle laughed, unsure whether Anders was serious or not. He felt certain though that if given the chance, the young man would shoot their prisoner. "No, we have to take him back to camp. Hopefully, he'll tell us everything we need to know."

"What about my arm? I can't ride with a broken arm!" Clifford protested.

"Oh, you can ride all right; you just won't be able to go very fast. We'll take a look at it once we make camp. Then you can tell us why you shot me." Kyle said.

"So, I did hit you," Clifford said, his voice tinged with satisfaction.

"No, you just grazed me. You're a sloppy shot." Kyle laughed. He positioned the horse next to Clifford and held the reins so he could climb up. "Get on up there. We haven't got all day."

Clifford glared at Kyle and then reached up to grab his saddle horn. He failed at his first attempt to climb up, but on the second, Kyle gave him a push from behind and Clifford landed hard in the saddle. "Son of a --!"

"Watch it!" Kyle warned. "We'll have none of that language. There are ladies and children back at camp. Let's keep it clean." Kyle managed to climb up onto his horse with his injured arm and took the lead. Clifford rode behind him with Anders following, holding his rifle on the rider in front of him.

It was past noon when the group had gathered back together and spotted Kyle, Anders and the shooter coming back through the woods. Walt was on his horse, preparing to go find them when he spotted them. "Where in Sam Hill!" he shouted, but when he saw Clifford, he understood. He greeted Kyle and took the reins from him as he dismounted. "I'm surprised Anders didn't shoot him," Walt chuckled, but when he saw that Kyle was bleeding, he called out, "Morgan, your husband's home!"

Kyle grinned, "Thanks, Walt. It's just a graze, really."

Morgan ran up to them. When she saw the blood on Kyle's arm, she nearly screamed but caught herself when she noticed the cautionary stare from her uncle. "Kyle, what happened?"

"It's not bad, Morgan, just a scratch. This fella's a lousy shot." Kyle waved Chris and Ronnie over to help pull Clifford from his horse. "Be careful with him, he broke his arm when he fell off his horse. Where are Sandy and Ben?"

"I'll get them," Walt said, and hurried to find them.

Morgan took a closer look at the horse Clifford was riding, "Kyle is this --"

"Pilgrim!" Sandy ran to the gelding, threw her arms around his thick neck, and buried her face in his mane.

"Mom, where did he come from?" Ben asked, confused.

"Kyle?" Sandy questioned.

"Take a good look, Sandy; do you remember this face, too?" Kyle said, nodding toward Clifford.

Sandy looked hard at Clifford; his face wrenched in agony. "Clifford! You were in Berkley Springs, and you escaped that night. Is this the guy who shot at Anders?"

Anders' bitterness escalated when he recalled the incident at the stables. "That gives me two reasons why I should shoot you!" "Two reasons? What's the first?" Sandy asked.

"He shot Kyle," Morgan said, daggers firing from her eyes at the man.

Sandy's hands flew to her mouth, "Oh my gosh!"

"C'mon," Kyle said. "I've got to get a band aid on this before I ruin my shirt and I'm sure our friend here would like to get his arm set properly."

After nearly two hours were spent dressing Kyle's wound and setting Clifford's arm, Walt pulled Kyle aside. "We lost a lot of time this afternoon and we've only got about five more hours of daylight left. I'm pretty sure more than that's needed to get to our next stop."

"I'm open for suggestions, Walt. Now that we've got Clifford here holding us back, we won't be able to ride as fast as we have been." Kyle said.

"I say we make camp here and interrogate him." Walt suggested.

Kyle maintained his point, "Clifford's not going to be able to ride fast tomorrow either, Walt. We'll lose even more time."

"I've got another idea then, but I don't think you're going to like it, son." Walt said.

Kyle's expression turned somber, "What do you suggest, Walt?"

"We'll have to leave him behind with a security detail." Walt explained, "The rest of us can make up for the time we lost today. Of course that means we'll have to push the horses, but they could all use a good, hard run."

Kyle shook his head, "You're right, I don't like it. Are you saying we'll need to leave someone behind?"

"I was thinking more like leaving two behind." Walt stated matter-of-factly.

Kyle was clearly discouraged. "Well, who did you have in mind, Walt?"

"Chris and Gus, but we'll have to run it by them first."

Kyle nodded. "Is that our only option?"

"It's the only one I can think of at the moment," Walt answered.

"Okay, after supper we'll begin the interrogation." Discouraged, Kyle kicked a small stone on the ground and went back to the campsite.

After their meal, Gus and Chris stood watch while Anders, Walt, and Kyle gathered around Clifford. Walt began the questioning. "Who do you answer to, Clifford?"

"Why should I tell you people anything?" Clifford said, stuffing a piece of hard biscuit in his mouth.

"For starters, why not consider the fact that we didn't let you die out there in the woods, with a busted arm, and no food or water?" Kyle said.

"I'd have been fine if your man there hadn't run his horse into mine," Clifford argued.

It was Anders turn. "Oh, so I should have just let you kill my friend? And where do you come off saying the horse is yours?" Anders's blood pressure was going up. He felt Kyle watching him. "Sorry, man, I really don't like this guy."

Kyle understood. He put his attention back to Clifford. "Are you going to cooperate or not? Really, Clifford, what have you got to lose?"

"Absolutely nothing," Clifford answered.

"Then why go back?" Kyle asked. "What could possibly be there for you?"

"I won't be going back," Clifford said quietly.

Walt raised his eyebrows. "And why's that?"

"If I failed this mission, and it's pretty obvious I did, then Garrison would send me to the smokestacks."

"Who's Garrison?" Walt asked.

"Garrison is the head of the Regulators; he oversees everyone and everything in The City. He answers to Baroam himself."

"Have you ever met Baroam?" Anders asked.

Clifford suddenly grew anxious, fearful. "No, and God help me if I ever do! He's evil. Look, I'm just the messenger, as they say. I do what I'm told and that's all. Garrison doesn't tell me anything about what his plans are." Clifford paused abruptly as a new revelation came to him.

"It looks like you have more to say, Clifford." Walt said, "Go on."

Clifford was disappointed with himself that he gave in to these people, but the kindness they showed him by sharing their food, shelter, and mending his arm made it difficult for him to be cruel to them. "The night before I left, Garrison told me that Baroam would be there in three days." He glanced quickly around the group, "That was the day before yesterday. He'll be there tomorrow."

A sudden urgency struck them. "What time! Day? Night?" Kyle demanded.

Clifford shook his head. His arm ached and he was angry that he had told them about Baroam's coming. "I don't know! That's all I have to say! I won't say anything else. Kill me, if you want to."

Seeing the extreme pain in Clifford's face, Kyle held back the questioning. "That's enough for now," he said. "Finish eating, Clifford. We'll talk later."

"No, we won't." Clifford mumbled and withdrew from speaking for the rest of the night.

Walt walked with Chris and Gus to a quiet area away from the group. "We won't get any more out of him and we certainly won't be able to bring him with us. Kyle and I discussed it earlier, and we both agree that a team will have to stay behind with him."

"I'll bring him back to the ranch," said Chris.

Walt stared back at him, "Well I was about to ask, but since you volunteered."

"I was never comfortable leaving Joann and David alone on the ranch," Chris explained. "Besides, at least there, we can keep him under lock and key until the rescue mission is over." Chris turned to Gus. "What about it, my friend? You and I could easily handle him."

Gus bobbed his head, "Yep, I suppose we could. Sure, I'll go back with you, but what about our responsibilities? Who are you going to get to fill our spots?"

"We'll have to address that tomorrow," Kyle said, joining them. "It'll be dark before long, and you should put as many miles behind you as you possibly can.

After loading their saddlebags with a few supplies and helping Clifford up onto his horse, Gus and Chris quickly said their goodbyes to everyone. Sandy and the others watched as the men disappeared into the heavy brush. We've lost two key people from our group, Kyle. Is that going to be a problem?" Sandy asked.

Kyle looked frustrated. "Oh, it'll be a problem, Sandy, but, hopefully, not a big one."

Day 3

The day's ride was uneventful, and the riders were grateful. Because of the time lost with Clifford, they rode hard until nearly dark when they finally arrived at the same campsite where Tom and Joe had stayed last winter. The men set up camp and collected more firewood, Sandy and Morgan prepared the fire in the fire pit, and Ben and Ronnie took care of the horses.

Once camp was set up and the horses settled, the group gathered around the fire to finalize the plans and make adjustments for the loss of Chris and Gus. Before starting off, Kyle smiled as he accepted a cup of coffee from Morgan. "Okay folks, we're short two, now that Chris and Gus are gone. Chris was going to supervise the security outside of the fence and Gus was going to drive the truck for the infirmary. Does anyone have any ideas?"

"How about we have Joe open the gate and have Boss Daddy fill in for Gus?" Walt suggested.

Kyle shook his head, "No, Joe is going to be helping with the infirmary."

After nearly an hour of discussion, they decided that Ronnie would handle the gate as soon as he and Ben arrived at the animal shelter. They will have to grab someone from inside to drive the truck from the motor pool to the infirmary. Walt was visibly agitated. "We need to hear what your buddy, Nelly can add to this, Kyle. Even if they do have back up, we don't know what those boys will be walking into."

"I agree," said Kyle. "Later tonight we'll try to reach them on the radio. In the meantime, I want to look around here. I've got a feeling Tom may have left some things behind." After a thorough search around the campsite with his flashlight, Kyle came up empty. He shook his head, obviously disappointed.

"Ask him when you radio him later," Morgan suggested. C'mon, let's eat. I'm starved." She grabbed Kyle by the hand and led him toward the campfire where everyone else had gathered.

After their meal and Bible reading, Kyle pulled out the radio and stood atop the boulders that marked the center of their campsite. Sandy and Ben stood by, hoping to hear from Joe and Tom, too. "Sandman calling Boss Daddy, do you read me; over?" He paused; nothing. He tried again, but still no answer. He looked at the people surrounding him. "I don't want to try too long. They are obviously not around.

We'll try again in a little while."

Another hour and he tried again, "Sandman to Boss Daddy, do you copy; over?" The radio crackled and he motioned for Sandy and Ben. "Come on up. I think we reached them."

A crackly voice came over the speaker, "This is Boss Daddy, Sandman. We read you. What's your situation; over?"

"In position, but short two; we had a run-in with a visitor from your neck of the woods." Kyle paused, and then continued, "The situation is under control, but we had to send two of our own back to base with the perpetrator. We believe we have remedied the problem but need input from your end; over."

Red radioed back, "I'm glad you've got it under control, Sandman. Whatever you decide will have to work. We are short-handed here, with injuries and old folks. What positions needed to be filled; over?"

"One of our drivers and one from security are missing; over." Kyle said.

"And your solution; over?"

"We'll have to do without the extra security but thought you could find some-one to fill the driver position; over."

Red thought for a moment. He still had to figure out how to deal with the guards that would be on duty that night. He would have to take care of them first, before he left for the far corner of The City. He sighed heavily. "I'll find someone; over."

"Very well. Is Nelly around; over?"

"Negative. Standby; over."

"Ask him if he and Little Lamb forgot something. He'll know what I'm talking about; over." Kyle smiled and waited.

"10-4, Sandman; over." Red turned from the base station and picked up the two-way police radio they used throughout The City,

"Connelly, are you there?"

"I'm here, Red. What's up?"

"Are you alone?"

"Affirmative."

"Sandman wants to know if you forgot something." Red had to chuckle at the question. He was looking forward to meeting Sandman and the others. The connection they all shared was rare these days.

Tom laughed into his microphone. "I certainly did and if he's calling from where I think he is, he would need a clear signal. Tell him to look under his feet."

"Will do. We'll need to talk soon. There's been a change."

Tom sat up in his cot, "What's up?"

"Get some sleep. I'll see you in the morning."

Red got back on the radio to Kyle, "He said to look under your feet, son."

Kyle laughed aloud, "Affirmative. Oh, by the way, the perp told us you would getting an unexpected visit from the Supreme City. Were you aware of that; over?"

Red's face went flush, "Negative, Sandman. I was not aware. Thanks for the heads up; over."

"Anytime, Boss Daddy. We're out."

Tom was restless. The old adrenaline rush was kicking in, reminding him of how he had felt before patrols in Iraq. He went to the only window in the unit and peered out. Raging smoke billowed from the smokestacks darkening the moonlit sky.

Kyle was on his knees with Ben holding the flashlight next to him. "Okay, Ben, I think I see something. Hold on a minute." Kyle stretched his arm deep between the rocks, hoping he wouldn't disturb any snakes. Suddenly, he felt the heavy canvas and grabbed hold. Yanking with all his might, the bag finally came loose, and Kyle was able to free it. Everyone gathered around to see what Kyle found. He pulled out the weapons wrapped in the flag. He handed the flag to Ben. "I believe this belongs to you."

Ben took the worn Old Glory, held it close, and looked at his mom.

"I think we should fly this when we leave tomorrow," Ben said.

"I agree," Sandy said.

"The weapons look like they are in good working order, but we'll check them better tomorrow morning," Kyle said, straightening up. Looking around the campsite at the others, he said, "We've got a big day tomorrow, folks. We'll see you at dawn." Then he turned to his wife, smiled, and took her hand. "Ready?"

Morgan returned his smile and followed him to their tent.

Sandy laid an arm across Ben's shoulders as they walked to the tent he shared with Ronnie. "How are doing, honey?" "I'm a little scared, Mom," Ben confessed.

"I think we are all a little scared, Ben. You'll do fine. Just remember, 'I can do everything through Him who gives me strength.'"

Ben smiled, "Thanks, Mom. Good night."

"Good night, Ben."

Philippians 4:13 "I can do everything through him who gives me strength."

CHAPTER 49

Tom made his way quickly down the sidewalk. The crowd seemed thicker today and with every eye he caught, he could tell whether they were followers of Baroam. Those that were followers could not look him in the eye. Those that were not, looked directly at him as if to say, "I'm in," acknowledging that this was the day. The last thing Red had told him was that they needed to talk. Those words had never settled well with Tom and he was anxious to see his friend. On his way, he stopped by the hotel to check in on Jason.

When Jason heard the heavy metal door open and quick footsteps coming down the hallway, he prayed that it wasn't Smith or Garrison. His ribs were beginning to feel better, but another beating would surely inflict more damage or kill him. He was relieved when he saw Tom. "Hey, Officer Connelly," he said, not bothering to hide his relief.

"Hey, Jason, did you think I was someone else?" Tom said, smiling at him.

"Yeah, I thought you were Smith."

"How are you feeling, son?"

"Much better; my ribs aren't as sore as they were yesterday. Tonight's the night, right?"

Tom looked quickly around him, "Yeah. I'm going now to see Red and tighten up the plan, but for now your job will be to get the rest of the prisoners out of here and lead them to the gate. Once they are safely there, we need you to help Joe's brother at the stables."

"Okay, no problem. I'm going to meet Joe's brother, that'll be great. What's his name?"

"Ben Parker," Tom replied. "I gotta run, but Red or I will be back to let you know if anything has changed, as far as you are concerned."

Jason looked apprehensive and unsure. "Tom, do you think this will work?"

"It will work according to God's plan. We can only do the footwork."

Jason sighed, "I'll see you later." He watched as Tom strode back down the hallway and through the doorway. During the time spent in his cell, he had done a lot of soul searching and praying. Unfortunately, he did not have a Bible with him, so he could only pull his strength from the few verses that Joe had taught him. "Acts 4:12 Salvation is found in no one else, for there is no other name under heaven given to men by which we must be saved." Jason prayed for an opportunity to see Joe again.

Tom found Red in the security office with two guards. He recognized them as the officers who would be on duty that night. When they saw him, they nodded 'hello' and shifted their attention back to the map of The City that Red was going over with them.

"Okay, boys, are you clear on everything?" Red questioned, folding up the map and handing it to one of them.

"We're clear, sir. We'll see you back here at twenty-two forty-five hours," the guard holding the map answered. The two of them turned and left the room.

Tom's eyes were wide with curiosity and concern, "What's going on, Red?"

"Connelly, our prayers for help may have just been answered!" Red grinned enthusiastically. "Want a cup of coffee?"

"Thanks," Tom said, reaching for the cup Red offered.

"A visitor is coming tonight," Red announced happily.

Tom was taking a swallow and looked up over his cup, "Who?"

"Baroam."

"This just keeps getting better and better, doesn't it?" Tom retorted sarcastically.

Red continued, "He's expected at around twenty-three hundred hours, but he'll most likely be late."

"Of course he will." Tom said, "So where does that leave us, and how can that be an answer to our prayers?"

"Those two guards who just left were scheduled on duty tonight. I would've had to deal with them one way or another before the others got here, but with Baroam coming, the guards now will be his security detail instead. I'll open the gate at the proper time and the others can do what they came to do without having to worry about a couple of overzealous night watchmen."

"Okay, that sounds like it will work," Tom, agreed.

Red leaned against the counter and lowered his voice. "There's more. When I talked to Kyle last night, he told me they ran into someone from our neck of the woods. Apparently, Garrison is still sending out spies. Long story short, the guy was injured, and they had to send him, with a couple of their riders, back to base camp in Willow Creek."

Tom listened intently, shaking his head. "Now they are short two people!"

"Correct," Red continued. "One would have been the driver for the infirmary and the other was going to supervise the security outside the gate."

"So, now what?"

"They'll have to recruit someone else to run the security. As far as the driver goes, once I open the gate, I'll hop in a cart skedaddle over to the motor pool, and I'll be the other driver. I can get it as far as the infirmary and then someone else will have to take over. I can't leave The City until I know everyone is out who wants to be out."

"What about the security cameras; they aren't due to start the loop until twenty-three fifty-five?" Tom questioned.

"When Baroam clears the gate and the guards are on their way, I'll call Garrison and tell him that Baroam has arrived, and then I'll call Mac. With Garrison in a tizzy over the big boss's arrival, I doubt he will be standing in front of the monitors like always. The transition should be seamless, and Garrison will never know. Once Baroam is in the building—and Mac will be able to watch for that—the building will go on lockdown, securing Garrison and everyone else inside. That should allow us those few extra minutes."

Red paused as Tom ran the whole exercise through in his head, "What about Jason? We'll need to get him out of there before they lock up the building." Tom said.

"That'll be your job. On your way to meet up with your people at the back gate, stop at the hotel and leave the keys and a rifle with Jason. He can release the rest of the prisoners and lead them out the back of the hotel. Just be sure to tell him that he only has a couple of minutes. We'll have a window of less than ten minutes to get everyone well on their way out and set off the explosions. Are you clear on this entire plan, Tom?"

Tom drained his coffee cup. "I'm clear. Have you told Joe about the changes?"

"No, I haven't seen him yet." Red said.

"I'll tell him."

"All right then, while you do that, I'm going to get on the radio and check on the guards for Charlotte and Dr. White."

Tom left the security office and went looking for Joe. He was in the stables, already sweating shoveling last night's straw into a wheelbarrow. When he saw Tom, his face brightened. "Hey, Tom." He stopped and leaned on his pitchfork. "What's the word?"

"I stopped and saw Jason on my way here."

Joe stood straighter and leaned the pitchfork against the stable wall. "How's he doing?"

"He's actually doing a lot better," Tom said. "His ribs aren't as sore as they were, which is good news." Tom took a step closer. "There's been a change of plans."

Remembering the cameras were still on them, Joe picked up his pitchfork and continued mucking out the stall. "I'm listening."

Tom went over the plan that Red had just told him including the change of plans. "Red will bring the truck from the motor pool to the infirmary, but he will need someone else to drive the truck out. Do you have any ideas?"

Joe thought for a moment, "Dr. White can drive it out. I want to make sure Jason and Ben get horses and dogs out."

"Sounds good." Tom said.

"What about Jason?" Joe said?

"He's my next stop. Hopefully, I'll see you again, but if not, stay alert and I'll see you on the other side." Tom smiled at Joe and left.

Joe watched Tom leave. The M16 slung over his shoulder bobbed casually against his hip as he walked. Joe prayed that the escape would go well and that no one would get hurt. With the possibility of freedom and a reunion with his family right around the corner, it had been difficult for him to concentrate on his work. There were so many things to look forward to, one of them being to spend more time with Tom. Perhaps they could go hunting or finally catch that grandaddy bass in the pond. Joe couldn't believe that it had been nearly a year since their meeting. In that time, Tom had become like a father to him. Joe put his attention back on his work. There would be plenty of time for dreams of fishing and hunting, but right now he had to put in his last full day of work in the City.

Sandy fell in line behind the last rider. They were on the final leg of their journey and would reach the edge of the woods by dusk and wait. The hardest part would be the waiting while the anticipation of the coming escape ate at her gut and tugged on her heart. Seeing his mom riding alone with worry etched on her pretty face, Ben drew back and rode alongside her. He, with the rest of them, was feeling the anxiety as they rode in silence, contemplating the coming night and the events that would follow.

Psalm 27:3 "Though an army besiege me, my heart will not fear, though war break out against me, even then will I be confident."

CHAPTER 50

THEY STOOD JUST INSIDE the tree line and watched as the black SUV sped down the dirt road, the headlight beacons slicing through the black of the moonless night. Adrenaline had peaked for the riders and their mounts. The skittish horses stamped their feet and pulled at their reins, ready to make the race to the gate.

When he spotted the SUV, Red checked his watch. "Right on time." He left the security office and went to stand by the gate. The vehicle pulled up next to him and the blacked-out window on the driver's side hummed slowly downward. The driver stared impatiently at Red, expecting him to open the gate.

Red ignored him, moved to the rear window, and waited as that window buzzed down. The man in the back seat didn't scare him. All Red felt for him was contempt. "Evenin,' gentlemen." Red glared at Baroam sitting in the dark, pulling off his gloves one finger at a time.

"Good evening, Mr. Dalton. Mr. Garrison is expecting me, and I would prefer not to be late. Kindly raise your gate so my driver can proceed through."

Red wanted to slap the smugness off the fat little man's face, but he let it go. "You can't be too careful these days, Mr. Baroam. You gentlemen have a nice evenin' now." Red straightened up and sneered at the driver, and then he returned to the office and raised the gate. Once Baroam's car was clear, he waved his two security guards to follow then radioed Tom. "It's a go, Tom; it's a go!" Then he called Garrison. "Mr. Garrison, Baroam just passed through the gate. He should be at your building directly."

Nick Garrison felt like vomiting. "Thank you, Red." He hung up the phone. He couldn't think of anything, except what he was going to tell Baroam.

Tom was waiting at the security bunker with Gabe when he got the call. "Okay, Mac, we're on. God speed my friend. I'll see you on the other side." Tom shook his friend's hand, grabbed an extra rifle, and quickly escaped out the door and through the fence. Just as he turned the corner toward the hotel, he spotted John

Smith leaving the building. "What on earth is he doing?" Tom hissed. He pressed the mike on the radio. "Red, we have a situation. Do you copy?" he whispered as he ran.

"What's the problem, Tom?"

Tom cut around the building the other way and entered from the back, "Smith is on the loose. I repeat Smith is out of the building."

"Get Jason out of there before Mac locks the building down and then you'll have to go after him, Connelly!"

"Copy that." Tom raced up the hallway, pulling his keys out as he approached Jason's cell.

Jason was waiting at his cell door when he heard Tom come in through the back.

"Jason, it's time." Tom said as he quickly unlocked the cell door.

Jason caught the rifle as Tom tossed it to him and took the keys, "You go on, Tom, I've got this." Jason hurried down the dimmed hallway, unlocking cell doors as he went. The captives inside followed closely behind him. When they reached the back door, Jason spoke quickly, "Follow me to the front gate, and whatever you do, don't fall behind. This is it, folks. We're all getting out of here!" Jason opened the door and moved out as quickly as he could. His ribs were starting to ache again. He knew he would not be able to run as fast as needed to get these people to the gate. Then he recognized the young man who had been arrested the same day that he was. "Hey, man. How's your head?"

The kid grinned. "Not bad now, but I had a killer headache for a while. Thanks for doing this."

Jason shook his head. "It's not my doing. I'm just one of the workers, but I need a hand."

"Sure, what do you need?" the boy said, eager to help.

"Get these people the gate. I have to go to the stables." Jason winced.

"Yeah, no problem. Hey, are you hurt?" The boy asked.

"Just some sore ribs. I'll be all right." Jason gave the boy a shove. "Get going! You're going to hear a couple of blasts soon, but don't worry about 'em. Just get these people to the gate!"

"Okay! I'll see you later!" The kid turned and directed the people to follow him.

After Tom left Jason, his concern went immediately to Smith. How was he going to stop him? Tom had a feeling that Smith was heading for the security bunker. He called his friend. "Mac, do you copy?"

"Loud and clear, Connelly. Baroam and his security detail are in, and I'm about to lock the hotel doors. Are you clear?" "I'm clear."

"What about Jason?" Mac asked.

"He should be clear in a minute."

"He's got thirty seconds. Wait a minute." Mac paused, "What's Smith doing? He's coming this way. Tom, please advise!" Gabe McCloud had precious few minutes to spare and knew that the others would soon be arriving at the motor pool. He watched helplessly as Smith drew closer. Suddenly Tom appeared from nowhere and struck Smith sharply on the back of the head with the butt of his rifle. Smith fell to the ground, never knowing what, or who, had hit him. Tom quickly grabbed him by his arms and dragged him up against a building. He had to meet up with Sandy and Morgan. He would have to come back for Smith. When Tom turned around to leave, he found Mac was standing next to him with a length of rope. He grinned, "Good thinking, Mac. This may not hold for long, but it should be long enough for the others to get out."

When they finished tying up their prisoner, Mac quickly made his way to the motor pool to prepare the trucks while Tom sprinted toward the rear gate.

Psalm 27:1 "The Lord is my light and my salvation whom shall I fear?"

CHAPTER 51

ONCE THE SUV HAD passed, the riders charged from the woods, into the open field toward the road. There was no time for recollections or contemplations. It was time to put their training and knowledge to the ultimate test. Failure would be grave, not only for them, but for the captives inside who were depending on them to succeed. Onward they raced with the American flag leading them, proud and high. Ben gripped tightly to the pole he'd fashioned out of a tall hardwood branch. The flag pulled and jerked from the wind and speed of his horse, but Ben didn't feel the extra effort he had to put forth. He only felt the pride of raising her up again for his father, his brother, his family and his country.

Sandy and Morgan, riding at full speed, split from the rest of the group to carry out their assignment. All of a sudden, a split rail fence came into view as they drew closer to The City. Sandy looked over at Morgan, "It must be the pasture for the livestock; we'll have to jump it!"

Morgan was exhilarated by the run and grinned. "You first!"

Sandy kicked her horse, and it burst forth with renewed energy. As they rapidly approached the fence, Sandy threw up a quick prayer, "Lord, give these horses wings!" Her horse sailed effortlessly over the fence, lit gracefully on the other side, and kept running. She rode low against Annie's neck and turned her head quickly to see Morgan's horse, Skye, jump the fence with the same grace. "Thank you, Father, so far so good."

Kyle and the others rode along the outside wall until they saw the gate rise, giving them the signal that it was clear to come in. The rider, who replaced Chris, sent the security details to their assignments, while Walt tied off their horses.

Red came forward to meet Kyle and the others. He couldn't keep the smile from his ruddy face when he put his hand out to them. "It's a great honor and pleasure to meet all of you," he said. The men shook hands firmly. "And you must be Little Lamb Two."

Ben grinned at the nickname, still out of breath from the ride. "Yes sir."

Red held out his hand, "Son, what do you say we put this flag where everyone can see her?"

"Sure," Ben agreed and handed it over to Red.

Red took the flag on its makeshift pole and slammed it hard into a patch of soft dirt, just outside the security office. "There, now folks can see her as they're coming out." He turned back to Kyle. "I'm Boss Daddy, also known as Red Dalton. Let's go, folks, we've got work to do."

He instructed Ben and Ronnie, "For now, just turn the animals out into the pasture. The lead ropes for the horses are in the tack room. By the time you get them all out, your help should arrive, and you guys can round them up and bring them through a gate in the fence up yonder." Red pointed across the pasture. "Just keep them pointed to the end there and you'll run right into it." He looked down into Ben's and Ronnie's young faces and saw determination, "Understood?"

The boys nodded, "Yes sir." Without turning back, the boys went straight to work. They disappeared into the tack room, confident in their work and trusting the rider assigned to cover them.

Red motioned the other men toward a golf cart. "Let's go. We've got folks waiting for us."

The men piled into the golf cart and rode silently through the streets of The City. Finally, Anders spoke, "What a depressing place, Red. How long have you been here?"

"Since day one and believe me, nothing has changed since then." The minutes ticked by until finally, they arrived at the motor pool where McCloud, standing among the idling trucks, was waiting for them.

"Pleasure to meet you all," Mac said. "We'll have to wait until later for the formal introductions. There are two rifles in each truck, but I suspect you are well armed already." He grinned. "I'm heading to the old folks building. Two of you take a truck to the infirmary and the other two take a truck to the rear of The City. We're just waiting on the signal now." He paused and scanned the area beyond the fence toward the gas station, "It should be coming any time now."

Tom was anxious to see Sandy and Morgan as he sprinted to the section of the wall hiding the secret gate. Quickly, he found it and crept into the bushes. He waited. Almost immediately, he heard soft, muffled voices from the other side and a light knock on the gate. He knocked back and whispered, "Challenge and pass."

Sandy couldn't contain the excitement of finally seeing her friend again, "Lion."

He recognized Sandy's voice instantly; his heart leapt. "Lamb" And he quickly unlocked the gate. Sandy and Morgan passed their packs to Tom, and then quickly wiggled their way through.

Once they were able to stand, Morgan threw her arms around Tom's neck. "Tom, I've missed you. We've all missed you." She stepped away knowing their time was short.

Sandy took a step forward, trembling, tears filling her eyes. She did not realize until that moment just how much she missed him. Tom couldn't take his eyes off her. He wanted to memorize every line and curve of her face. He reached for her, and she fell into his arms, holding tight to him. She savored every second, listening to his heart beating rapidly beneath his jumpsuit. Reluctantly he pulled away. "Sandy, you know what to do. I can't come with you right now, but I'll catch up to you before you reach the gate." His voice was thick with emotion.

"What is it, Tom?" Sandy asked.

"One of the head Regulators left the building before it locked. He's indisposed for the moment, but I need to go back and take care of him."

Sandy shook her head. "No, Tom. It doesn't feel right. Why do you have to go? Isn't there anyone else?"

"You know me better than that," he said softly.

Sandy was downcast. He was right. She did know him. She knew he was the kind of man who would do whatever it took to get the job done, even if it meant that he would have to make the ultimate sacrifice. A long time ago, he had offered up a blank check to help those who were less fortunate. A check he signed in his own blood. It was who he was. They weren't at war with a foreign enemy, but with an enemy, nevertheless, who was hell bent on destroying the country he loved. He was still a United States soldier. She turned her tear-stained face up to him. "I do know you, Tom, and that's what frightens me. I don't think I could stand to lose anyone else right now."

Tom gazed lovingly into her eyes and stroked her cheek with the backs of his fingers. "I'll do my best."

Sandy took a deep breath and let it out slowly. "That's all any of us can do." She reached up and kissed his cheek and allowed him to slip his arms around her again. His closeness comforted her, and she tightened her arms around him. To Tom, it suddenly felt like goodbye, and he pulled away quickly. Sandy felt it, too. She gave him one last look and then ran toward the gas station.

***

Garrison opened the door to his suite and greeted Baroam with a bow, "Your Excellency. I trust our Supreme Leader is doing well." For a moment, he wondered about the long overcoat that Baroam wore and then suddenly realized that his handgun was in his desk.

Baroam caressed the butt of the nine-millimeter stuffed snugly in his belt; his plump belly slouched over it. "Mr. Garrison, our Supreme Leader is not doing well at all." His voice was low and controlled. "He and I expect a full explanation of the goings-on here over the last week. In fact, our leader is increasingly disappointed, and I am not in the habit of bringing him bad news when he is in such a state of mind. I'm sure you understand."

"Yes, Mr. Baroam, I certainly do." Garrison casually walked over to his desk and moved behind it. At least from that vantage point his gun was within reach. He continued, "We have been running a full investigation all night and we believe we have found the culprit. He is in our custody now, in a cell downstairs."

Baroam seemed pleased. "Very good, we shall go see this culprit soon."

"Why not right now sir? We have a top-of-the-line express elevator that will take us straight to the basement level." Garrison looked nervously at the two guards flanking Baroam. He wanted this business with Baroam done as quickly as possible. His hope was that the fat man standing in front of him would see that they were progressing with their inquest and that he would leave, but Baroam had another idea. His opinion of Garrison had collapsed, leaving only a bad taste in his mouth. He wanted Garrison gone, not only gone from The City, but also gone from his sight, gone for good. This was not only Baroam's wish, but also the Supreme Leader's order.

Baroam turned to the guards. "Kindly wait for me outside, gentlemen. I won't be long." His thick lips smiled, but his eyes did not. From behind thick glasses they glared, evil and cruel.

Garrison watched the men leave. He knew his time would be up if he didn't act fast. Suddenly, in a flash, he reached into his drawer and withdrew his .357

revolver. He pointed it at Baroam's wide chest, certain that he wouldn't miss such a large target.

Baroam watched him coolly, unaffected by the gun. "Frankly, Mr. Garrison, our Supreme Leader feels that you have failed. I, too, feel that you have failed. Where does that leave us, then? You were entrusted with a very small responsibility and yet you still managed to fall short. What would you have our Leader do?"

"Why not just give me another chance?" Garrison said, the gun trembling in his hand, "Or better yet, if he's not happy with what I've done, then he can give it to someone else. I'll take the demotion."

"Of course you would. You have no pride in your work and that is why you have come up wanting. No, Mr. Garrison, there is no other option. You have disappointed the Leader one too many times." While Baroam spoke, he continued to stroke his gun. He grasped the weapon and pulled it from its holster.

***

Joe left his unit at the precise time that he had been instructed and hoped that Charlotte and Doctor White wouldn't have any problems with their guards. Once they were in position, they would bring the sick and injured to the front doors of the hospital and wait for the signal. When he arrived, he was relieved to see Charlotte and the doctor waiting for him. He went to his girlfriend and hugged her tightly. "How are you feeling?"

"Good," she said. "Excited. I'll be so glad to be out of here." She smiled at Dr. White.

"Okay, let's move," Joe said. "We need these folks to be ready to roll when the truck gets here."

Galatians 6:9 "Let us not become weary in doing good, for at the proper time we will reap a harvest if we do not give up."

CHAPTER 52

IT WAS FIVE MINUTES to midnight. Barbara sat on her bed with her backpack next to her. She watched the clock on the bedside table nervously. The knock on the door would come any moment, telling her it was time to go. And although she was expecting it, she still jumped when Sam Valdez rapped lightly. She rose from her bed, grabbed her backpack, and opened her door to Sam. He helped her with her backpack, and they went quickly to each floor, quietly rousting the residents from their rooms. Nervously clutching their few possessions, they trailed after Barbara and Sam. Inside the elevator, one of the women began to weep. Barbara wrapped her arms around her, "There now, darling; why are you crying, when we will be out of this horrible place soon?"

"I only wish my Harold could have been here," the woman sobbed.

"Harold is in a much better place, ma'am." Sam assured her. "Don't you worry; we'll all be free soon."

The elevator came to rest on the ground floor and the doors slid open with a thud. Sam pulled his gun and peered out the elevator door before allowing the others to come out. "Okay, Barbara, you're clear." He stepped aside and held the elevator doors open while Barbara ushered the people out. "You wait right there by the door," Sam instructed. "I'm going to go check on Mr. Harris. He should have been here by now."

Sam pulled the metal door open to the stairwell and was relieved when he heard voices. Mr. Harris had his group under control, and they were making their way down the concrete steps. Sam stepped just the stairwell and motioned for them to hurry. "Time is growing short, folks. You need to get a move on." Sam looked up and grinned at the exasperated look on Mr. Harris's face. "Are you all right, Mr. Harris?"

John Harris returned the smile. "Yes, I'm just fine." Then he nearly tripped on Dorothy, who was just in front of him and taking the steps one at a time.

Once they reached the bottom floor, Sam gently took each one by the arm and guided them over to where Barbara was waiting. Finally, at the last one, Sam pulled Mr. Harris aside. "When the truck gets here, I'll need you to hold the door open while I help them up into the back of the truck. Can you handle that?"

Harris laughed. "Officer, I just played caboose on a geriatric train of eighty- and ninety-year-olds, down three flights of stairs. I think I can handle holding a door for them."

Sam roared with laughter. "I guess you can at that." Sam patted him on the back and they both proceeded to the front door to wait for the signal.

***

Sandy wiped the remaining tears from her eyes. Her meeting with Tom was unsettling and she was afraid for him. Kneeling beside the gas pumps, she pulled a quarter block of C-4 from her pack and made a small hole in it for the fuse and blasting cap. She glanced quickly at Morgan, who was across the lot, next to the power sub-station. They held up three fingers . . . two . . . one! Simultaneously they popped the cap and raced toward the infirmary, three blocks away. When they were nearly there, the percussion from the explosion buffeted past them. The blast rocked them forward to the ground. Sandy picked herself up, gave Morgan a hand up, and both women continued their dash to their next destination.

With a distressed heart, Tom left Sandy and ran back to the building where he had left Smith. He had already decided that he would not kill him. He had seen too much bloodshed in his lifetime and didn't want to be a part of it anymore. When he arrived at the back of the building, he was horrified to see the rope lying on the ground. Smith was gone. Tom searched frantically. The lot had one truck, and an ambulance left. The plan was proceeding. The others had taken the trucks to evacuate the people. The gate to the security bunker stood askew. Tom made his way toward the bunker, but suddenly changed direction. Smoke from the fuses at the substation and gas station swirled in the light summer wind. They were about to blow. He spun around and raced to the infirmary where he knew Sandy should be. He would have to deal with Smith when he saw him. For now, all he could think of was Sandy.

Joe, Charlotte, and Doctor White went from room to room in the infirmary, wheeling out those who could not walk and helping those who could walk to get out of bed. Patients who were able to move freely helped those who could not. Joe was disheartened when, on more than one occasion, he found a patient that had died waiting for care. He gently covered them and prayed silently over them, before moving on to the next patient. When he looked up, he saw Charlotte coming down the hall toward him, pushing a mother and her newborn in a wheelchair. "Charlotte, what's the status; how many more do we have?"

Charlotte brushed a lock of hair off her face, "One more floor, Joe, but it should go easy. Is someone coming to help?"

Joe looked over his shoulder. "My Mom and a friend should be here any minute." Suddenly the building shook as two enormous blasts blew out the windows. Charlotte instinctively covered the mother and baby with her body while Joe protected Charlotte. In an instant, the hallway went black until the emergency generators kicked on. Joe slowly, cautiously, lifted his head to see the area bathed in dim red lighting and the exit signs above the doors flashed red. He gently pushed Charlotte, the new mother and infant, toward the exit. "That was our signal. Time to go folks. Go! I'll be right behind you!"

Charlotte quickly pushed the wheelchair to the exit, passing two women in her hurry, she exclaimed, "Mrs. Parker!"

Sandy quickly turned. "Charlotte!" Sandy noted the ugly purple bruises on Charlotte's face and stroked her cheek gently. "I'm so sorry. Where's Joe!"

"I'm fine, Mrs. Parker. Joe's up the hall. Not far."

Sandy gave her a quick hug. "The trucks are on their way, Charlotte. Please hurry!"

Sandy didn't wait for a response but kept running. Suddenly she saw her son. "Joe!"

Joe heard the familiar voice and turned around. "Mom!" He ran to her and hugged her, then hugged Morgan. The severity of the moment did little to mask his expression of joy and determination. "We've got one more floor!"

Finally, with the infirmary fully evacuated Joe helped the last of the patients board the truck. He quickly realized that the transport had no more room. He shouted to the others, "Dr. White, you're driving. The rest of us will have to make a run for it." Joe grabbed Charlotte's hand as they raced for the gate, amid the terrified people running for their lives away from a monster they couldn't see but knew was there. To him the scene looked like something out of a horror movie. They raced to the stables, and he prayed that his little brother and Jason were all right.

Ben and Ronnie let the large dogs out to the pasture first. The attention starved animals were grateful to see the new friendly faces and wanted to play. Ben spun around when he heard someone shout, "Ben Parker!"

Ben turned quickly and saw a young man, obviously hurt, coming toward him. "I'm Ben!"

"Ben! I'm Jason, a friend of your brother's. I'm here to help." Jason swiftly began rushing the dogs through the gate, and then hurried to Ronnie who was holding the lead ropes. "Here, give me those," Jason said, reaching for the ropes. "The horses know me. I'll hitch them and then I'll pass them off to you. Remember to take off the lead rope before you turn 'em loose."

"Got it," Ronnie answered. Jason's arrival brought a sudden urgency to the situation that he hadn't felt. Now his eyes were wide with fear and uncertainty as he absently took the lead rope from Jason and started down the aisle to the pasture with two horses.

"Hey, kid!" Jason called.

Ronnie turned around, "Yeah?"

"It'll be all right, kid. You'll see." Jason smiled broadly at Ronnie and passed off another horse to Ben. "I'm glad I got to meet you, Ben. Your brother is a good man."

Ben nodded as he took the rope from Jason. "Yes, I know. I'm glad to meet you, too. There's going to be a lot to talk about when we get out of here."

All of a sudden, the two blasts came from further inside The City and the stable went dark. Jason ducked into the tack room and grabbed a flashlight. When he turned it on, particles of dust and straw were falling from the rafters of the stable. "That was it," Jason said. "We really have to hurry now. Save the last three, Ben. I'll saddle them so we can round up these animals away from here."

Ben snatched the ropes from Jason, "Okay, I've got these two." Ben was at the exit in no time and released the mare and gelding into the pasture. He grabbed Ronnie by the collar, pulled him back into the stable, and pushed the gate closed before the horses and dogs could come back in. He shoved his friend urgently up the aisle to where Jason was saddling the second horse. "I've got the last one, Jason," Ben said. He could see that the pain from Jason's injury was worsening. "Ronnie, finish saddling that horse. Jason, are you going to be all right?"

"Yeah, I'll be fine," Jason said. "I'm going to go check the front one more time. You and your buddy go out the back now!" Jason said as he pulled himself up onto his horse. He needed to find Joe.

***

Dorothy screamed when the explosions shook the building, and the others began to wail. Barbara peered out the window as she comforted them and spotted the truck coming. She took a deep breath when she saw that Gabe McCloud was driving the truck. "Matthew 6:12 'and forgive us our sins, as we have forgiven those who sin against us." Gabe pulled the truck around to the front and backed it up to the front door. Barbara turned to Mr. Harris, "The truck is here."

Sam stepped outside first and checked up and down the sidewalk. "We're clear, everyone! Move out!"

Mr. Harris followed and held the door open while the others made their way out. With the help of her former antagonist, Gabe, Barbara gingerly climbed in. She smiled at him as he took her hand. Gabe was relieved to see her forgiving smile and patted her hand after she took her seat.

When they were all loaded, Sam turned to Mr. Harris. "Okay, you're next." When he glanced past him, he saw one of Garrison's Regulators taking aim at Harris. "Get down!"

John Harris turned to look behind him, but never saw the man who shot him. His gaze immediately shifted back to Sam, then up to Barbara as he slumped against the glass door and slowly dropped to the sidewalk.

Sam leapt into the back of the truck and returned fire; the Regulator fell, dead. "Mac! Move out now!" Sam sat down heavily, keeping his eyes averted from the others as he grieved. Gabe sped through the narrow street toward the main gate, cursing the powerful people that created this hell. Then he realized that he used to be one of them. Barbara Beechum cried bitterly.

***

Jason emerged from the stables just in time to see Joe running past, "Joe!"

Joe quickly turned and saw his friend's pale, pain-stricken face. "Jason! Let's go, man! We're almost out of here!"

Jason dismounted from his horse and ran to Joe while grasping his side. "Joe, I don't think I can make it, but I need you to do something for me."

Joe's eyes stung and his throat tightened when he saw the blood flowing from Jason's side, "You're talking nonsense, Jason! C'mon, we're almost free."

"I can't make it, Joe. I need you to baptize me. Now! I need get right with God!"

Joe looked around, confused. He spotted Jason's horse but knew Jason would never be able to get back on him. "Morgan! Take this horse to the exit!"

Morgan grabbed the reins from Jason and swung up, landing hard on the saddle. She dug her heels into the horse's side, and they took off for the gate. "Lord, please protect them."

Joe tossed his rifle to Sandy. "Cover us, Mom!"

Sandy positioned herself in front of the water trough. Joe and Charlotte now stood behind it, and Jason was standing in it. Joe helped his friend sit in the trough, then took him by the hands with one hand and placed his other hand behind the boy's neck. "Jason, repeat after me. I believe that Jesus is the Son of the Living God and that he died for my sins."

Jason repeated the words with tears flowing freely down his face. Joe couldn't tell whether the tears were from the pain of the broken ribs that punctured his lungs, or if they were from joy in the fact that soon he would have everlasting life in the arms of his Lord and Savior.

Joe continued, "Jason O'Malley, I baptize you in the name of the Father, the Son and the Holy Spirit, for the forgiveness of sins." Joe immersed Jason completely into the cold water, now turned crimson. With Charlotte's help, they raised him out of the water. Carefully, Joe helped Jason step out of the trough. The boy immediately crumpled to the ground. Joe knelt down next to him. "Jason, you can do this. We've got to go, now!"

"Joe," Jason was crying now. "I can't breathe."

Joe carried his friend inside the stable and propped him up against the wall. The boy's shirt was soaked in blood. "Jason, you'll be all right here. I have to get my mom and Charlotte out of here." He looked hard into Jason's eyes. "I'll come back for you, Jason. I promise." Joe held back the tears that threatened to spill over and stood quickly.

Jason's breath was short and labored. Blood poured from his mouth now. "Okay, Joe. I'll wait for you here." What he thought was a shout, had been merely a whisper.

Exodus 15:2 "The Lord is my strength and my defense; he has become my salvation."

CHAPTER 53

GARRISON PULLED THE TRIGGER just as the buildings outside exploded. The room shuddered and the monitors shattered behind him. The room suddenly went dark. Garrison dove beneath his desk, shielding himself from the glass raining down from the monitors. When it was safe for him to come out, he crawled out from beneath the desk among the debris on the richly piled carpet. He peered through the thick smoke and dust and found himself staring down the muzzle of Baroam's gun.

"As I said, Mr. Garrison, you mustn't disappoint the Supreme Leader." Baroam squeezed the trigger and Garrison collapsed. Dead.

Joe and Sandy started toward the gate, "I'll have to come back for him," he yelled over the screams. Sandy tried to hand his rifle back to him, but he pulled a revolver from his belt. "Keep it, Mom. Charlotte, let's go!" The trio continued making their way through the crowd. They were only ten yards from the main gate when, above the din, Sandy thought she heard someone call her name.

"Sandy!"

She turned suddenly and saw Tom racing toward her. Her heart leapt with joy. "Tom!" She began running towards him. Looking past him, a half dozen Regulators were swiftly gaining on those rushing to the exit, including Tom. Something just beyond Tom caught Sandy's eye. A man, an evil looking man, was raising his pistol and aiming it at Tom! Her world began to spin down to slow motion. "Tom! Behind you!" A flurry of bullets flew around her, but still she ran to him.

"Sandy, go to the gate! I'm right behind you!" He shouted over the gunfire. All of a sudden, Tom jerked forward. His face wrenched in pain as he fell to the ground.

The bullets continued to fly. Sandy screamed, "Tom!" After what seemed like an eternity, she was kneeling beside him.

Tom' fingers tenderly brushed her cheek and touched her hair; his breath was coming in quick gasps. He tried desperately to hide the pain in his voice, "Sandy, go. Please. I'll be all right."

Sandy shook her head violently, "I won't leave you, Tom!" She wept and a tear fell on his face.

Suddenly, John Smith was standing over them. He turned a sardonic grin on Sandy, and she froze. The intense training she received did not prepare her for something like this. Once again, someone she cared for had fallen. Her life lay in the balance and all she could see was the muzzle of a gun and Tom's face distorted in pain and sorrow. Smith held his aim on Tom, relishing the moment. Finally, he had power over the man. Suddenly, someone grabbed Sandy by her arm and jerked her to her feet, pulling her back from the depths of grief.

Furiously Sandy struggled to pull away, but realized it was Joe. He drew his pistol and passed his mom over to Charlotte. "Run!"

Charlotte grasped Sandy's arm pulling her away from the gunfire, her bruised face drawn with determination and purpose. "Hurry, Mrs. Parker! Run!"

Sandy couldn't bear the agony; she had to go back to Tom. Just as she tried to get free from Charlotte's grasp again, she heard another shot. "No!" She struggled to get free, but Charlotte gripped her arm tighter and dragged her toward the gate away from the danger.

Joe turned to Smith, who already had Joe in his sights, but Joe was faster. He fired with deadly accuracy and John Smith dropped to the ground. With the madness and the chaos surrounding them, Joe knelt next to Tom and prayed.

2 Timothy 4:7 "I have fought the good fight, I have finished the race, I have kept the faith."

EPILOGUE

A COOL AUTUMN BREEZE floated gently over the Parker family gravesite. Two fresh graves now lay next to Staff Sergeant Parker, each adorned with fresh wildflowers. The survivors of the biggest political catastrophe in United States' history were scattered throughout the newly freed states. They were putting their lives back together with much fewer resources than they had before the disaster. Many of the people, especially those who were rescued from the various 'Cities' around the country as well as those who came back to Willow Creek, had learned that their faith should never be put in any government entity. The only One who could save them was God through the Lord Jesus Christ.

Sandy left the family plot, taking her time going back to the farmhouse. After the rescue, the original group returned to the ranch to regroup, and then left to go back to their homes to rebuild their own lives.

Clifford remained at the ranch long enough for his broken arm to mend and was then taken back to the City where he chose to stay. Tanya and Steve decided to stay in Berkley Springs through the winter and return to Willow Creek in the spring. Sandy, Joe, and Ben returned to the ranch, while Kyle, Morgan, and Charlotte settled into Steve and Tanya's old Victorian house. It had been a bittersweet good-bye when Anders and Walt parted with promises from Kyle and Morgan that they would return in the Spring to West Virginia and start a home there.

Sandy was glad to be back at the ranch, but at the same time it was somehow even more painful than before. She took a walk through the stables to calm her heart. This is where she found solace these days, in the quiet company of her horses and with her God. Pilgrim nickered softly when he saw her, and she went to him. He was always the one Tom would choose to ride. "I know, boy. I miss him, too." Sandy said softly. She took a deep breath and kissed him on the nose before she went to Annie and then Cheyenne. By the time she had made it through the barn, it was nearly sundown, but she wasn't quite ready to go inside yet. She went back around to the other side of the barn and sat on a bench that overlooked the empty pasture. "I'm going to have to get more livestock," she thought to herself. Suddenly her heart broke again, and she wept. She had done a lot of that lately and missed her sister's comforting words.

Joe watched his mother from the kitchen window while Charlotte prepared the coffee pot. "I'll be right back, Charlotte." He slipped out the mudroom door and approached her, slowly. "Mom, it's getting dark. Why don't you come in the house? Charlotte just made some coffee."

Sandy looked up at her grown son and smiled through her tears. "I'll be right in, Joe."

Joe smiled sadly and hesitated before he turned and went back to the house. He also grieved for the loss of Tom, and his friend Jason, but with Charlotte in his life now, the difficult times were becoming easier to get through.

Sandy finally got up and went into the house. It was bright and smelled of fresh coffee and dinner. Ben looked up from the kitchen table when he saw his mom. He, too, had grown since the disaster and her little boy was no longer a boy. He sensed how his mom was feeling; he could see it in the new lines on her face and her eyes that once danced with joy were now dull from sorrow. He stood and pulled a chair out for her at the table. Charlotte busied herself with the meal preparation, leaving Sandy to relax and talk with her sons.

After supper, Joe pulled out his dad's tattered Bible and began the reading, "From the book of Revelation, grace, and peace to you from Him who is, and who was, and who is to come."

Sandy rose early the next day, feeling refreshed and rested. The morning was cool and clear with a blue, cloudless sky. She put the coffee on the stove and decided to take a walk before her boys woke up. She stepped outside, felt a chill still in the air, and reached inside for her husband's jacket. She wrapped herself in it and headed out the door. Yellow, red, and orange leaves littered the driveway and crunched softly beneath her boots. A good hearty walk would be nice before breakfast, but she was curious why she began her walk down the driveway. When she reached the end of the driveway, she noticed the mailbox door was hanging open. "When was the last time I checked the mail?"

As she moved closer, her heart sank, and her stomach twisted into knots. On legs heavy as lead, she moved toward the mailbox. She paused before crossing the road and looked up and down. The action was eerily familiar, but she continued to move forward. She stood in front of the oversized box, once again staring at the single envelope that lay in the shadows. She reached a trembling hand in and pulled it out. "It's got to be left over from before," she thought. She held the envelope in her trembling hands and opened it.

"You may have won the battle, but the war has only begun."

Sandy scanned the letter frantically until she found what she was looking for. There, in the upper right-hand corner, dated two days ago.

Find out what happens next in THE CONSEQUENCES OF CHOICE - RISE OF THE REBELLION

About the Author

SHERYLL GENT WAS BORN in Kearney, Nebraska, grew up in Maryland, and relocated to Florida three years after the death of her first husband. She currently lives in Vero Beach, Florida, with her husband, Tim, and their two dogs, Earl and Bailey. She loves spoiling her grandchildren and cherishes family time with her two sons and daughters-in-law. After retiring from her years as a legal assistant, Sheryll now works in transcription while dedicating herself to her true passion—writing. She enjoys horseback riding, listening to live music, and crafting stories that reflect God as the loving and merciful Being that He is.

.

www.ingramcontent.com/pod-product-compliance
Lightning Source LLC
Chambersburg PA
CBHW030240030726
47493CB00023B/310

9 798990 965263